'Clever, generous and ...
crime no...

'Mesmerising and powerful, with an extraordinary sense
of time and place and characters you will never forget'
Elly Griffiths

'With obvious debts to both *A Star is Born* and *All About
Eve*, this is the full-on book equivalent of a classic
Hollywood "woman's picture"' *Sunday Times Crime Club*

'I loved this elegant and enthralling novel . . .
A spellbinding read' Louise Candlish

'A gorgeously written novel which evokes the atmosphere
and glamour of old Hollywood while including utterly
modern themes' Sinéad Crowley

'Grey brings to life a plot that is as dramatic as its
characters, rich with 1960s period detail . . . With clear
homages to film noir, this intriguing read will grip
you from the start' *Woman & Home*

'A stylish and page-turning mystery' Rachel Hore

'Delia, the heroine of V. B. Grey's gripping and subtle novel
is a fabulous study in ambivalence, guilt and yearning'
Elizabeth Buchan

'A nuanced and moving portrait of ambition, manipulation,
and the emotional havoc created by those unable to

'Inspired by women-centred narratives and the
noir thrillers of the 40s and 50s, Grey invites readers
into a glamorous, dark world of ambition,
manipulation and revenge' *Culturefly*

'Takes elements of classic mystery novels with
the glamour and pizzazz of celebrity and turns
both on their heads. Captivating'
Woman's Way

V. B. Grey is a pseudonym for Isabelle Grey, a novelist and television screenwriter whose credits include Jimmy McGovern's BAFTA award-winning *Accused: Tina's Story* as well as over thirty-five episodes of *Midsomer Murders*, *Casualty*, *Rosemary and Thyme*, *The Bill* and *Wycliffe*. She has also written non-fiction and been a magazine editor and freelance journalist. Isabelle's previous novels include two psychological thrillers, *The Bad Mother* and *Out Of Sight* as well as four books in the DI Grace Fisher series, *Good Girls Don't Die*, *Shot Through the Heart*, *The Special Girls* and *Wrong Way Home*. Isabelle grew up in Manchester and now lives in London.

tell me
how it ends

V. B. GREY

Quercus

First published in Great Britain in 2020 by Quercus
This paperback edition published in 2021 by

Quercus Editions Ltd
Carmelite House
50 Victoria Embankment
London EC4Y 0DZ

An Hachette UK company

A CIP catalogue record for this book is available
from the British Library

PB ISBN 978 1 52940 543 9
EB ISBN 978 1 52940 541 5

10 9 8 7 6 5 4 3 2 1

Typeset by Jouve (UK), Milton Keynes

Printed and bound in Great Britain by Clays Ltd, Elcograf S.p.A.

MIX
Paper from
responsible sources
FSC® C104740
www.fsc.org

Papers used by Quercus are from well-managed forests and
other responsible sources.

For E. B.

PROLOGUE

England, early 1950s

I have lost everything a person can lose. And, should I ever attempt to forget, my failing body will remind me. I've lived in the cramped attic flat of this big house in Birmingham, where I work as a housemaid, since the Red Cross parcelled me up and sent me here seven years ago.

I see her face for the first time as I'm tidying up after Miss Irene and her brother had entertained some friends the previous evening. I'd heard them laughing as they danced to some of the records Miss Irene loves to buy, and later slamming the front door, starting up the growling engines of their sporty little cars and crunching the gravel on the driveway. It doesn't matter how much noise they make. I seldom sleep for more than an hour at a time.

They've left most of the records scattered across the side-board and, before I can dust and polish, I must match the black platters to their colourful sleeves and put them away on their allotted shelf.

I've heard the name Delia Maxwell, have caught snatches of her singing on the radio, but I haven't seen her face before.

Although her hair, always naturally wavy, is now a shining halo of blonde, and her heavily made-up eyes make her appear older, I recognize her instantly for who she really is.

She wears a strapless bodice of pearl-white satin and has been posed smiling over one naked shoulder, her lips pink and glossy. I feel a spasm of hate such as I'd never felt for even the most sadistic guards in the camp.

I shuffle quickly through the other album sleeves, my hands shaking with shock and fury. There is only one other image of her. She has been photographed as if on stage, smiling and stretching out arms encased in long white gloves that match a floor-length gown embroidered with a thousand sparkling diamanté jewels. To one side of the cardboard square is simply the name *Delia* in a curling script of vivid pink. The image speaks of beauty and sophistication, of comfort and safety, of all the things she has taken away from me.

I'd never known what happened to her, whether she made good her escape or perished with so many countless others. The revelation that she is alive reminds me of why I have survived. I have a purpose after all.

1

FRANK

London, April 1963

'You've heard of Delia Maxwell?'

'Who hasn't?' I replied.

My old friend Peter Jenks and I were sitting at a corner table in a Soho jazz club. He'd rung me earlier in the day and said there was something I might be able to help him with, so I'd driven over in my new green MGB, checked my name, Frank Landry, off the members' guest-list and made my way down the narrow stairs to the low-lit basement. I had no idea why he'd begun by asking if I'd heard of his most successful recording artist, so I drank some of my beer and waited for him to explain.

'She was supposed to come into the office last week to sign a big new contract.' Peter kept his voice low, even though there was little chance of being overheard. 'It's a wonderful opportunity for her, a real change of direction. We had champagne on ice, the works, but she never turned up. And now she's not answering her phone and no one seems to know where she is.'

I assumed such temperamental behaviour was to be expected

of such a big star. 'Has she ever pulled a stunt like this before?' I asked.

'Never. She's hard-working, professional, and this is something she really wants.'

'I take it you've already checked the hospitals? Made certain she's not ill or had an accident?'

'Discreetly, yes,' he said. 'And I've spoken privately to a chap I know at Scotland Yard who looked into it for me.'

That brought me up short: Peter wasn't easily rattled.

'He checked with all the London morgues,' he continued. 'No unidentified remains match her description, although he warned me that, if a body goes into the Thames, it can sometimes be several days before it washes up. Anyway, there's not much more he can do. He says she's a responsible adult who has every right to go missing if she wants to.'

It was clear that this official response had done little to reassure him. I'd known Peter for nearly twenty years, ever since, fresh from school, we'd shipped out to Canada together for pilot training during the war. The thick glossy hair he'd once been so proud of was thinning and beginning to show some grey, but he'd kept his wiry runner's physique. We'd stayed in touch after demob when I'd gone up to Oxford, then headed to the Far East to work for a rubber company, and he'd been the first person I'd looked up on my return a few weeks earlier.

He graduated from Cambridge, married his childhood sweetheart and went straight into RMJ Records, the classical-music recording company his grandfather had founded. He'd always been crazy about American music, so it was no surprise that he'd signed as many of his favourite jazz, blues, and country-and-western singers as he could. Thirteen years later, the once nearly defunct label was thriving and Peter was running the company. I guessed he'd take just as good care of his artists as he'd done of his men after he was made up to squadron leader at the grand old age of twenty-two, so clearly something more serious than an unsigned contract was bothering him.

'Is she the type to go on a bender?' I asked. 'A lost weekend?'

'Not Delia. The last time I saw her, she seemed fine, but this isn't like her.'

'Who's the man in her life?'

'There isn't one. Or not that I know about, anyway.'

That she was discreet didn't alter my hunch that there'd turn out to be a man at the bottom of this somewhere. Delia Maxwell was just too lovely for there not to be.

'Any family?' I asked.

'Lost in the war. It's not something she talks about.'

I summoned up what I could recall of Delia Maxwell. A cloud of white-blonde hair, cinched-in waist and wide-skirted, spangled dresses; black-and-white newsreel of her smiling for the cameras outside a premiere, white mink draped over a bright satin evening gown, diamond earrings glittering in the flashlights, and eyes full of suggestion and mischief. She was probably still only in her early thirties yet had been famous for a long time. She was always on the radio, singing with various orchestras, and more recently on television, too. My ideal woman was less showy, but Delia's rich, silvery voice had a tender catch to it, and had often been a poignant reminder of home when I'd been out in Malaya or rattling around some other outpost of a fading colonial empire.

'And no one knows where she is?' I asked.

Peter shook his head. 'No. Which is where you come in, Frank.'

Recognizing Peter's boyish grin, I suspected I was about to agree to something rash. 'You're not expecting me to find her for you?'

'Why not? You haven't landed a permanent job yet, have you?'

'No,' I admitted. I'd been drifting since I got back, and he knew it. 'Although I have had a decent offer from a rubber concern that's opening up new estates in West Africa and wants a head of security.'

He frowned. 'I thought you wanted to stay away from political hot-spots, to think about settling down at last.'

He was right. The struggle for independence in some African countries threatened to be as brutal as the Communist insurgency in Malaya, where I'd ended up working alongside British military intelligence as they 'won hearts and minds'. I wasn't sure I could stomach much more of that kind of trouble.

'Stay in London,' Peter cajoled. 'Do a little discreet asking around for me. You can be our new head of security.'

I laughed. 'Private eye, more like.'

But he saw that I couldn't resist. And I *was* ready to settle down and take a job where I could sleep at night. I'd somehow missed out on what Peter had – a rewarding job, a home with wife and kids, and a place in a world where the worst that could happen was a *chanteuse* going walkabout.

'Good man!' he said.

'So what was this big new contract Miss Maxwell was due to sign?' I asked.

'It's to star in a movie.' Peter lowered his voice again in spite of the bearded young men jamming on saxophone and double bass on the tiny stage. 'We're keeping it under wraps until the contract is signed, but it'll be a major Hollywood motion picture, mammoth budget, the whole shebang.'

'Surely that would mean you *losing* her as a recording artist.'

'You obviously don't appreciate how much money the album of a successful film musical makes.' He smiled, although the tension didn't leave his eyes. 'In the movie she'll play a singer, so the soundtrack is an essential element in the story.'

'From crooner to movie star is quite a leap,' I said. 'Perhaps she's simply taking some time to think it over.'

Peter shook his head. 'If that were the case, she'd say so. She never lets people down. Look, I don't mean to pry into her private life, but if she's in any kind of trouble, I'd like to help. The American producers are only here for the rest of this week. They have to be certain she'll be reliable. So far I've managed to make excuses, but I'm a hopeless liar and—'

'That's true enough,' I said, with a grin.

He didn't laugh. 'Seriously, Frank, I can't afford to be left with egg on my face. I really do have to find out why she's fallen off the radar.'

At least a couple of good reasons came to mind, but I didn't know the lady and he did.

'I can't honestly believe there's any kind of scandal involved,' he went on, as if guessing my thoughts, 'but if there is, then I need to be the first to know. I can arrange for you to talk to her friends, and for her daily woman to let you into her house. She has a mews cottage in Knightsbridge. Most of all, I just want to be sure that she's safe and sound. I'm very fond of Delia. Everyone is.'

I had to admit I was intrigued. Delia Maxwell was too glamorous to be the girl next door, but I couldn't remember hearing any dirt about her. Maybe her absence was a ploy to win a better deal, or she simply had cold feet. Meanwhile her true reasons for dropping out of sight remained a mystery.

Peter caught my eye and punched me lightly on the shoulder. 'I knew you'd go for it,' he said. 'You've always been my wingman. Let me get you another beer.'

2

The next morning, as I climbed out of my car, Delia Maxwell's daily woman was waiting on the doorstep. She greeted me and held up a set of keys.

'Good morning, sir. Door's open, but Mr Jenks telephoned and said to let you have these so you can lock up. I'm all done here, so, unless you need me, I'll be off.'

I thanked her and, judging that she wasn't the type to gossip to a stranger about her employer, told her she could go, yet she remained, clutching her handbag in front of her with both hands.

'Miss Maxwell has always been very good to me,' she said in a rush, 'and it's not like her to go away without letting me know, so I can cancel the milk and everything. I do hope nothing bad has happened to her.' She walked quickly away.

I looked around. Although Delia's home was tucked away behind the busy thoroughfare of Knightsbridge, I was surprised to find the cobbled mews less smart than I'd imagined. Only a few of the upper windows had fresh curtains or boxes with greenery and spring bulbs coming into flower, and some of the garage doors were in need of a lick of paint. I pushed open her unlocked front door. In spite of Peter's assurances, I wasn't all that keen on snooping around an unknown woman's house, and yet I had to confess, now the moment was here, I was as curious as any gossip columnist to see inside the home of an international singing star.

I'd spent an hour over breakfast reading the magazine spreads and yellowing newspaper columns that Peter had sent over. They had been compiled by a press-cuttings agency and included dozens if not hundreds of photographs of Delia Maxwell, often on the arm of a handsome actor, racing driver or minor aristocrat. Each picture was accompanied by a description of the singer's clothes, shoes, hair and jewellery, along with details of where she had just dined or whose party she was about to attend. Yet the few sparse responses from Delia revealed only her favourite colour, her ideal holiday destination, or the venues of a forthcoming tour.

When I came across some early speculation about her background there was no attempt to contradict even the most far-fetched of stories, not even when each fresh account cancelled out the one before. She was a Russian émigrée, a barefoot Sicilian contessa, who had learned to sing with a band of roving gypsies, a runaway Greek orphan, who had grown up in poverty, and yet was simultaneously the loving little sister who had never got over the loss of three handsome brothers, all of them wartime resistance heroes. What all the stories captured, however, was that a hint of tragedy lay behind the alluring images.

Although I had found nothing in the press cuttings to hint at why she might choose to vanish – or why anyone would wish her harm – what so many photographs confirmed was that, even captured unawares, Delia was truly beautiful. Not pretty but with the kind of fine bone structure and generous eyes and mouth that would still be striking in old age; the kind of beauty that could indeed belong to a Greek goddess or a wild gypsy girl. The kind of beauty that, in my somewhat limited experience, a woman might too easily hide behind.

I climbed the steep staircase that rose straight from the front door to the living quarters over the double garage. At the top there was a narrow corridor with four doors opening off it and a further even steeper staircase leading up again at the far end. It was hardly the extravagant interior I had been expecting.

I opened each door as I went by and looked in: kitchen, bathroom, bedroom and what appeared to be a dressing room. I felt uncomfortable lingering in the bedroom and didn't like to disturb the accumulation of pots and potions that adorned the vanity table in the dressing room. In any case, I could see no sign of violent disarrangement or hasty departure.

I had to duck my head to negotiate the tight bend of the next flight of stairs, which opened into a surprisingly large room with huge windows on three sides looking out over a cityscape of brick chimneys and haphazard slate roofs. Smoke curled into a cloudy blue sky and a cat stared at me, unblinking, from where it lay curled in a sunny corner of an adjacent roof. It was a nostalgic view. During my absence abroad, gleaming new office blocks and high-rise hotels had replaced the bomb damage, creating a London I sometimes barely recognized. But here there were no tall buildings close enough to overlook the space, making it feel oddly private, given how tightly packed in it was among the surrounding streets.

The room was easily big enough for a party. The decor was lovely, and no doubt expensive, yet not at all in the sumptuous, flashy style I had expected. Nevertheless, this must be where, according to the press coverage, Delia entertained visiting American movie stars and world-famous entertainers, who all coveted an invitation to her home. She was renowned, I had read, for her omelettes.

The wooden-framed sofas, chairs and a comfortable-looking daybed were flamboyantly curved but upholstered in plain grey-and-white-striped fabric. The style reminded me of something middle-European, perhaps Viennese. Beneath the windows ran low lines of built-in shelves crammed with books and records. A modern upright piano stood against the single wall, its white lacquered top scattered with sheet music. Above it hung paintings and drawings, all of different sizes and in unmatched frames. In one corner, at an angle, a wide desk was piled neatly with unopened post. In another I saw a spanking new stereo console. Pale spring sunshine streamed in, yet I could imagine how at night, with the lamps lit and the curtains drawn, the room must feel warm and intimate. Not a place, it seemed to me, that anyone would be in a hurry to leave.

Something made me walk across the cream-coloured rugs to select an LP from a shelf. I tipped it out of its sleeve, set it to play on the turntable, and took a deep breath as Delia's silky voice spilled into the room. I was transported back to a dinner-dance in Kuala Lumpur and the first time I ever held Evelyn in my arms. I closed my eyes, giving way to longing and regret. The effect of the music was so potent it was all I could do not to glance over my shoulder to make sure the singer wasn't standing in the doorway.

Pulling myself together, I went to the desk and flipped through the pile of letters. Nothing struck me as odd and I wasn't yet ready to start steaming open Delia's private correspondence.

A framed photograph on top of the desk caught my eye. I knew the man in it from some of the captioned images in the press cuttings. Although he'd died about three years ago, Conrad Durand had been the musical and theatrical impresario who'd launched Delia's career and managed all her affairs.

The man in the photograph had thick grey hair and a square Slavic face. He looked easily old enough to be her father. The picture had been taken outdoors, although the background was out of focus. He was gazing directly into the lens and smiling, his eyes crinkling against the sun, smoke from his cigarette half obscuring one side of his face. In most of the newspaper images his expression had been grave and watchful, and I wondered if it was Delia he'd been smiling at behind the camera. I looked away and, surveying the room once more, realized there were no other photographs and, other than on her record sleeves, no images at all of Delia herself.

It was an orderly room, yet also untidy in a lived-in sort of way, which strengthened the impression that its owner had just stepped out and might be expected back at any moment. As the poignant chords of 'My Hidden Heart', one of her most famous numbers, began to play, I went to look at the bookshelves. She seemed to have eclectic tastes, ranging from recent green paperback crime novels to older hardbacks, including several recipe books, some recent, some with Hungarian titles. I'd learned from the snippets I'd read that Conrad Durand had been Hungarian. Had they perhaps lived here together, or had she inherited and kept some of his books?

'Who are you? What are you doing here?'

The music had prevented me from hearing anyone on the stairs, and I spun around, my heart pounding with shock.

Framed in the doorway was not Delia but a young girl, little more than a teenager. There was something balletic in the upright way she stood, her hands thrust deep into the pockets of her unbuttoned khaki trench coat – indeed, the flat pumps she wore, with tapered black slacks and a matching roll-neck sweater, looked like ballet shoes. She had short dark hair, arresting grey-green eyes and an extremely fierce expression. 'Who are you?' she repeated.

'My name is Frank Landry,' I told her, still breathless from the unpleasant sensation of being caught out. 'Peter Jenks has asked me to look into Delia Maxwell's disappearance. Who are you? I wasn't aware that anyone else had keys.'

She ignored my question. 'Disappearance? Can't she simply go away for a few days without everyone making such a fuss?'

'Do you know where she is?'

'No, but I don't see why her record company has to set the hounds on her. Who said you could come poking around in her house?'

'Miss Maxwell was supposed to sign an important contract last week,' I said. 'People are concerned about her.'

'Oh, that,' the girl said. 'Well, maybe she just wants a life of her own.' She walked calmly over to the stereo console and lifted the arm. The music stopped and the room fell quiet. 'Maybe she's tired of being a money machine for other people.'

I tried not to smile at her youthful indignation. I noticed that her upper lip protruded slightly over the lower, a small imperfection that seemed simultaneously wilful and faintly comic. With her cropped hair and black garb, I guessed the kid saw herself as one of those coffee-bar beatniks who liked to argue about existence while listening to Juliette Gréco.

'Perhaps you'd like to tell me who you are?' I suggested.

'Lily Brooks. I've been helping Delia pack up and get everything in order before she leaves for Hollywood.'

'So you know about that?' I asked.

'Of course.' She held my gaze with a coolness I wouldn't have expected in one so young. I found it oddly offensive.

'Well, since you must know where things are, perhaps you can help me so that I don't have to go poking around,' I said, equally cool. 'Could you check whether she's taken her passport, chequebook, a suitcase, or any other essential items?'

'She keeps her passport and chequebook in here,' Lily replied, walking over to the desk and opening a drawer. She held up one and then the other for me to see before returning them to their places and shutting the drawer. 'Her suitcases will be downstairs.'

Once Lily had left the room I went to the desk and took out the passport, wanting to make sure that Delia Maxwell's was the name written by hand in the paper window on the cover. It was. I flipped through the pages and saw stamp upon stamp from all the foreign countries she had visited, presumably on tour. Many of the readable dates were close together, suggesting a pretty punishing schedule. Being Delia Maxwell looked like hard work.

I then flipped through the stubs in the chequebook and saw nothing that seemed out of the ordinary. The last two stubs hadn't been filled in, but it wasn't uncommon to tuck a couple of blank cheques away in a pocket or handbag rather than carry around the whole book. It wasn't uncommon for blank cheques to be stolen, either.

Lily returned promptly. 'So far as I can tell, all Delia's suitcases are still here,' she said, glancing suspiciously at my position beside the desk. 'The only things that seem to be missing are her toothbrush and face cream.'

'Does she have a car?' I asked.

'Delia doesn't drive.'

'When were you last in contact with her?'

'She telephoned early on the morning she was due to sign the new contract and told me not to come in that day because she had too much else to do.'

'She didn't mention anything about going away? Or leave a note for you?'

'No. She simply hasn't been here.'

'And she didn't sound upset or frightened when you spoke?'

'Not at all. Why should she?'

Lily's gaze was expressionless and I couldn't fathom what was going on in her head.

'I've never met Miss Maxwell,' I said. 'Why don't you tell me about her?'

Lily frowned as she pushed her hands back into the pockets of her trench coat. 'They all believe that they care about her, but what they really care about is keeping the show on the road. They won't let her stop.'

'And you think that's what she'd like to do?'

'Yes, except she feels responsible, because so many people depend on her and have a stake in her career. But what about what *she* wants?'

The girl spoke with fervour but her defiance only made her appear childish.

'So what does Miss Maxwell want?' I looked around. 'Seems she already has pretty much everything that most people wish for.'

'How does anyone decide what they really want?' she asked in return. 'After all, isn't it often when you're right on the brink of getting something you've always dreamed of that you start to doubt whether it was ever what you really wanted in the first place?' A scornful smile curled the edges of her mouth and she lifted her chin in challenge. 'What if she's discovered there's more to life than being number one in the charts or even being a movie star? Isn't she allowed to choose what she wants?'

'Delia Maxwell is free to do whatever she likes,' I said mildly. 'But it's also true that she isn't someone who can simply disappear and *not* expect people to ask questions.'

Faced with the girl's disdain, the argument sounded feeble even to my ears. What justification did I have to meddle in the affairs of a woman I'd never met? I was close to apologizing and slinking out of the house, like the trespasser she so obviously thought I was. Loyalty to Peter prevented me – as well as my refusal to be put in my place by such a slip of a girl. It struck me then how neatly Lily had managed to sidestep my questions, using her display of childish outrage to distract me. Whether or not it had been her conscious intention, there was something in her attitude that made me question how much she was holding back.

4

Gowns by Celeste occupied the ground floor of a narrow town-house in Mayfair. I gave my name to an attractive young assistant who disappeared to summon the proprietor from a basement workroom. As far as Peter was aware, Celeste Burns was Delia Maxwell's oldest and closest friend, and I was curious to learn what insight she could offer into the star's disappearance.

As I waited, I took a look around. The two interconnecting rooms were embellished with gilding, mirrors and lavender velvet: Delia's signature costumier must know her own clientele, yet even to my eyes this pampered interior seemed hopelessly out of date. Perhaps it spoke of Delia's loyalty that she had not yet abandoned Gowns by Celeste for one of the trendy new boutiques opening in Chelsea.

Celeste soon appeared. She looked about my age, late thirties or perhaps a few years older, neither plain nor pretty, but with a neat figure and elegantly dressed. Clearly she had the skills to present herself to best advantage. She gave me a shrewd up-and-down look and asked how she could help.

'My name is Frank Landry,' I said, offering my hand. 'Peter Jenks has asked me to speak to you concerning Delia Maxwell.'

She shook my hand, then nodded to her assistant, a signal for her to disappear. 'And why has Peter sent *you*?' Celeste asked, with a slightly mocking smile.

I returned the smile. 'He and I go back a long way, so I guess he trusts me with the security of his artists. He's becoming a little anxious about Miss Maxwell's whereabouts.'

'Her whereabouts?' Celeste was immediately taken aback. 'Whatever do you mean?'

'Miss Maxwell missed an important meeting last week,' I explained, surprised that she – unlike Lily Brooks – didn't already know.

'But she's all right?' she asked anxiously.

'As far as we know.'

'Delia was due to come in two days ago for a final fitting,' she said. 'The dress is for an event when she's due to receive a special music award. I assumed she was too busy with the film producers to let me know she couldn't make it. But you're saying that Peter Jenks doesn't know where she is, either?'

'That's correct,' I said, wondering if Celeste's reluctance to get in touch about a missed appointment suggested that Delia might in fact be more client than friend.

'I see.' She gestured to one of the carved French sofas. 'Do sit down, Mr Landry.'

'Can you tell me when you last spoke to Miss Maxwell?' I asked.

'Last week. I'd also made her a new suit – she'd wanted something special to wear for her signing – and I rang to check she was happy with it.' Celeste took a seat opposite, crossing her shapely legs. 'You said Delia missed a meeting, but she did go ahead and sign the contract, didn't she?'

'No, not yet.'

This increased her concern. 'But you know all about it?' she asked, shooting me another penetrating look. 'How important it is?'

'Yes,' I said. 'It's partly because the American producers are leaving on Friday that Peter's asked me to try to find out why she's gone silent.'

'It makes no sense at all,' Celeste said. 'Delia is simply dying to make that movie. It's a fabulous opportunity for her.'

'She hasn't expressed any doubts to you about it?'

'None at all.' She sounded shocked. 'Why would she? She's been really excited. She enjoyed the screen tests, has been taking acting lessons, and talks all the time about moving to California. She can't wait for it to be officially announced. Are you sure nothing terrible has happened?'

'Peter's made enquiries with hospitals and the police,' I said. 'We can only assume she's safe.'

'But you've been to her house to check? I mean, when you think of awful things like the death of poor Marilyn Monroe last summer . . .'

'You're not afraid that Delia—'

'No, no,' she broke in, before I could finish my question. 'Not at all. It's only that you do hear of accidental overdoses and so on.'

'I went to her house this morning,' I reassured her, filing away the implicit suggestion that Delia might rely on sleeping pills. 'Everything appears to be in order.'

'Thank goodness.'

Celeste's relief seemed at odds with her insistence that Delia was happy and excited about her future. 'Has anything happened recently to upset or worry her?' I asked.

'I don't think so.'

'But you're not sure?'

'She's actually a very private person, you know.'

'Peter thought that, if anyone knew where Miss Maxwell is, it would be you,' I told her, hoping this might encourage her to reveal whatever was clearly on her mind.

Peter's tribute seemed to please her, although she inspected her immaculately manicured nails for a few more seconds before speaking. 'The truth is that Delia and I had a blazing row a week or so ago,' she admitted. 'That was why I didn't chase her when she failed to come for her fitting.'

'What was the argument about?'

'Oh, nothing that really matters now.'

I recalled my sense that Lily, too, had been concealing something, and I dangled a hook. 'I met a young woman at Miss Maxwell's house.'

'Not Lily, surely.' Celeste looked displeased when I nodded. 'What was she doing there? Who let her in?'

'She had her own keys.'

Celeste's face tightened. 'I can't believe Delia would have given her the run of the place.'

It had struck me as odd, too. 'Lily told me she's been helping Miss Maxwell. She seems rather young for such responsibility.'

'She is, although it does make sense. Delia's paperwork has got into a bit of a mess since Conrad died, and there's been a surprising amount to do to get everything in order before she leaves for California. I suppose, really, that Lily's been invaluable, but—' Celeste shook her head. 'One minute Lily was merely one of those faces waiting in the dark outside a stage door and the next she's Delia's personal assistant. I simply don't understand it.'

I wondered if this might be what they had argued over. 'Did you say anything like that to Delia?'

'Yes.' She paused to stare out of the heavily draped window. 'I shouldn't have interfered, but I felt I had to say something. After all, Delia knows almost nothing about her, yet has got her virtually living in her house and has given her access to all her private affairs, her banking, and the lease on her house – everything.'

'And how did Miss Maxwell react to you pointing that out?' I asked, remembering the two blank cheque stubs.

'She accused me of being jealous. She told me that if I wasn't nicer to Lily she'd have to find a new costumier.'

'How long was this before Miss Maxwell disappeared?'

'The row?' said Celeste. 'The week before she was due to sign the film contract.'

I wondered if Delia had told Lily about the quarrel. 'Lily seems to think that, far from being excited about taking a new direction, Miss Maxwell wants a break from it all,' I said.

'That's nonsense,' said Celeste, firmly. 'Delia's life is being Delia Maxwell. It's all she knows.'

'Lily seemed equally convinced that she's the one who understands what Delia really wants,' I said.

'Rubbish,' declared Celeste. 'She's only known Delia for the blink of an eye. And, besides, Delia needs this movie role. She's only too aware of how fast everything is changing.'

'My old man has a shop in Bromley that used to sell wooden radio cabinets,' I told her. 'Before that it was pianos. Now it's transistors and portable record players.'

'Then you understand,' she said. 'It's the same for all of us – music, fashion, magazines, even hairstyles. If we don't keep up we'll all be swept aside. This week Delia's a huge star, a fixture in the firmament. Next week, it could all be over.'

'So what would make Miss Maxwell risk throwing away such a huge opportunity?'

'I don't know.'

'Is it something to do with Lily? How much do you know about her?'

'Only really that she's a fan. A particularly adoring fan. Although Davey did give her a pretty good grilling when he first met her.'

'Davey?' I interrupted. 'Miss Maxwell's musical director? Peter suggested I speak to him, too.'

'Yes, Davey Nelson,' she said. 'He made Delia ask to speak to Lily's parents. Turns out the girl was fostered, although she'd lived with the family for several years. He also told Delia she must ask to see the certificate Lily got for her shorthand, typing and book-keeping course.'

'And did she?'

'She said she did. After that, there wasn't much else we could do. We have to follow Delia and take Lily at her word.'

Celeste stood up and went to consult a leather appointments diary on the antique desk. Her back was turned and she didn't seem to realize that I could observe her in one of the many mirrors. I caught a glimpse of how swiftly her polite mask fell away when she supposed herself unobserved. 'My next client isn't for another hour,' she said, recomposing her smile. 'Perhaps it would be helpful if I told you how Lily arrived in Delia's life.'

I settled down to listen, curious to discover what lay behind the mirror's fleeting revelation of Celeste's bleak despair.

'It all began one evening a couple of months ago,' Celeste continued, as she returned to her seat. 'I'd gone to meet Delia in Portland Place after she finished a broadcast in the BBC concert hall. We were going out to supper afterwards. The weather was horrible but that didn't stop the usual gaggle of autograph hunters waiting for her on the pavement outside the stage door.

'Fans are all sorts, young and old, male and female, and Lily was just another among them. Anyway, Delia started signing their books and programmes as she always does, and I was trying to keep my umbrella over her, but the wind caught it, blew it inside out, then dragged it out of my hand and into the road where a car ran over it, so that was that.'

I waited for Celeste to gather her thoughts.

'What you have to understand is that fans are selfish little beasts,' she said, 'utterly ruthless, most of them. Once a perfectly respectable-looking woman even brought out a pair of scissors and tried to hack off a lock of Delia's hair. So, that night in Portland Place none of them cared about their idol getting wet or cold, except this one girl, a dark, elfin little thing, who wormed her way through to the front to hand me her umbrella.'

'This was Lily?' I said, recognizing the girl's determination from my brief encounter with her.

'This was Lily,' Celeste agreed. 'Meanwhile the others just kept thrusting their stupid autograph books in Delia's face, even though her fingers were so frozen she could barely hold the pen.

'Then Lily rounded on them. "Let her go home!" she shouted. "She's just left a hot concert hall. She'll catch her death standing in the rain like this. Can't you see how tired she is?"

'And she darted away to flag down a cab, then returned to usher us into it, ignoring how the other fans protested and gave her dirty looks or even a nasty push and jab. She was about to close the taxi door without even waiting to be thanked but Delia stopped her. Delia was laughing, delighted by this little terrier. She told Lily to get in, to come and join us for supper.

'Lily said she couldn't possibly, but the rain was pouring down, and I still had her umbrella, so she had no choice but to climb in, although she insisted we were to drop her at the nearest Tube station.'

The way Celeste related her story somehow suggested that she'd raked over these events often, as if they contained some puzzle or mystery she had yet to resolve.

I shifted about, trying to make myself more comfortable on the elegant little sofa, and my fingers found a patch at the edge of the seat where the velvet nap had worn away. I took a closer look around the salon and saw that the carpet was thin in places and the edge of one of the window curtains had frayed. I studied Celeste anew. She wore no wedding ring and I reckoned it must take guts for a single woman to hold together a business like this on her own.

'We told the driver to go straight to the restaurant,' she went on, 'and Delia persuaded Lily to come in with us. Of course she was shy and star-struck to begin with. Delia had to order for her and even then we both had to coax her to eat and even more to tell us anything about herself. Once she got over her nerves, she soon admitted it was her dream to sing like Delia, and maybe to act, too.'

'Presumably she also has a level-headed streak,' I said. 'You mentioned she has a certificate in typing and book-keeping.'

'She said her foster parents persuaded her do that,' said Celeste, drily, 'but she'd fled the provinces and come to London as soon as the course finished.'

'Does she have friends or family here?'

'No one. When we dropped her home after dinner – Delia insisted – it was to digs in a row of bedsits in Earl's Court. She told us that, when she was lonely of an evening and knew Delia was performing, she'd buy a ticket whenever she could afford to, and if none were available, simply go to the stage door in hope of seeing her. She said that even just a fleeting glimpse of Delia coming out and waving to her fans made her feel a part of something, and less alone.'

I pictured the newspaper cuttings I'd left in my flat. I'd learned next to nothing from all those gushing words, yet I couldn't see why it should matter if a star-struck and friendless young girl wished to believe that knowing Delia's favourite colour somehow created a connection between them. Except that I'd met Lily, and she certainly hadn't struck me as the gooey-eyed type.

'Is that why you're worried about Lily having access to all Miss Maxwell's personal papers?' I asked. 'Because such a zealous fan might find out something about Miss Maxwell that she'd prefer to keep hidden?'

'No, of course not! There's nothing to find.' Celeste fell silent, pulling at her skirt to straighten the hem by a fraction of an inch. I waited to hear how much she would reveal. 'I'm sure Lily does care about Delia,' she said at last. 'She's always very sweet and attentive, and Delia couldn't have managed without help, but it would have been simpler to employ someone from a secretarial agency.'

'So what made Lily stand out?'

'Well, that's the thing,' Celeste replied. 'I'm not sure it was really anything to do with Lily. That night in the rain outside Broadcasting House, I think Lily reminded Delia of something in herself. You see, she and I were meeting for dinner because it was Conrad's birthday. You know about him?'

'Only what I've read in the press cuttings.'

'He was an old family friend,' she said. 'He'd known Delia all her life. After her family were lost in the war, Conrad was all she had left. He brought her to London, which was where I met them both soon afterwards. He seemed to know everyone, and he gave me my first commission, creating costumes for her – and Davey his, too. Davey Nelson wrote all her early hits. Anyway, since Conrad's death it's become a tradition for us to raise a glass to him once a year.'

I may be cynical, but a middle-aged man's reasons for choosing to saddle himself with someone else's teenage daughter might not have been purely philanthropic.

Celeste gave me a shrewd look. 'If you'd met him you'd have liked him,' she said, as if reading my mind. 'Everyone did. He was civilized, educated. Delia was devastated when he died – a heart attack at sixty-two.'

'He had no children of his own?' I asked.

'He was never married,' she said. 'Anyway, my theory is that Lily's appearance presented Delia with an opportunity to take someone under her wing, just as Conrad had done for her. But now I worry that Lily's convinced herself they're soul-mates.'

'How old is Lily?' I asked.

'Seventeen or eighteen.'

'So there's time for her to grow out of her teenage crush?'

'If that's what it is,' said Celeste, darkly. 'I simply don't believe she's the wide-eyed ingénue she makes herself out to be.'

'What do you mean?'

'Well, one night about a month ago,' she began almost reluctantly, 'I came upon Lily backstage when Delia was on the bill for a command performance at the London Palladium. I don't often go to Delia's shows – first nights, obviously, and otherwise only if a gown isn't behaving itself and I need to see what alterations to make.'

'And Lily?' I prompted.

'She was standing in the wings where she could watch. I was about to go up to her when I saw she was not only silently mouthing the words of the song but also mimicking each gesture. She went through Delia's entire set, copying every move. There's a little kick she does when she has to pull the microphone cable closer, and it was as if Lily couldn't get it quite right so kept repeating it until she'd mastered it. As the curtain came down I slipped away and Lily never knew I'd seen her.'

'But you said yourself that she's a fan.' I was becoming impatient. After all, I was there to discover why Delia had disappeared without signing her movie contract, and the story of Lily's fixation didn't seem to be leading anywhere.

'I didn't think too much of it, either, at the time,' Celeste agreed. 'But then, a day or two later, at Delia's house, I found Lily sitting at her dressing-table, using her cosmetics to make herself up just as Delia does. She didn't see me immediately, so again I waited and watched her reflection as she angled her face to the light, posing her head at exactly the same slant as Delia. They're not really alike, but she'd caught the look so perfectly that it gave me a real start.'

'You don't think it was just the familiar surroundings?' I asked. 'That if Lily hadn't been in Miss Maxwell's dressing room, you'd never have thought she was aiming for such a likeness?'

'I saw what she was trying to do,' Celeste replied stubbornly. 'It was as if Lily wants to *be* Delia. Anyway, then she spotted me standing in the doorway and jumped up. She blushed with embarrassment that I'd caught her, apologized profusely and begged me not to tell Delia.'

'And did you?'

'I was very reluctant to make such a promise, but then Lily poured her heart out, all about how she'd never felt as if she belonged in the small town where she went to school. She said that when all her friends went on about Elvis or Billy Fury or Cliff Richard she had worshipped Delia, convinced that, if she ever got to meet her, Delia would understand her like no one else could and she wouldn't have to be lonely any more. Eventually I agreed not to mention it, on condition that Lily promised never to touch her things again without permission. Not that it really mattered. Delia likes having Lily around and probably wouldn't have minded.'

'Then what's the problem? And what could it possibly have to do with Miss Maxwell's disappearance?'

Celeste hesitated for a long time. 'You should speak to Davey Nelson.'

'About what in particular?'

She bit at her bottom lip. 'Davey reckons . . . The fact is, Delia's been so happy recently, and so excited about the future . . . I'm sure Davey's barking up completely the wrong tree, and it's only because he has a tendency to assume other people are like him, but he thinks . . . he thinks that Delia and Lily are lovers.'

This was an explanation I had not seen coming. Except that Delia had been prepared to fall out with an old friend over the girl, Lily had spoken to me of her employer in a strangely proprietorial way, *and* she had keys to the house . . . Perhaps Delia's sudden absence was due to a lovers' tiff, or she was regretting the entanglement and, fearing a scandal, had gone away to think it over. I waited to hear what Celeste would add to this revelation.

She hesitated for a long moment. 'I suspect Davey's right about Lily having those kind of feelings towards Delia. But I honestly don't believe there's anything like that on Delia's side. She's discovered she can play Lady Bountiful and that it's fun to have a protégée, that's all.'

My instinct told me that Celeste didn't believe her own words, and didn't really expect me to, either. I felt out of my depth. I'd only ever come across one or two female couples in my travels, and I can't say I'd ever given them much thought. I could only suppose, however, that any love affair gone wrong would cause the same pain and confusion. My own barely healed heartbreak had remained private: how much worse if such humiliation and regret could potentially be played out in the full glare of publicity?

Celeste looked exhausted after telling her story, and I remembered the despair I'd glimpsed in the mirror. I had supposed that her business meant more to her than a husband and family, but what if she had never wanted a man in the first place? What if she herself had tender feelings for Delia – unacknowledged, perhaps, but real enough to make her jealous of a younger woman?

I appreciated all too well how hard it was to go on and on trying to keep such feelings hidden. I'd hated the despicable but necessary lies I'd had to tell as the secret lover of a married woman in the tight-knit ex-pat community in Malaya, but I'd never been able to make myself stop loving Evelyn. Instead, I'd done my best to mislead the gossips and, to this day, had never told a living soul of our affair. Right up until that final afternoon in a hotel room in Kuala Lumpur, I had never seen the end coming. I'd been so sure I was the only person in the world who truly knew her that I'd completely failed to see that, forced to choose between us, she would opt to stay with her husband. It was nearly seven years since I'd last seen her, yet I was no closer now to making sense of her decision.

I knew too little about Celeste to judge whether she harboured feelings for Delia that might have left her similarly unable to discern the truth about what Delia really wanted. I needed to speak to Davey Nelson. Perhaps he could finally shed some light on the truth behind Delia's increasingly disquieting disappearance.

6

When I telephoned, Davey Nelson claimed to be too busy to meet me, and sounded blithely unconcerned about where Delia might be. In fact, he seemed rather annoyed that she'd missed rehearsals and a recording session for her new album, and made out that she was wasting his time, which I guess she was. He did, however, stress his conviction that Delia was a survivor and would no doubt show up again when she was good and ready.

With no further leads, I reported back to Peter, who suggested I meet him the following morning at an Italian coffee bar in Frith Street near the Soho offices of RMJ Records. I'd have preferred somewhere more private, but discovered that he had his own regular table at the back and, with the noise of the espresso machine and intermittent music from the jukebox, we could speak freely. It was just as well, for Delia had now been gone for more than a week, and the poor devil was clearly in an anxious state.

'What have you found out?' he asked, as soon as I sat down.

I summarized what I'd learned so far. When I began to explain about Lily Brooks, starting with how enthusiastically Delia had taken the girl under her wing, he broke in to say that he knew who she was.

'Davey Nelson's been working with her,' he added.

'And what does he say?' I asked, curious to hear how widely Delia's musical director had shared his theory about the women's relationship.

'He's rehearsing her for Delia's spot at a big annual awards ceremony tomorrow,' Peter said. 'Delia was supposed to be launching her new number that evening, so now Lily's going to sing instead.'

'Really?' I couldn't hide my surprise. 'Are you sure that's a good idea?'

'It was Lily's suggestion, apparently.'

Was it? Perhaps I should have been more receptive to Celeste's anxieties about the girl's ambitions.

'Davey's written a slightly different arrangement to suit her voice,' Peter continued. 'He thinks she'll do fine, says she's a natural. And, of course, if Delia suddenly reappears, it means she can take her rightful place without any last-minute panic about lighting and timings and so forth. And if she doesn't, then at least we have an alternative story to offer the press, something to draw their fire away from Delia's no-show.'

'Don't kid yourself,' I said. 'The story will still be about Delia's disappearance even if you get Doris Day to take over her spot.'

'I know, Frank, but it's better than doing nothing at all.'

He looked miserable. I understood how desperately he was hoping Delia would simply come back and carry on, so was clutching at any straw to keep things on track.

'Celeste Burns thinks Lily might be a little too infatuated with Delia,' I said. I waited to see Peter's reaction.

He nodded and gave a wry smile. 'Can't blame her for that.'

'No,' I agreed, 'but what if it also goes the other way?'

'What do you mean?'

'When Celeste suggested that maybe Delia was placing too much trust in a teenager hired to help organize some paperwork, they had a terrible row and Delia hasn't been in touch with Celeste since, not even about a missed fitting.'

'That doesn't sound like Delia,' he said, with a frown. 'And Celeste is her oldest friend.'

'Has Davey Nelson spoken to you about how he thinks Delia might feel about Lily?'

He looked at me sharply. 'No. Why?'

'Is it possible that Delia's gone off to escape an affair that's gone wrong?'

He frowned. 'An affair?' Then he got it. 'Oh. Is that what Davey told you?'

'It's what he told Celeste,' I said.

'I admit Delia's never shown much interest in men,' said Peter, 'but I've never heard any rumours that . . . Besides, it's none of my business. Her love life has nothing to do with her recording contract.'

'It might if the girl's foster parents make a fuss,' I said. 'Lily's not legally an adult until she's twenty-one.'

Peter's frown remained in place. 'There's a standard morals clause in Delia's new movie contract. That sort of thing would need to be hushed up.'

'Plus there's always the possibility that Lily could use their relationship to blackmail Delia,' I said, 'which might explain why Delia's made herself scarce.'

He chewed on that for a while. 'No,' he decided at last. 'I'm sure it's not that.'

'All the same,' I said, 'are you certain you want to put Lily on stage in Delia's place, given how little you know about her? Especially if she does well, in which case the press will want to know an awful lot more about her.'

Peter shook his head. 'It's supposed to be a nice tribute to Delia,' he said. 'And whatever Celeste says, it's likely their row had much more to do with Celeste being left behind when Delia goes to Hollywood. I happen to know Celeste is concerned about her tenure in Curzon Street. It's a short lease that belonged to Conrad, which means Delia inherited it, and it's up for renewal soon.'

I remembered Celeste's frayed curtains and worn carpet. 'Business and friendship are often a bad mix,' I agreed. 'And Celeste's anxiety would contribute to her mistrust of the girl. On the other hand, I haven't found any more convincing reason for Delia to run away, if that's what she's done.'

'Well, I can't change our plans for the awards ceremony yet again,' said Peter. 'I'm to accept the special achievement award on Delia's behalf and Lily will sing the new number. Davey will keep an eye on her.' He sighed. 'But you're right. We're flying blind, aren't we?'

'Rather,' I agreed. 'Where are you up to with the American producers?'

'I've got a final meeting with them this afternoon. That's why I was keen to see you now. They fly back tomorrow. I'm hoping they might keep their options open, but what the hell do I say to them, Frank?'

'The truth?'

'I guess I'll have to. But I fear it will mean Delia kissing goodbye to her movie career before it's even begun.'

'Maybe that's what she's wanted all along,' I said, 'and just couldn't face telling you.'

'Delia's not afraid of anything,' he said. 'And certainly not of me.'

It struck me then, with a pang of sadness for Delia, that each of those close to her had their own kind of investment in her and felt that some part of her belonged uniquely to them. Even Peter, certain though I was that his concern for her was genuine, must also have a duty to the other family shareholders in the company, which meant that, in her absence, the show had to go on.

Becoming aware of our surroundings, I noticed that, aside from the owner behind the hissing Gaggia, Peter and I were pretty much the oldest people in the coffee bar. The other customers might be advertising executives, or actors and musicians, students or secretaries. The way they dressed, the way they gestured and spoke to one another, even the way they smoked, all showed that they belonged to a new and very different decade. Celeste had been accurate in her remark that if our generation didn't keep up we'd all be swept aside. I remembered the visa stamps in Delia's passport and all the years of train journeys, airports, new theatrical venues and unfamiliar hotel rooms they represented. Maybe Lily was right, and Delia had simply had enough.

Peter pushed his empty cup around the surface of the Formica table. 'I keep hoping she'll come back,' he said, 'and that she's somewhere safe.'

'And, meanwhile, you're sure you don't want to reconsider handing over her spot to Lily?'

'It's too late now.' He stood up, leaving a few coins on the table for our coffee. 'You will come to the ceremony, won't you, Frank?'

'Never missed a mission yet.'

He smiled and clapped me on the back. 'Come over soon for Sunday lunch,' he said. 'Mary and the kids would love to see you.'

As we parted in the street, I wished him luck for his meeting with the Hollywood producers. I could only cross my fingers that Lily's appearance at the awards ceremony wouldn't blow up in his face.

7

The event was held in the banqueting suite of one of the big hotels in Park Lane. I brushed down my old dinner jacket and drove over there in good time. It was a rather chilly evening in the last week of April, and a slight mist hung about the darkening trees across the road in Hyde Park. Maybe it was the unseasonal nip in the air, but I was reminded of Peter's reluctance to speak of how his contact at Scotland Yard had enquired if Delia had been found in any of the London morgues.

Where was she? And what had really happened to drive her away? Could she be dead? Murdered in some crime of passion and her body as yet undiscovered? Or a suicide? Neither Peter nor Celeste seemed to believe she was the type to throw herself off Beachy Head, yet too often the people who killed themselves were those you least suspected of harbouring such despair.

I realized that I, too, was beginning to care about her fate. Did that make me merely one more among Delia's legion of fans, someone who experienced a non-existent connection as somehow meaningful? Nodding to the doorman as I entered the hotel, I caught myself humming under my breath. I recognized the tune and had to smile. It was a Sinatra number that Delia had also recorded: 'I've Got You Under My Skin'.

I didn't expect to meet anyone I knew, other than Peter, so made my way straight to the ballroom. It was magnificently decked out, with dozens of circular lamp-lit tables, each laid with crisp white linen, sparkling glass and shining silver, spread out beneath rows of magnificent chandeliers. Pedestals placed at intervals between the tables bore dramatic flower arrangements. I couldn't name the vivid blooms but they reminded me of the tropics. Men in black tie stood or lounged beside women wearing brightly coloured evening dresses, the most stylishly attired presumably recording artists and starlets.

A stage had been set up at the far end of the vast room, fringed by further banks of flowers. Above it hung a shimmering banner bearing the event's name and logo, and to one side, chairs and music stands were set out ready for a small concert orchestra and piano.

Unable to spot Peter in the crowd, I went to consult the seating plan and discovered he had put me on a table with Celeste Burns. I found her already seated. The striking effect of her sleeveless black velvet gown, set off by the ornate quantities of witty and extravagant costume jewellery that adorned her neck and arms, made me admire her pluck and be grateful that I wouldn't have to sit out the evening with strangers.

She rose to greet me with an anxious look. 'Delia's not going to appear, is she?'

I shook my head but gave her an encouraging smile. 'The night is young.'

'It's no good pretending,' she said. 'Besides, word is already out. Everybody's talking and the press are lapping it up.'

'Then let's not add to the rumours,' I said, taking my seat on the gilt chair beside her. 'Unless you've remembered something else that might be useful?'

'I've been racking my brains as to where she might have gone,' she said, 'but, no, I've nothing more to tell you. Except – I imagine you've heard what Lily and Davey have cooked up?'

'Peter told me,' I said.

'She's got everyone wrapped around her little finger,' Celeste said angrily.

Thankfully a regiment of black-and-white-clad waiters descended on us, and she had to stifle her objections. We ate smoked salmon followed by lamb cutlets, and I knocked back a couple of glasses of wine and exchanged small-talk with the lady in pearls on the other side of me. As soon as dessert had been served the dance band took their places and the master of ceremonies bounded onto the stage.

He kept up a smooth flow of topical jokes while holding to a tight schedule, introducing each act followed by the celebrity whose job it was to open the golden envelope and declare the winner of each award. With a third glass of wine, and released from the obligation to be sociable, I managed to relax a little and began to enjoy the show. It was fascinating to see so many well-known entertainers at close range and watch them perform for a receptive home crowd. It helped me to appreciate the possible attractions of such a starry life.

The ceremony had been due to end with the presentation of Delia's special achievement award, so when the MC dropped his patter and invited Peter to the stage, the entire ballroom fell so silent you could have heard a pin drop. I even noticed a group of waiting staff craning over each other's heads at one of the service doors, trying not to miss a word.

The MC introduced Peter and formally presented him with Delia's gold trophy before stepping back out of the spotlight. Peter thanked all the right people on her behalf, then took a deep breath. I don't think anyone present envied him the task of accounting for her absence, yet I was more than confident that he was up to the job: this, after all, was trifling compared to all the times he'd had to brief the squadron on raids from which we understood that not everyone would return.

'Although I know how grateful Delia Maxwell would be for the honour of this award,' he began, 'most of you will have heard by now that she won't be joining us tonight to accept it in person.' He paused for the rustle of whispering to die down. 'Believe me, I would like nothing better than to hand on her apologies and regrets, and to tell you that I know where Delia is right now and that she is safe and well.'

Whatever he had been going to say next was drowned in thunderous applause, with many in the audience rising to their feet, including not only Celeste but also all the dance-band musicians. Peter stood fighting down his emotion until the tumult died away and people settled back into their seats.

'Thank you,' he said, clearing his throat. 'Thank you. I know you all love Delia as much as I do, and as ardently as do her many devoted fans throughout the world. I hope she's aware that we're all wishing her well, and that, whatever her reasons for not being here with us tonight, they are not due to any unhappiness or pain.

'What I can tell you, however, is how much Delia had been looking forward to singing her new number for the first time this evening, exclusively for you, her friends and colleagues. After a great deal of heart-searching, we at RMJ Records have decided to go ahead and offer you the musical experience she had planned for you. A young friend of Delia's has generously agreed to appear in her place, accompanied at the piano by Delia's musical director, the celebrated songwriter Mr Davey Nelson.

'Lily Brooks is a complete novice. She is singing tonight only as a homage to a star she so deeply admires. So I will leave Delia's music to speak for her. And I introduce to you Miss Lily Brooks, singing "Tell Me How It Ends".'

8

As Peter left the stage to further applause, Lily quietly replaced him in front of the microphone. She wore a knee-length sleeveless dress of emerald green, with matching high-heeled satin shoes. Her dark hair was freshly cropped and she wore minimal make-up and no jewellery except earrings which, from the way they reflected the light, had to be diamonds.

Celeste leaned in to whisper to me: 'Davey wanted her in one of Delia's stage gowns, but I insisted she wear this.'

'Well, it works,' I whispered back. The simplicity of the dress gave Lily's slight figure a fresh grace and sophistication. She looked stunning. I certainly couldn't imagine her in any of the curvaceous, spangled outfits in which Delia always looked so glamorous. In fact, the idea of it made me feel mildly queasy: it would have been like dressing the girl up in a dead woman's clothes.

Lily placed both hands on the microphone and stood looking down at her feet, waiting for Davey Nelson, at the piano, to begin playing the intro. The room fell silent.

'*Tell me how it ends*,' she sang, raising her wide eyes to the audience. '*Tell me I won't be blue, That the moon won't shine on you with somebody new.*'

Lily's clear, sweet notes hit me in the pit of my stomach. The words were trite yet she sang them as if she were the first young lover ever to experience such raw longing. Delia's voice might have been stronger and more richly beautiful but even she couldn't have sung the foolish lyrics better.

'*I never dreamed our love could fade. Oh, please, just tell me how it ends.*'

A shiver ran down my spine, and I found myself wanting to look around, just as I had in Delia's rooftop living room when I'd listened to one of her records, to make sure she wasn't watching her protégée from an unlit corner of the ballroom.

As Lily began the second verse, she removed the microphone from the stand and, giving a little kick as she pulled the cable free, began to move across the stage, angling her face perfectly to the spotlight.

Celeste leaned in close. 'I told you!' she breathed into my ear. 'She's been rehearsing Delia's every move!'

I glanced around the room, now hazy with cigarette smoke. People were staring at the stage in rapt attention. I looked back at Lily and studied the extraordinary confidence with which the girl wielded her power over the audience. Remembering the insolent defiance she had shown in Delia's rooftop living room, I felt a first ripple of suspicion and even fear. Could Celeste be right, and had this moment, or some version of it, always been the true objective behind Lily's steady insinuation of herself into Delia's life?

I drank the last of my wine and waited for the song to finish. As Lily wrapped up the number, Celeste caught my eye and gave a despairing shake of her head.

The piano chords died away. There was absolute silence for a moment. Then the applause began and went on and on. Whether it was for Lily or Delia, I don't think anyone knew. And when Lily reached out her slim arms to the audience in an oddly stagey gesture that even I recognized as one of Delia's signature movements, the noise threatened to bring the ballroom's heavy chandeliers crashing to the floor.

Lily bowed her head, looked down at her feet, and simply stood still and waited for silence.

'You do see now that I'm not making it up, don't you?' Celeste hissed in my ear. 'This is what she's been after from the very beginning.'

On stage, a spotlight sliced Lily diagonally in two, putting half of her face in shadow while accentuating the delicacy of her collarbone and one slim wrist where she still held the microphone. Was she angel or devil? Or were Celeste and I merely projecting our own fears and concerns onto the blank canvas of her youth?

'Thank you,' Lily said at last, her eyes huge and her speaking voice faint and rasping, despite the amplification. 'Thank you for accepting me. I know that Delia would thank you, too, for the welcome you have given me, and that she would be especially glad of it because I am her daughter.'

I thought I had misheard. Her *daughter*? At the back of the room, I noticed two or three reporters stand open-mouthed, then rush out, each no doubt aiming to be the first to telephone the news to their editor.

Lily continued to speak. 'I was the baby Delia Maxwell was forced to give up, and, while I wish more than anything in the world that my mother was here now beside me, I am proud to stand before you on her behalf.'

Celeste's eyes were wide with shock and she clamped both hands over her open mouth, her skin paling against her red lacquered nails. I made a quick calculation. Delia must have been very young, but it was possible, and it would certainly explain how Lily had been able to evoke the older woman's physical presence with such intensity.

I looked around for Peter but couldn't locate him among so many astonished, staring faces. No one moved or spoke, and then Davey Nelson stood up from the piano and very slowly began to clap. Others followed his lead, and in an instant the entire ballroom had once again risen to its feet, clapping and whistling, stamping and shouting, 'Bravo,' while Delia Maxwell's long-lost daughter stood alone on the little stage with a faltering smile, white-faced, her arms limp at her sides.

9

The MC returned to thank the sponsors and bring the ceremony to a close, but no one was paying attention and all the other award winners were forgotten. People rose from the tables and began to regroup. A sparse few were preparing to leave, intent on retrieving coats and wraps and securing a taxi before the crush. The rest either appeared dazed or gathered with friends and colleagues to chatter eagerly about the implications of Lily's astonishing revelation.

I turned to Celeste. She had tears in her eyes, and a stricken look. 'How could I have got it so wrong?' she asked. 'What kind of terrible person am I not to have seen it?'

I could only shrug.

'Poor Delia,' she said. 'When I think of what I said to her . . .'

'Is it true, do you think?' I asked.

Celeste nodded. 'Oh, yes. She's never spoken of it, but Conrad told me in confidence years ago that she'd had a baby when she was very young and gave it up as soon as it was born. He wanted me to understand so I could help her if she ever needed it. I should have remembered, but it's something that happens to so many girls, isn't it? If only I had, I wouldn't have been so blind and stupid when she must have needed a friend.'

'Was Conrad Durand the father?' I asked, thinking angrily of the photograph on Delia's desk.

'No!' Celeste sounded shocked. 'He loved her, but not like that.'

I wasn't sure I believed her. And, in any case, it must have been Conrad who encouraged the teenage Delia to give up her new-born baby. This certainly explained why she was so guarded about her past in all her press interviews. And perhaps also why the tender feelings she poured into her music had been so powerful. In my head I heard the ache in her voice as she sang of feeling blue, of foolish dreams of happiness and lost love – not dreams of a lover but of a child.

And yet her daughter had been found. So where was Delia? Why wasn't she there to witness Lily's debut and to join in the celebrations?

'I need to speak to Peter,' I told Celeste.

'I'll come with you.'

We wove our way through the crowd, which was finally beginning to thin out. Peter hadn't moved far from his table, on which Delia's award trophy stood forlornly. Besieged by people asking questions, including three or four reporters scribbling shorthand in their notebooks, he shot me a look of grim resignation.

As I waited on the periphery until the hubbub died down, Davey Nelson detached himself from the far side of the circle and approached Celeste, a cigarette dangling between his fingers. Up close, I was able to study him better: he was thin with wavy dark hair and a sardonic glint in his eye. His single-breasted DJ had fashionably narrow lapels and the trousers tapered at the ankle. He wore unconventional Chelsea boots rather than formal Oxfords, yet sported gold cufflinks and an expensive wristwatch. I assumed, as Delia's principal song-writer, he must earn hefty royalties from her success.

'So what did you think?' he asked Celeste, turning sideways to avoid blowing smoke at her. 'She was good, wasn't she?'

'Lily?' said Celeste. 'Yes, yes, I suppose she was.'

'Oh, come on,' he scolded, 'admit it! She was magic. She's really got that something extra.'

Davey spoke with the cavalier drawl that I – a grammar-school boy – associated with a top public school. His slightly camp tone and exaggerated gestures also signalled that he was not abashed by his homosexuality. I couldn't help but admire his self-possession.

'She'll never have Delia's voice,' said Celeste.

'Maybe not,' he agreed, 'but that hardly matters. She's got something else that's all her own, something that will really appeal to the kids. And how about that announcement for a finale? What a publicity coup!' He turned to me and smiled. 'Timing is everything in this business.'

His words made it very clear that loyalty didn't count for much, although perhaps it couldn't, with popularity and record sales in the hands of a fickle public. *The Queen is dead,* I thought, as Celeste introduced us. *Long live the Queen.*

'How on earth did Lily learn to sing like that?' I asked, as we shook hands. 'You've only had a few days to prepare.'

'She sang in the school choir,' he said. 'And in front of her bedroom mirror, too, I'm sure. But the truth is, if you have to be taught, you haven't got it. And she's got it. Lily would be a sensation regardless, and as Delia Maxwell's daughter, she's been handed a blank cheque. If Lily doesn't have a number-one hit within weeks, I'll eat my hat.'

I was curious to know whether he'd had prior knowledge of Lily's announcement and, if so, what other of her secrets he was party to. But then I recalled how he'd shared with Celeste his belief that Lily and Delia were lovers – and, in an emotional sense, had been right – so, if he had known the truth, it hadn't been for very long.

'And the dress was a triumph, too,' he said, turning back to Celeste. 'It was absolutely spot on to pare it down to the bare minimum.'

Perhaps Celeste resented his condescending tone, for she did not respond. He seemed used to her coldness, however, for he leaned past her to stub out his cigarette, then turned away to survey the ballroom.

Many tables had been abandoned and waiters were already clearing away empty plates, glasses, ashtrays and discarded napkins. Several knots of people remained, small islands in a growing expanse of carpet, and even they were edging slowly towards the exit. I felt a hand on my elbow. It was Peter.

'We can't talk here,' he said quietly. 'Come to my office first thing tomorrow morning. Is that OK with you?'

'Yes, of course.'

'Our public-relations team is going to be working flat out, but I could really do with your help on this, Frank.'

Before he could say more, there was a movement, like a flock of starlings wheeling in an empty sky, as everyone who remained in the room turned at once in the same direction and seemed to hold their breath.

They were gazing at Lily, who had emerged from backstage and was walking towards us. She looked waif-like and vulnerable, yet simultaneously assured and triumphant, almost like one of those puzzle drawings where the silhouette of a wine glass becomes the profile of an old crone. I felt sure that, in future, her ambiguity would endlessly intrigue audiences and help propel her to stardom. She went first to Davey and held out her hand.

'Thank you for believing I could do it,' she said. 'I was so scared, so sure I had no right to be there, and yet, out on that stage tonight, I felt alive for the very first time.'

She moved to stand in front of Peter. 'It's all because of Delia,' she told him. 'She helped me to find something in myself I was never aware of before.'

I imagined that everyone was dying to ask where Delia was, but not even the reporters taking down her every word dared to interrupt the moment.

'You were perfect, absolutely spellbinding,' Peter said, taking her hands in his. 'Delia would be immensely proud. I think we should all have a glass of champagne to celebrate.'

'Oh, no, really, thanks all the same, Mr Jenks,' said Lily. 'If you don't mind, I'd just like to run away home now and sleep.'

And she had such a faraway look in her eyes – as would any starry-eyed kid from the sticks who'd found herself transported into a make-believe world where dreams came true – that it would have been cruel to break the spell.

'Whatever you prefer,' he said. 'But, if you don't mind, I'll send a car to pick you up in the morning so we can have a proper talk.'

'That would be great.'

'I'll come with you now and find you a taxi.'

As he took her elbow to escort her to the doors, the reporters rushed forwards.

'Where is your mother?' one called out. 'Do you know?'

'Why wasn't she here tonight?'

'Did she know you'd be singing her song?'

'When did you find out you were her daughter?'

'When is Delia coming back?'

Peter held up his free hand. 'Hey, chaps, not now, OK? Don't worry, we'll organize a press conference tomorrow and you can ask all the questions you want but, for now, Miss Brooks is going home for some well-earned sleep.'

The reporters followed them to the door, repeating their questions, but Peter waved them aside and shepherded Lily safely away. I slipped out behind them, leaving Celeste with Davey.

It was late and there wasn't much traffic along Park Lane as I walked back to my car. A nearly full moon had risen above the trees in the park and cast sharp, strange silhouettes on the pavement in front of me.

Davey was right that, tonight, Lily had been handed a blank cheque: this was a modern fairy tale the press and the fans were going to adore. But why hadn't Delia been there to play her part and publicly reclaim the child she'd given up? And why didn't Lily know – or was unwilling to say – where Delia was?

Imagining Delia's rush of love for her lost child, I realized that, if I knew what was best for me, I ought to put the whole business out of my mind and accept the job in West Africa. In truth, there was little enough to keep me in the country, except my parents in Bromley, a married sister in Nottingham and a ticket for the Second Test at Lord's in June. But tonight, as I shivered in the night air, I was haunted by the memory of Evelyn walking out of our hotel room in Kuala Lumpur.

I'd left Malaya and been in Ceylon for four months when,

nearly six months after Evelyn had so abruptly ended our affair, I heard that she'd given birth to a son. She'd never even told me she was pregnant. I often thought about the boy. He'd be old enough to go to school now. Not for the first time, I wondered if he looked at all like me.

10

A few days afterwards, at Peter's request – and this time with Lily's permission – I unlocked the door to Delia Maxwell's mews house in Knightsbridge. It was late afternoon and there had been heavy rain all day. I left my wet brolly in the tiny hallway and looked up the narrow stairs.

Although Lily had dropped her bombshell at the awards ceremony too late for the next morning's papers to run more than a short inside column, her announcement, linked to Delia's disappearance, had been front-page news in all the Sundays and each day since. Yet, in spite of the hysterical coverage, there was still no clue to explain Delia's absence. At the press conference Peter had set up, Lily had calmly repeated to the clamouring reporters that she was as mystified as everyone else as to where Delia had gone, or why. She had also deftly evaded questions about when and how she and Delia had discovered their true relationship, and remained strangely enigmatic about her mother's state of mind other than to say that, in the days before she left, Delia had told Lily she was happier than she'd been in years. Not that Lily's reticence had prevented speculation from running wild.

Meanwhile Peter was at pains to explain to anyone who would

listen that the reason he'd beaten his rivals to be first in signing Lily to a label was because it was what Delia would want and he owed it to her to do everything he could for her daughter. I guessed that he felt guilty about the indelicate haste with which the deal had been struck. Twice he reminded me that Delia had given him his first really big hit after he had joined his grandfather's company, and that when her recording contract had come up for renewal, she had become a huge international star who could take her pick of offers yet had chosen to stay with him. He would never do anything to betray her loyalty.

Finally, for want of any other possible action, he'd asked me to make a thorough search of her papers for any hint of where she might be. I told him I had no idea what he expected me to find but, now the story was out, he was adamant that he couldn't go on doing nothing. He had to be sure that she was safe.

And so, once again, I found myself climbing the stairs to the first floor. The house was silent in the way that only an unoccupied home can be, and I imagined Delia coming in after a performance, or at the end of a long foreign tour. I could still vividly remember from my flying days how hard it could be to return to solitude and silence after experiencing intensity and fear, to be shut in a room alone with the adrenalin still coursing through my veins, the noise of the ack-ack guns and the light of roving searchlights trapped inside my head. Stepping out alone into a spotlight on stage in front of an expectant audience must in many ways be similar to taking off on a mission, with the dread of making a mistake and being shot down in flames almost as crippling, and the relief of coming back unscathed just as great. What did Delia do with herself to dispel such emotions?

I also thought about her returning here after dropping Lily off in Earl's Court on the night of Conrad's birthday. Had she sensed straight away that Lily was hers? I often imagined what it would be like if I were ever to come face to face with Evelyn's son, convinced I'd know immediately whether or not he was mine. Sometimes I encountered him in dreams in which my deep and primitive jolt of recognition was almost unbearable. Surely Delia's happiness at finding her child at last would have been just as intoxicating.

So why wasn't she here? If she had been afraid of scandal over her teenage pregnancy, then a glimpse of any of the recent front pages would surely convince her otherwise. And she must have realized that the story would only grow bigger the longer she stayed away. What other reason could prevent her return? Why had she not been found? The more time passed, the more reason there was to fear the worst.

Feeling like a peeping Tom in the unlit first-floor corridor, I steeled myself to enter her bedroom. It was a square, white-painted room, unexpectedly small and simple. The rain-streaked window overlooked another mews passage at the back. The bed had crisp white sheets and a rose-pink satin eiderdown. The lamps on the bedside tables had glass drops and pleated fabric shades in the same colour, matching the flowers on the chintz curtains. The pale blue dressing-gown hanging on the back of the door did not look as if it had been chosen for seduction.

I opened her bedside drawers and looked under the bed. A clock, a book-marked novel, an eye-mask, a bottle of aspirin, a dropped handkerchief: nothing to tell me where she was now. And almost nothing to add to the little I already knew about the woman who slept there. I began to feel it was a hopeless task: if a woman chose to conceal herself, there was little any man could do about it.

In the bathroom, recalling Celeste's anxiety about an overdose, I checked the mirrored cabinet where, among talcum powder, hand-cream and shampoo, I found a half-empty container of Benzedrine, a prescription label on the canister, and a bottle of Nembutal. Marilyn Monroe had died from just such a cocktail of pep-pills and barbiturates, so I was relieved to see that the bottle of Nembutal was still three-quarters full.

As for the Benzedrine, I could easily imagine how a seasoned performer like Delia might appreciate the extra kick of a bennie or a purple heart. After all, I'd happily taken the wakey-wakey pills doled out by the RAF quacks when we were flying constant bomber-support operations. I'd been only too glad to be kept alert. On the other hand, I'd also seen how getting hooked on them had made one or two perfectly good pilots so reckless or paranoid that no one wanted to fly with them. And coming down from them could be like slamming into a brick wall.

Perhaps, after all, the most obvious explanation for Delia's abrupt and silent departure was that she'd booked herself into one of those discreet private clinics to undertake a cure, although my hunch was that an addict would never have left surplus drugs behind.

I closed the cabinet and moved on to the dressing room. The wall of deep built-in cupboards was packed full of coats, including furs, dresses, shoes, handbags, silk scarves and gloves. Opening the doors released a powdery fragrance of lemon and violet and a deeper floral scent I couldn't identify. The trace of her perfume offered my first direct experience of her physical presence, and made me recoil from what I was doing, a clumsy

stranger prying into an unknown woman's life, and simultaneously want to inhale that fragrance deeply enough to pull her
closer and pierce her mystery.

I reviewed how little I still knew about her, and asked myself
whether it was in her nature to be elusive, or whether she had
been forced to become so to cover her tracks after giving up her
illegitimate child. Either way, my intelligence skills, such as
they were, had been honed on the interrogation of Communist
sympathizers in Malaya, which certainly hadn't left me with
the subtle investigative techniques required to track down a
woman who remained so enigmatic.

To begin with, her original name was not Delia Maxwell, and
not even Peter knew what it had been. However, Conrad Durand,
the old family friend who'd brought Delia to England after the
war, had been Hungarian. And when Peter had spoken to Lily's
foster parents about her contract with RMJ Records, they'd
explained that Lily had taken their name, Brooks, because in
the children's home where she'd been before coming to live
with them, she'd been bullied about her birth mother's unpro-
nounceable Hungarian surname.

Although Peter had said Delia didn't like to talk about her
past, and he'd never pressed for details, he had the impression
she'd been some kind of refugee before Conrad had taken her
in. Perhaps she'd even been in a camp. I'd ended up as a prisoner
of war for a few months after being shot down and, when the
Nazis evacuated Stalag Luft III ahead of the Soviet advance, I'd
seen many a long line of poor souls being forced to trudge along
the snowy, bombed-out roads of Europe, some of them little
more than ragged skeletons in their striped cotton uniforms. I
might have had to march for six days in freezing weather but at

least I'd received Red Cross parcels and still had a home and a country to return to.

It was possible that she'd already been pregnant when Conrad had rescued her, if that was what had happened. We'd all heard stories about the brutality of the Russian troops, raping any woman they could find; I reckoned our side weren't always too scrupulous, either, although it was unpatriotic to say so. Or, in spite of Celeste's faith in him, was Conrad Lily's father after all? Whatever the truth, Delia had had plenty of good reasons to remain silent about her past.

Needing a stronger sense of connection to my quarry, I turned to her dressing-table. Among the abundance of brushes, cosmetics, hairspray and night creams was a flat-fronted perfume bottle, Guerlain's L'Heure Bleue. I removed the ornate glass stopper and inhaled the scent. It was the same fragrance that clung to the clothes in the cupboards, heady and mysterious, impossible to describe. I sat on the stool in front of the angled mirrors, listened to the rain patter against the window, and tried to picture Delia dabbing a spot on her wrists or at the base of her throat. I hoped that, if her reflection could look back at me, it would forgive me for being there.

11

The papers in Delia's desk upstairs had all been neatly filed and labelled in a round childish hand that I guessed was Lily's. When I'd finished looking through them I took the liberty of going down to the kitchen and helping myself to a large glass of Delia's excellent whisky. I wasn't sure that I had learned anything new, but reading Delia's handwriting and touching so many objects she had held made her seem more real than a photograph on an album sleeve or some dimly remembered television appearance.

Back in the rooftop living room, I put another of her records on the stereo, settled in an armchair, loosened my tie and stretched out my legs in front of me. The LP I'd chosen was her most recent album and some of the tracks were new to me. The strength and purity of her voice could not hide the underlying threads of passion and vulnerability that were woven through all of her music. This, if anywhere, was where Delia truly revealed herself.

I stared out through the streaming windows at the cloudy grey dusk gathering beyond the smoking chimney stacks. I couldn't stop myself thinking about Evelyn. We had spent hours – occasionally days – in each other's arms and yet now I realized how far her physical presence had faded from me. I strove to recall the touch of her lips, the smell of her hair, and how I would push back a strand, dampened by the steamy heat, which had stuck to her forehead. I thought of her son, and tried to imagine the two of them together, Evelyn reading to him, throwing a ball in the garden or handing him over to his *amah* before dressing to go out for the evening. I could almost hear the swish of the stiff silk of her skirts.

I was sure Delia, too, must have sat here and thought about her child – until Lily had miraculously walked back into her life. I'd have given a lot to know whether that had been coincidence – some divine Providence – or if, outside the BBC concert hall that night, Lily already had some inkling, later confirmed, that Delia was the mother who had given her up.

I found it impossible to believe that, having found her child again, Delia wouldn't want to stay as close beside her as she could. If, as Lily claimed, Delia *had* become disillusioned with her fame, then surely Lily's presence in her life offered an alternative of inestimable value. Wouldn't Delia relish the ability to wave her magic wand and open up her charmed world to her daughter? And even if her absence had been some kind of deliberate stunt to launch Lily's career, that was now accomplished – and, besides, why would Delia choose to go on the very day she was supposed to sign her new movie contract?

I turned my head to look at the photograph of Conrad Durand: if he was Lily's father, there was little physical resemblance. I had, however, discovered more about him from the desk's contents than I had about Delia herself. I'd learned, for instance, that he'd been born in Budapest before the turn of the twentieth century, that he wasn't Jewish, which was presumably why he'd been able to protect his commercial interests and to travel through Nazi Europe, and that he'd died a wealthy man and left everything to Delia. He must have known her – and her secrets – better than anyone else.

Perhaps I shouldn't have had that drink, or I had fallen too much under the spell of the melancholic song Delia was singing on the stereo, but I began to resent Conrad almost as much as Evelyn's brute of a husband. What gave any man the right to control a woman's life, and that of her child? I got up and went over to the desk. It was puerile behaviour, but I laid the photograph flat so I didn't have to feel his eyes watching the back of my head.

As a track ended and another began, I sat sipping my drink and listening to Delia sing of her lonely heart and her yearning to see her lover one more time. The words were shallow, yet I was convinced that the woman singing them shared my own hopes and longings. I'd have given anything at that moment to be transported back to that final afternoon with Evelyn in Kuala Lumpur and to be given the chance somehow to end our affair differently, or at least to understand why she had rejected me. I'd never spoken about it to anyone, yet Delia's voice was telling me that she, too, had suffered in similar ways. I sank lower in my chair and closed my eyes, allowing her rich tones to swell and fill the room.

I must have fallen asleep, for when I awoke it was dark and the music had stopped. The rain had eased a little and I wasn't aware that anything had roused me, but as I straightened my back and ran my hands over my face I was sure I heard a floorboard creak somewhere below me.

I got quietly to my feet, feeling like a burglar caught in the act, and tiptoed to the doorway. A light shone from the corridor below. I had not switched it on. I felt cornered and sick. A figure appeared at the bottom of the stairs. Backlit, I couldn't see a face, but the outline looked too slight to be a man.

'Lily?' I called. 'Is that you?'

'Who are you?' A woman's voice, high and afraid. 'What are you doing here?'

'My name is Frank Landry. I'm retained by RMJ Records. I can explain.' My brain was working far too slowly, but I knew enough to retreat back into the room, away from the top of the stairs, so as to appear less threatening.

More lights went on. Footsteps ascended and then the woman stood framed in the doorway. She had brown hair, still damp from the rain, and wore flat shoes, a sensible tweed skirt and matching oatmeal-coloured twin-set. She cast a frightened look around, as if expecting to find the place ransacked, then back at me, gripping the door-frame and sizing me up with real fear in her eyes.

Sobering up, I took in what she must see – my dishevelled hair, loosened tie, an empty glass on the floor beside my chair – and held up my hands in appeasement, taking another step back.

I could only stare at her in astonishment. She was smaller, and her face more delicate and fine-boned, than I'd expected, but the perfect skin and dark, lustrous eyes were every bit as beautiful as they were in her photographs. Delia had come home.

12

DELIA

She'd been terrified when she'd first heard him call out from upstairs – she'd been so careful to check there were no lights on before she'd let herself in – yet as soon as she'd understood who he was she had stopped being afraid. Nevertheless, she now remained standing behind her front door listening to his departing footsteps until all she could hear was the rain.

After a minute or so she roused herself and went upstairs to the kitchen where she stared at Frank Landry's empty whisky glass in the sink. Peter had often spoken of how he and Frank had met as trainee RAF pilots during the war, only eighteen years old, and how Frank had saved his life in an aerial dogfight at the cost of getting himself shot down and captured. Knowing this, she wasn't able to mind as much as she should about the uninvited stranger having made himself at home in her house.

After she'd cut short his embarrassed apologies, he had picked up his glass and carried it downstairs, placing it in the sink on his way out. She'd warmed to something in his manner, the genuine contrition in his blue eyes. That was when she'd made him promise to delay telling Peter of her reappearance until she'd had time to do so herself. She liked that, conscious of his loyalty to his old friend, he'd been reluctant to agree. All the same, it didn't leave her very long to come to a decision about the future.

She had returned this evening intending to stay only for as long as it took to pack a couple of suitcases and retrieve all the documentation required for Delia Maxwell to vanish for ever. But now she was trapped. Frank Landry was bound to tell Peter sooner or later that she'd come back. Besides, if Peter had cared enough to send the man to whom he owed his life to find her, she couldn't let him down by running away again. She owed him that much at least. She couldn't start to think about what she owed Lily.

She hadn't planned her initial escape. To begin with, she hadn't dared to believe the possible significance of some of Lily's stray comments about the circumstances of her birth. And then, when Lily's answers to a few of her own deliberately tentative questions seemed to confirm that Lily might really be the baby Delia had given up for adoption, she had feared being overwhelmed by long-buried emotions. When Lily, the hope showing clearly in her eyes, first hinted that she, too, was beginning to suspect the truth, Delia had frozen, unable to decide which way to turn.

Long accustomed to keeping her emotions hidden, and sensing that Lily was on the point of speaking, of seeking confirmation, Delia had felt as if everything was rushing towards her too fast. Plus, once she signed the new contract, the madness of making a Hollywood movie would further engulf her, leaving her no time to spend with Lily, get to know her daughter and make amends.

A further pressure was her dread that she had been deluding herself and it would turn out that Lily was not after all her child. How would she be able to hide such crushing disappointment from an audience, let alone in front of a film camera? She simply couldn't imagine acting on a forty-foot screen when her heart was broken.

Whether Lily was hers or not, some kind of resolution was fast approaching and Delia hadn't been able to face it. So she had run away.

She'd always kept a wig similar to the natural colour of her hair that, worn with dark glasses, had been useful for incognito visits to her doctor or dentist. She had added some dowdy new clothes, packed a few essentials, and taken a random train north. She'd crisscrossed the country many times for singing engagements, but this time, as she'd looked out of the carriage window at unfamiliar stations and landscapes, and heard the iron beat of the wheels, she'd been unable to withstand a flood of memories of an earlier journey. The old feelings of grief and guilt confirmed she had been right to flee.

By the time a taxi dropped her off at a small hotel beside a lake, she was filled with fear that she would be exposed for what she truly was – a sham, a thief and a murderer. She had crept into a chilly bed and hidden away. When she eventually ventured out, she had spoken to no one except the elderly waiter who served her meals.

Work, Conrad used to tell her, work was the thing, the only thing. He'd been her father's closest friend, an impresario who had spent his professional life in theatres and opera houses. He had first praised her voice and encouraged her to sing as a child, and later, after the war, when she had had to think about her future, he'd told her to sing. He'd introduced her to Peter, and told her to trust him and to work hard for him. He had found people like Celeste and Davey to support her. And so she had worked, been glad to work. It had been a relief, and work finally offered her something she could have some control over. And everyone had been happy. Starting with house orchestras at hotel dinner-dances, then appearing in local theatres, and later in international concert halls and fabled Las Vegas hotels, she had found eager audiences who clapped and cheered; in each new town she saw her name in lights; she'd hear her voice on the transistor radios of passing cars; she'd marvel at the crowds who turned out to welcome her at airports on far-flung continents; and the money rolled in. All she ever had to do was sing.

And she was happy to sing. She was never lonely when she sang. She could tell the truth and reach out to ask forgiveness for the terrible thing she'd done. Yet, at the same time, the singing had created someone who was not really her at all and allowed her original self to disappear. When she was among other musicians, Delia Maxwell could be nothing but the music. It became as natural as breathing. Except that she was still breathing when so many from her past were not.

Her father, Oskar, used to smile when she attempted the popular songs of the day. She could still hear him cracking his arthritic knuckles as he sat and listened. He wasn't old, and he'd been able to employ assistants in the fashionable photographic studio he ran in Budapest, until all Jewish businesses were banned, but his hands still suffered from so many hours under cold running water in the darkroom,

She was his first-born and he had chosen to save her by sending her away. He'd promised she would come back as soon as it was safe.

She had never stopped having nightmares about the platform

at Budapest's Keleti railway station where, at fourteen, she had clung to the lapels of his greatcoat, inhaling the scent of its damp wool along with the tang of ash from the engine as the waiting train hissed and blew clouds of white steam. Sometimes she could barely remember being that child, yet the emotions of that morning remained as sharp as ever. She had begged him to let her stay, but he had prised her fingers loose and forced her up the steep steps into the carriage. She would never forget the sound of the door closing before the train carried her away from everything and everyone she knew.

As arranged, Conrad had met her in Zürich, although not before she had spent forty agonizing minutes waiting alone in the teeming hall of the Hauptbahnhof. Occasionally, as she waited in the wings for her cue, she'd be seized again by the alarm and growing panic of those long minutes when she had believed herself abandoned. The first time that happened, she didn't think she'd be able to move, but, by focusing on her first glimpse of Conrad approaching through the crowd, she'd been able to force herself out on stage.

In Zürich, he had kept assuring her that her stay would be temporary, that she would see her family again, until it was no longer possible for anyone to make such promises. Within two years, it seemed as if everyone she knew – her parents, Oskar and Eva, and her younger sister Zsofia, her uncles and aunts, many of her school friends and their families – was dead. Conrad was all she had left. Others had paid for her survival, and only her beloved father had believed the price worth paying.

She'd never been sure what Conrad knew of how her deliverance had been contrived, and she had never felt able to ask him. She depended on him too much. If he had rejected her, she would have had to join the tens of thousands of other displaced persons milling around Europe, just one more kid with a suit-case (if she was lucky) and a Red Cross label pinned to her coat. She was grateful for the travel permits and visas he managed to obtain for her. He later confirmed her suspicion that they were recompense for his activities couriering secret docu-ments and information to and from Allied officials based in Switzerland.

Not long after she and Conrad arrived in London, the official confirmations began to come of all the deaths in the Nazi camps. Soon after that her labour pains began. Then those women who only pretended to be kind came and took her baby away, and she wanted to die so she could be with all the others who had died. It wasn't until much later that she allowed her-self to know or care what had happened to her daughter, who became yet one more person she had lost through her own cow-ardice and inaction.

After the birth, and when the fall of the Iron Curtain exiled her from Hungary, Conrad had new papers drawn up for her, granting her British citizenship. Even her name, Irma Székely, was forgotten. And then work had to be the thing, the only thing, as Irma Székely learned to sing her heart out to people who loved Delia Maxwell.

Until, years later, a rainy night outside the BBC concert hall led to a bittersweet promise of redemption. Delia had never been consciously aware of being safe and happy before the war because she had never needed to be. But when the sparse infor-mation about Lily's past – the date of her birthday, that her original surname was Hungarian – first began to cohere into miraculous possibility, and she watched Lily move about her house or wait for her to come off stage, she experienced tiny heart-stopping moments of thankfulness and relief. They reminded her of the early weeks of peacetime when rosebay willowherb began to soften the London bomb craters, and strangers would recognize in each other the same jolt of surprise that the war was truly over at last.

Except, if the miracle was real, she had no idea how to be a mother. Her own memories of family life seemed too distant and hazy. She was afraid of getting it wrong. After all, why on earth should Lily love her? Lily admired Delia Maxwell, but Delia Maxwell was not Irma Székely. And Irma Székely did not deserve to be loved.

With mousy hair and dull clothes, Delia had been sitting unrecognized in the lounge of her lakeside hotel when she saw the newspaper headlines about Lily's triumphant debut and her announcement that she was Delia Maxwell's long-lost daughter. She had felt nothing but relief that Lily had come to her own decision about her true identity. Reading the following day about the recording deal Lily had signed with Peter, Delia had convinced herself that Lily's future now lay in the best possible hands. She'd heard Lily sing, picking out chords on the piano in Delia's living room, and was sure that, with Peter and Davey's help, she could use this publicity to launch a promising career. Delia's kindest gift would be to leave the stage to her daughter, this time by vanishing completely. Her decision had given her a feeling of release as if, by disappearing, she could give back something of what she had taken when she'd obeyed her father and climbed into that train in Budapest.

However, now that Frank Landry had witnessed her brief return, she would have to stay. It would be unreasonable to disappear a second time, and they would only try all the harder to find her.

As she rinsed his empty glass and set it aside, she felt her heart squeeze and then release. She gripped the edge of the sink, recognizing the sensation as both pain and joy. Now she would have to reclaim her child.

13

Early the following morning she dialled the number for Lily's digs in Earl's Court. She wasn't sure if Lily would still be living in her shabby bedsit, but the landlady who picked up the receiver in the hallway grudgingly agreed to fetch her. While Delia waited for the woman to climb one flight of stairs and call up the next, she felt more nervous than before the most daunting performance. At last she heard descending footsteps, then Lily's voice on the line.

'Hello?'

'Lily, this is Delia.'

The pause was agonizing.

'You're back!'

The warmth in Lily's voice was unmistakable. Delia unclenched her fingers from around the phone. 'Yes, I'm back,' she said. 'Are you busy this morning? Can you come and see me?'

'Straight away!'

'Jump in a cab,' she said, excitement washing over her. 'I'll give you the money when you get here.'

She dressed and made herself up with care, needing the assurance of being Delia Maxwell, and half an hour later stood facing Lily in the centre of her rooftop living room.

'Let me look at you,' she said, holding out her hands.

As she drew Lily closer, a surge of exhilaration made her giddy. She was more accustomed to being on the receiving end of enthusiasm and adulation, and it felt strange and unnerving to experience the welling up of such extravagant emotion from within.

As Lily smiled at her shyly, Delia took time to study every feature as if she'd never seen the girl before. 'I only had a few hours with you when you were born,' she said, stroking Lily's fingers, 'but I remember your hands being so wondrously small. I'd never seen anything so tiny. Each little nail so perfect, and your eyes, fixed on mine, staring up at me. It seems like yesterday. Can you ever forgive me?'

'For what?'

'For giving you up.'

'You must have been younger than me,' said Lily. 'What choice did you have?'

'At the time, it certainly didn't feel as if I could choose anything,' said Delia. 'I could only do what they told me was best. But then, as the years passed, I kept imagining you growing up without me and blaming me for—'

'Don't,' said Lily. 'There's no need.'

'Are you sure you don't hate me?'

Lily squeezed Delia's hand and let it go. 'I'm here now. We're together at last. Anyway, what am I to call you? "Mother" seems too formal.'

'In Hungarian it would be "Anya".'

Lily seemed almost to recoil. 'No, not that. I'd like to go on using your name. I'm used to it now and, after all, I've been besotted with Delia Maxwell for as long as I can remember, ages before I had any notion of who you really were.'

'Whatever you like,' said Delia. 'If I'd been allowed to name *you*, I'd have given you my mother's name, Eva.'

Lily nodded. 'When I first saw your original name among your papers, I told myself I must be dreaming.'

'It's a long time since I answered to Irma Székely,' said Delia, 'and I assumed that, after I'd given you up, you wouldn't be told my name. But why didn't you say something when you saw it?'

'I suppose I was scared.'

'Of what?'

'That you might not want me. But not only that,' she went on hurriedly, before Delia could respond, 'I just couldn't believe it was true.'

'That's how I felt, too,' said Delia. 'At least at first, until some of the dates and names you mentioned began to add up. If only I'd kept my own name, you would have known straight away, and maybe found me sooner.'

Lily laughed. 'It wouldn't have made any difference. In some strange way I think I've always known who you were to me. I always believed you were singing just for me.'

'If only that were true.' Delia faltered. 'Singing is the one thing I'm any good at, but then, when I think of you, growing up without me – well, everything I've done feels so pointless.'

'If you hadn't sung,' said Lily, 'I'd never have found you.'

Delia smiled. 'That's true. It was a kind of miracle. To think that, if it hadn't been raining, we might never have met. I'm sorry I ran away. I feel so stupid about it now. But when I finally began to understand that I really had found you again, I panicked. It was so hard to work out how to think about you properly.'

'Where did you go?' Lily asked.

'The Lake District.'

'Why there?'

'No reason. I'd never been and people told me it's very beautiful. They were right.'

Lily looked down at the floor, uncharacteristically diffident. 'Why didn't you come back sooner?'

'As soon as I'd read the papers, you mean?'

'Yes. Were you angry that I told everyone?'

'No, of course not! I was proud that you wanted people to know, that you *wanted* to be my daughter, and wanted *me* to know. It was thrilling that you stood up there on stage and said so in front of everyone.'

'I didn't plan it, but when I saw all those faces, and knew that the applause was really meant for you, I had to tell the truth.'

'You're much braver than me.' Delia walked over to one of the windows and looked out, her back to the room. 'I spoke to Peter this morning. He said you were in a children's home before you went to live with Mr and Mrs Brooks. I had no idea. I'm so sorry.'

'I don't want to talk about the past.'

Stricken with guilt, Delia turned to face Lily again. 'Were you very unhappy? They said you were bullied. You mustn't spare me. You must tell me the truth.'

'It's over, gone. Promise me you'll never ask again.'

'If that's really what you want. But were Mr and Mrs Brooks kind to you? Did they—'

'No, you have to promise not to ask questions.'

'Very well. But if you feel differently another day, then you can talk to me about anything you want.'

'OK. But you won't go away again without telling me, will you?'

Delia smiled. 'I promise.'

'You'll be off to Hollywood soon,' Lily said ruefully.

'Maybe you can come with me.'

Lily shook her head. 'You'll be busy. I'd hardly see you. Can't you postpone it?'

'I'll have to speak to Peter,' said Delia. 'But I won't ever leave you. I want to make up for everything you've been through. We must find you somewhere nice to live. What if I buy a big house with gardens and a swimming pool? Then we can live together. Would you like a cat or a dog? And holidays. Where would you like to go? Let's go on a shopping spree – to Paris or Rome or New York. What do you say?'

Lily looked at the floor again, pointing one foot and digging the toe of her flat pump into the cream-coloured rug.

'Tell me!' said Delia. 'What would you like? We can fly off somewhere together. Have you ever been in an aeroplane?'

Lily looked up from under her lashes. 'You'll think I'm silly.'

'No, I won't.'

'You know that Peter has given me a recording contract?'

'Yes. I was so pleased when I read that in the papers,' said Delia. 'Oh, I so wish I'd been there to hear you at the awards night. You must have been so nervous, particularly in front of that crowd. Showbiz people are hard to please. But you must have done well, and I'll do everything I can to help you learn the ropes. Maybe you'd like music lessons.'

'I don't want lessons,' Lily said shyly. 'I want to record "Tell Me How It Ends". I know Davey wrote it for you, but he says I should make it my first single, that I should sing it just the way I did at the awards ceremony. That was before you came back, but you will speak to Peter, won't you? He says it's your song, but if you tell him that you can find something else and don't mind giving it to me, he won't mind, will he?'

Delia felt an unexpected surge of protest rise in her throat, but subdued it instantly, hoping her selfish impulse hadn't betrayed itself to Lily. After all, it wasn't really so much selfishness as a professionally honed instinct. Conrad had taught her too well and, after half a lifetime devoted to the creation of her stardom, it had become second nature to seize every opportunity. Yet how could her career weigh a jot against the chance of enabling her daughter to fulfil her dreams?

And, after all, Lily had no real comprehension of what she was asking. She was a child. How could she understand the way the music business operated, and how much effort had already been poured into laying the groundwork for the new release?

'Come here.' Delia held out her hands again. 'I'm sure I can persuade Peter. I'll talk to him first thing tomorrow.'

14

Peter was overjoyed to see her enter his office. 'Delia!' he cried, coming out from behind his desk to embrace her. 'It was such a fabulous surprise to hear your voice on the phone but even better to see you with my own eyes!'

'I don't know what to say.'

'Mary sends her love. And congratulations, if that's the correct expression.'

'I'm so sorry that I worried everyone so much,' she said. 'You must be furious at how I let you down. Can you ever forgive me?'

'Stars are allowed to be a little temperamental once in a while.' He waved her apology aside and ushered her to one of the buttoned leather sofas placed beside the grand marble fireplace, a draughty relic that he had refused to let the architect tear out during the recent modernization of the Edwardian building. 'You're looking great. Motherhood obviously suits you!'

Delia was pleased. The new pink-and-white-check suit Celeste had made for her was a deliberate copy of an outfit she'd seen worn by the American First Lady, Jackie Kennedy. Delia had hoped such homage would strike the right note with the Hollywood producers when she'd been supposed to sign the contract. Well, that hadn't happened, yet wearing the suit, with its oversized black buttons and three-quarter-length sleeves, made her feel satisfyingly chic and contemporary.

'I do at the very least owe you an explanation—'

But Peter cut her short, holding up his hands in a gesture of mock surrender. 'You don't have to tell me anything at all. We're simply delighted to have you back.'

Delia thought his cheerfulness seemed a little strained and, feeling responsible for the anxiety she'd caused, tried to sound reassuring. 'I can't really improve on Lily's announcement, anyway,' she said, with a smile.

'Very true!' he said. 'She'll be joining us in a minute. I have a proposition to put to both of you.'

Delia was surprised: Lily hadn't mentioned that she would be coming, but then Delia reflected that Lily's presence would make it easier to break it to Peter that she didn't intend to record what was supposed to be her new single. She felt bad about letting him down, especially after leaving him in the lurch with the Americans, but she'd made up her mind. Lily had to come first.

'Besides, I owe you an apology,' Peter continued. 'You must have been petrified, coming home to find Frank Landry snoozing away like Goldilocks in your house. He told me all about it. He was mortified, poor chap.'

'It was fine, really.'

'I'm glad,' he said. 'Ah, Lily, here you are.' He leaped up as if taken by surprise when his secretary opened the door and showed Lily into the room. She wore her usual flat black pumps, white jeans, an over-large black sweater and no trace of make-up. She went straight over to kiss Peter familiarly on the cheek before going to Delia and accepting her embrace. She took a seat on the sofa opposite, making herself at home by tucking one leg up beneath her and nestling into the corner.

Peter sat down beside Delia and looked from one woman to the other. 'Extraordinary!' he declared. 'It's so amazing to see the two of you together that I can't wait to tell you my proposal.' He turned to Delia. 'If only you'd heard Lily sing the other night. She's your daughter, all right. Not the same voice, not at all, but the same rare ability to reach the heart and soul of an audience. Everyone who was there is still talking about it. So my suggestion is this, that we record "Tell Me How It Ends" with both of you and release it as a mother-daughter duet.'

'What a wonderful suggestion,' said Delia. 'That never occurred to me, but I love it!'

'Davey's already putting together a new arrangement,' he told her. 'It'll be sensational.'

'I can't wait to get started.' Delia was thrilled. She couldn't imagine anything better than to go into a recording studio with her daughter and help her to master the subtle, difficult process of making a popular ballad appear simple. 'What do you think, Lily?'

'I'm not sure,' she said.

'Don't worry,' said Peter. 'Davey will work with you again, just like he did before.'

'It's not that.' She looked at Delia in helpless appeal.

Delia had to admit that she was disappointed by Lily's lack of enthusiasm, but she was determined to keep her word and smiled back reassuringly. 'Lily had an idea she might record it by herself.'

'But for you to sing it together will be the ideal answer to everyone's questions. "Tell Me How It Ends", all captured in one simple, bittersweet refrain,' said Peter. 'The title couldn't be more apt. The fairy tale ends happily. I guarantee it will shoot straight to number one. It can't fail!'

'I think your proposal is brilliant,' said Delia. She was already imagining how she might blend their voices to create new harmonies. 'Seriously, Lily, Peter's right. It tells such a great story that it really would be a far more remarkable and original launch for you than singing by yourself.'

'I don't think it would,' said Lily. 'I don't know how to say this without sounding—' She broke off, looking at Peter as if for help, and clearly upset by the difficulty of explaining herself.

'Go on,' said Delia. 'Whatever it is, we won't mind.'

'It's just that there's a new music scene now.' Lily twisted her hands in her lap, then shifted her gaze to Delia, almost deliberately taking in the pink-check suit. 'The kids want what's young and new.' She looked down at her hands, her voice dropping so they had to crane to hear her. 'The kids don't want to look like their parents.'

Delia felt as if she'd been slapped. But then she looked at Lily and suddenly understood that the girl wore her hair cropped short and slouched around in simple jeans and a sweater not because she had no money to spend on more formal clothes but because this was her style: this was the future. Lily didn't want to look like her mother. Or to be seen singing a duet with her, either.

'It's fine.' Delia ignored Peter's inarticulate protest. 'Don't say another word. I understand completely.'

Conrad had taught her that, if she wanted to succeed, she had to curb other desires – for rest, for food, for time to lay aside the mask – but she'd seldom been asked to sacrifice something she wanted in order to grant someone else's wish. With a rush of mingled tenderness and regret, she recalled how her mother had spoiled her and her sister when they were little. Yet she had given away all those sweet moments of indulging an imperious child, of laughing when a parent ought to be strict, of bestowing an ice-cream or reading one more bedtime story. She had so much to make up for, and was determined to savour every precious moment.

'The duet is a lovely idea, Peter,' she said, 'but Lily's right. "Tell Me How It Ends" should be her song. Her first hit. And it would be a shame to waste all the hard work that she and Davey must already have put into it.' She held up a hand as Peter opened his mouth to protest again. 'No arguments.'

Peter wrestled silently with his objections for a moment, then gave in. 'Very well, Delia, if you're absolutely sure that's what you want.' He gathered himself together and turned to Lily. 'And you'll do it beautifully, just as you did at the awards ceremony. It's not that I ever feared you wouldn't, it was just such a unique opportunity to do something rather special.'

'Thank you,' said Lily, her eyes bright with pleasure. 'Thank you both. I won't let either of you down, I promise.'

'I'll let Davey know the change of plan,' Peter said. 'The recording studio's already booked for today, and he understands we need to release a single as soon as possible so we don't lose the momentum of all this publicity.'

Lily leaped up and kissed each of them in turn. 'I'm so happy! This is all such a dream!'

'I need a quick word with your mother,' he said stiffly. 'Would you mind waiting for her outside?'

'It's OK. I want to run over to Carnaby Street and look at a new boutique that's just opened. I won't be long.' Lily blew more kisses and closed the door behind her.

Delia smiled at Peter. 'I know your plan was perfect, but I can't resist making her happy.'

'Fair enough,' he said. 'But to be honest, Delia, it's your career I'm more concerned about.'

'You think it will hurt me with the fans?' she asked. 'That I was an unwed mother?'

'No, not that. The irony is, of course, that Lily's announcement has been a great human-interest story and the press will go on lapping it up. No, I'm afraid it's about wooing back the American producers. I did my best, but they weren't at all pleased at being stood up.'

'I know I chose the worst possible moment to play truant,' she said apologetically, 'but they'll give me a second chance, won't they?'

'We can try.'

'Everything just came at once,' she said. 'I haven't changed my mind about wanting to act. I'm still really looking forward to making the movie.'

'Good,' he said, visibly relieved. 'I'll let them know straight away.'

'Only, do you think they'd let us postpone for a while?' she asked. 'I can't leave the country now, not for six months or so, not now that I've found her again.'

Peter frowned, clearly hating what he had to say. 'You've not forgotten why we went after the movie deal in the first place?'

Delia sighed and sat back against the hard, buttoned leather of the sofa. 'Of course not,' she said. 'My style of stardom belongs to the Fifties and I have to reinvent myself.'

'The music scene is changing faster than ever right now,' he said. 'If we don't change with it, we risk being left behind.'

Recalling Lily's pronouncement, she smoothed her pink check skirt over her knees and smiled wryly at Peter. 'The kids don't want to look like their parents.'

'I'm afraid she's right,' he said. 'Look, I can talk to the Americans and see what they say, but they're ready to go into production. They won't wait for ever. What if you and I were to fly out and meet with them? We don't have to stay for very long, only a few days. It might just do the trick.'

'Oh, Peter, I don't know. I have to do what's right for me for once, rather than what's best for my career.'

'They're the same thing, aren't they?' he asked gently.

'I'm not sure I know any more.'

Delia wanted to explain to him how, the previous week, when she'd been able to walk by the wind-ruffled lake or sit in a tea-shop entirely unnoticed, she had expected to enjoy the novel liberation of anonymity but instead had felt strangely invisible. She hadn't experienced that in years, and wasn't sure she'd liked it, any more than she could honestly admit that she'd welcomed having to manage without all the little attentions and considerations that constantly smoothed Delia Maxwell's path through life. The realization that she no longer knew how to live an ordinary existence had been unsettling.

'My life suddenly seems so selfish and self-absorbed,' she said. 'I've seen other women, big stars, out on the road and trying to juggle being a mother to their children. It doesn't look easy.'

'Lily's not a baby.'

'I know. But I'm a mother now. I have someone else to put first. I don't want to get it wrong.'

Peter frowned. 'You're not saying you want to ditch your career?'

'No, no, of course not. I still want to go into acting, only there are other things I want to do before I go to California, like making sure Lily is properly settled. I'm thinking about buying a new house.'

'All right,' he said. 'Let's say that you don't make this movie. How would that help Lily?'

Delia smiled. 'It wouldn't. I'm only asking for a little time.'

'I'm afraid you may not have that luxury now. Especially after you've given away the number we had all nicely lined up with the radio stations and DJs. Lily will benefit from that, which will help keep your name in the news, but if you leave a vacuum for too long, don't be surprised if others rush to fill it.'

'I do understand,' she said. 'It's just that finding Lily is all so new and bewildering. I feel like I'm Rip Van Winkle, falling asleep for twenty years and waking up to discover I've grown a long white beard and missed the revolutionary war.'

'We'd only have to stay in Hollywood a couple of days,' he urged. 'The sooner we go the better.'

Delia rose to her feet. 'Let me think about it.'

At the door, he turned and placed a hand on her arm. 'May I give you some advice?'

'Please do.'

'I love my children,' he said. 'I want to offer them the best life I possibly can. But – well, I came out of the war in one piece. I'm still here. Sometimes I think that's all anyone can ever really give their children. Just to be there.'

Delia tried to shut out the urgent sound of the hissing engine and her father closing the carriage door. She forced a smile. 'Yes, but you've been right next to your children since the day they were born.'

'And you,' he said, returning her smile, 'are Delia Maxwell.'

15

Delia stared at her reflection in the dressing-table mirror as she slipped off the pink-check suit jacket she had put on with such pleasure only a couple of hours earlier. She laid it aside, certain she would never wear it again.

Lily had not returned to Peter's office by the time she was ready to leave. Assuming the girl would go directly to join Davey at the studio, Delia had gone home, telling herself it didn't matter that Lily hadn't wanted them to go together.

After all, it wasn't as if Lily needed her mother to take her by the hand for her first day at school. All the same, if Lily was serious about a singing career, then surely she must appreciate how much Delia had to offer. Delia might not have been there to teach her how to tie her shoelaces – she had forfeited that – but she could still show Lily how best to survive in the hothouse world she was about to enter. She wondered if Lily was shy about asking for help. If so, perhaps she ought to find a taxi and simply turn up at the studio. Davey wouldn't mind. More likely he would be glad to have her there. After all, she could judge better than he how far Lily's untrained voice should be pushed. They were probably waiting for her, annoyed that she hadn't shown up.

First she must change her clothes. When rehearsing or recording, she usually wore a simple sweater with slacks or a skirt, but suddenly she felt self-conscious. She was hardly old, only thirty-four, yet she no longer belonged among her daughter's generation. They were teenagers and she'd look silly if it appeared she was trying to imitate their style.

Then a wave of protest bubbled up deep inside. She wasn't ready to stand aside, to be relegated to being square and out-of-date. For years she had led the way, a Pied Piper of fashion, with magazines and newspapers reporting her every change of hairstyle, lipstick or hemline. Her presence on any street instantly drew awe-struck crowds. Although occasionally oppressive, the attention had made her feel connected, admired, *loved*, and despite Peter's warnings that her heyday might be over, she refused to believe the adulation she'd earned could simply disappear overnight.

A renegade idea insinuated itself. Where should her loyalties truly lie? She had known Lily only a few months, while her fans had loved her for years. She rejected it immediately, shaken by the unpleasant sense of betrayal. Lily was her *daughter*, her flesh and blood. Had she become so inured to the lack of any real familial bond in her life that she was now incapable of embracing the presence of her own child?

And yet she knew in her bones that Peter was right: she wasn't ready to give up everything she had achieved. Was it so wrong to want both? Yes, she must do everything in her power to help and guide her daughter to the life she dreamed of, but *she* was still Delia Maxwell. She would telephone him later and agree to his suggestion that they fly out to Hollywood to discuss her movie project.

She was pulling on a sweater when the doorbell rang. Before going downstairs she took a precautionary look out of the window. Returning earlier by taxi, she had noticed a couple of reporters with cameras prowling around the entrance to the mews, and had no wish to encounter them. Instead she was dismayed to see Celeste holding a large bouquet of roses. Their last meeting had been difficult and they had parted in anger, but it would be unkind to reject this gesture of friendship.

'Peter rang and I came straight over,' Celeste exclaimed, as soon as Delia opened the door. 'I couldn't wait to see you! And these are for you.'

'That's sweet, thank you,' said Delia, accepting the flowers but drawing her quickly inside away from prying eyes.

'I can't tell you how glad I am that you're safe,' said Celeste. 'I've been so worried, and so very sorry about the things I said. Now that I understand about Lily, of course everything makes perfect sense. I hope you can understand that I was only trying to look out for you.'

'Come upstairs,' said Delia, trying to cut the apologies short. 'We both lost our temper, so we're equally to blame. And I'm sorry, too.'

She led Celeste into the kitchen, glad of the distraction of arranging the flowers at the sink. 'I'm due at the studio,' she said, 'but there's time to make you a quick coffee.'

'No, I'm fine. I won't stay. I only wanted to welcome you back, and to congratulate you.'

Seeing Celeste glance at another flower arrangement on the table, sent by Frank Landry the day before with a note of apology, Delia made a show of inhaling the scent of Celeste's roses. She never understood what made her withhold affection from her oldest friend. She had long ago guessed Celeste's secret – that she had feelings for Delia that Delia could never reciprocate – but she wasn't sure whether this was the reason or whether her failure to love was something that had become entrenched after her father had sent her away. The warmth and security of her childhood had become so entangled with abandonment and grief that she'd all but forgotten the simple pleasures of loving – until Lily had reminded her.

'I love champagne roses, and these are magnificent,' she said. 'You always know what I'll like best.'

Celeste visibly relaxed. 'Oh, Delia,' she said, clasping her hands together, 'I saw Lily sing! It was thrilling. You must be so proud.'

'I can't take much credit,' Delia said drily.

'Perhaps not. All the same, she was wonderful. She's certainly inherited your star quality. Tell me, when did you find out she was your child?'

'I'd rather not talk about it now, if you don't mind.'

'One more Delia Maxwell mystery?'

Delia laughed and, turning away from the sink, kissed Celeste's cheek. 'I know you understand,' she said. 'I'll tell you everything another time.'

'Of course,' Celeste said brightly. 'Life will be very different from now on.'

'It will.' Aware of how she was shutting Celeste out, she yielded. 'There's been so much to take in. I haven't worked out my own feelings yet – except that I'm over the moon.'

'I'm so happy for you,' Celeste said. 'For you both.'

'I'm glad to hear you say that. I already feel that my life will be so much richer. And I won't be all alone in the world any more.' Delia instantly regretted her words. 'I meant family,' she said, reaching out to touch Celeste's hand. 'I've always been very lucky to have such good friends.'

Celeste gave a wan smile. 'So what happens next?' she asked. 'You'll still go ahead with the movie?'

'Yes, I hope so,' said Delia, 'although we're going to ask if the producers are prepared to delay for a little while.'

'Why?'

'Some breathing space before I dive in, that's all.'

'But right now you're more famous than ever,' Celeste protested. 'You really should be riding the crest of the wave.'

'You sound like Conrad,' said Delia. 'If he were here, I'd already be on set: lights, camera, action!'

'And enjoying every minute.'

It was true, and Delia laughed once more, feeling lighter than she had in weeks. Suddenly she was sure of what she really wanted. It had been Conrad who'd first brought Delia and Celeste together and it was good to be reminded of how they'd always supported and encouraged one another. In a still-rationed England, desperate for some style and pizzazz, it had been the glamour of the young dressmaker's extravagant gowns, stitched from parachute silk and beads unpicked from old clothes she'd found in street markets, and following the stylish lines of Dior's New Look, that had played a vital role in creating the image of Delia Maxwell. Her fame in turn had boosted the new salon Conrad had helped Celeste to establish. Perhaps, in making a movie, in trying something new, Delia could not only reinvent herself but also recapture the adventurous spirit of those early years. Besides, if she wanted Lily to go on admiring Delia Maxwell, then Delia Maxwell had to go on being a star.

Delia gave Celeste an affectionate hug. 'I'm glad you came over. It's really helped.'

Celeste's cheeks flushed with pleasure, the same delicate pink as the champagne roses she'd brought. 'Good. I'm so pleased.'

'But, look, if you don't mind,' Delia apologized, 'Davey's expecting me.'

'Back to work!' Celeste embraced her. 'Call me any time. I'm so happy you're safe and well.'

Delia accompanied her downstairs. 'Before I forget,' she said, as Celeste reached out to open the door, 'did I leave my diamond earrings in your salon after the last fitting? I looked for them this morning but couldn't find them anywhere. The fitting was the last time I remember wearing them.'

'Oh, but Lily has them,' said Celeste. 'She wore them to the awards ceremony. She said you gave them to her.'

'Oh, yes, of course I did,' Delia lied. 'How stupid of me. I'd completely forgotten. Goodbye, Celeste. It was kind of you to come over. And I love the roses.'

Delia bundled her out into the mews before Celeste could notice or remark upon her confusion.

16

As the taxi drove north towards St John's Wood, Delia tried to subdue the panicky feelings of guilt that had resulted from her natural impulse, as soon as Celeste had gone, to run upstairs and check whether any other jewellery was missing. She'd stifled the urge immediately, but was ashamed that she'd even entertained such suspicion.

She couldn't believe Celeste would seek to cause trouble by inventing the story, so perhaps she had misunderstood or misreported what Lily had actually said. And even if Lily *had* claimed Delia had given her the diamonds, she must have known that Delia would have lent them gladly if she'd been there to grant permission.

Delia would never have dreamed of taking anything from either of her parents without asking, but that had been a different era. After all, mothers and daughters borrowed clothes and suchlike from each other all the time, didn't they? Delia was sure she could remember her mother scolding her, albeit while laughing, for playing with her lipstick or parading around in some expensive new hat.

She was vexed. It was all so trivial! Why should it matter even if Lily, full of nerves before the awards ceremony, *had* chosen to tell a little fib? After all, she could hardly explain why she could assume Delia's consent when no one yet knew that Delia was her mother.

Delia was relieved when her taxi drew up outside the white stucco villa that formed the deceptive frontage of the recording studios. As she paid the cabbie and walked up the front steps her irritation faded and she couldn't help smiling. Some of the best hours of her life had been spent here.

'Miss Maxwell!' The receptionist rushed forward to greet her. 'Oh, my goodness, is it really you? Welcome back!'

'Hello, Janet.' Delia was touched by the young woman's excitement.

'Are you here to see Mr Nelson? He's in Studio Two.'

'Thanks. I know my way!'

Delia walked through the original Regency building to the modern studio complex beyond. She was stopped first by a technician and then by a horn player: each greeted her with surprise and genuine delight. There was no warning light over the entrance to Studio Two, so she tapped on the door and looked in. Davey, seated at the grand piano, frowned at the disturbance and turned to see who it was. At the sight of her, he raised his eyebrows in exaggerated surprise and beckoned her in before going back to making annotations on a page of sheet music.

She was amused by his response. Used to his ways and aware that his greeting was anything but dismissive, she moved quietly to sit in the nearest chair. Lily, in her white jeans and black sweater, stood at a microphone. Two guitarists sat nearby. Old friends, they welcomed her silently with a nod and a hand raised in greeting. Lily gave Delia a nervous smile. Delia smiled back and gave her a small thumbs-up.

As she breathed in the familiar musty air of the cavernous space, she recalled all the magic she and Davey had created there. For her, the scuffed parquet floor, overflowing ashtrays and muddle of metal music stands, wires, speakers and microphone booms would always be exhilarating and even glamorous. Alone on stage in front of an audience, even with Davey nearby, she was on her own. Here, however fast they raced through the numbers, sometimes recording two or even three tracks a day, the work was shared: whether fooling around with silly running jokes or enduring hours of frustration and exhaustion, everyone was in it together. It was thrilling to think that Lily was now part of Delia's professional family.

She saw Davey look over at her daughter. 'Let's try it one more time,' he said. 'Ready?'

Lily took a deep breath and, gathering herself together, gave a resolute nod. Delia clasped her hands tightly as Davey played the opening chords and Lily began to sing.

'Tell Me How It Ends'. Delia knew exactly how she would have sung it. She closed her eyes and listened carefully as the guitars began to fill in. The arrangement had been altered to accommodate Lily's lighter, inexperienced voice, but the change from minor to major chords gave the number an immediacy that was young and fresh. Lily sang well. She was good, a natural! Delia's heart swelled with pride and she blinked back tears as they came to the closing refrain. She could still hardly believe, after so many years, that her child was not only in the room with her, but looking to her mother for reassurance as she sang.

Davey held up a hand, watching the sound engineer in the control room above. Given the nod, he relaxed.

'We'll play that one back,' he said, 'but it sounded pretty good to me.'

'It was wonderful!' exclaimed Delia, hurrying to embrace Lily as Davey ran up the steep stairs that flanked one wall.

'Did you think so?' Lily asked. 'Really? Truly?'

'Yes, my darling, really and truly wonderful.'

'Oh, I'm so glad. I've sung it so many times already this morning that I can hardly hear myself any more. And with you listening, I so wanted to get it right. I'd hate to let you down.'

Lily stuck her hands into her jeans pockets and hunched her shoulders. Delia was struck by the poignancy of the gesture, as if the girl was trying to make herself smaller. Had she first adopted this pose in response to some frightening or threatening situation in her childhood? Delia hoped not.

Lily glanced up the stairs to the window of the control room. 'I'm parched,' she said. 'Do you think it's OK for me to nip and get a drink before he comes back?'

'Of course. Go.'

As Lily ran off to the canteen, the guitarists came to say a proper hello to Delia. She was glad of a chance simply to gossip like old times, and to catch up on what had been going on in her absence, so she didn't notice Davey come up behind her, cigarette in hand.

'So the lost sheep returns,' he said drily. 'And what do you make of your protégée?'

'I think you've got another sure-fire hit on your hands.' She and Davey never embraced one another, a habit so long ingrained that neither noticed it. Delia simply took it for granted that he was happy to see her, and that he would assume the same.

'I'm considering whether to add some instrumentation to the intro,' he said. 'Maybe a woodwind, what do you reckon?'

'I don't think it needs it,' she said. 'I like the simplicity.'

'Hmm.' He looked doubtful. 'We'll see.'

'There were a couple of phrases that could maybe do with sharpening up, though. Would you like me to show her?'

'No, thanks. We're fine. We'll probably run with that last recording.'

Hurt by this rejection, she reminded herself of how prickly Davey could be about any challenge to his authority. Status of whatever kind mattered to him and he had a tendency to defend it unnecessarily.

'We must talk soon about what I'm to record now my darling daughter has stolen my number,' she said, with a laugh. 'I hope you've got something good for me up your sleeve.'

'Not right at the moment,' he said. '"Tell Me How It Ends" needs a flip side, which we'll do tomorrow, then Peter wants us to have a follow-up in the pipeline.'

Delia felt rebuffed in a way she hadn't experienced in years – she wasn't used to taking second place to anyone other than another star famous enough to top her on the bill – but reminded herself of Davey's essentially kind, if deeply buried, heart. 'You know, I was Lily's age or younger when you and I first worked together,' she reminded him. 'It's so lovely for me to see you bring on my daughter as you did me.'

'Sure,' he said, softening a little. 'And, as it happens, I still think Peter was right and the two of you should've sung it together. Your voices would blend brilliantly.'

'Another time, perhaps.'

'Yes. I—' He broke off as Lily came back into the studio.

'Sorry,' she said. 'I was just getting some water.'

'That's OK,' Davey told her. 'We played it back. It's all good, so you can run away and play.'

'Really?'

'Yes, but back here tomorrow at nine sharp.' He turned to the guitarists. 'Thanks, boys, you can go home now.'

The musicians immediately started to pack away their instruments. Delia turned to Lily. 'Want to share a cab back into town with me?'

'Great!'

Lily fetched her bag and coat, then turned to say goodbye to Davey, but he was already halfway up the stairs from where he gave a casual wave before disappearing into the control room. Delia could see that Lily was not yet accustomed to his lack of pleasantries, so as they left the studio and walked back along the corridor, she linked her arm with Lily's and pressed it against her.

'Don't mind Davey,' she said. 'I can tell that he's really pleased.'

'I never thought recording a number would be such hard work.'

'Davey can be tough,' she said. 'But he's the best. It'll be worth it.'

In the reception area the commissionaire was looking out for them. 'Miss Maxwell?'

'Yes, Harry?'

'I'm afraid the taxi driver who brought you up here must have tipped off the press,' he said, frowning in disapproval. 'There's a few of them waiting for you outside and they won't budge. I've got a cab waiting, which I can send around the back, if you prefer.'

'That's all right, Harry. I'll have to face them sometime.' She turned to Lily. 'Won't be a moment.'

A few minutes later Delia emerged from the bathroom having brushed out the blonde waves of her hair and applied fresh lipstick.

'Right then, let's face our public!'

It was annoying to be ambushed like this, but dealing with the press had become second nature, so she straightened her shoulders, plastered on her sunniest smile and led the way out onto the front steps. Camera bulbs flashed and reporters shouted questions. Before she could speak Lily stepped in front of her.

'My mother is delighted to be back in London,' Lily informed the eager gathering, 'but she won't be taking any questions today. I've just successfully finished recording my debut single, and of course I can't begin to tell you how lucky and happy I am to have her guidance and support.' She turned to Delia, her eyes shining, and paused just long enough for the photographers to get their shots. 'I still can't believe that I have this incredible woman in my life. It's a miracle that we're reunited at last. Thank you very much.'

As more flashes went off Delia became aware of Davey coming up behind her and whispering something in her ear. She turned to look at him in surprise, but he had already taken a step back into the doorway. Had he really said what she thought he had? *Better watch yourself. She gets what she wants, that one.* She must have misheard.

17

Delia handed Frank Landry a glass of wine. When he'd called to invite her for dinner, explaining that he wanted to make a proper apology, she had rashly offered to cook a weekend kitchen supper instead of going out. Her main intention had been to avoid further unnecessary press attention and, after all, he had already made himself comfortable in her home, but now she was regretting the unintended intimacy. Perhaps she should have refused him outright – except, she reminded herself, he was Peter's friend.

Frank seemed equally nervous when he arrived, calling her 'Miss Maxwell' and repeating his remorse at having scared her in the dark of her rooftop living room. However, as she led the way upstairs, each of them carrying a glass of wine, it was her turn to be embarrassed: so many people had now sent flowers that one side of the room resembled a florist's shop. Seeing such a show of starry excess through his eyes, she wished she'd had all the blooms sent over to the hospital at Hyde Park Corner. Her reaction made her realize that she cared about his opinion and had actually been rather glad to hear from him again – an admission that increased her disquiet over what he might have learned about her during his enquiries.

'So I have you to thank for my career,' she said lightly as they sat down on one of the grey-and-white-striped sofas.

He looked confused. 'How so?'

'Because I owe so much of it to Peter,' she said, 'and Peter wouldn't be here if not for you.'

'Oh, that.'

'But you did get shot down after saving his life?'

'I bailed out and was captured.'

'And then what?'

'I sat around for four months in a rather draughty hut in Germany.'

'Bad luck.'

'Better luck than a lot of others. And Peter wrote to me faithfully every week, telling me to keep my chin up.'

'What did you think about in your draughty German hut?' she asked.

'We tried not to think too much about anything.'

'Did it work?'

He caught her look of amusement. It made him laugh. 'No,' he said, 'of course not.'

'So what were the things you tried not to think about?'

Frank looked embarrassed. 'Food. Beer. Women. Missing out. Fear that we might yet lose the war.'

'I sat out the last years of the war in Switzerland. It was impossible for me to go home and then I had no home to go back to. I had a great deal not to think about.'

'Why Switzerland?'

'My father was Jewish. It was enough to put his whole family in danger, so he sent me to Zürich where I'd be safe. His best friend, Conrad, took me in.'

'So you'd grown up in Hungary?'

She'd remained silent about this part of her life for so long that she hesitated before replying, yet something about this man tempted her to abandon her habitual reserve. 'Yes,' she said, 'in Budapest, although Delia Maxwell wasn't born anywhere. That's why I'm so used to not talking about my past.'

'You don't have to tell me, either, if you don't want to.'

She took another moment to consider – it was a novel experience to feel shy when speaking about herself, and to reveal anything of her real self – and then smiled. 'No. I don't want any more secrets. Lily's seen to that! In fact, it's a relief to feel able to talk about people I loved. My father was a portrait photographer in Budapest. He and my mother knew all the actors and singers and musicians. We lived in a beautiful apartment. I had a little sister, and aunts, uncles, cousins. I had a very happy childhood.'

'Until you went to Zürich?'

Delia nodded. 'Not long afterwards they all perished and I had no one except Conrad.'

'I'm sorry. It was a rotten war.'

'Conrad would never allow me to admit it, but it's a dreadful thing to be the only one to survive. I'd known Conrad all my life, and he looked after me, but it's not the same as family or the school friends I grew up with.'

Frank nodded. 'I went straight from school into flying, mainly Mosquitoes as bomber support over Germany. I lost a good few friends. Those of us who made it asked ourselves the same question: why did I get to live and they didn't?'

'At least you were doing something useful.'

'I suppose so. And the actual flying was fun in a way, but the rest . . . Once it was over and I went up to Oxford—'

'Oxford!' Delia interrupted him. 'I would have loved to go to university.'

'What would you have studied?'

'History, perhaps,' she said. 'Tell me what it was like, all those ancient libraries and learned professors.'

'It was fine,' he said, 'except I was surrounded by men who seemed like children, even though they were only a few years younger than me. They regretted losing out on what they saw as glamour and excitement, and only wanted to hear our adventure stories. I never knew what to tell them.'

'Easier to pretend,' she said.

He smiled wryly. 'I've never been much good at that.'

'I'm very good at it,' she said, with a laugh. 'Or, rather, Delia Maxwell is.'

'Are you not Delia Maxwell?'

'You ought to know,' she said. 'You're the one who's been investigating me.'

Frank coloured. 'That's not fair.'

'You're now one of an extremely select group,' she said. 'Only a handful of people have ever seen me without blonde hair. I wonder what other secrets you uncovered.'

Her teasing had a sharp edge to it, and he didn't return her smile.

'It was only to make sure you were safe,' he protested.

'It's still a rather strange position to be in.'

'I don't blame you for being angry. I hope you can forgive me.'

His candour stirred her heart. 'Tell me, why did Peter send *you* to track me down?' she asked.

'I've worked in intelligence,' he said. 'I was head of security for a rubber company in Malaya for several years. This was before independence.'

She saw his face harden, and was curious. 'What was that like?'

'My job was to help ferret out Chinese Communist sympathizers, keep one step ahead of the guerrilla insurgents, and try to look after the local villagers who worked as rubber tappers.'

'A big task.'

He nodded. 'It was jungle warfare, and I also had to liaise with the British military, many of them inexperienced conscripts all too aware they were only getting shot at so they could protect British commercial interests. Anyway, I'm sure people on both sides were keeping a close eye on me, too, so I understand what it's like to be spied on. I didn't like it, either.'

He sounded bitter, and she sought to distract him. 'You were listening to one of my records when you fell asleep.' She recalled how her discovery of the disc on the turntable the following morning had somehow cast a softer light on the presence of the stranger in her house. 'Was that part of your enquiries?'

'Absolutely,' he replied, with a look of relief. 'I discovered that you do sing rather well.'

'That's good to know,' she said, deadpan. 'But tell me, honestly, what *did* you find out about me? I would prefer to know.'

'I couldn't find a cupboard, let alone any skeletons in it, if that's what worries you,' he said. 'You do understand how anxious Peter was about you? He even had a pal at Scotland Yard check all the morgues.'

'I do, and I'm grateful,' she said, trying to hide her shiver at the image of a mortuary slab. 'As well as genuinely sorry that I caused such trouble.' She stood up. 'Would you like something to eat? I wasn't joking when I said it would be a kitchen supper.'

Frank followed her downstairs where she made him sit at the small table while she took out eggs, butter and an omelette pan. She stood at the stove with her back to him as she cracked the eggs into a bowl but, glancing around, saw him looking in some bemusement at the stick of French bread, bottle of wine and plate of sliced tomatoes dotted with herbs and minced shallots already set out on the table. She poured the eggs into the pan and, turning to reach for the pepper, caught him staring at her. He nodded towards the food as if to distract her.

'I've read about your omelette-making skills,' he said. 'They're famous.'

'You'd better taste it first.' She handed him a little white jug of vinaigrette. 'For the tomatoes.'

However accustomed Delia had become to the effect of her fame on people at close range, she still found it obscurely hurtful and was aware how, perversely, it tended to make her stiff and artificial. *See me!* she wanted to cry out. *Look beyond the fame and talk to me!*

She finished cooking the omelette and divided it onto two plates. As she laid his before him, she gave him a full-beam Delia Maxwell smile.

He blinked, then remembered to thank her. As he offered her the tomatoes before helping himself, he shook his head as if confused. 'I can hardly believe it,' he said. 'I'm sitting here with one of the country's most dazzling stars as if it were the most natural thing in the world.'

'I'm not a freak, you know.'

'No, oh, no, I'm sorry, that's not what I meant. It's just – well,

I assumed, before the war, that I knew exactly what my future would be. I'd leave school and help my father in his shop. It's in Bromley and he sells radios and record players. As a kid I could never have dreamed of having the life I've led. And now here I am, drinking wine and eating French bread with you. But then I guess one way or another the war made exiles of us all. So many imagined lives that no longer exist.'

'You must have had dreams for yourself before the war?' she asked.

'Nothing special, although once the action started I couldn't wait to be old enough to join up. Flying a Spitfire became every schoolboy's dream.' He stared at the wall behind her, lost for a moment in the past. 'My mother hated me being a pilot. I can understand that. But when I was a prisoner of war, I resented how, in her letters, she couldn't hide her happiness that I was out of harm's way. I knew then that I could never go home because the old life no longer made any sense to me.' He speared a piece of omelette with his fork. 'This is delicious, by the way. I can see why your skills are so renowned.'

'Good.'

'What about you?' he asked. 'What did you dream of?'

'My best friend Anna and I were either going to be Nobel Prize-winning scientists, like Marie Curie,' she said, 'or join a circus where we'd be bareback riders and trapeze artists and wear coloured tights and spangled costumes.'

'There's still time.'

'Not for Anna.'

Delia hadn't intended to voice the thought aloud, but Frank nodded sombrely and made no reply. She fought against the sudden tide of guilt and fear that threatened to suck her under.

Striving silently to regain equilibrium before Frank noticed her distress, she rushed to change the subject, grabbing the first question that came to mind. 'You haven't been married?'

'No,' he replied. 'I've led too rootless a life for that. Not like Peter. He only ever had eyes for Mary.' He hesitated, and Delia found she was curious to know what he might add. He looked at her more directly than he had yet. 'But I may have a son.'

'Ah,' she said, wondering if she'd been drawn to him by some intuitive recognition of mutual loss. 'So you can understand what it's like for me to have found Lily again.'

'I hope so.'

'Do you see him?'

'No.'

She nodded in sympathy. 'For so long I've belonged nowhere,' she said. 'I have no one who shares my memories, or who looks like me, or laughs just like my sister, or even speaks my language. And now – now I have Lily. I have to hold my breath in case the spell breaks and it all melts away like mist.'

'Like that Greek myth,' he said. 'Orpheus and Eurydice. If he looks back he'll lose her again.'

'Exactly. I've never been so happy and afraid at the same time.'

'Not even on stage?' he asked.

'No.' Delia spoke firmly. 'That's just limelight and grease-paint. This is real.'

'I envy you,' he said.

Frank's unguarded smile held such comprehension that when, an hour later, he stopped at the front door and gazed down at her, seeking permission to kiss her, her returning smile granted it. She hadn't allowed herself to be kissed like that in a long time.

18

Delia sat alone in her corner banquette, the only unaccompanied woman in the Savoy Grill. She didn't mind that Lily was late: it gave her a chance to appreciate the ripple of covert interest and the surreptitious glances of recognition from her fellow diners.

She had invited Lily to lunch to celebrate the success of 'Tell Me How It Ends'. Released within a month of recording, the single had shot straight to the top of the charts, thanks to the story of Lily's extraordinary debut, and looked set to remain there, engulfing the girl in a whirlwind of photoshoots, interviews and live radio and television appearances. Delia's first hit had created just such a stir – television, of course, had barely existed then – and although she recalled being glad that it had made Conrad so happy, mainly she remembered feeling constantly bewildered and unable to keep up with all the rush and excitement. Lily, however, appeared to love every second of the merry-go-round, and, over the past couple of weeks, had grown in confidence and poise before Delia's eyes.

She was overjoyed at Lily's success, pleased that her daughter possessed such a healthy appetite for life. Yet, while she revelled in the novel emotions of maternal pride, Delia had to admit that it was pleasant to receive some attention on her own account. She just wasn't saintly enough to live contentedly in her daughter's shade. Peter was still waiting for the American producers to agree dates for their trip to Hollywood and, although he worried that they were being stonewalled, she remained confident that a meeting would be fixed up soon. She felt ready now for a new challenge.

Another responsive quiver ran through the restaurant as the maître d' finally led Lily to Delia's table. Lily's clothes alone would have attracted notice, even among those diners who failed to recognize the girl who had shot to fame. The scalloped hem of her primrose-coloured crochet-knit dress ended above the knee. She wore off-white stockings and flat black-and-white Mary-Jane shoes, the outfit topped off with a floppy-brimmed hat. Delia was sure the clothes must have come from Mary Quant's Bazaar in the King's Road. She had bought some things there herself, but knew she could never have carried them off with such youthful panache. Lily was simply a breath of fresh air blowing through this stuffy world. She rose to greet her daughter eagerly and pulled her in to sit beside her on the banquette, wanting everyone to look at them together.

As Lily removed her hat and sent it skimming above the array of glass and silverware to land safely on the opposite seat, Delia gasped. The gesture suddenly brought to mind her spoiled little sister throwing aside a sun-hat she refused to wear. Delia laughed, turning to search Lily's face for vestiges of Zsofia's dark hair and soft grey eyes. If her sister had survived, she'd be Lily's Aunt Zsofi. Delia felt again the visceral reality of the link between her daughter and the family she had lost.

'I can't stay too long,' said Lily. 'I have another meeting at half past two.'

Delia smiled indulgently – Lily was too excited to have noticed her late arrival – and summoned a waiter. 'Then we'd better be quick about ordering.'

Lily picked up the menu. 'Oh, but it's all in French,' she said. 'You'll have to choose for me. What ought I to have? Do they have things like lobster and oysters?'

'They do,' answered Delia, laughing, 'but if you don't have much time, you should pick something a little simpler.'

She ordered two Dover soles with new potatoes and then turned once more to look at Lily. It was all she could do not to reach out and stroke her short, soft hair. 'Everyone in London will be wearing that hat and dress within the month,' she told her. 'And what about your birthday party? Have you decided what you'll wear?'

'No, not yet.'

'There's plenty of time to go shopping, if you'd like. I've made all the other arrangements.'

'I'm doing a magazine feature tomorrow, so maybe they'll have something,' said Lily, carelessly. 'And I spoke to a movie director this morning. He wants to meet me this afternoon. He's just back from Hollywood. Some American producers want to make a film, a musical. They already have a script but, rather than shoot it there, they've asked him to come up with ideas for doing it here, on location, in the new gritty black-and-white style.'

'Like *A Taste of Honey*?' Delia suggested.

'Yes, and *The L-Shaped Room*,' said Lily, 'although I didn't see either of them. Our local cinema was really strict about age limits.'

'I went to both the premieres,' said Delia, with a smile.

'Well, anyway, apparently the producers have told this British director they're looking for a new face and suggested me.'

'You certainly fit that bill.'

'Peter keeps saying I ought to get a proper agent,' said Lily, 'someone to handle all the different things that people want me to do.'

'That's good advice. And you can always rely on Peter to do what's best for you.'

Lily waved a hand. 'Oh, yes, he'll do whatever I want. And I'd really like to try acting. The director said, if they go ahead, they'll want to start shooting as soon as possible to make the most of the good weather.'

Delia felt a stab of concern for her. She was young, and believed too easily that this deluge of attention would be solid and lasting. She tried to work out how best to warn her without spoiling the magic of the moment.

'It's good to keep all your options open at this stage,' she said lightly, 'certainly until you discover what kind of work you really enjoy, as well as the way of life that suits you best. What looks glamorous from afar can turn into a daily grind if you don't love what you're doing.'

'I love it all!' Lily exclaimed. 'I want it all.'

Delia was surprised by her own envy and regret. She had never had the steeliness of Lily's desire. She had worked hard to please Conrad and been grateful to the audiences for accepting her, but had shied away from admitting how much any of it actually mattered to her. The things she had really wanted – home, safety, peace of mind – had seemed always unobtainable.

A waiter served their fish. Lily picked up her fork and started eating immediately. The rich lemony smell made Delia realize she was hungry, too.

'I've been looking at houses,' she told Lily. 'If you're going to be busy, you may be glad of a steady base. There's a lovely place I've seen for sale in Denham. Quite a few show-business people live out that way, so it must be convenient. And it's near Pinewood. If you do start making films, then being on set will mean a lot of early mornings. Would you like to come and look at it with me?'

Lily paused in her eating. 'I'd like a flat in Chelsea but Peter says I'm not old enough and I'd need your permission.'

'Wouldn't you like to live with me?'

'I could come at weekends,' said Lily. 'But you'll let me rent my own place, won't you? I mean, it's not as if I haven't managed on my own before. I'm quite used to that.'

Lily's candid gaze pierced Delia's heart. She assumed this was the ruthlessness of youth – the supposedly maladjusted young of today who expected everything life had to offer to be poured straight into their laps – and hoped it wasn't evidence of the damage inflicted by Lily's unhappy childhood. She would have to remember that motherhood also involved difficult and confusing choices, between making her child's life sweet and easy and doing what was best for her.

'This is good,' said Lily, oblivious, as she finished her fish. 'Is there time for me to order some dessert?'

'Yes, of course,' she said, summoning a waiter for the menu. Rewarded by Lily's smile, she decided that, as long as she could help to fulfil Lily's dreams, she would let the future take care of itself.

'I think the producers behind this picture may be the people you've been talking to,' Lily said casually.

'And it's also a musical?' asked Delia.

'Yes, a doomed love story about a rags-to-riches ingénue discovered by an older and troubled star. The director's going to tell me more about it when we meet.'

Delia felt a chill run through her. Surely Lily would remember that this was the story of the movie she was to make. Had Lily forgotten the correspondence she'd handled between Delia and the Americans, or had she paid no real attention to the letters she'd typed and filed? Should Delia remind her? After all, if the British director, whoever he was, was unaware that Lily's mother had already been cast, it might become awkward for Lily at a later date. Surely the producers wouldn't be offering Delia's role to someone else – to her own daughter – without telling her first. It must just be one of those odd coincidences, with two similar projects in development at the same time.

And yet an unpleasant aftertaste rose in the back of Delia's throat as the words Davey had whispered on the steps of the recording studio came unbidden to her mind: *Better watch yourself. She knows what she wants, that one.*

She turned to take a fresh look at Lily, who was studying the dessert menu, and forcibly reminded herself how she *had* initially misinterpreted Lily's reasons for stepping in front of her to speak to the reporters that afternoon outside the recording studio. Afterwards, in the taxi, Lily had said she hoped Delia hadn't minded – she'd only wanted to protect her from having to answer impertinent questions – and had gone on to explain how she felt responsible for any press intrusions, afraid she'd been reckless and naive about revealing Delia's past without her permission. Realizing how much the slightest misgiving about her daughter's sincerity could hurt Lily, Delia had been happy to rebuke herself for paying any attention to Davey's catty comment.

'By the way,' she said, determined to confront her one final niggle, 'I don't suppose you have my diamond stud earrings? I can't find them anywhere.'

Lily had made her choice: 'Peach Melba.' She met Delia's gaze self-consciously. 'I'm afraid I borrowed them without asking and then forgot to give them back.'

'For the awards ceremony?'

'Yes. I'm so sorry.'

Delia felt only relief. 'It doesn't matter. And, if you like them, you should keep them.'

'Oh, no, I couldn't possibly.'

'Please. They're yours.'

'Really? You're sure?'

'Absolutely.'

Lily leaned forwards and gave her an impulsive hug. 'Thank you.' The touch of her lips on Delia's cheek was as light as a butterfly's wing. 'And I'm so glad that, if I do make this film, they want to shoot in London. I couldn't bear to be away from you.'

Moved by her daughter's declaration, Delia felt a bond as fine and strong as spider's silk stretching between them. She waved to the waiter to order the Peach Melba.

19

Before pressing the lift button to go up to Celeste's fifth-floor flat in Kensington, Delia took a deep breath, mustering her determination to carry through the awkward conversation that lay ahead. When she'd inherited the lease on Celeste's Curzon Street salon along with the rest of Conrad's estate, she'd pushed the implications out of her mind, but now the lease was coming up for renewal with the freeholder. Leaving a discussion about her future plans to a solicitor seemed cowardly and, sensitive to how Celeste's business was struggling, she knew she shouldn't postpone it any longer.

Celeste was waiting at the door. She took Delia's jacket and led her into a living room decorated in pale colours softly reflected in mirrored panels enhanced by glass teardrop wall lights. Two cocktail glasses and a shaker sat ready on the grey-and-white-marble coffee-table.

'Too early for a drink?' asked Celeste.

'Not if it's one of your specials,' Delia replied, sitting in her usual place on one of the comfortable sofas facing each other across the low table. 'But just a small one.'

Celeste poured and handed her a martini. 'What shall we drink to?'

'Old friends,' said Delia, holding up her glass.

'Fifteen years,' Celeste agreed, chinking their glasses together.

'How young we were!'

'You'd already had Lily,' Celeste reminded her.

'That's true.'

Celeste took a deep breath. 'Did you know Conrad had told me about her?'

'What? No!' Delia was astonished. 'When?'

'Years ago. He thought someone else ought to know, in case you ever needed help.'

Delia silently absorbed this new information. After she'd recovered from the birth neither she nor Conrad had ever mentioned it again, and yet he had told Celeste.

'It must have been three or four years after we met,' Celeste continued. 'He said not to tell you I knew unless it became important. So then, to my shame, I pretty much forgot.'

'So much has changed since then.' Delia didn't know what else to say.

'Do you want to talk about it?' Celeste asked gently. 'About Lily's birth?'

'Not really.' Delia sighed. 'But nor do I see the point in keeping it wrapped in mystery any longer. And sooner or later I expect Lily will ask, too.' She took a fortifying sip of her drink. 'It's an old and simple story. An actor friend of Conrad's used to come to the apartment in Zürich. One day he came on his own when he was sure I'd be there alone. I had no idea what was happening until it was too late. I certainly never thought I might have a baby as a result.'

Celeste reached out across the table. 'Oh, darling!'

Delia squeezed Celeste's proffered hand. 'It's actually a relief to say it aloud,' she said shakily. 'What do you think? Do I tell Lily the truth or invent some teenage romance?'

'Tell her the truth,' said Celeste. 'She's old enough to understand that none of it was your fault.'

Delia nodded. 'By the time Conrad discovered I was pregnant, it was too late to do anything except have the baby. The war in Europe was nearly over, and he managed to bring me to England where no one knew me and there'd be no gossip about what had happened. And afterwards we stayed here.' She smiled at Celeste. 'And then he found you, and Davey, and here we are, still together.'

Celeste raised her glass. 'To Conrad.'

Delia smiled. 'To Conrad.'

Each drank her own silent toast.

'He decided everything,' said Delia. 'It never occurred to me that I might have any choice about what happened after she was born. At first I just tried to forget, but then, all through the years, I've felt a thread stretching out into the darkness. And then she found me.'

'A fairy tale.'

Delia nodded. 'Which is why I have to try to give it a happy ending.'

'What about you?' asked Celeste. 'Are you happy, Delia?'

'Of course!'

'Only – the way you went away so suddenly – I hope you don't feel I let you down.'

'You've always been a good friend to me.' Delia raised her glass. 'The best.'

'Just ... even before you disappeared, you seemed anxious. You've lost weight, you—'

'That's just the pills,' said Delia. 'I decided I ought to lose weight for the film cameras.'

'What pills?' Celeste asked sharply.

'Benzedrine. Lily says all the kids her age take them. She gave me some, and then I went to my doctor for a prescription.'

'Purple hearts!'

'Similar sort of thing. Lots of people use them when they're dieting. My doctor says they're perfectly safe.'

'But you will be careful, won't you? Especially once you go to Hollywood. You hear such terrible stories about drugs there.'

'Well, I have some news about that.' Delia's pride made it agony to speak, but she would have to get used to the humiliation. 'It looks like Lily might become the movie star, not me.'

'Really?'

'Yes, she told me at lunch today. If she's offered the part, she'll be playing my role.'

'No! They can't do that, can they?'

'Of course they can. I spoke to Peter this afternoon. He only found out this morning, but it's why the American producers have been stalling us. As soon as they heard about Lily, they decided to rewrite the story around her, bring in a new British director, and shoot the whole thing in London. They think it will give it a more contemporary feel.'

'You can't let that happen!'

Delia shrugged. She had never suffered such a serious professional failure before and had been totally unprepared for how bitterly it stung. 'I didn't sign my contract. They were all ready to start shooting when I went AWOL. What were they supposed to do?'

'What does that matter? You mustn't stand for it! You must

fight!' Celeste rose to her feet and paced the small room. 'I'm sorry, I shouldn't have said that, but you're the star, Delia! You've earned it. Lily knows nothing about performing, let alone acting. She's an amateur. No one would have heard of Lily if it weren't for you.'

'Every woman knows how to act,' Delia said, with a wry smile, hoping to deflect Celeste's outrage. Yet she was touched by her friend's ferocity. Since Peter – reluctantly, shamefacedly – had confirmed Lily's bombshell, she had swung from anger and even a kind of grief to panic that perhaps, all these years, she'd been kidding herself and was simply not good enough. And, of course, it was only once she'd lost her future as a film star that she knew for certain how desperately she'd wanted it.

'But don't you mind?' Celeste pressed.

'Yes, of course I do. I'm horribly disappointed. But I have only myself to blame. Meanwhile, I want what's best for Lily.'

'Even if you have to stand aside?'

'She's my daughter. All the years I was building my career, I should have been taking care of her.'

'What does Peter say? I hope he's standing up for you.'

'He's not in an easy position.'

Celeste shook her head indignantly. 'You mean even he's fallen under her spell. Nothing's been the same since that night you met her.'

'I told Peter he has to support Lily in every way he can,' Delia said firmly. 'I'm absolutely thrilled for her, and I want you to be, too.'

Celeste went to sit beside Delia, taking her hand. 'Darling, of course you love Lily, but how much do you think she loves you?'

Delia disengaged her hand. 'Don't be silly. Of course she loves me.'

'All the same, it wouldn't be entirely unnatural for her to blame you in some way for giving her up, would it?'

'No, it wouldn't. I think she's had a hard time. She has every right to blame me, if that's how she feels.'

'But it's no excuse for being so inconsiderate and only thinking about what *she* wants. Not when you're doing everything you can for her.'

'She's done nothing wrong.'

'Have you spoken to her about stealing your role in the film?'

'She hasn't *stolen* it.' Delia angrily recalled how Celeste had all but accused Lily of stealing her diamond earrings. 'She merely accepts what people offer her.'

'But she must have known it was yours?'

Delia was about to respond sharply, except she had no defence for Lily's behaviour. 'I'm not going to upset her,' she said, struggling to subdue her conflicted feelings. 'I can't risk losing her again.'

Celeste must have sensed Delia's turmoil. 'It won't come to that,' she soothed. 'But what about your career? And what if—'

'What?'

'What if she's seriously trying to get back at you in some way? I mean for giving her up. Children who feel rejected do act like that sometimes, don't they? And Lily's young, too young to fully understand herself. Plus you don't really know all that much about how she grew up.'

'She won't talk about her childhood, and made me promise not to ask,' said Delia. 'That speaks for itself, doesn't it?'

'Whatever bad things happened, you can't take it all on your shoulders,' said Celeste. 'I worry that she wants to take something away from you, that maybe she's had something like this in mind since you first befriended her.'

'Had what in mind? Lily's little more than a child. A greedy child sometimes, I admit, but she grew up without proper love. You can't blame her for acting as if she's been let loose in a toy shop.'

'And if it's more than that?' Celeste clasped her hands until her knuckles whitened but evidently decided to go ahead and say what she wanted to say. 'I found her once at your dressing-table, making herself up to look just like you. I never told you because she made me promise that I wouldn't, but—'

'Then you shouldn't break your word now,' Delia said, a note of warning in her voice

'Can't you find out a bit more about her childhood?' Celeste pleaded. 'If only to help you understand her better, to give her the best possible support.'

'She has a hit record and is about to star in a film,' said Delia. 'She told me she's never been happier.'

'Very well.' Celeste got up and returned to her seat on the opposite sofa. 'So how are you going to get your own career back on track? Not by playing a supporting role, I hope.'

'I'm working with Davey on a new single,' said Delia. 'It's not as if Delia Maxwell is going to be singing to empty seats.'

Celeste sipped her martini. The look in her eyes suggested she wasn't as confident as Delia might wish.

'We all have to change,' Delia went on, deciding that, however brutal, the matter of the lease had to be faced sooner or later. 'And I wanted to warn you that I won't be renewing the Curzon Street lease. The freeholder wants a great deal of money for it, and I need to gather my capital ready to buy a house where I can offer Lily a proper home. My place is too small so she's in a service flat for now, but she can't go on living out of a suitcase. I'm really sorry.'

'Of course you must do whatever you think best.' Celeste picked up the cocktail shaker. 'Another drink?'

She rose and turned away but not quickly enough to hide her face. Glimpsing Celeste's expression, Delia was shocked by the depth of the hurt she had inflicted.

20

Sitting in the passenger seat of Frank's green sports car, Delia glanced at his profile and wondered what he was thinking. She hadn't seen him since the night he'd kissed her more than a month ago. He'd called twice but, nervous of taking on further emotional complication, she'd made excuses not to see him, only to regret doing so when he didn't call again. She'd initially asked Peter if he'd accompany her on a second viewing of the house that was for sale. He'd been too busy and had suggested Frank, who'd sounded pleased to hear her voice on the telephone. Although he insisted he knew very little about bricks and mortar, he'd immediately agreed to drive her out to Denham.

He drove fast and confidently, intent on the road. His brown hair was thick and soft-looking, his mouth attractive, and he possessed a diffidence that made her feel she could trust him. For years after Lily's birth she had avoided men until, on tour, she had fallen lightly for a horn player, who turned out to have a wife in Streatham. Nevertheless the experience had been fun and had later emboldened her enough to embark on a mutually discreet fling with a famous American crooner. There had been no one since: partly because her life was too public and, she had discovered, not many men liked being in a woman's shade, but also because of her own terror of loss. Her reunion with Lily seemed to have unlocked her emotionally and, now that she'd had a little time to get used to motherhood, she felt ready to be wooed. It was disappointing, therefore, to find Frank rather withdrawn and preoccupied. She hoped it was merely because, with the top down, they had to shout to be heard above the rushing wind.

They reached Denham and she directed him through the pretty, wisteria-clad village to where the house lay behind a high wall. The imposing metal gates had been left open for their arrival, and they went slowly along the driveway between wide lawns. Seeing the house for a second time, she realized its size was absurd. What was she thinking? What would she possibly want with six bedrooms, especially if Lily clung to her desire for her own flat in Chelsea?

As she untied her headscarf and put away her sunglasses, Frank swung the car around, spraying gravel over the curving steps that led to the imposing entrance. The estate agent, who must have been watching for them, appeared at the front door as Frank leaped out and came around to open her door and help her out. Delia liked the touch of his hand at her elbow as they mounted the steps together to greet the agent. Frank kept close beside her as they toured a procession of over-furnished rooms that smelt of lavender and furniture polish, the agent hovering discreetly in the background, darting ahead only to draw up window blinds that cut slanting shadows across the parquet floors. When they reached the domestic offices he suggested they might like to wander the grounds by themselves. The vendors, he said, were abroad so they could take as long as they liked.

Glad to escape into fresh air, Delia led the way to the sheltered outdoor swimming pool, which Frank duly admired. 'You could throw some splendid parties out here,' he remarked. 'Do you like giving parties?'

'For friends, yes,' she replied. 'I thought it would be fun for Lily to have somewhere to invite people. There's a tennis court over there, too.'

He surveyed their surroundings solemnly, a slight frown on his face.

'And the pool is heated,' she said, wishing he'd show more enthusiasm. 'Warm enough to swim even in an English summer.'

'It's all beautifully kept,' he agreed. 'It might be worth asking how many of the staff will want to stay on.'

'I hadn't considered that,' she said, recoiling from the idea of being constantly watched over by housekeepers and gardeners. She already put up with quite enough fussing from hairdressers, make-up artists, lighting technicians and the like, and always rejoiced in returning to the privacy of her own home. And goodness knows what it would cost to maintain the staff that such a house and grounds would require.

Frank fell behind as she led the way towards the magnificent cedar of Lebanon that dominated the lawn. Although she was grateful for his practical comments and welcomed his opinion, she worried that his distracted mood was dispelling the rosy glow she'd felt when she first viewed the house. She turned to look back at it from the vantage point of the lawn. A red-brick Victorian pile, she saw now that it possessed none of the charm or elegance of her first impressions. Perhaps it was because the high ceilings and parquet floors reminded her of her parents' apartment in Budapest, but in reality not even the bars of light that spilled across the floor as the agent pulled up the blinds had succeeded in brightening the far corners of the stuffy rooms. Could she honestly imagine herself living here, let alone being happy?

She turned to Frank. 'Tell me what you really think.'

He hesitated before giving his answer. 'I can't see much wrong with it. The only question is how much you really want to live here.'

'I need a family home,' she said. 'My mews cottage isn't big enough for the two of us.'

'Has Lily seen it yet?'

'She's been too busy. Maybe she'd prefer somewhere modern. What do you think?'

'I wouldn't know. But is that why you want a place like this? For Lily?'

'Yes, although perhaps with six bedrooms and a two-acre garden I'm getting a bit carried away.'

She laughed but he remained serious.

'Has Lily said she wants you to buy a big house?'

She was taken aback by his directness, even though she had requested it. 'She'd like to have somewhere out of London to come to at weekends. Why? What's wrong with the idea?'

'There's nothing wrong,' he said. 'It's just whether it's also what you want.'

Why did he have to look so downcast? First Celeste and now Frank – no one seemed to want to celebrate the miracle of finding her daughter!

'OK, so maybe not this house,' she said brusquely. 'But I can't stay where I am. I have to find somewhere I can offer Lily a home.'

She turned to walk away but he remained where he was, in the shade of the cedar's wide branches. She stopped and looked back. 'Shall we go?'

'I often dream that I'm living with my son,' he said. 'In some dreams his mother is there, too, and we're a happy family. In others I'm furious that she's kept him away from me. And then I wake up and remember he might not even be mine.'

'You don't know?'

'It's complicated. But I do understand what Lily means to you.'

Delia wasn't ready to unbend. 'Let's go and ask the agent what other houses we can look at in the area.'

'Tell me,' he said, still not moving, 'what is it you think Lily wants?'

'Everything!' She laughed. 'And why shouldn't she?'

'What does she want from you?'

Delia was annoyed. 'I think she's young and everything's happening so fast that she's barely had time to think. I think she needs me there simply as her mother. And that's where I want to be.'

He nodded, the frown back on his face. 'Your daughter was born in a nursing home in Barnes?'

Delia flinched at the shock, at the intimacy of this man revealing a fact she had never shared with anyone. 'So you *did* investigate me.'

He ignored her. 'Is it correct?'

'Yes. But how did you find that out? Until Lily came back, only Conrad knew my real name.'

'It's my job,' he said. 'There's usually an official trail if you know where to look. You have British naturalization papers.'

She waved that aside. 'So you discovered where Lily was born. What does it matter?'

'Has Lily shown you her birth certificate?'

'No,' Delia said angrily. 'She doesn't want to talk about the past. And she doesn't have to prove herself to me.'

'When your daughter was a few weeks old she was adopted by a couple in Richmond.'

'Even I never knew that. I was never told.'

'The adoption society was very helpful,' he said. 'The couple who took her had been married for ten years and desperately wanted children. With the war coming to an end, they were eager to build a family as soon as possible.'

'How dare you go spying on me? Does Peter know? Did he pay you to do this?'

'No. Celeste asked me to find out more about Lily's childhood because she was worried.'

Delia winced. She knew Celeste's concern was genuine, however misplaced, but her agitation overcame her compunction. 'I don't believe this! You've no right to conspire with each other behind my back!'

'Would you like to know what else I found out?' he asked gently.

'I imagine you've already told Celeste!'

'I haven't told her anything, and she hasn't asked.'

Trapped by what felt like an assault, Delia walked around in a small circle. 'She's only doing this because I'm evicting her from Curzon Street!'

'She never mentioned anything about that. She only said you might need looking after,' he said patiently. 'I think you should hear what happened to your daughter.'

'Only if it will help Lily,' she said. 'Otherwise I'd thank you to keep your nose out of my business!'

'It won't be what you expect.'

Delia was trembling with fear and anger. 'I don't care. I'm her mother. Whatever happened to her, I can bear it. I have to. The more I know, the better, so I can help her.'

'A year later the couple who adopted your baby also adopted a little boy, Michael.'

She frowned. 'Lily never mentioned a sibling.'

'When your daughter was five years old,' Frank continued almost tonelessly, 'she contracted polio.'

'And they abandoned her? Is that why she had to be in a children's home? Poor Lily. I should have been there to take care of her!'

'No, that's not what happened. Maybe *Lily* was in a children's home, but not your daughter. I'm so sorry, Delia. And I'm even more sorry to be the one to tell you. Your daughter died.'

'Died? Don't be ridiculous.'

'The child you gave birth to died of polio at the age of five.'

'That's not possible.'

'I can take you to her grave, if you'd like.'

Delia's hands flew to her mouth and she sank onto her knees on the grass. 'No!'

'I don't yet have any idea who Lily really is,' said Frank, coming to crouch beside her, 'but I'm absolutely certain that she cannot be your daughter.'

21

FRANK

The party Delia threw to celebrate Lily's eighteenth birthday in early July was in full swing. I was surrounded by expensive flower arrangements and besieged by a fleet of waiters, who glided between guests pouring champagne and offering silver trays of smoked salmon and caviar canapés. The only thing missing amid the crush of famous faces gathered in the private room of the Mayfair hotel was the birthday girl herself. In front of all of Delia's friends and show-business colleagues, Lily was at least an hour late, and counting.

Delia, however, was acting as if she hadn't a care in the world. She looked stunning in a shapely ruby-coloured dress overlaid with a fine black net that rustled faintly, and seductively, when she moved. Yet, even among friends, she radiated a kind of self-contained energy that left her solitary in the midst of all the noise and movement. I noticed how pale she was beneath her flawless make-up. Others would probably attribute it to the stress of being the indulgent mother of a wayward teenager; I could only guess at her real feelings.

She had greeted me without a flicker of acknowledgement of what had passed a week or so ago beneath the spreading branches of the cedar of Lebanon when, heartbroken, she had bound me to secrecy: no one was even to suspect that Lily was not her child. Her grief at the death of her young daughter had left me feeling so clumsy and useless that I could see no way to offer comfort other than to promise to stay silent. We had barely spoken on the drive back to London and I had not seen her again until tonight.

Had she told Lily? Delia had been certain that Lily would be as shocked and upset as she was, although privately I was doubtful. Perhaps the girl's reaction to my revelation of the facts explained her delayed arrival. It was also possible that Delia had not yet found the right moment to break the news, in which case this party threatened devastating exposure. I refused to believe that Delia would actively plan to reveal the truth in front of everyone here tonight.

I watched as, with carefree peals of laughter, she dragged various celebrities over to the grand piano and jokingly commanded them to play or to sing, either solo or in duets with her. Her guests loved the impromptu entertainment, making it possible for another half-hour to tick by without too much awkwardness.

So far I'd also managed to avoid more than a passing word with Celeste Burns. She was a nice woman, and I disliked the necessity of having to lie to her, but I was aware that she'd be curious to find out if I'd yet learned anything that would allay her concerns or raise further alarm about Lily. Luckily she knew plenty of people, and seemed happy to smile at me occasionally from the far side of the room.

It was an unusual space, designed for parties. One wall was taken up with a double-height bay window dressed with theatrical blue and gold velvet curtains. Opposite, an ornate staircase led down from a gallery where new guests could be seen arriving and from where they in turn were able to take the time to survey the people gathered below. A few women, accustomed to making an entrance, made the most of the opportunity to pause for dramatic effect before descending to the room below.

I found a quiet spot in the shelter of the bay window from which I could watch Delia and try to puzzle out yet again whether or not Celeste's apprehensions about Lily were well founded. Who was she? And could she really have studied Delia's stage gestures, and made herself up to look like her, not because she wanted to identify more closely with her, but so that she would appear more convincing as her daughter?

I was lost in my suspicions when I felt a hand on my arm and looked around to find Mary Jenks beside me. I was glad of the distraction, and was in any case always happy to spend time with her. We'd first met during the war when she, too, had been in uniform and was already engaged to Peter. I'd liked her immediately, swiftly appreciating that she was one of those rare women who could be good friends with a man without losing one iota of her fun or femininity. She'd always been attractive and, if anything, the softening lines of motherhood had made her even more so.

'She's amazing, isn't she?' she said, tilting her champagne flute in Delia's direction. 'I'd have been in tears by now.'

'Have you met Lily?' I knew Mary had little appetite for show-biz extravaganzas, which was why she had not attended the awards ceremony.

'No, not yet,' she said, 'although I get the impression from Peter that she can be a bit tricky. What do you make of her, Frank?'

I was strongly tempted to tell Mary the truth. I'd hated not going straight to tell Peter everything; he was, after all, employing me and, given how newsworthy Lily was, the reputation of RMJ Records would be at stake if any kind of scandal erupted. With difficulty, I kept my counsel, assuring myself that the evening couldn't possibly end without some kind of announcement from Delia.

'Delia would say that Lily's had a difficult childhood,' I said instead, 'and has now been thrust into the limelight without any real preparation.'

'Very diplomatic,' laughed Mary. 'Young and inconsiderate she may be, but in my book not turning up to her own party is plain rude. I wouldn't let one of my children get away with it.'

I smiled, feeling her good sense wash over me like a tonic, while she glanced at Delia, sitting at the piano beside a legendary American blues singer and laughing as she tried to pick up the chords he was playing.

'Mind you, I can't even begin to imagine having either of mine taken away,' she went on. 'I'd have ripped my own heart out first. I feel awful when I think of all those times I regaled Delia with the children's latest antics without any thought as to what she might have been feeling.'

At that moment, as if a grenade had exploded, the door on the gallery above us flew open and Lily, wearing an eye-catching dress of vivid colours in a swirling geometric pattern, made a dramatic appearance at the top of the staircase.

'Hello, Delia,' Lily laughed as she stumbled slightly on the steps and had to clutch at the silvered handrail to steady herself.

Mary whispered in my ear. 'She's tight!'

Following her, a nonchalantly elegant figure was instantly and, even in this company, almost shockingly recognizable: Guy

Brody, at this moment probably Hollywood's most sought-after leading man. He was shorter than the impression he made on screen, with a head slightly too large for his body, yet he instantly drew, and retained, the gaze of everyone in the room. And he knew it.

'He should've behaved better than to let her get so drunk,' I whispered back.

'We're not late, are we?' Lily demanded of the assembled guests. 'So sorry if we are!'

'What possessed her to bring him?' Mary asked. 'It's selfish and cruel. Everyone here knows he was meant to have been Delia's leading man.'

Celeste had told me about Lily taking Delia's role in the movie – it was what had prompted her plea for me to do something to protect Delia – but I hadn't known her future co-star's identity. Before I could respond to Mary, the blues singer at the piano struck up the opening chords of 'Happy Birthday'. Everyone joined in, their professional voices effortlessly finding harmonies or bass notes, but all were happy to relieve what might otherwise have been a mortifying moment for their hostess. The song ended with everybody clapping and cheering.

Delia went to embrace Lily before turning to welcome Guy Brody. I was curious to watch their interaction. Clearly she and Brody already knew one another, for he kissed her cheek affectionately and finessed it beautifully so that Delia and Lily presented a happy tableau to all her guests.

Now that the moment of truth was here, I was impatient to see what Delia would do and how she would handle the inevitable revelation. However difficult, now was the moment to explain the misunderstanding. Not wishing to inhibit her in any way, I moved further into the depths of the window embrasure so as to be out of her direct line of sight.

She took both of Lily's hands in hers and held her out at arm's length. 'Happy birthday, my darling daughter.'

Mary must have caught my sharp intake of breath, but I dared not look at her. What on earth was Delia doing?

'Only in my wildest dreams did I expect to be able to celebrate your birthday with you,' she continued blithely, 'although I have silently wished you every happiness on this day in each year that's passed since your birth.' Letting go of Lily's hands she swept a fresh glass of champagne from the nearest tray and held it up. 'I ask you all to drink to the health, happiness and success of my beautiful girl. To Lily!'

My mind was racing, trying to work out what had possessed Delia to take such a course. Had she simply refused to believe what I'd told her? She must realize that I had only to speak to force her to retract her words. What made her so certain that I never would?

As far as I was aware, I was the only person present who knew she had just told a momentous lie. But at that instant I had no option but to raise my glass with the rest.

'To Lily!'

As Lily demurely thanked everyone for being so kind, she appeared not to be so very drunk after all. There was something about her manner that I didn't trust. It struck me that she might be an accomplice in this inexplicable charade. Why? Did she wield some terrible power over Delia that had forced her to lie?

As I watched Delia standing beside Lily, her beautiful face apparently lit up with joy, I saw her glance across in my direction. I thought myself well shielded by the velvet curtains, and it took me a moment to grasp that she was staring behind me at my reflection in the darkening glass of the window. I stared back at her, but couldn't fathom any meaning in her expression.

I felt Mary's hand on my arm. She was studying me rather too perceptively and I forced myself to relax my shoulders and smile like everyone else. Then she very deliberately directed her gaze back towards Delia. 'Don't go breaking your heart, Frank,' she said quietly.

22

Immediately afterwards, the birthday cake, an extravagance of pale blue icing decorated with pink and yellow water-lilies, was wheeled in to further applause. I was relieved to be released from Mary's scrutiny when Peter came over to join his wife. He looked distressed at the unmistakable whispers and covert glances people were directing to where Delia, Guy Brody and Lily stood chatting insouciantly together.

'I feel rotten about the way Lily's taken Delia's movie role,' Peter said. 'What would you have done in my shoes, Frank?'

I shook my head. 'It seems that Delia can't deny Lily anything.'

'No,' he agreed, with a sigh. 'And I do understand why the producers went with Lily when they saw their chance. They'll be working to an incredibly tight schedule but, commercially, it was absolutely the right decision.'

I was burning to tell him the truth and felt terrible at keeping it from him. I would most certainly have to tell him soon, but right now I was too confused, too unsure of the implications of what I'd witnessed. I needed to get it straight in my own mind, and to speak to Delia, before discussing any of it with Peter.

'Do you think Lily will be good enough to carry off a starring role?' asked Mary. 'Does anyone know if she can act?'

I had to stop myself replying cynically that, so far, she'd managed to perform her chosen role to perfection. And yet, as a ceremony was made of Lily cutting the first slice of cake and making her birthday wish, I watched her close her eyes and tilt up her chin; with her face at rest, she looked so young and incapable of guile that it felt ridiculous to accuse her of some devious, carefully laid and malicious plot. In that moment, she was just a kid, not a criminal mastermind.

'So what's Brody like?' I asked Peter, as I watched Delia respond to the deployment of Brody's famous lop-sided grin with a regal radiance of her own. 'Is his charm purely professional, or is it the real thing?'

Although I'd seen a couple of the films in which the American actor had made his name, all I knew about the man was that he'd been a war hero, wounded twice and commissioned on the battlefield when fighting through Sicily and France.

'Well, he saw some tough action as a soldier, as I'm sure you know,' said Peter.

'I think it's rather wonderful how openly he's spoken about his psychological scars.' Mary placed a light hand on my arm and looked up at me. 'Too many of you boys kept all that to yourselves.'

'Maybe,' Peter conceded. 'But he's also supposed to have a rather murky personal reputation. Kept under wraps, naturally. I hope he respects how young Lily is.'

'Delia would have known how to manage him,' said Mary.

Delia and Guy Brody seemed genuinely at ease with one another although, as I was learning, that could simply have been the ability of stardom to create its own bubble. 'He must be more than twice Lily's age,' I said.

'Yes,' said Peter, 'but that's the story of the film they'll be making. All the same, I may have to ask you to keep an eye on her for me, Frank.'

'Of course,' I replied, and in truth I welcomed any opportunity to help me resolve the girl's unsettling ambiguity.

Waiters began circulating with slices of cake, and Peter led Mary away, eager to introduce her to the American blues singer, who was one of his all-time heroes. My mind was buzzing with questions, as well as an uneasy feeling of betrayal, but Celeste slipped into their place beside me, leaving me no time to straighten out my thoughts.

'They really would have made the perfect screen couple,' she said regretfully as she looked over to where Delia remained beside Brody as Lily left them to talk to Davey Nelson.

'I can hardly bear to think about what she's thrown away,' she continued. 'I wish I understood why she thinks it's a mother's job to let her child walk all over her.'

I made a noncommittal murmur that she seemed to take as assent.

'So what have you found out?' she asked. 'Anything interesting?'

'Not really.'

'But you have been digging into Lily's past?'

'A little,' I answered, hoping she would judge it too impolite to press harder. Luckily we were interrupted by a slight commotion on the other side of the room, where Lily stood facing Davey defiantly.

'Why shouldn't I say it?' she demanded loudly. 'It's true, isn't it?'

Davey tried to hush her but people around them turned to

watch. Aware that she had everyone's attention, Lily raised her champagne glass imperiously, spilling some wine over her hand. I held my breath, wondering what she was going to say.

'To retirement,' she declared.

Davey again attempted to quieten her down, but she refused. 'Go on, Delia, tell them your plan, about retiring to domesticity in a big house in the country.'

All eyes turned to Delia. I sensed the greedy, expectant hush of an audience hoping for a spectacle, the bloodier the better.

'Don't be silly, darling,' Delia said, with a shocked laugh. 'Whatever gave you that idea? The only reason I'm thinking of buying a house in the country is for you.'

'But you don't need to work any more,' Lily said gaily. 'You can leave me to earn the money now.'

'Lily, it's sweet of you to wish to support me, but I love my work and have absolutely no intention of giving it up.' Delia's voice, low and resonant, compelled respect.

'Of course not!' Peter stepped into the middle of the room. 'Your millions of fans around the world would never allow you to abandon them, and nor would I!'

'Hear, hear,' echoed Guy Brody, coming forward to clink his glass to Peter's. 'Let's all drink to our brilliant hostess. To Delia Maxwell and her many future triumphs!'

I raised my glass along with the rest of her guests, all the while keeping a close eye on Lily. I was unable to decipher the fleeting look I caught on her face as she joined in the new toast: was it confusion at her gaffe or a glint of secret satisfaction?

It was Mary who acted swiftly to prevent an awkward silence. She whispered in the ear of the American blues singer, and he immediately glided back to the piano and began a Fats Waller number that everyone would know. Delia's guests politely re-focused their attention and soon began to sway and tap their feet to the upbeat rhythm.

'That sort of talk will cost Delia her career if she's not care-ful.' Celeste was clearly upset. 'It's disgraceful behaviour. Who does Lily think she is? Why on earth does Delia tolerate it?'

On the other side of the room, Delia walked over to Lily, took her arm and led her aside. As they stood talking quietly together, Lily, in her gaudy dress and flat shoes, looked exactly like an over-excited child being soothed and gently chastised by her mother. Studying her, I could detect no sign of embarrassment or contrition, yet when Delia touched her cheek in a gesture of either forgiveness or appeasement, she gave Delia an impulsive hug and seemed, with shining eyes, to be thanking her for the party.

'It's what I've said from the beginning,' Celeste continued. 'Lily is out to steal her career.'

'And what Lily has always said,' I pointed out, trying to deflect Celeste from asking *why* that might be Lily's intention, 'is that perhaps Delia *would* like to quit, but feels too responsible for everyone who depends on her.'

'People like me, you mean?' Celeste asked sharply.

'I'm only playing devil's advocate,' I protested. 'But maybe Lily really does believe that Delia is weary and would like a break. Delia did run away, after all.'

I had no idea what I believed. Did Lily know that Delia was not her mother? Had she always known? In which case why set out to destroy the golden goose? What did she really want? Or did she believe she *was* Delia's daughter? I could just about under-stand an abandoned and angry child seeking such attention and behaving so badly – maybe needing her long-lost mother all to herself – and yet ...

'Delia should put a stop to it before it goes any further,' Celeste insisted, as Lily hastened away to reclaim Guy Brody. Observing the girl link her arm familiarly through his, Celeste shook her head contemptuously. 'I wonder if he has the faintest idea what he's letting himself in for.'

Delia went to stand behind the blues singer at the piano, pushed back her shining blonde hair, smoothed down the curves of her ruby dress, and began effortlessly to harmonize with his gravelly vocals. As everyone fell silent, allowing the air to fill with the silvery magic of her voice, an unwelcome doubt hit me: why did I distrust Lily so much when it was Delia who had deliberately lied to everyone at this party?

23

I sat in the hotel lobby, watching the final guests depart and waiting for Delia to appear. I needed to catch her alone. I felt baffled and disturbed by her purpose in staging such a performance. I also had every right to be angry that she had co-opted me, unasked, into her lie. I deserved an explanation, and to know how long she expected me to keep quiet. For her sake I had deceived Peter, my oldest and most loyal friend. That had to stop.

The most innocent explanation was that, unwilling to face the truth, she had convinced herself I had got my facts wrong. Although I couldn't help being stung by her lack of trust, I wanted to reassure her that I would only ever have her best interests at heart. I kept thinking of how she'd sunk to her knees on the grass beneath the cedar of Lebanon. Her grief had been horribly real, and I'd wanted desperately to take her in my arms and comfort her. We'd driven back to town in silence, but I knew then that I'd fallen in love.

But what of Lily? She and Guy Brody had shown no scruples in being among the first to leave the birthday party, so I hadn't been able to observe her for very long. In the end I had to assume that, whatever she might or might not know of her true parentage, Delia hadn't told her that she now also knew the truth.

After all, what possible reason could Lily and Delia have to conspire deliberately in perpetrating such a fraud?

I brought to mind Lily's face as she'd cut her birthday cake and made her wish, how the youthfulness of her features masked any possible darker motive. And then it came to me, like a blinding flash. How could I have been so stupid? The day that Delia was celebrating was the day she'd given birth to a daughter. Today would have been the birthday of a five-year-old polio victim. Unless, by some far-fetched coincidence, Lily had been born on the same day, then Lily *had* to know that today was not her birthday.

I got to my feet and paced around the lobby, where my agitation drew wary glances from the tail-coated young man behind the reception desk. A chattering couple came out of the ground-floor bar and headed for the street. I returned to my seat and tried to remain still.

What part had Lily really been playing tonight? How long had she known? The heartlessness of her deception shocked me. Who was she, and what was she after? Fame and a career, or something more deeply twisted? Might she be insane? In which case, what kind of danger was Delia in?

I took a deep breath. It had been Lily who had announced at the awards ceremony in front of hundreds of people who knew and worked with Delia that she was Delia's daughter. Such premeditated audacity took guts, as well as a cool head and a calculating mind. If she was insane, then her madness was of a very special kind.

I was even more anxious for Delia to appear. I had to warn her, to discover if Lily had any kind of devious hold over her, and to offer my protection.

I blamed myself. Peter had given me the job of looking into Delia's disappearance and ensuring her safety, yet I had failed to establish the most basic credentials of the young woman who was all but living in her house.

My anxiety raised an old and familiar rush of panic, a flashback to another occasion when I had fatally overlooked a vital detail. My mouth went dry, my palms began to sweat, and I could almost smell the steamy vegetation of the Malayan jungle, hear the gunshots and see the torn flesh of the eight unarmed villagers shot dead by young British conscripts who had wrongly believed them to be guerrilla insurgents. I had always felt responsible because I had failed to establish that the inexperienced patrol – jumpy from a recent and bloody ambush – had been properly briefed. And all this carnage was for what? To protect British interests in rubber and tin.

I pushed away the all-too-vivid memory, trying to catch my breath. Desperate not to succumb, I looked around for something to distract me and found it: Delia was coming slowly down the stairs. She looked heavenly in a pearl-white satin evening coat and long matching gloves. Thankfully she was alone.

I must have appeared a little strange, or perhaps she wondered why I was still in the hotel, for she looked alarmed.

'What is it?' she asked.

I made an effort to smile as naturally as I could. 'I thought you might like a lift home.'

She hesitated a moment. 'Thank you. That would be kind.'

I let her go ahead of me into the heavy revolving door that led outside. The July weather was mild, but there must have been a shower during the evening, for there was a damp sheen on the pavement. Delia shivered slightly after the heat of the party and pulled the collar of her coat close around her neck. My car was parked nearby, and we both remained silent until I had fired up the engine.

'I suppose I owe you an explanation,' she said, turning in her seat to look at me as I drove through the Mayfair streets.

With no clue what to say, I concentrated on waiting for a gap in the traffic at the turn into Park Lane.

'You'll think I'm foolish,' she went on, 'and I'm not disputing what you told me, but it doesn't matter. I can still be a mother to Lily. She's found something in me that she needs and longs for. When it came to the point, I didn't have the heart to take it away from her. And why should I? It's real. I am a mother. Or I was. I abandoned my own baby. I won't abandon her.'

'Lily's real mother might still be found,' I said carefully. 'If that's what matters to her.'

'In that case, I'd stand aside,' she said. 'Of course I would. But, for all she tries to cover it up, you can see how fragile she is emotionally. She's coming into a very tough business and needs me to protect her.'

'And when someone else gets to the truth?' I asked. 'It won't be long before some reporter digs it up. What then?'

Delia tilted her head and shrugged her shoulders. 'Love gives you faith in the impossible.'

Her words sounded like a line from a song. She might believe such simple sentiments while she was singing, but her naivety had left her wide open to Lily's cold-blooded duplicity.

We rounded Hyde Park Corner and turned off towards Knightsbridge along the side of the new underpass. I wanted to be able to look at her properly when I told her what I'd realized about Lily's birthday, so I said nothing until I had parked outside her house in the darkness of the unlit cobbled mews. When I didn't get out to open her door, she reached for the handle.

'Wait,' I said. 'I have to ask you something.'

She folded her hands in her lap and sat quietly.

'Lily's birthday,' I began.

She turned to look at me, a sharp gleam of alarm in her eyes. 'It's the same,' she said quickly. 'It must be. How else did she come to believe that she's mine?'

'Except she's not your daughter,' I said gently. 'And it's yet another extraordinary coincidence. Not only adopted, and from a Hungarian mother, but with the exact same date of birth, too. Let's not forget that she's had access to all your papers.'

'So did you,' she shot back.

I had tried to forget the night I had riffled through her cupboards and helped myself to her whisky, but regardless of how deeply her accusation cut, I had to make her understand that Lily could pose a real threat. 'I think she came across a reference to the daughter you gave up and decided she could exploit it.'

'Did you find anything like that?'

'No,' I admitted, 'but she had more time for a thorough search. Or maybe she covered her tracks and removed whatever she found.'

Delia frowned and looked away, nervously smoothing her satin coat across her knees.

'Did you keep papers relating to the adoption?' I asked.

'Conrad might have done,' she said. 'I honestly don't remember. I have a box of papers from when he died that I haven't looked at yet.'

'Then I think you have to take seriously the possibility that she has duped you deliberately.'

'Very well,' she said, raising her chin and turning to look at me directly. 'So Lily knows it's not real. But she has no family, had an unhappy childhood, and chooses to believe in a fairy tale. It's clear she really has been following my career for years. She was a keen enough fan to hang around a stage door in the rain. I mean, how often do adopted kids fantasize that their real family is royal or famous or fabulously wealthy? There are far worse things than convincing yourself you're Delia Maxwell's daughter.'

'Particularly when it offers you a meteoric rise to fame.'

'She has real talent.'

'So do lots of girls her age. They don't get to commandeer a glittering awards ceremony, or steal a starring role in a movie. And what was all that nonsense tonight about you retiring?'

Delia impatiently waved aside my objections. 'Nothing. Wishful thinking. She wants a mother, a home.'

'It'll be easy enough to check Lily Brooks's date of birth.'

'No.'

'Delia, you've just said you think she's delusional. You need to know what kind of fantasy world she's living in. She could be dangerous.'

She smiled. 'That's silly. I've known her for months now. You've only met her a few times. And you've forgotten that I know what it's like to lose your family, to feel abandoned. I understand her. There's not a day I don't wake up and ask myself why I am here when none of my family or friends are. I've been so lucky.' She lifted her arm, displaying the diamond bracelet clasped over the white satin of her glove. 'The ones who are gone should be enjoying all this, not me.'

The warmth of the car had released the lemon and violet

fragrance of her perfume and I longed to gather her in my arms and show her what I thought she was worth. 'You mustn't think like that,' was all I said.

'But I do.' Her smile was beautiful and also heart-breaking. 'Don't you see? There has to be a reason why I alone survived, and this is it. It's so that I can hand on some of my good fortune to Lily. You have to promise not to tell anyone the truth, not even Peter.'

'But what if—'

She silenced me with the touch of her gloved hand on my cheek. 'You have to promise me that you'll let Lily go on being my daughter.'

She had tears in her eyes. What else could I do?

'Goodnight, Frank.' She slipped out of the car and disappeared into her house before I could hold her back.

As I drove to Maida Vale, it began to spatter with rain again. Maybe it was the rhythmic action of the windscreen wipers, but I felt strangely disconnected from the world around me: elegant mannequins in a department-store window, slowly changing traffic lights, and human faces staring blindly out from the lit interior of a passing bus, all melded into a brightly coloured blur against the blackness of the glistening streets. I switched on the radio in an attempt to subdue my wilder thoughts. Lily was singing 'Tell Me How It Ends'.

24

LILY

Lily was alone in her dressing room waiting for her first call on set. She could hardly believe that it was finally about to happen. Although Peter, Delia and Guy had all sent flowers, the room was hardly glamorous, and she'd already come to loathe all the hanging about. Everyone kept talking about the whirlwind of activity required to get the project off the ground in record-fast time so they could make the most of the English summer, but the past few weeks of endless pre-production meetings about wardrobe and hair and lighting had been irritating, and now she just wanted to get on with it. It wasn't as if she'd ever entertained dreams of acting: she had never even been much of a movie fan. And now this whole business of making a film was turning out to be far more complicated than she'd ever imagined. She wasn't afraid of a challenge. She just wasn't sure that she saw the point of rising to meet this one, now that her primary goal of robbing Delia of the part had been accomplished.

Perhaps she ought to take another look at her lines while she waited. But that was another reminder of her ignorance. She'd naively assumed they'd start at the beginning of the script and work through to the end. Of course, now she'd seen how much work was involved in setting up each scene, working like that made no sense at all. Although James Sinclair, the youngish and trendy British director, had made his name by shooting several of his films on location, they were kicking off at Pinewood Studios with all the scenes that required specially built sets. It might be disorienting for the actors to tell their stories out of sequence, but it was also another signal that, far from being a star and the centre of attention, as she'd thought she'd be, she was just one more, if equally important, cog in a complex and intricate machine.

She couldn't sit here waiting any longer. Although perfectly clean, the dressing room reminded her unpleasantly of the dingy bedsit in Earl's Court that had smelt of mould and other people's unwashed clothes. She was so glad she'd persuaded RMJ Records to rent a much nicer flat for her in Chelsea. Maybe, if she crept out onto the sound stage, she could watch and learn a bit more about how it all worked.

Her first surprise was how just many people filled the huge, lofty space. They were nearly all men, moving purposefully about and each intently focused on carrying out a separate specialist task about which she understood almost nothing. Above her head the lighting riggers took shouted instructions from the camera team below. Other members of the crew moved around with clipboards and stop-watches, microphone booms and camera tracks. There were carpenters and set-dressers and men reeling out yards of cable across the floor.

James spotted her but merely nodded before returning to the earnest discussion he was having with four technicians over adjusting some hefty piece of camera equipment. She hadn't yet worked James out. His manners were impeccable but impersonal. He was tall and rangy, with long sideburns and a Carnaby

Street shirt, yet he spoke with the cut-glass accent of the English upper class. She shivered in her skimpy costume of black Capri pants and a short-sleeved black jumper. Outside it was a fine summer day but inside the draughty sound stage it was cold. She hadn't been prepared for that, either.

As she rubbed her bare arms, trying to generate some warmth, she heard the ever-present voice in her ear: *What have you got to cry about?* Nothing, she told herself. This was nothing. She was a bit chilly, but she wasn't going to freeze to death any more than she was about to be beaten or starved or attacked by dogs or shot in the head. She was still alive, wasn't she? She must show no fear and accomplish what was required without fuss. Crying only ever made everything worse.

'Lily.' It was James. 'Since you're here, be an angel and help me block out this scene.'

She went to stand obediently on the spot he indicated. He took her by the shoulders and gently pushed and pulled her into the position he seemed to want. He stepped back to allow an assistant to approach. Without making eye contact, the assistant stuck a tape-measure under her nose, then called out the result to the focus puller perched on his rig.

'That work for you?' James asked, turning away to address the lighting cameraman. When the other man nodded, the assistant darted forward again to stick a bit of coloured tape to the floor by her feet.

'That's your mark, dear,' said a drawling female voice, as the men returned to their discussion.

Lily turned and found the red-headed woman who had introduced herself at an earlier costume fitting as Vivien, the actress who'd also be playing in the scene they were about to shoot.

'You're new to all this, aren't you?' Vivien linked her arm in Lily's and led her away from the activity around the camera. She was tall, willowy and impeccably groomed, even though she was in costume as the waitress girlfriend of a down-at-heel pianist.

'I hadn't expected it to be so technical,' Lily admitted, liking the gleam of sharp wit in Vivien's eyes, and deciding it would be useful to encourage her patronage. She was right: within ten minutes Vivien had given her a complete run-down of who was who and how the whole process generally worked.

'The two people never to get on the wrong side of,' said Vivien, 'are the script supervisor and the props master. They can make your life hell if they choose. Oh, and watch out for Guy Brody. But you've probably worked that out for yourself by now.'

'Really?' Lily asked, feigning innocence to encourage the older woman's indiscretion. Lily had not only recognized within seconds of first meeting Guy how deftly he used his charm to get what he wanted but had admired him for it. She was happy, though, to listen to whatever Vivien wished to tell her about this unfamiliar world: three years in a children's home had taught her that knowledge was power.

'Don't be fooled by that slow old Gary Cooper smile,' said Vivien. 'Have you noticed that Guy never laughs? Not properly. Never trust a man who lacks a sense of humour, I say.'

Lily laughed. 'I'll remember that, thanks.'

'He's married, of course, so strictly OLDC.'

'OLDC?'

'On Location Doesn't Count. And you can rule him out, too.' She nodded towards James. 'He bats for both teams.'

'Really?' Lily hadn't yet picked up on that, and filed it away for future usefulness.

'But maybe you're in less of a rush to find a good husband.' She gave Lily a sideways look. 'You're young, and it can't do any harm to have a mother like Delia Maxwell behind you, especially when you're starting out.'

Lily decided to turn the tables. 'Is that what you want? To get married?'

'A little security never hurt anyone, darling, and I've been kicking around for a while now.'

Lily would have placed Vivien as no older than twenty-five, but if she was still playing supporting roles after a few years in the business, then maybe an ambitious marriage became a sensible option.

Vivien seemed to guess her thoughts. 'Don't kid yourself,' she said. 'We girls are all just so much interchangeable window dressing. In the end, if you want any influence around here, you have to marry it.'

Lily didn't agree, but she smiled anyway. In her experience, power was easy as long as you didn't care what anybody thought of you. Yet most of the women she'd met seemed convinced they had to sacrifice all hint of ambition if they wanted to be lovable. That was certainly the moral of the picture they were about to shoot: the only reason why the character Lily played had to end up as a lonely and tragic heroine was because the silly young woman gave in to pathetic sentimentality about her lover and his fading career.

But then, as if to bear out the truth of Vivien's advice, Guy Brody made his entrance, causing an immediate ripple of heightened alertness and attention among everyone on the floor.

'See what I mean?' Vivien whispered, arching one flawless eyebrow.

Guy strode straight over to James. The director draped an arm around the actor's shoulders before turning to walk a few paces away from the camera team. Anyone left in the vicinity of the two men quickly melted into the depths of the vast studio.

Lily watched, smarting at her own relegation and furiously assessing how best to confront it. Yet what did it matter? She was almost tempted not to bother with the effort of making this work. She could easily feign illness or come up with some other excuse to make her escape, but she was held back by the fear that doing so might create an opportunity for Delia to step back in. Until Delia's defeat was established beyond recall, Lily must hold firm.

But how to approach the turned backs of the two powerful men who had excluded everyone else from their charmed circle? Lily glanced at Vivien, who responded with an ironic shrug. She mentally reviewed what experience she could draw on and came up with her return to the hotel ballroom after dropping her bombshell at the awards ceremony. She pictured again how every head had turned to watch her walk across the expanse of carpet to join Peter Jenks. Holding in her mind the potent hush that had fallen on that occasion, she stepped out towards James and Guy.

It worked. As if sensing some change of pressure in the air, the two men turned to face her. Guy smiled with amused appreciation as Lily, head up, fearlessly met his gaze and kept walking towards them. She saw with satisfaction that, when James came halfway to meet her, every other man present took note of the capitulation. She'd gained mastery of nastier playgrounds than this. It was easy when you didn't care.

25

The boost to Lily's confidence didn't last long. As soon as the crew swung into action, she felt as if she was the only one who didn't know what she was doing. On paper, it was a simple enough scene, the one in which Guy's character, a disillusioned and increasingly heavy-drinking Hollywood star visiting London in search of some meaning to life, first enters the club where Lily's character, a coffee-bar bohemian, sings with a blues trio. It was the additional presence in the scene of Vivien, as the aspiring singer's older and wiser friend, that confused Lily. Every time she had to turn from looking at one actor to the other, James would shout, 'Cut!'

'You looked at the camera,' he said each time. 'Try again.'

She waited for the familiar chant.

'Quiet.'

'Turn over.'

'Speed.'

'Action.'

On the fourth take, she made sure she kept her gaze at the correct level, but James yet again called, 'Cut!' before they were even halfway through.

'What did I do?' she asked, bewildered.

'You started your line before I'd finished mine,' Vivien explained gently. 'They can't pick it up in the loop if we speak over one another.'

Lily wasn't exactly sure what that meant, but stored it away as one more thing to learn and then remember not to do. On the next take, trying not to blink as the clapperboard snapped in front of her, she knew her voice was stiff and artificial and her movements wooden. The more she berated herself and tried to relax, the more impossible it became to break the intense and concentrated silence around her. She had to be clever, think on her feet. If she was going to indulge in self-pity she might just as well roll over and die. She'd never survive if she didn't force herself to do things she didn't want to do. This was nothing compared to—

And that was always the point at which all choice stopped, where she'd learned to close off whatever feelings she might have and to do only what was required. No grazed knee, lost toy, sore throat, school bully or other childish woe was ever worth pursuing once it reached that stage.

Lily stuck it out and made it to the end of the sixth take without further mistakes. As soon as James was satisfied, the crew began setting up for the next shot and, happy now to be ignored, she was able to take a breather. She knew her performance was pedestrian, but had not the first idea how to make herself believe that this huge chilly space at half past nine in the morning was a small, stuffy bar after midnight, let alone convey that her character had just met the man who would alter her life for ever.

Guy ambled over to stand beside her. 'Want some good advice?'

'Anything!'

He leaned in close. 'They'll bring the tea urn later. Whatever you do, don't eat a biscuit if your throat's dry.'

It was a relief to laugh. 'Good tip, thanks.'

'There's a lot to learn on your first day.'

'Yes.'

'Don't lose your nerve. Believe me, I wouldn't be here if I didn't think you could do it.'

Self-interest was a language Lily understood. 'Thanks, Guy. Any other tips?'

He shook his head. 'Not really. Don't act it, just think it and let the camera pick it up. You'll be surprised how little you have to do. Oh, and keep an eye on where the light's falling. That's where the magic will be.'

This was something Lily already understood how to do. When she had been about eight years old her mother had taken her to see Delia Maxwell on one of her provincial tours. It had been the first time Lily had ever visited a theatre. She had never forgotten walking from the station through a rancid winter fog that had made her mother cough and gasp for air, before entering the expectant atmosphere of the darkened auditorium. She'd watched the musicians assembling in the orchestra pit, tuning instruments she'd never seen before. Then the heavy curtains had swept aside and the theatricality of the spotlights and applause had heightened the fervour with which her mother kept whispering in her ear, repeating over and over that the singer on stage was worse than the devil and that, from now on, Lily's mission in life was to destroy her. Lily had felt as if not only she but the entire audience was responding to the drama not of the performance but of her mother's words.

After her mother's death, obeying the instruction to know

her enemy, Lily had spent her young teenage years studying magazine features on Delia Maxwell and, as she grew older, took every chance to watch her perform so she could scrutinize her stage and television technique before trying to reproduce it in front of the bathroom mirror. In the end, her fixation had given her an instinct for how to angle her face into the perfect spot for any light-source. She already knew where the magic would be. All she had to do here on set was add in a camera lens and then be Delia. She'd done just that when she had stood alone in the spotlight on stage at the awards ceremony and sung 'Tell Me How It Ends'. It had been easy. She knew precisely how to do it. It was what she'd spent so much of her life preparing for.

When they were called for the new scene, Lily was ready and played it effortlessly. She could instinctively feel that she'd done well, and when the crew simply turned away, back to their own tasks, preparing to set up the following shot, she took the absence of comment or congratulation as professional accept-ance. She went happily to her dressing room to wait for the next call.

Later, after they'd wrapped for the day, Guy drove her home to her Chelsea flat in his silver Jaguar. Arriving in Smith Street, he leaned across to open her door. 'I told James he has to show you the rushes tomorrow,' he said. 'In fact I insisted.'

She turned to him for an explanation.

'Just watch,' he said, with a smile. 'You'll see.'

Early the following morning she sat nervously between James and Guy in the front row of the little screening room and watched take after take play out on the unedited reel of film. She had idiotically forgotten that the producers had agreed to

James shooting in black-and-white, in homage to modern French cinema as well as James's revered American *noir* dramas of an earlier era. The actors' voices had already been synched, but no ambient or background sound had yet been added, making their actions on screen seem strange and almost dream-like. Lily didn't mind how glaring her early mistakes were because it was so incredibly useful to see how what had seemed like tiny errors were indeed grossly magnified on screen. Slowly, as they reached the footage shot the previous afternoon, she began to understand why Guy had insisted she see the rushes, and to watch how, once she'd found her confidence, the camera began to love her. Everything she'd learned from studying Delia Maxwell had been caught on film. Her make-up appeared minimal and her short hair made her eyes unnaturally large and luminous, yet the more she turned aside from the camera's gaze, forcing the audience to seek her out, the more interesting her features became. The less she did, the deeper the lens tried to delve into the elusive world behind her eyes.

Lily had never truly seen herself before. She'd dismissed all the fuss and fame that had followed her announcement that she was Delia's daughter; it had scarcely mattered to her that the movie script had been rewritten and rushed into production in hope of building on the overnight success of her hit single; that Guy Brody had agreed to star alongside her because she was the so-called face of the future; that Davey kept telling her she had 'that something extra'; or that even Delia's praise had sounded genuine. She'd paid no attention because she cared only about her ultimate goal.

Now, for the first time, Lily caught a glimpse of something novel and intriguing, something other than her focus on Delia, something that promised to repay hard work and study – that she might actually want for herself.

She caught her breath and froze in her seat. Wanting something for herself felt dangerous and forbidden, as if, should she dare to reach out to take it, her life would spiral terrifyingly out of control.

She still had a few minutes before they reached the final frames in which to steady her breathing and return to the familiarity of an existence where her own needs and hopes could not exist because the monsters under the bed were real and the world would end in ashes. She had to make herself forget what she had glimpsed of the potential Lily up on the silvery black-and-white screen. Her life could not permit anything so trivial as what *she* might want from it.

But she couldn't do it. Something in her rebelled. She couldn't stop looking at this alternative self. She felt an overwhelming urge to step up into the image, to merge with it and escape into a world in which that image of freedom existed, and the shamed and silenced Lily of her childhood could be abandoned and forgotten.

Lily repeated over and over that it didn't matter what she wanted, that she had no right to want anything, but for once the incantation had no effect. A genie had escaped from the bottle.

The reel ended and the lights came on. She heard as if from a distance Guy and James telling her how extraordinary her screen presence was, that it was movie magic and she was going to be a star. And she was flooded with the certain knowledge that she wanted this and, what was more, that she intended to have it.

26

'I've got a surprise for you.' James seemed particularly pleased with himself when he greeted Lily on her arrival at the studio at the end of the week. 'It's about shooting your first song today. Working to playback can be tricky when you've not done it before, so I had the brilliant idea of asking your mother to come and lend moral support.'

Lily's heart sank. 'And she said she would?'

'Yes. She'll be here in about half an hour.'

'That's wonderful. So kind of you.'

'See you later,' he said, whistling as he walked away.

Lily didn't want Delia there. It was the last thing on earth she wanted. Neither could she imagine why Delia would wish to visit the set of the movie from which she had been so ruthlessly dropped. If only Lily had known earlier, she could have found a way to fob her off. But perhaps Delia had decided to come because she hoped to upstage Lily in some way. Might it even be an attempt to win back the role?

Sitting in make-up, her costume protected by a freshly laundered white gown, Lily stared at her reflection in the mirror.

'Try not to frown, dear,' said the woman dabbing at her

forehead. 'This foundation dries quickly and needs to go on smoothly.'

Lily's mission had never allowed for the possibility that Delia would turn out to be generous and caring. True, Delia's kindness had given Lily an unforeseen advantage because it made her the perfect dupe. Right from when Lily had seized the opportunity to make Delia notice her that night outside the BBC concert hall, Delia had actively enabled Lily's steady infiltration. She had insisted Lily take shelter in the taxi, invited her to supper, even dropped her home.

Lily would never forget the cab ride to the restaurant: sitting sideways in the jump seat so her knees wouldn't come into contact with Delia's; the steamed-up windows; and Delia, the mythical beast Lily had been hunting for so long, laughing as Celeste tried to prevent the soaking wet umbrella dripping on their shoes. Her mind had been a whirl. She had spent so much of her childhood learning all she could about her quarry. Until she had let Delia drag her into the taxi, her hatred had remained abstract; now she had abruptly to come to terms with Delia's physical reality. The star had seemed both bigger and smaller than she'd expected, less mythic and more complicatedly and intractably human.

Over an expensive dinner she'd barely been able to swallow, she'd done her best to watch and learn. Celeste was possessive and over-protective but also shrewd and a little too observant for her liking. But Delia was surprisingly open and suggestible, and it had been all too easy to prompt her into requesting Lily's assistance in sorting out her papers and preparing for the move to California. And once Lily had won unfettered access to Delia's house, the rest had simply fallen into place.

She couldn't believe her luck when, in an untouched box of Conrad Durand's papers, she came across a receipt for the nursing home where Delia had given birth. The existence of a daughter given up for adoption, who would now be the same age as her, offered an undreamed-of opportunity. Armed with that discovery, she made a thorough search of all Delia's documentation and unearthed a few other useful snippets she could weave into her own fictitious story. It had been so easy to drop a few apparently stray hints about her supposed background, and Delia's reaction quickly confirmed that she'd chanced upon a rich seam of longing and regret that could be worked to her advantage.

As time went on, however, Delia's increasingly eager hope and unwavering kindness had begun to wear her down. She had a visceral distrust of it. She found it so cloying that at times she doubted she could go on playing the role of grateful orphan without going mad. It had been a relief, frankly, when Delia ran away.

Her disappearance had unnerved Lily initially, all the more so once Peter's old war-time buddy had begun sneaking around, but she soon realized that Delia's absence provided the ideal conditions in which to gamble everything on a single high-stakes roll of the dice. That had paid off so well that, by the time Delia reappeared, Lily's position was unassailable.

Since then, regardless of how much Lily took or how rude or ungrateful her behaviour, Delia had gone on being unfailingly benevolent. Her evident remorse over the baby she'd cast aside only provoked Lily into further defiance.

Of course there were times when Lily itched to fling the truth in her face, to tell her that the cuckoo fattening herself up in the nest had no connection whatever with the daughter Delia had abandoned, but she had successfully fought off the desire to see what would happen then to Delia's saintly act of motherhood. It was fine: she could wait.

'There we are,' said the make-up artist, with relief. 'All done now.'

Released, Lily made her way back to her dressing room. As she passed across one corner of the sound stage she heard laughter. Peeping between two flats she saw Delia and Guy standing together in conversation. From what she could overhear, it was merely small-talk, but she remained still so she could listen, just in case.

'Lily, whatever are you doing skulking behind there?'

It was Vivien, following on her heels from the make-up department. Delia and Guy turned and peered about, trying to see where she was. As Vivien arrived at where Lily stood, Lily could tell from her raised eyebrow that, also spotting the other two through the gap, she'd guessed that Lily had been eavesdropping.

'My mother's here,' said Lily, clearly.

'Oh, I do hope you'll introduce me,' said Vivien. 'I'd love to meet her.'

'Lily!' called Delia, laughing. 'Where are you? Come out and show yourself!'

Lily didn't mind so much being with Delia when there were other people present. Then it was clear to her how to act, and she was able to channel her real feelings into a performance. Watching herself through Vivien's eyes, she stepped out where Delia and Guy could see her.

Delia held out her hands. 'Hello, darling.'

Lily accepted the embrace, closing her eyes as she inhaled the older woman's perfume, a scent she had come to detest. Freeing herself, she caught Guy's amused glint that suggested he, too, assumed she had been spying on them.

'This all seems like a dream.' Lily indicated the busy sound stage. 'And it's entirely thanks to you, Delia!'

'I'm so proud of you,' Delia responded. 'And I'm delighted if I can help in any way today. I'm so glad James thought to ring me.'

'Wait till you see how much the camera loves her,' Guy said to Delia. 'You know, there's a scene later in the script where my character's name is taken down from over the marquee and hers is put up in its place. I'm beginning to worry that's going to happen in real life!'

There was a silence as Guy realized the crassness of what he'd just said, and to whom he'd said it. Lily did her best to look oblivious. Delia coloured, but managed a smile, raising her chin and standing even straighter.

'I seem to remember another line from the script I was sent to read,' Delia said lightly. ' "Don't settle for the little dream. Go on to the big one." That comes soon after you sing your first song, doesn't it, Lily?'

'Yes, that's what we're shooting today.'

'Well, it's good advice,' said Delia. 'I hope you'll take it.'

Stop being so nice, Lily wanted to scream. *Stop trying. I can't stand it.* She was suddenly overwhelmed by the hopelessness of maintaining her fledgling sense of self with Delia present. It was impossible to act one part at the same time as playing another.

For what the camera had so far captured and then revealed to

Lily was a person she barely knew. She hadn't got a firm enough grip on this emerging new persona to make it real, and was suddenly and horribly afraid that, if she let go of it even for an hour, she would never recapture it. *Stop this fuss*, said the voice in her head. *There's no point in crying. What did you ever have to cry about?* The voice was always right. It didn't matter what she wanted. She had a more important promise to keep.

James arrived and everyone hustled to get into position as he greeted Delia and arranged for a chair for her to be placed beside his.

Lily and Davey had already recorded 'Kiss Me Tomorrow', the first of several musical numbers in the film. She was to sing it in the scene in which the aspiring singer's true talent is revealed to Guy Brody, playing the older disillusioned star. Davey had reassured her that, even if her voice turned out not to be strong enough for some of the bigger set-pieces, her role in the film would remain secure because they could always dub in a 'ghost' singer. But James had been pleased with this first recording, and told her that a natural sound was more 'real' and better suited to the style of film he aimed to make. Lily had given a lot of thought to how she might play a character who voices her innermost feelings through song and, now she'd learned from the rushes how to achieve some of the effects she wanted, was eager to try out her ideas.

She readied herself to begin miming to playback. There were a lot of shots and camera angles to cover, so she knew she would spend the morning hearing herself singing the simple ballad over and over again. The presence of Vivien and Guy, whose characters had to watch and listen with rapt attention during every take, added to the pressure. The clumsiness and embarrassment of her first day on set came back to haunt her as, on her first try, she came in late. On the third take she looked at Vivien when she was supposed to be looking at Guy. Her tense limbs began to jerk like a marionette's.

'Cut!' James called resignedly, for the umpteenth time. 'Delia, can you help us out here?'

Lily wanted to yell at Delia not to come near her, but she didn't dare, too afraid that, if she started telling the truth she might not stop. Instead she forced a grateful smile as Delia walked over to her and waited to hear what advice an experienced performer could offer.

'Think of your audience,' Delia said quietly. 'Forget all this and just think of the people who'll be sitting in their cinema seats watching you on screen. Give *them* what they want and you don't need to worry about this lot.'

'This isn't a stage,' said Lily in irritation. 'I have technical stuff to get right.'

Delia smiled. 'I know. A theatre stage isn't as straightforward as it looks, either. But take your time. Leave room for the magic. Trust me, if the audience loves you, the only job all these people around you have to do is to make that magic work.'

James stepped forwards. 'Delia, I think—'

Delia held up a hand to silence him, never taking her eyes off Lily. 'You lead, they'll follow. Just do your job, the job only *you* can do, and leave them to do theirs.' She turned to face James and the camera team behind him, treating them to a full-beam Delia Maxwell smile. 'Come on, gentlemen. All your years of skill and experience, and you're telling me you'd let yourselves be beaten by a mere slip of a girl?'

The camera operator laughed. 'No, ma'am.'

'That's better,' said Delia, returning to her chair. 'Over to you Mr DeMille.'

Lily could feel the tension leave the chilly air as everyone nodded, grinned and settled back to their tasks. Guy gave her an encouraging wink as she took up her mark once more. Even though she had never hated Delia more venomously than at that moment, she could also feel the adrenalin of it run like fire through her blood. In striving to repress her hatred and conceal its nakedness from the rolling camera she remained oblivious to how its intensity would unconsciously reveal itself on screen, or to how that almost indiscernible intimation of a secret inner passion would one day have cinemagoers queuing around the block.

27

Guy Brody was teaching Lily to drive his long-nosed Jaguar coupé. He didn't seem to care that she might damage his expensive car, let alone that she didn't have a licence. He insisted it didn't matter because the studio grounds were private property. In any case Lily had learned by now that no one ever tried to stop Guy doing whatever he wanted. And, once she'd mastered bringing up the clutch without stalling, she'd loved the sensation of controlling the throaty engine, and had badgered him for another lesson every chance they got.

The late July weather had been changeable, so James had decided to leave the London location scenes until the end of the shooting schedule in hope of more settled conditions. They would only be at the studios for a couple more days. The following week they would move on to Rome. Lily had already noticed a kind of holiday atmosphere among the crew, especially the younger ones who would now disperse, presumably to work on other projects, as only James and his heads of department would be required in Italy. Now that Lily was to leave the great draughty sound stage, she marvelled at how quickly it had grown so intimately familiar. It would be a wrench to start again somewhere else. And she had never been abroad. She had hardly been anywhere in England, come to that.

She had panicked briefly when she discovered she'd need a passport and, to apply for one, would have to produce her birth certificate. Her surname on most official documents had been changed to Brooks a few years earlier. She'd been happy to keep it, especially as it made a good professional name. Her birth certificate was the only thing that could give her away. So far as she could tell, Delia had always kept her Hungarian name out of the public eye, so there were presumably very few people in a position to spot a discrepancy even if Lily's original surname came to light. It was reassuring that her foster mother had never managed to pronounce the Hungarian syllables well enough to remember the name, so why should Lily fear that the overworked production assistant who'd be taking the documents to the Passport Office in Petty France would be any different?

Lily had tried in vain to deny that a tiny part of her almost hoped that her fraud *would* be exposed. She was growing tired of keeping up the pretence. She'd done all she could so far to fulfil the promise she'd made and, for the time being, had run out of ways to inflict further damage. It might be a relief to be so far away that she'd no longer have to make excuses to avoid seeing or speaking to Delia. Secretly, she longed to be free to embrace wholeheartedly the new Lily she'd discovered in the highly technical dream factory that was the film industry.

But, in the small hours of the night when she couldn't sleep, the admission of her desire to escape brought on an agony of guilt. She was weak, a coward, a traitor. She had never really cared. She was just as bad as those who had persecuted and tortured and killed.

Then she'd been grateful for the limited supply of drugs pre-scribed by the private doctor she'd consulted, especially during bad nights when only a dose of Nembutal offered any relief. However, the barbiturates left her drowsy, and some mornings she wouldn't have made it to the studio on time without the extra boost of a pep-pill. Taking a bennie, she thought now, was just like pushing her foot down on the accelerator of Guy's silver Jaguar.

'Go on, take her on one more spin around the lot,' Guy urged, from the passenger seat.

Lily was happy to obey. Taking a bend in the driveway a little too fast, Guy reached for the steering wheel to guide her back to safety. He kept his hand on hers a fraction longer than neces-sary as she headed into the final straight and drew to a halt in front of the white stucco mansion. She pretended not to notice his touch, just as, earlier in the day, she had played the ingénue when raising her mouth to his for their characters' first on-screen kiss. She had judged – she was pretty sure correctly – that Guy was more likely to be aroused by naivety than experience.

She'd discovered some time ago that arousing desire in a man – all the more so once he had acknowledged it in himself – tended to work in her favour. It had paid off with Peter. She'd beguiled him into a fairly passionate kiss when he'd said good-night after dropping her home on the night of the awards ceremony. Afterwards, he'd been too full of remorse ever to approach her again, so much so that she needed only to look at him in a certain way for him to fall into line with whatever she wanted. Guy Brody was no Peter Jenks. The first couple of times she'd become aware of Guy's gaze lingering on her hips or mouth, she'd caught his eye and waited for him to respond.

When he'd merely smiled and turned aside, as if refusing to yield so readily, she'd realized that her advantage lay in doing nothing.

'Photographer at three o'clock,' Guy warned, nodding across to the shallow entrance steps where a man garlanded with cameras, light meters and flash bulbs stood waiting. 'Let's give him his shot and get back to work.'

It still amused Lily how brazenly photographers would call out or beckon her closer while apparently avoiding eye contact as they peered down into their view-finders. She swung her legs out of the driver's seat and, as she stood up, saw and heard the now familiar sequence of adjustment, click, wind on and reset repeated in swift succession. After the man had exposed half a dozen frames or more, Guy waved a hand to block his face.

'OK, that's enough. Thanks a lot. Come on, Lily.'

He held out his hand for her to run around the car and join him. As they walked away, back to the sound stage for the final long sequence that was to be shot on set, he kept hold of her hand just long enough for her to hear two more rapid click-and-rewinds. Guy didn't appear to have registered them. She'd noticed that he was a tiny bit deaf. She thought it might be from an explosion in the war. She'd noticed many things about him over the past week or so. For one, he never mentioned his wife or children. For another, unexpected loud noises made him tremble. However hard he tried to hide it, he was still afraid of whatever terrifying events he'd witnessed as a soldier. And, perhaps because his current work was cast into relief by his past heroism, she suspected that, deep down, he believed acting was a shameful career for a man.

'I'm a circus animal,' he'd confessed once, in the darkness of the car taking them both back into town when, exhausted after a long day, he'd hitched a lift with her driver. 'It's all just a glorified trick.'

'That's not what you've been saying to me,' Lily had replied teasingly.

'No, that's because you're different.' He took a long sip from the silver flask he kept in his jacket pocket. 'And, besides, women like being looked at. That's your purpose in life, isn't it?'

Was it? Lily had wondered sleepily in the back of the car. It wasn't hers. Or maybe Guy meant that the role of every woman was to perform for men?

'What *is* the trick?' she'd asked.

'Oh . . .' He'd waved his hand airily. 'You know.'

If there was a trick, Lily had decided, there was more to it than angling your face to the key-light. Perhaps it was about having something to hide. She hid her hatred and Guy his fear. And Delia? Well, Lily had the power to decide when *her* secrets should be revealed.

As they walked back across the parkland to the sound stage, Lily could feel the sun on her back. They'd warned her how hot it would be in Rome but she still couldn't imagine it, and she disliked being at a disadvantage. She'd seen travel brochures and posters, and had watched Audrey Hepburn in *Roman Holiday*, but surely the ornate and crowded streets in the film had been partly contrived. It couldn't really be like that.

'Tell me about Rome,' she asked. 'What do I need to know?'

Guy turned to her with his slow sideways smile, the Gary Cooper smile, as Vivien had dubbed it. 'The Eternal City,' he said. 'Hollywood on the Tiber. Watch out for pickpockets and only drink bottled water.'

'You were there in the war?'

He shook his head. 'Never got that far. Invalided out before we got to Rome.' He paused. 'The production team's going to be based at Cinecittà, the film studios Mussolini built. Ironic, no?'

Highly attuned to what it took to *survive* the war, Lily had never before given much thought to those who'd fought it. Their struggle, it seemed to her, had been clean and equally matched, with clear rules of combat, a professional enmity that was over and done with once the fighting stopped. But now she tried to imagine what it must be like to walk the streets of a city you'd killed people to get to, and to rub shoulders with those who had in turn tried to kill you. Guy couldn't have been much older than she was now when he'd enlisted. She thought again about the trembling, and how hard he tried to disguise it.

'Do you mind going back to Italy?' she asked bluntly.

'I've been before. We shot that Tennessee Williams film there.'

'The movie you won the Academy Award for?'

'Yes.' He stopped at the cavernous entrance to the sound stage. From inside came the sound of a stagehand whistling 'Tell Me How It Ends'. Guy turned to place his hands lightly on Lily's shoulders, treating her to his best smile. 'The way you're going, I reckon we'll be in the running again with this film. What do you think? Best Picture? Shall we aim high? Are you up for being a winner?'

She saw in his eyes not admiration for her but his own hunger for the accolade, the validation. She returned his smile. Life was always easier once you were certain of what someone really wanted. Knowledge was power.

28

Lily stood beside Guy on the roof terrace of their hotel above the Spanish Steps. It was early morning but the sun was already high in a cloudless sky. She was wearing the first pair of sunglasses she had ever owned. Through them she could see St Peter's Basilica in the distance and, closer at hand, the bright white marble steps leading down to a square bordered by ochre-coloured buildings with green shutters. Sounds of traffic, car horns and church bells drifted up to them. Unfamiliar pink flowers bloomed in terracotta pots along a ledge that was only a few feet away across the shadowy chasm of the narrow street below. To her right were the dark umbrella pines of the Borghese Gardens. Yesterday's free day, granted for sightseeing, had taught her how grateful she would be for their shade later in the day.

She felt foolish that she had been so unprepared for Rome to be so overwhelmingly *foreign*. She could make no sense of the babble of voices or the mysterious exhortations on the stylish advertising posters. The hanging baskets bore the reddest, bluest and most yellow flowers she'd ever seen, and the rows of table-cloths along the pavement cafés were blindingly white. She barely dared raise her eyes to the churches, fountains, Roman columns and larger-than-life sculptures of bearded gods, avenging angels, smooth-breasted women and warriors on horseback. Even the pungent smells, good and bad, were unfamiliar.

She loved it. She loved it all. She imagined spreading her wings and soaring over this rooftop view with nothing to hold her down.

'Breakfast?' Guy asked.

They took their seats at a table with an uninterrupted view over the city. Recalling the delicious sugar-dusted rolls and sweet blood-red orange juice they had been served the day before, Lily realized she was hungry.

'Help yourself,' said Guy, as a waiter laid out a feast before them.

She watched enviously as Guy piled his plate high and, without a second thought, reached for butter, jam and fruit, then poured frothy warm milk into his coffee. She longed to allow herself such harmless greed without being crippled by shame and guilt. It had been so unexpectedly easy and pleasurable to take whatever she wanted from Delia – her purpose was to take away what Delia had – but, without that excuse, she found it enduringly impossible to eat more than the minimum she physically required.

She placed a single roll on her white and gold plate, pushed aside the tempting dishes of honey and apricot jam, and surreptitiously reached into her purse for one of her little triangular pills, quickly swallowing it with her orange juice. When she looked up she found Guy watching her.

'Got one to spare?' he asked.

She was caught. Unless he assumed it was merely an aspirin, in which case, did she have one of those in her purse to give him? She hesitated that bit too long, and he laughed.

'I know they're not lady pills,' he said, holding out a hand, palm up. 'Come on, I haven't had one of those in a while.'

He crooked his outstretched fingers in a gesture that left her little choice but to hand over one of her precious remaining stock. He tossed it into his mouth and washed it down with a mouthful of coffee.

'That'll get the day off to a good start,' he said.

She was surprised. His alcohol consumption had never appeared to her excessive, mainly because, she'd assumed, he was too preoccupied with how he displayed himself to his audience to risk losing self-control – and, to Guy Brody, every person he met was an audience. This new evidence of his willingness to abandon a measure of self-restraint shifted her view of him somewhat.

Not that Lily regarded her amphetamine use as lessening her own self-control: quite the opposite. An older boy at a youth club had introduced her to the various candy-coloured pills when she was sixteen, and she'd immediately welcomed how they smoothed over her emotions, cut out a lot of extraneous noise and left her better able to focus. Over the past two weeks it had been especially useful to discover how a single bennie was enough to reduce the world to just her and the camera lens.

'Don't look so shocked,' Guy teased her. 'You teenagers may be taking over the world, but don't imagine you've invented anything new.'

By the time the waiters began to take away their breakfast dishes, Guy was buzzing from the hit. He stood up, snatched the last pastry from the basket and bit into it.

'Let's play hooky,' he said, brushing the crumbs from the front of his shirt.

Lily looked at her watch. 'The car will be collecting us in ten minutes.'

'Never mind.' He took her arm. 'There's a place I'd like to show you.'

'James will be waiting.'

'Let him. We do enough hanging about for them. Let them sit around for us for a change.' Guy gave her the full smile before cramming the rest of the pastry into his mouth.

A barricade deep inside Lily cracked and threatened to give way. Her instinctive reaction was to clamp down on it instantly. 'We can't.'

'Why not? Give me one good reason.' Guy licked his lips, spearing a sugared flake at the corner of his mouth with the tip of his tongue. 'It's not as if they can start without us.'

The temptation to abandon her defences was overwhelming. Guy held out his hand to her and she took it.

'Where are we going?'

He raised a finger to his lips.

Outside the hotel Guy commandeered the car that was waiting to take them to the studios. Powerless to object, the driver touched his cap and pulled out into the traffic. Lily had no idea where they were going and, for the first time in her life, felt it might be possible to abandon herself gladly to that sensation. Guy didn't speak as they pressed on through narrow streets and then along a wide boulevard with shops and offices before diving back into smaller streets where at last the driver pulled over and stopped. Guy ordered him to wait and led Lily across a road, dodging a stream of skidding and weaving motor scooters and noisy little pastel-blue or bright-red cars, and on into the bustling heart of a market. Rows of stalls stretched in both directions, crammed with flowers, fruit and vegetables. People were pushing, pointing, and shouting in loud Italian. She'd been in street markets in England but had never before seen such Mediterranean colour and abundance.

'Don't get lost,' said Guy. 'Keep hold of my hand.'

Sometimes she followed, hanging onto him amid the crush; sometimes he directed her from behind, guiding her by the shoulders or waist, and stopping to point out a display of sunflowers with seed-heads larger than her face, or Bacchanalian heaps of green and black grapes, peaches and lemons, or the perfect classical profile of the young man pushing a barrow of melons and shouting at the crowd to make way. They emerged into the centre of a square where a huge stone bowl brimmed with clear water. She dipped her fingers, enjoying the sensation of cold and then, imitating a gesture she recalled from a film, flicked a few drops at Guy.

He seized her tightly by the wrist. There was no laughter in his eyes. 'Don't think you can play with me,' he said. 'Don't confuse acting with real life.'

She was shocked, although less at his reaction than at her own failure to see it coming.

'I'm not the besotted has-been who'll promote his woman's career at the expense of his own,' he continued, describing his role in the movie. 'I'm not making way for you. You're only here to draw a new audience and make me look good. Understood?'

Lily nodded.

'And I didn't bring you here to shower you with roses and watch your face light up with joy – although that's the little script you'll act for James's benefit half an hour from now. You're merely my pretty little excuse for turning up late.'

'When the real point is to remind him who's in charge?' She lifted her chin and gave him a straight look.

It was Guy's turn to be surprised. His reaction turned to laughter. 'You're quite a clever little bitch, aren't you?'

'Yes,' she said, keeping her gaze level. 'I've had to be.'

It was rare that she misjudged someone, but she'd been wrong about Guy preferring innocence to experience. She watched the coldness behind his eyes turn to desire as he pushed her back against the rim of the fountain. With one hand hard on her breast, he pressed himself against her and thrust his tongue into her mouth.

She was jubilant. It was the first authentically strong reaction she'd elicited from him. And it was precisely how she needed him to look at her on screen. Their audiences would love it.

29

'You're late,' James announced unnecessarily.

Guy nudged Lily forwards. She held up the huge bunch of pink-tipped lilies he had bought. By the time they'd arrived at Cinecittà, a few miles south-east of the city, the director and his entire crew had been waiting for over an hour.

'I'm so sorry,' she said. 'We made a detour to the flower market. Guy bought me these. Aren't they beautiful?'

Beside her, Guy shrugged helplessly, as if to suggest that no sane man could have had the heart to refuse her.

'Very pretty.' James, tight-lipped, was plainly furious, but had little choice but to give in gracefully. 'Perhaps next time you could confine your tourist trips to the return journey.'

Overpowered by the sickly scent of the blooms, Lily was glad to hand them to an assistant. As she and Guy went their separate ways to costume and make-up, she caught his eye, but he returned her ironic look with bland innocence.

She knew that James had every right to be annoyed. His time at Cinecittà was limited and they had a lot of work to get through. The studios were doubling as the production base for the sequence of scenes to be shot in the streets of Rome, and the scripted location for the scene she was now preparing to shoot.

At this point, late in the story, Guy's character has been offered a last chance to rescue his failing career by playing a supporting role in a big-budget spectacular being filmed at Cinecittà. He is by now married to Lily's character, whose successful singing career has eclipsed his movie stardom. She arrives by limousine at the iconic modernist entrance to the studios and catches her husband, hot and exhausted, in the mortifyingly short-skirted costume, sandals and helmet of an ancient Roman general.

With sophisticated make-up and dressed in a silk couture suit, Lily sat in the back of the stuffy limousine waiting for the driver to receive the signal to start moving. She could tell immediately from the way Guy tramped into view that he barely needed to act his resentment and humiliation. She was pleased: she'd hoped they'd be able to hook into the aggression of his bruising kiss in the Campo de' Fiori – exacerbated, she was sure, by the amphetamine he'd taken at breakfast – and was now certain they'd give James a high-octane performance that would make him forget their late arrival.

The car moved off, covering the few yards into shot. Lily opened her door and rushed to her mark. 'Surprise!'

Guy's outfit had deliberately been made half a size too big in order to accentuate its foolishness. He shot her a look far more venomous than the script warranted as he spoke his lines. 'Darling! What are you doing here? Aren't you supposed to be in London?'

'I was, but I had a free day and flew out to see you!'

'Check up on me, you mean?'

'No, no.' Lily's eyes had to give away her wifely concern that he might be drinking again. They would pick up her close-ups once the master-shot was in the can.

Guy's animosity was almost palpable, and when James called 'Cut' and then 'Print', Lily could see that the director was pleased.

She went up to Guy, touching him lightly on his bare arm. 'That was brilliant,' she told him. 'Thank you.'

So far as Lily was concerned, the rest of the day went equally well. A scene in which Guy's character is elbowed aside while people crowd around his wife to beg for her autograph propels him back to the bottle. His late-night drinking will lead him to be thrown into jail where he gets beaten up for insulting the guards. Lily's character will cancel her concert in London so she can stay in Rome to bail him out. The scene in which, after refusing her help, he stumbles away into the dark maze of Trastevere would be shot on location that night, with James using the decadence and decay of the crumbling, shadowy streets to mirror the nightmare of the washed-up movie star's alcoholic breakdown.

Lily would not be in those scenes – her character's own moments of despair would be shot separately the following night – so she was free to spend her evening as she wished. Except that she had no idea what to do with her free time. Everyone else would be working and she knew no one in Rome. As she was driven back to the hotel she remembered the young tourists she'd seen the previous evening sitting on the Spanish Steps in the cooling night air. Perhaps if she changed into her most inconspicuous clothes, she could go and sit among them, listen in to their conversations or maybe window-shop along the boutiques that lined the streets that led off the square below.

She bathed and changed, then went down to the hotel lobby. The doorman stepped smartly ahead of her to pull open the heavy door and she slipped out into the narrow street that led to the top of the Spanish Steps. Idly she noticed several men lounging by some scooters parked opposite the hotel entrance. She hadn't gone three paces before a shout went up and they came running towards her, raising their lightweight cameras and reeling off several frames before she knew what was happening.

'Ciao, signorina!'

'Guardami!'

'Ciao, bella! Sorridi, per favore!'

She didn't understand what they were saying, yet they kept shouting and gesticulating, barring her way forwards.

She retreated back into the safety of the lobby where the doorman closed the door firmly against the insistent paparazzi. She felt him looking at her disdainfully as if the ambush had been her fault. The lift was slow to arrive and she was grateful to regain the privacy of her suite.

Lily knew the studio press agents were keen to use the glamorous setting of La Dolce Vita for publicity stills, and an official photographer had discreetly followed them on the choreographed sightseeing tour that had filled their first day in the city, but she hadn't expected her presence to incite such unauthorized attention, or at any rate not so soon.

She could order room service if she was hungry, but she had hours to kill before she would feel like sleeping, and it would be late before Guy and James returned to the hotel. A selection of glossy magazines had been left artfully fanned across the coffee-table, but she'd already flicked through most of them. When she'd first seen her suite two days earlier the rooms had been the most luxurious she'd ever inhabited. Now they were four walls. It wasn't that she minded spending time alone, it was the frustration of being denied the chance to explore this tantalizing foreign city. Rome had already offered her a glimpse of freedom, and she didn't want it taken away before she could make sense of what it might mean.

Deciding she would be safe from unwanted attention within the confines of the hotel, she discarded her slacks and cotton shirt in favour of a cocktail dress suitable for the roof terrace bar and restaurant. About to open her door, she hesitated, then returned to the bathroom where she swallowed a pill.

Seated alone at a table where she could turn her back on the rest of the diners, Lily ordered first one and then a second glass of wine, exacerbating the effects of the barbiturate she'd taken. The following couple of hours passed easily as she stared drowsily out across the twinkling cityscape to the balmy darkness of the distant hills beyond the Tiber, not really thinking about anything.

Eventually she made her way somewhat unsteadily into the lift and along the corridor back to her suite. Managing to find her key and open the door, she kicked off her shoes and curled up on the enormous double bed.

She had no idea how long she'd been asleep when she was awoken by hands on her shoulders and a soft voice in her ear.

'You left your door unlocked. You shouldn't do that.'

It was Guy. He seemed to be putting her to bed.

'Roll over.' His breath was warm and smelt faintly of garlic and brandy.

She tried to do as he asked, but her limbs felt too heavy to obey her brain. She felt his weight on the mattress as he knelt behind her and heard rather than felt him unzip her dress.

'That's it,' he said, as he awkwardly pulled her arms free of the fabric. 'Lift yourself up a bit.'

He dragged the dress down over her legs, taking her pants with it. She wasn't wearing any other underwear. She expected him to tuck the bedclothes around her but he just shuffled backwards off the bed. She waited to hear the door close behind him. When the sound didn't come, she let herself begin to drift back into sleep. But then he returned, kneeling on the bed beside her once more. This time she could feel the naked skin of his thighs. Did he mean to sleep here beside her?

'You're not a virgin, are you?' he asked, using his knees to push her legs apart.

Sleepily she shook her head. She'd dealt with that when she was fifteen. She'd done it several times since, when it had seemed expedient. Fumbling youths with hot hands inside her underwear, no big deal.

'Good.'

But he didn't want her to sleep. He shook her shoulders until she opened her eyes. There were no lights on but moonlight streamed in between the open curtains.

'What are you doing?' she asked, suddenly alarmed.

'Having you,' he said. 'Come on, wake up. I don't want to screw a corpse.' He slapped her cheek hard enough for it to sting.

Did she want this? She'd assumed she'd go to bed with Guy sooner or later, but like this?

'Open your mouth,' he said, rearing up over her. She had no idea what he was doing or what he wanted her to do until she was nearly choking. 'Come on,' he repeated. 'You're in Rome, lick up your *gelato* like a good little girl.'

30

There was no point in crying, Lily told the bathroom mirror in the morning. She'd been shocked and disgusted at the way Guy had used her, but no one would listen if she cried. It wasn't important. She had nothing to cry about. No one had been starved or beaten or killed, so it didn't matter what had happened to her. Nothing had happened. That was what her mother would have said.

Guy had returned to his own suite to wash and dress, so Lily decided to go ahead and have a rooftop breakfast as if nothing had changed. She popped a bennie, brushed her hair extra hard and took the lift to the terrace. Their table was ready for them, and she chose the seat Guy usually took, facing the entrance where she would be able to see him coming. He appeared soon afterwards, as the waiter was pouring her coffee. He gave her a warm smile and came around the table to kiss her cheek.

'I hope you slept well,' he said, placing his hand lightly on her shoulder. 'I enjoyed last night.'

He seemed sincere, but then he was one of the world's most highly paid actors. She stared at him in confusion as he sat down and shook out his snowy linen napkin.

'I'm starving,' he said. 'Aren't you?' As he reached for the basket of sugar-dusted rolls he made a little tut-tut shake of his head and grinned at her with a raised eyebrow. 'All your fault. You're a bad girl for giving me that little pill yesterday.'

Lily watched him busy himself with butter and jam. He seemed entirely natural and relaxed. After a moment he raised his head from his plate, caught her looking at him and smiled.

'I'd like nothing more than to take you somewhere special for dinner tonight, but of course you'll be working.'

She blinked rapidly. Had she misunderstood? He spoke as if he'd made love to her. Perhaps she was simply naive about how experienced adults behaved in bed. After all, last night's encounter had not been with an adolescent behind the youth club but with a mature and worldly Hollywood star.

She forced herself to eat one of the rolls. She tried desperately to recapture the exhilaration of the previous morning, but it wouldn't come. Her senses felt dead. When she shifted in her chair the soreness between her legs brought back unwelcome images that took away her appetite entirely.

'Now don't mope.' There was a harsh note in Guy's voice. 'You have to eat. We've a picture to make, remember, and I want the best out of you.'

She washed down each bite of bread with a mouthful of coffee until her plate was empty.

'That's better,' he said.

A thought came unbidden to Lily's mind: *I wish Delia were here. She'd know how to handle him.* She dismissed it angrily. It was Delia's fault that she was here at all. Everything was Delia's fault and always had been. It was invigorating to be reminded of her purpose.

Lily sat up straight, reached for a second roll and managed to eat it without reluctance.

'What will you do today, while I'm working?' she asked Guy.

He acknowledged her recovery with a nod of approval. 'I shall see friends,' he said. 'There's a cocktail party. You've got the scene on the bridge this evening?'

'Yes.'

After Guy's character has rejected his wife's attempt to help him, she takes refuge in a nightclub where, by unlikely coincidence, she finds the blues trio she used to sing with in London. Her three former friends, who had supported her when she was poor and undiscovered, insist on walking her safely home across the river from Trastevere. Lily savoured the irony of the film fantasy. In real life, she had no friends to walk her anywhere.

'Location night shoots are always tricky,' Guy said. 'I'll look in on you when you get back and you can tell me how it went.'

Lily looked at her watch. 'I'd better go.' She pushed back her chair and walked away.

'Hey, Lily?'

She turned to see what he wanted.

He gave his slow smile. 'I just wanted to take another look at you.'

He delivered the line without a hint of self-consciousness, as if he'd forgotten that she'd recognize it from one of the first scenes they'd acted together.

She smiled back, her expression as full of hope and joy as when she'd performed the exchange on the sound stage at Pinewood.

The drive out to Cinecittà gave her time to calm down. Guy was a distraction. Nothing. Or, rather, he was right, and all that mattered was that they made a great, award-winning picture together. That was why they were here, and that was what she wanted, too. There was nothing to cry about. Crying only made everything worse.

Yet she still couldn't manage to recapture the intoxicating sense of freedom she'd felt the day before. That thrilling breach in her usually well-guarded defences had already been walled up again. And the effect of the pill she'd taken before breakfast was beginning to wear off. She didn't have many left so, even though they didn't seem to last as long as they used to, she'd have to wait until the evening before taking another. She'd need one to prepare for the important scene they were to shoot later.

She and the crew arrived at the location as darkness fell. The air above the Tiber was slightly foetid, a sweet smell that was not entirely unpleasant. Bats flitted across the water and wheeled up over the trees that lined one bank. They were not filming on the bridge that in reality led directly from Trastevere, but on the more picturesque Ponte Sant'Angelo, where James wanted the combination of old-fashioned street-lamps and Bernini's winged angels, high on their stone plinths, to create eerie shadows to accentuate the vulnerability of Lily's character. In the scene, as her old musician friends escort Lily's character home across the river, after her drunken husband has stumbled off into the darkness, she was to break into an impromptu reprise of 'Kiss Me Tomorrow', transforming the hopeful number she had sung for him when they first met into a ballad of desperation and regret.

The song was already recorded and, after talking to James, Lily was excited about how they would film it. She was to remain still and inward-looking, leaving the lighting and camera angles to create the drama as James focused close in on her face. Now that she understood how to do less and less in front of the camera, she knew just how powerfully such stillness would translate onto a cinema screen.

Small crowds were gathering at each end of the bridge, held back by a couple of equally curious *poliziotti*. As she'd left the hotel that morning she'd been snapped again by the paparazzi, who had followed her car on their scooters, weaving dangerously in and out of the oncoming traffic and laughing as they drew level and snapped random pictures through her window.

As Lily waited for James to finish his consultation with the cinematographer she looked over at the actors playing the trio of musicians. They seemed to regard their one-day shoot in Rome as more holiday than work and were leaning over the stone balustrade in the middle of the bridge, flicking coins into the river in competition to see who could get his coin to fly the furthest before hitting the water below. One of them, a puckish young man in tight trousers, kept glancing at James and smiling hopefully whenever he caught the director's attention. He seemed smitten by the older man's charisma, and she hoped he'd have the good sense to know that he'd be joining a long line of James's extras.

The young actors were only a few years older than her, and they'd already shot several earlier scenes together in London, yet it hadn't occurred to them to invite her to join their game. She was the star. She didn't belong with them. Later, after they'd wrapped for the night, they'd be free to go off and explore, to go drinking and dancing with the rest of the crew, to have an adventure before catching a plane back to London the next day.

It would be fun to go along with them, but they wouldn't want her. The attention she'd gather would only cramp their style. They were pleasant, courteous young men, probably tactful enough to wait and slip away when she wasn't noticing, but it would still feel like a rejection. She was on her own, trapped and isolated, just as she had always been.

She could hardly wait for the clack of the clapperboard, for the quiet moment when everyone around her ceased to exist and she could begin, in miming the song, to confide her character's conflicting feelings of tenderness and determination to the starry sky, watched by the all-seeing lens of the film camera.

31

Guy, casually dressed in loose linen trousers and a white shirt, was waiting in Lily's suite when, exhausted, she got back to the hotel late that night.

'The chambermaid opened the door in return for an autograph,' he said, with a grin.

She hid her dismay. Would she be able to leave instructions not to let Guy into her room again, or would that provoke unwelcome gossip?

'I'm so tired,' she said, flinging her bag onto the nearest chair. 'The moon kept going behind clouds and out again, upsetting the lighting. We had to do take after take.'

'So much for James's vaunted realism,' he said. 'Go have a bath and I'll bring you a drink.'

'Please, Guy, I really just want to sleep.'

'Sure, sure. I know exactly how you feel. I'll give you a little massage after your bath and you'll sleep like a baby.'

Lily bowed to the inevitable, afraid that, if she tried to push him out, it would end up the worse for her. She went to run the bath, grateful at least that he didn't object when she shut the door behind her. Inside, her fingers hovered over the lock but she decided against it. She wondered if taking a sleeping pill might help, but regretfully decided against that, too.

The hotel provided an array of little flasks of sweet-smelling toiletries that had delighted her on her arrival. She shook some of the scented salts into the water and watched them dissolve. As the steam rose she looked at herself in the full-length mirror. Her face was pale, her eyes huge, and traces of her film make-up remained along her jawline where she'd been in too much of a hurry to wipe it off properly. As she began to unbutton her shirt, the mist of steam on the glass thickened and slowly obscured her image. She smiled, rather liking the idea of becoming so insubstantial that, for tonight at least, she could vanish entirely.

She dropped her clothes onto the floor and stepped into the bath. She might as well get it all over with. She lay back in the hot water, trying not to notice the faint bruises on her inner thighs, then shut her eyes and tried to relax her body. She heard a tap on the door and Guy entered, carrying two glasses of champagne.

'Might as well enjoy ourselves,' he said.

He placed her glass beside the taps and went to sit on a stool against the opposite wall, out of touching distance. For ten minutes he chatted about her day, asking how she thought her scenes had gone, giving his opinion of the rushes of his own work from the night before, as if the naked intimacy of the bathroom was unexceptional. At last he held up a big fluffy white towel and gestured for her to step into it. Taking his glass, he left her to dry herself. Lily brushed her hair and her teeth and was finally left with no choice but to wrap herself tightly in a dry towel and walk out into the bedroom.

'Here.' Guy patted the mattress beside him.

Lily couldn't control her ragged intake of breath, but then saw that he meant to draw her attention to a small gift-wrapped package lying on the coverlet.

'I went shopping today. Bought you a present.'

Confused, she picked it up and untied the silken bow. Beneath the paper was a case stamped *BVLGARI*. Opening it, she found a delicately coiled snake, its skin a pattern of turquoise stones set in gold, with two small diamonds for its eyes.

'It's not exactly original,' he said. 'Elizabeth Taylor made them all the rage last year. But I thought it would suit you.'

A *snake*? She felt as if she'd been slapped. Yet he was looking at her as if he expected her to be pleased and was evidently awaiting her thanks. She lifted the necklace out of the box and, feeling it drape itself around her fingers as if it were made of silk rather than metal, she saw how beautifully it had been made. She looked into his face again and could detect no hint of irony.

'Thank you,' she said. 'It's amazing.'

'Let me see it on you.' He took it from her and, rising to stand behind her, curled it around her neck. 'Turn around,' he ordered.

She did so.

He nodded approvingly. 'Perfect. Now come to bed.'

It was not what she wanted or would have chosen but, as he moved on top of her – less aggressively than he had the night before – she reminded herself of how kind he had been to her in other ways, that Guy Brody had a million adoring fans who would swoon at the very thought of being kissed by him, and that, with a few weeks still to go before the film was finished, it would be pointless to make trouble for herself. And, above all, if this was the only price she had to pay, then there were far, far worse things that human beings had had to endure.

Lily was woken some hours later by the sound of Guy screaming. For a moment, as she struggled up out of a deep sleep, she thought she must be back in her childhood bed, with its iron frame and thin mattress. The muffled screams were just as she remembered them from her childhood: thin and strangled, too full of fear to draw enough breath, filled with the terror that this breath would be the last. She knew exactly what to do.

She sat up and shook him gently but firmly, rocking his shoulders against the soft mattress. 'Wake up,' she instructed him. 'You're having a nightmare. Wake up.'

She teased the edge of the sheet into a point and used it to tickle his face. Sure enough, as he thrashed about, he also tried to bat away the feather-like touch. The tiny physical irritation caused him finally to open his eyes.

'That's it,' she said. 'You're awake now. Come on, wake up. You were having a nightmare.'

'Oh, God,' he said, curling into a ball beside her.

She slid out of bed, found her dressing-gown, and put on all the lights. As soon as she'd been old enough to lift the heavy kettle and light the gas, she used always to fetch her mother a warm drink, but now a glass of water would have to do.

'Sit up,' she commanded. 'Drink a little of this.'

He groaned but did not move.

'Guy!'

To her surprise he laughed and shook his head, muttering something into the pillow.

'What did you say? I can't hear.'

'Not Guy Brody.'

He turned his head but she wasn't sure whether he was actually looking at her or whether he was still in some dream world of his own.

'Nathan Kubelsky,' he said. 'Lieutenant, United States Army.'

Lily frowned. Was this the name of a character he'd played in a film she hadn't seen? He saw her perplexity and laughed again.

'That's my real name,' he said. 'Ohio, born and bred. Guy Brody's the invention. He was never in the war.'

'Drink some water,' she urged.

He sat up enough to take hold of the glass and swallow a few mouthfuls before handing it back. 'What did I say?' he asked, clearly more awake now. 'Nothing you can sell to the scandal sheets, I hope.'

Although he spoke flippantly, he hung his head away from her. Lily thought he looked ashamed. She recognized that, too.

'You were screaming, that's all.'

'That's all?'

'I've heard worse.'

'You? How? Where? You're not old enough.'

'My mother,' she said. 'You should go back to sleep now, before you start thinking too much about it.'

'You're not repulsed by the supposed war hero screaming in fright like a child?'

He studied her face as if trying to read her true feelings. She thought perhaps it was her first glimpse of a man who might be real, not acting even to himself.

'No,' she said. 'Go back to sleep.'

Guy lifted Lily's hand to his lips and kissed it. 'Thank you, my darling.'

In that moment she believed he might even mean it.

32

FRANK

I leaned back on my elbows on the tartan rug and stretched out my legs. I'd already taken off my jacket and rolled up my shirt-sleeves. Delia and I were picnicking on a grassy slope below the terrace of Kenwood House, surrounded by magnificent English parkland trees. Below us was a little lake, choked with water-lilies, some already in flower, and above a few wispy clouds drifted across the August sky. I couldn't believe my luck. Me, Frank Landry, here alone with Delia Maxwell for an entire after-noon! I had enjoyed one or two lazy days like this with Evelyn, although the necessary secrecy of our affair usually made such outings impossible. Now I could feel only dimly the pain and misery of those last months in Malaya after she'd ended our affair. Loving Delia made me believe I must be the happiest man alive.

'Are you sure I can't get you an ice-cream?' I asked.

She smiled. 'I couldn't eat another thing.'

Delia's appetite had been modest and we'd barely reached the bottom of the Fortnum & Mason hamper I'd bought. I looked at her again. She sat upright, her bent legs tucked sideways under the wide skirt of her patterned cotton sundress. The fluffy white cardigan she had thrown over her shoulders added to the halo effect of her white-blonde hair. I wished she'd take off her sun-glasses so I could see her beautiful eyes.

'Happy?' I asked. I couldn't stop myself.

'It's so peaceful,' she said. 'An inspired suggestion, coming here.'

She tilted her face up to the sunshine. Surely she must sense how much I wanted to kiss her. As I turned to lean closer, I caught sight of two teenage girls approaching over the grass, both holding pens and bits of paper. They saw I'd spotted them, stopped and began giggling and nudging one another, trying to summon the courage to advance the rest of the way. They seemed magnetized by the sight of Delia. I couldn't blame them.

'I think we have company,' I said quietly. 'A couple of auto-graph hunters.'

She sighed and looked over her shoulder. Removing her sun-glasses, she beckoned to the girls, who immediately came forward. It was foolish, but I couldn't help sitting up straighter, proud to be her chosen companion.

'Oh, Miss Maxwell,' exclaimed one. 'Please can we have your autograph?'

She held out out her hand for the pen and paper. 'Is it for you? What's your name?'

'Can you write it to Carol?' said the girl. 'That's my auntie.'

Delia's smile didn't alter. 'Of course.'

'She adores your music. She chose one of your songs for the first dance at her wedding. I was a bridesmaid,' the girl added, with a hint of pride.

'Well, I'm very honoured to have been part of such an import-ant and happy occasion,' said Delia. 'What colour was your dress?'

'Blue. There were four of us and we all wore the same.'

'I'm sure you looked very pretty.' She added a flourish to her signature and held out her hand to the other teenager. 'And what about you?'

'It's for my mum,' said the girl. 'Her name's Peggy. She'll be so cross she wasn't here. Just wait till we tell her!'

'There you are,' said Delia. 'I hope you enjoy the rest of the day.'

The first girl piped up again. 'Lily Brooks isn't here with you, is she?'

'I'm afraid not, no.'

'But you're her mum, aren't you? Tell her we think she's fab!'

'Oh, yes!' agreed her friend. 'We love "Tell Me How It Ends"! We know all the words.'

'I will, of course. Bye-bye.'

The girls left, although we could hear their high voices chattering excitedly all the way back up to the terrace. Delia sat still, her hands in her lap, looking towards the lake, although I couldn't help noticing that she was breathing more rapidly than before. I couldn't bear to see her upset by such thoughtlessness.

'You don't have to put up with this,' I said. 'You could put an end to her career in a single moment!'

She laid a warning hand on my arm. 'Frank, you promised.'

'I know I did, but—'

'No,' she said. 'No buts. Besides, if those girls weren't crazy about Lily, it would only be someone else younger than me. And I meant what I said to that girl: it *is* an honour to touch the lives of strangers. Her mother will always remember dancing to my song at her wedding.'

I was sensible enough to recognize my spurt of anger as jealousy that Delia should care so openly for the feelings of strangers when I still had no real idea what, if anything, she felt for me. The girls' intrusion had broken the dreamy solitude of our picnic and I didn't know how to recapture it.

'Where is Lily?' I asked. 'Is she still in Rome?' I was pretty sure she was, and that, if she'd been back in London, Delia might not have agreed to spend the day with me.

'She's due home tomorrow, I think.'

Her uncertainty suggested that Lily hadn't been in touch to let her know. My anger flared again: Lily had chosen to create the fiction of herself as Delia's daughter, yet couldn't be bothered to fulfil the basic requirements of the role.

'I don't suppose you managed to see her passport before she left?' I asked.

Delia's eyes flashed as she turned to me. 'No, I did not. And I don't want you to talk like this, Frank!'

'But someone will see it, sooner or later,' I urged. 'Unless she's forged new documents, the truth will eventually come out. And then what?'

She ignored me, busy tidying away the remains of our picnic and packing the basket.

'If you're going to go on pretending ignorance of the truth, then I need to know what you expect me to do,' I said. It was unkind, but I had somehow to pierce this dangerous make-believe.

She stopped what she was doing and, still holding the cast-off sandwich paper she'd been folding, dropped her head. I felt like a bully.

'No one really knows anyone else, do they?' she asked at last. 'We don't know why Lily is doing this. But she has no mother, and I have no daughter. Why can't you let it go at that?'

'Simply because you're both famous,' I said. 'Your fans want to know everything about you. It won't stay secret.'

She looked up and smiled sadly. 'There are worse secrets than this.'

I saw the pain in her expression and immediately the image of Conrad Durand, half hidden behind the smoke of his cigarette, jumped into my head. What had he done to her? Why had Delia's father trusted such a man? Why had the birth certificate of Delia's daughter, the little girl who died of polio, recorded *Father unknown*?

'Please let me tell Peter,' I begged. 'Give him the chance to be prepared for any story that might break. It's his job to protect you. Both of you,' I added reluctantly.

'It's not fair to compromise him.'

'But it is fair to ask me to lie to my oldest friend?'

'I didn't ask you to go digging into my private affairs!'

'I did it to protect you. Don't you see that I'm in love with you?'

She softened immediately. 'Oh, Frank.'

Trying to blot out her look of concern I moved to take her in my arms. She let me kiss her but I could feel no answering desire. I retreated enough to take possession of her hands, deciding to risk all by voicing a hope I knew was probably no better than a pipe dream.

'It's not too late to marry and have another child of your own. You don't have to go along with this charade.'

She snatched her hands free, but then relented and touched my cheek with her fingers. 'You can't save my life like you did Peter's, you know. It's not that easy.'

'But you'll let me try?'

'I sing about love,' she said. 'It's my job to make people yearn and dream and cry. Outside work, I'm not sure I really know what that means.'

'You seem to love Lily,' I protested.

She looked surprised. 'It seems I do, yes.'

'So you could love me?'

As she studied my face, I studied hers in return. For all her fame, she retained an aura of innocence, convincing me that much of her reticence stemmed from inexperience, from ignorance of how incendiary a lover's touch could be. I ached to kiss her again, to show her what two people making love could become.

'Don't pin your hopes on me, Frank,' she said.

All I saw was a halo of blonde hair, her lips, her breasts, her perfect skin. I didn't care what happened to my hopes: she hadn't said she didn't love me. All I heard was her telling me there was a chance that one day she would.

33

In the car returning from Kenwood Delia told me that Gowns by Celeste would soon close and that she and Celeste had arranged to meet the following day to tie everything up. Although Celeste planned to reopen under another name with a shop near Sloane Square and seemed to be looking forward to the change, I could tell Delia felt bad about effectively evicting her old friend, especially as Celeste had given way gracefully in the continuing belief that Delia was, quite properly, putting her daughter first. Although Delia seemed to have shelved the idea of buying a country house, I suspected she felt trapped in the web from which she refused to free herself, unable to change her mind about surrendering Celeste's expiring lease without offering an explanation that might reveal too much.

Hearing the doubt and regret in her voice, and wanting to offer moral support, I suggested that I pick her up in the morning and drive her over to Curzon Street, brushing aside her protests that she could easily walk the relatively short distance and I must have better things to do with my time.

The day dawned as sunny as the one before and, when Delia came down to greet me, she suggested leaving my car and walking there together. Even though she wore a headscarf and sunglasses, I saw heads turn and people staring at her as we crossed Hyde Park Corner. She, however, seemed to exist inside her own unselfconscious bubble, and I reflected how, over the years, the need to create such a protective shell must have intensified her natural reticence.

'Do you want to come in and say hello?' she asked, when we reached Celeste's door. 'We're going to be looking at designs, so don't feel you have to stay if you find it too dull!'

The salon already had an air of desertion. Celeste seemed a little put out that I should see it like that, but quickly rallied and explained with eager enthusiasm that the designs Delia chose today to redefine her 'look' would also help Celeste to launch her new Chelsea boutique.

'I thought we could start by looking through this sheaf of photos I've put together for you,' said Celeste, sitting beside Delia on one of the lavender-velvet sofas and pointing to a pile of pages torn neatly from magazines laid out on a footstool beside a number of her own sketches.

I took a seat against the opposite wall where I could watch them as they began to work their way through the cuttings, exclaiming, laughing and occasionally handing a sheet across to me for my opinion.

'I'm not wearing a hemline that short!'

'No, but the fabric is pretty, don't you think?'

'I wouldn't mind that one in a lighter shade.'

'I thought these sleeves would look good on you.'

'I'll never make that flat-chested look work.'

'No, but it's the silhouette that really matters. I'm afraid waists are right out.'

'What about my hair? Maybe I should cut it short.'

'You'll certainly have to re-vamp your make-up.'

'Frank, what do you think? Would I suit short hair like this?'

'You look wonderful just the way you are. You don't need to follow fashion for the sake of it.'

'It's more than fashion,' said Celeste, pretending outrage. 'And you're assuming that "Delia Maxwell" came into existence all by herself.' She turned to Delia. 'Do you remember those fittings when Conrad kept insisting on bigger, wider, tighter, more sparkly and even more sparkly?'

Delia smiled fondly. 'Celeste's early dresses really helped to make me famous,' she explained. 'There was still some rationing, so such luxury and extravagance cheered people up and encouraged them to believe that better times were just around the corner.'

'And then they associated that optimism with Delia, and loved her for it.'

Delia nodded. 'It was never just fashion. Conrad always understood that, too.'

Talking about their early days together seemed to soften the two women and draw them closer.

'So what would Conrad advise now?' Hearing the sour note in my voice, I immediately regretted having spoken. I knew my jealousy was idiotic, but that was what my feelings for Delia had reduced me to.

Celeste shot me a sympathetic look. 'It wasn't only Delia he created, you know,' she said. 'He chose the name Celeste, too. Marjorie Burns from Balham was never going to cut the mustard.'

'And now we both have to reinvent ourselves again,' Delia said lightly. 'It's a shame he's not here. He'd have had such fun.'

She picked up one of Celeste's drawings and handed it to me. The minimally sketched figure was clearly Delia, even though her familiar curves were hidden by a straight fall of fabric from a single seam beneath the bust and her nimbus of blonde hair was reshaped into angular lines.

'Appearing on television is quite different now that they can zoom in close,' she said. 'They used to film me singing with a single fixed camera as if I were on a stage. Audiences focused on the dresses and the set far more than on my face. But now they often feature these new pop stars performing in the middle of a crowd, so the whole thing is just as much about the young people around them and what they're wearing and how they respond. I still have to be me, but I also have to look as if I belong in that world.'

Celeste riffled through the torn-out magazine pages. 'Here,' she said, finding what she wanted. 'What about these shoes with that outfit?'

The two women returned to their detailed discussion, their heads almost touching as they sat together on the gilt and velvet sofa sifting through the images, selecting and rejecting – what? Who was the Delia Maxwell whom Marjorie Burns and Irma Székely sought to reinvent? It hadn't been difficult to trace Delia's original name, the name Conrad had taken away from her along with her child, her language, even her hair colour. Who was she, really? Was he the only man ever to have known her? Would she ever reveal her true self to me?

She looked up and gave me a radiant smile. 'Poor Frank. You must be bored to tears! We'll be a while yet, so why don't you leave us to it?'

I accepted my dismissal with good grace and set off back to

where I'd left my car. It was good to stretch my legs and I kept walking west through Hyde Park until, before I knew it, I'd reached the Knightsbridge barracks. So much of this area of London was changing as the developers finished what the Luft-waffe had started, and I'd heard there were plans to demolish these old buildings, too. Nothing stayed the same, so why should Delia?

I remembered how I'd felt, sitting for four months in a Ger-man prisoner-of-war camp, wondering if my life would ever start again and, if so, what I would do with it. I certainly hadn't intended to go back my childhood home in Bromley as if noth-ing had changed. But maybe, after feeling such a misfit at Oxford, I'd run too far in the opposite direction. Looking back, I saw now that, in Malaya, I'd rather lost my way. Perhaps now I could find the right track again. Not reinvent myself, but grow into the man I'd meant to become.

I left the park at Rutland Gate and doubled back along Knightsbridge, heading towards Delia's mews. Passing Harrods, on a whim I went in. As I strolled between counters of skin creams, nail polish and perfume, a familiar bottle caught my attention and I stopped. Guerlain's L'Heure Bleue. I picked up the flat-fronted flask and removed the heart-shaped stopper. Along with the fragrance of lemon and violet came a wash of shame at the memory of opening Delia's cupboards and sitting at her dressing-table.

'Frank!'

Guiltily I spun around, almost dropping the bottle. It took several seconds for my brain to catch up with my eyes.

'Evelyn!'

I saw her gaze fall on the perfume bottle in my hand and,

embarrassed, I turned to replace it, barely aware of the sales-woman who took it from me. I wasn't sure how to greet my former lover. A handshake seemed insultingly formal, but would it be right to kiss her? She took the decision for me, step-ping close and, with her hands light on my arms, raised herself on her toes to touch her cheek fleetingly to mine. As she moved away I thought I detected a few grey hairs among the brown.

'You're back in England?' I asked.

'Only for a few weeks,' she said. 'Staying with my parents and . . .' She hesitated, then lifted her chin and spoke more firmly. 'I've been looking at prep schools. My son Simon will be seven this year.'

'I heard you had a child.' I could feel my heart knocking against my ribs. 'That's his name, Simon?'

She nodded, her serious grey eyes fixed on mine. 'An only child. He's with his grandparents today. We go home next week. Of course, it's all so much quicker and easier now one can fly.'

She was thinner and two worry lines had appeared on her forehead, but she retained the translucent skin, long lashes and delicate features that I remembered. That I had adored.

'You look well,' she continued. 'Are you settled here now? The last I heard, you were in Ceylon.'

'I rattled around all over the place, but I think I'm finally ready to stay in one place.'

She glanced behind me at the perfume counter. I felt myself colour.

'Are you married?' she asked. 'Do you have a family?'

'No. I never . . .' I didn't know what to say. 'What about you? Are you well? Are you happy?'

Her expression changed entirely, although whether to anger

or misery I couldn't tell. She shot me an imploring look, turned on her heel and walked away. I ran after her, pushing my way through the shoppers.

'Evelyn, wait!' I caught up with her and grabbed her arm. 'Why didn't you tell me? How could you just leave me like that when you must have known?'

While she searched my face, I agonized, transported back to that hotel room in Kuala Lumpur: the need to know *why*, to understand in what way I had failed, was suddenly as urgent as it had been then.

'You could have told me,' I pleaded. 'I would have done anything you wanted.'

'Oh, Frank,' she said, freeing herself from my grasp. 'You were such a mess you could hardly look after yourself, let alone me or a child.'

'I would never have let you down.'

'I know you would never have meant to. I do know that, if it's any comfort.'

'Then why?'

'You still don't understand?'

It was wrong to ask but I couldn't stop myself. 'Is he mine?'

There was pity in her eyes. 'Not here, Frank. Not like this.'

'I have to know. I have a right to know.'

She took a deep breath and, making up her mind, looked at her watch and told me she'd meet me at the Victoria and Albert Museum in half an hour.

I stood and watched her walk away. She was dressed in a summer coat the colour of forget-me-nots and held a brown crocodile handbag over one arm. Her court shoes weren't high, and her stockings had old-fashioned seams. She'd always been slight but her figure was no longer girlish and, perhaps deliberately, she no longer walked with the sashaying sway of her hips that used to drive me wild. Was she the mother of my son or merely a woman I'd known and loved in another country a long time ago?

It was only a ten-minute walk to the museum and I didn't know what to do with the remaining time. If I'd been a religious man I'd have sat in a pew in the Brompton Oratory and collected my thoughts, but my C of E family had never gone in for serious devotion. Reaching the front steps of the V&A, I was tempted to abandon the mission entirely. What was to be gained? I was in love with Delia. I already had sufficient complications in my life. Only the thought of the boy, Simon, propelled me through the door of the imposing entrance.

As a kid I used to love being taken to the Science Museum or the Natural History Museum, but I had no memory of ever visiting the V&A. It was quiet and everything looked dim and brown. What light there was came through grimy windows. Elderly warders in brass-buttoned uniforms dozed in the corners of the lofty courts. I wandered into the nearest chamber, full of dusty altar-pieces, Roman gods and Greek friezes, with a huge, decorated column rising in the centre. When I looked more closely, I saw that they were all plaster casts, not even the real thing. To eke out the next fifteen minutes, I made a slow circuit of the ground floor, staring randomly at all manner of exotic objects, mostly hidden behind yellowing glass like tigers in a zoo. When I returned to the entrance hall I found Evelyn already waiting.

'Let's go upstairs,' she said. 'There's never anyone there.'

She led me back to the plaster casts, then through a smaller room that seemed to have nothing but huge metal keys.

'I used to love coming here when I first came to London to

work,' she said, as we climbed some stairs. 'Some of these exhibits were the nearest I'd ever come to "abroad".'

I knew it was during her six months working as a secretary that she'd met her husband. She'd also told me that she'd only known him four months before agreeing to marry and accompany him to Malaya.

We emerged into a long, low gallery with windows along one side, looking into a deserted courtyard. Down the middle ran display cases of ornately decorated glass objects, engraved or enamelled, clear or in jewel-like colours.

'Is he mine?' I asked again. This seemed at that moment to be the only thing left to salvage from our shared past.

'Simon is my son,' she said calmly.

'And your husband?'

'Ian never knew I was unfaithful.'

I found that hard to believe, especially when the military authorities had kept a pretty close eye on me, but then Ian wasn't the sort of man who, if he *had* suspected he'd been cuckolded, would have done nothing about it. Which was why we had always been so extremely cautious. I closed my eyes against the bloody memories of the Malayan jungle that came flooding back, and stretched out a hand to steady myself against a corner of the nearest glass case.

'You're still having them?'

I heard her voice through the swirl. 'Having what?'

'The nightmares. Those horrible sudden changes in your mood.'

'No, no, of course not.'

'Have you forgotten what you were like, Frank? After whatever happened to you, or whatever you did out there, the things you'd never speak about?'

'I wasn't allowed to talk about it. And, anyway, I was fine.'

'You weren't. I tried to help, but you'd never let me in, never tell me what happened.'

'There was no need. I had it under control. I would never have let you down.'

'But you were impossible to be with,' she said. 'And sometimes you scared me.'

As if lemon juice had been poured on invisible ink, the words she'd said in that hotel room, the reasons she'd given for leaving, began to form in my mind. It was as if I'd never heard them before. I hadn't wanted to hear them then and I still didn't now. She came close and I backed up against the glass case.

'I understand a lot more now,' she said. 'They call it battle fatigue, don't they?'

I thought of Mary Jenks praising Guy Brody for speaking out. I'd reckoned his psychological scars couldn't go very deep if he was able to talk about them so easily.

'I also know more now about the kind of work you were involved in,' she went on. 'It must have been ghastly. In a way I was glad you reacted as you did. It showed you didn't take it lightly, that maybe you didn't even think it was right. After Independence the truth started to come out, about the killing of civilians, the burning of villages, the bombing. If that was the sort of thing you saw or did, then I'm not blaming you, but it left something dark inside you. You weren't a well man afterwards.'

'I would never have harmed you!'

'I couldn't save you from something you wouldn't own up to.'

'You were the one who needed rescuing, not me.'

Evelyn smiled. 'Still the same old romantic. You never would believe that women are the tough ones. We have to be.'

'You left me because I was weak?'

'Not weak, Frank. But hurt and traumatized. You simply stumbled from one war into another without learning how to deal with the damage.' Evelyn gave a sad little laugh. 'I know you're a good man. I've had a lot of time to think about you. Sometimes I think I only got to know you after you went away.'

'And now?' I wasn't sure I could live with her answer.

'Here.' She took a small white envelope out of her handbag. 'Let me know if you'd like to meet Simon. As I said, we fly home next week.'

She walked away, the tap of her heels echoing along the deserted gallery. I opened the envelope and pulled out a sheet of paper on which she'd written a telephone number. Folded inside was a small black-and-white photograph, its edges crinkled and sharp, probably taken with her old Box Brownie. A small boy peered up at me through the struts of a veranda, smiling into the camera.

34

Peter suggested I meet him upstairs at the Garrick where, as most members preferred the bar in the early evening, the morning room was seldom used. I found him sitting alone in a high-backed leather chair by a far window, brandy and soda ready on a tray in front of him, watched impassively by the rows of gilt-framed theatrical portraits that lined the walls.

'What's up?' he asked, as I sat down. 'Is it about Delia?'

'No,' I said with a sigh. 'Or not directly.'

'What, then?' He seemed apprehensive. I hoped whatever was troubling him had nothing to do with all the things I hadn't told him. I dreaded the day I'd have to admit that I could have warned him of impending problems. And it doubled my guilt at turning to him for help while withholding mine.

'I ran into an old friend this afternoon,' I said.

'Anyone I know?' he asked, brightening up. 'Someone from the squadron?'

'No, from my days in Malaya.'

'Help yourself, by the way.' He indicated the drinks tray. 'What's so urgent that we had to meet straight away?'

I reached into the breast pocket of my jacket and pulled the crinkle-edged photograph out of its envelope. I handed it to him without explanation.

Peter looked at it for a moment, nonplussed. 'Who's this? A godson?'

'You don't think he looks like me?'

Peter reacted with shock. I sometimes forgot how a traditionally moral upbringing underpinned his innate kindness and warmth.

'He's yours?' he asked.

'I don't know.' I came to the nub of it. 'And I can't decide whether I want to know.'

He nodded slowly, sitting back in his armchair. I poured myself a brandy, inhaling its woody tang while he studied the little picture.

'He doesn't *not* look like you, if you know what I mean,' he said, handing it back.

I replaced it in my inside pocket.

'What does his mother say?'

'She's asked if I'd like to meet him.'

'Does she need your help?' he asked. 'Is she able to support the boy?'

'Her husband is a rubber planter.'

'Ah,' he said. 'Now I see the difficulty.'

We sipped our drinks in silence.

'She never told me,' I blurted out at last. 'She ended the affair, and I never knew why. I only found out later that she was having a baby, by which time I was a thousand miles away.'

'Does she have other children?'

'No.' I realized what he meant. 'That will make it easier if she wants to leave her husband, won't it? If the boy *is* mine?'

'But if the boy regards her husband as his father, if he loves him, then—'

'The man's a brute!'

Peter gave a wry smile. 'He might very well say the same of you.'

I returned his smile. 'You don't have to throw the book at me. I've been doing that pretty effectively for myself.'

To my amazement, instead of the nod or laugh I expected, Peter turned away, a hand over his eyes, his shoulders bowed.

'Peter?' I asked in alarm. 'What's up? Whatever's the matter?'

He took a deep breath and turned back to face me, his jaw working as if fighting back tears. 'I'm in no position to lecture you.'

'What?' I had never seen him look like that. Upset, angry, grief-stricken at the loss of another airman, but never this guilty, hang-dog look.

'I'd like to say it was nothing,' he said, 'but it wasn't. It was enough. And she's right, I can't deny what I *wanted* to happen, that I wanted her.'

'Who? Peter, what are you talking about?'

Waiting for his answer, my guts began to clench at the possibility that he was speaking of Delia.

'Lily,' he said. 'The night after the awards ceremony. I took her home in a taxi, remember?'

I did. Peter had been given the job of escorting Cinderella to her golden carriage before the Fairy Godmother's enchantment could wear off. I should have guessed that, if there had been trouble, it had involved Lily.

'She was so happy,' he continued, 'and so ... It had been a

pretty emotional night. A magical night, really. But it's no good making excuses. I kissed her, and she invited me in, asked me if I wanted to stay.'

'And did you?'

'No. Although I did go in. And shut the door. And at that moment I wanted very much to stay. But, thank goodness, as soon as I kissed her again I saw sense. I went straight home.'

'You can't beat yourself up over a couple of kisses.'

'I've barely been able to face Mary since. Or Delia, come to that. How would I tell her that I was ready – more than ready – to take her teenage daughter to bed? I'm nearly forty. My kids are nearer Lily's age than I am.'

If I'd detested Lily before, I thoroughly hated her now. 'Forget it, Peter. You did the right thing. You went home.'

He shook his head miserably. 'She won't let me forget it.'

'Lily won't?' I had to be very careful. My instinct was to tell him everything, to put the poor man out of his misery immediately by assuring him that, whoever Lily was, she was no innocent little flower. But then he'd clearly already learned that for himself. And, when it came down to it, I wasn't ready to sacrifice my chance with Delia until I had no other choice.

'Lily's blackmailing me,' Peter said. 'Oh, not for money. She'll soon earn more than I do. But to make me do whatever she wants. If I refuse, she threatens to tell Mary what happened.'

'But nothing really happened,' I protested. 'Mary's not going to take Lily's word over yours. And even if she does, she'll forgive you. She's the best-hearted woman I know.'

'That's not the point, though, is it? I've let her down. I've not been the man she deserves.'

'We're none of us that,' I said bitterly.

'Oh, I'm sorry, Frank. You came to me for advice, and here I am pouring out my troubles.'

A new line of thought presented itself. 'Is that why Lily was able to walk off with Delia's movie role so easily?'

He nodded, shamefaced. 'Partly. The original suggestion came from the American producers, but I could have fought harder.'

'I don't suppose Delia has any inkling of this?' I asked.

'How could she?' said Peter. 'Although, you know, it's made me admire Delia all the more, the way she's taken it on the chin and been genuinely glad for her daughter. I only wish Lily was more deserving of her mother's loyalty.'

I wanted to smash my fist into the nearest wall. I drained my brandy, aware that my hand was shaking slightly. As Peter refilled our glasses, I tried to steady my mind. If Delia and Peter were to share what they each knew, Lily's shenanigans, whatever their purpose, would be finished in an instant. Surely Delia's loyalty to Peter would sanction my exposing Lily to him as an ambitious and scheming imposter. If only I could feel certain that she'd understand and forgive me.

'But what about your dilemma, Frank?' Peter's question broke into my deliberations. 'Are you going to meet the boy? Do you want to be with his mother? Do you still love her?'

I realized then that there was one simple answer to all my questions about Evelyn. It was too late. I was in love with Delia. And I was ready to do whatever it took to have Delia love me in return.

'I'm still your head of security, right?' I asked Peter.

'Of course.'

'Then let me find out more about Lily. Discover what happened to make her like this. We know she was in a children's home in the Midlands before being fostered in Worcester, but where was she before that?'

He looked confused. 'What has Lily to do with the little boy in the photograph?'

'I can't explain, but just give me the nod and I'll find out what she's really after.'

'I'm not sure that's an appropriate response,' Peter said. 'Whatever happened in the past, it's for Lily and Delia to sort out between themselves.'

I clenched my fists, willing my old friend not to be so blind, to ditch his chivalry for once and see Lily for what she was.

But he shook his head in resignation. 'Lily can't help being a mixed-up kid.'

'I saw Chinese boys younger than her blow up a truck full of British soldiers in Malaya,' I said angrily.

Peter instantly looked wary. 'The war's over, Frank. You can't think like that any more.'

I wasn't so sure. Somehow the secure and steady world Peter had grown up in had been preserved and had waited relatively unscathed for him to return to after he was demobbed – much like the values and traditions contained in the grand Regency room we were sitting in. Perhaps that was what Evelyn had also been trying to tell me in the museum, that even the most fragile objects could survive centuries of war and destruction. But my experience had been different, messier, the values our boys were fighting for less clear-cut. For people like me, whose lives had been thrown hopelessly off course, the world might be patched up but the true horror of the past never went away. I didn't say any of this to Peter, and it was far too late to change anything by saying it to Evelyn.

35

When I rang Delia the following afternoon, she said she'd be happy for me to call at her mews house. I'd spent the morning on the telephone and then at Somerset House, trying to learn everything I could about Lily's background. I'd not discovered anything dramatically significant, but I now had a copy of her birth certificate in a brown envelope in my jacket pocket along with a single sheet on which I'd written everything else I'd found out. The birth certificate would give Delia paper proof with which to confront Lily, and I also hoped that seeing the truth in black and white might persuade Delia to accept that Lily was a fraud who posed a real threat.

I found her bright and energized by the new plans she'd hatched with Celeste. She led me straight up to the rooftop living room where the final sketches were spread out across the floor.

'I need to talk it all over with Peter,' she said, pointing out her favourites. 'And Davey, too, because I think I should launch my new look along with my next single. I might do my hair differently, with more layers and a sort of short and tousled cut. In America they call it "the artichoke", apparently! What do you think?'

'You've got the cheekbones for it,' I said, taking pleasure in her excitement.

'I think it's right to change everything all at once, don't you, rather than bit by bit so that no one really notices? That will help Celeste, too. She's so full of plans for her new boutique and I'm so glad for her. And all I need now is the right song. I've put it off too long. I must get back in the studio with Davey and throw some ideas around.'

Ideas that would never see the light of day, if Lily ordered Peter to bury them. Perhaps that was why Peter hadn't rushed Delia back into the studio weeks ago. And she would never even know why her career was being run off the rails. She'd blame herself, see it as evidence that her star was waning, that her fans no longer wanted her. I feared it would break her heart.

'So you're not going to retire?' I asked, forcing myself to adopt a teasing tone.

Delia laughed merrily. 'Not at all. Quite the opposite, in fact. Maybe I will even still make a movie somewhere down the line, but I love live audiences. And, as you know, the plan is to do more television. Several of the radio DJs who have always championed my music are now involved with the new TV shows, and I'm sure they'll help me make the shift. I have a lot of kind and generous friends in the business.'

Thrilled to see her so positive, I beat down the selfish little voice that said she wouldn't have much time left for romance amid her re-launched career. I told myself not to care: I was the one here with her now and that would have to be enough. I held out my hands and she took them and threw them up into the air, spreading her arms wide as she did on stage.

'I feel better than I have in ages,' she said. 'I just know that it's all going to work out.'

'Then it will,' I told her.

She kissed my cheek and went over to sit at the piano. She picked out a few notes that soon became chords, then began to hum a melody.

'I didn't realize you wrote some of your own music as well,' I said.

'I don't, really. I come up with little fragments and Davey works on them.'

'And the words?'

'Both of us, I guess. We've worked together so long we don't really notice.'

'Have you ever worked with anyone else?'

'Only when I've covered a well-known song,' she said. 'Especially some of the American hits. It's fun doing that sometimes. But Davey and I have always been a kind of double-act.'

A chill struck me. I was convinced that, as soon as Lily caught wind of something necessary and precious to Delia, she would do her best to destroy it.

Before I could speak, Delia swivelled back to face the keys, playing soft, lilting chords that I didn't recognize until she began to sing. It was 'When I Fall In Love'. She turned her head to me as she sang, her voice low and tender yet powerful enough to fill the room. *When I give my heart it will be completely.* I daren't let myself believe she was singing these words to me. After all, she'd warned me that it was her job to make people yearn.

She paused before breaking the silence that followed. 'There's nothing to beat a favourite love song.'

'That's true.' I knew I had to protect her. 'And if you had to work with someone new, instead of Davey?'

She laughed. 'I'd hate it!'

'You're not worried that Lily will monopolize him?'

'Davey's always busy. It's never stopped him finding time for me before.'

He might, I thought, if Peter felt powerless to control the situation. 'What if Lily won't let him?'

'Stop this,' she responded angrily. 'I don't want to hear it.'

'I've been talking to Peter,' I said. 'I can't say more than that, but you have to accept that she's scheming and malicious.'

'You're imagining things,' she said. 'There's plenty of room for both of us, especially now she has her film career.'

'Which she stole from you.'

'I refuse to fight her.'

'And if she won't lay down her weapons?'

Delia rose to her feet, summoning all her stage presence, and stared me down. 'It was sweet of you to call round,' she said, 'but I mustn't keep you.'

'I'll go,' I said. 'But I want you to have this.' I took out the envelope containing Lily's birth certificate.

Delia refused to take it, so I walked across the room and left it on her desk, below the framed photograph of Conrad Durand. 'Just take a look,' I said. 'God knows, you deserve to have found your own daughter safe and well. I wish you'd been able to. But please believe me that championing Lily is not the way to make amends. She's not harmless, Delia. She's not the lost child who's invented her own fairy tale.'

'I'll see you out.'

I followed her down the narrow stairs. There was nothing

more I could say. I even felt an odd kind of relief as she closed the front door behind me. I hoped that my refusal to back down would give her pause for thought. I knew that she would never let herself love me until Lily Brooks had been fully exposed for what she was.

36

DELIA

Delia was furious. As if Lily could ever pose any kind of threat to her career now that she had recovered from the blow of losing the movie! And Frank was wrong about that, too: it had been entirely her own fault. The only part Lily had played was in resurrecting the past and reviving Delia's long-buried maternal guilt. And actually she was glad she'd finally faced it. In a strange way, although her own child was dead, she felt whole again. It was ridiculous to fear Lily or see her burgeoning career as competing with her own. Men always relished the idea that women had to be rivals, feuding and clawing each other's eyes out, especially if they were successful in other ways. That was all it was.

As Delia's anger with Frank ebbed away, regret seeped in. She liked him. She had liked the idea of something happening between them. She had often longed to overcome her habitual reserve, and his admiration had encouraged her to meet the future with renewed energy and optimism. His attentiveness had also forced her to admit how much she missed Conrad, how deeply she still mourned his loss. He'd been her bulwark, her family, her wisest counsel.

Returning upstairs, she went straight to the framed photograph of him. Holding it to her, she wondered what his advice would be if he was here now. He would surely want her to be happy and to have a rounded life. Her eye fell on the brown envelope that Frank had placed on the desk. She was tempted to throw it away unread, but the irony in Conrad's smile told her that would be the coward's way out.

She replaced his photograph, opened the envelope and drew out two sheets of paper. One was a birth certificate in the name of Lily Körmöczy, born in Birmingham in 1945.

Delia dropped the paper as if it had burned her fingers. It could not be. She must have misread. Her face was hot, her fingers icy cold. She sat in the chair beside the desk and bent forward to pick it up.

Lily Körmöczy.

She scanned the handwritten sections. There was no entry under 'Name of Father' but the mother's name was written in black ink in perfect copperplate: Anna Körmöczy.

Anna had survived the extermination camp. Anna had lived. Anna, too, had had a daughter.

Delia scanned the other sheet on which Frank had written Lily's brief biography. *Lily entered the children's home when she was nine following the death of her mother.*

By then Delia Maxwell had already become a household name, with several hit records and her picture endlessly reproduced in newspapers and magazines. Surely Anna must have recognized her and made the connection. If so, then Anna Körmöczy's daughter must know what Irma Székely had done.

*

On their first day at elementary school Anna and Irma were placed at adjoining desks and, when it came time to walk home with their mothers, discovered that they lived two streets from one another. By the start of the second term they had become inseparable. Anna, with her robust sense of fairness and justice, always stood up for the more easy-going Irma if she was picked on at school, while Irma consoled Anna when her quick temper got her into trouble. They remained each other's best friend throughout the following nine years.

Anna's father, a tall, quiet and kindly man, was a professor at the university where he taught chemistry. Her handsome and athletic older brother talked of becoming a doctor. Her mother was a talented watercolour painter and an avid reader, often forgetting her household duties because she was too lost in a novel. Anna's family lived in an apartment with the same high ceilings and parquet floors and almost identical lace curtains and wide-girthed ceramic stoves as that of Irma's family nearby.

Irma's father, Oskar, ran Budapest's most stylish photographic studio where he encountered leading figures from all walks of life. He loved meeting new people, always ready with a smile and a compliment. Her parents' social life revolved around the opera and the theatre, and they travelled often to Vienna – and sometimes further afield – where they also knew many actors, musicians, playwrights and directors. Irma loved to sing, and she and her younger sister Zsofia enjoyed regular dancing and music lessons. Their mother, Eva, loved stylish clothes and dressing up to go out, while Irma's father grew stout from too many convivial dinners.

Although the girls' friendship led the two families to meet fairly frequently, their parents never truly became friends.

In the winter they went skating on the frozen lake in the Városliget where in the summer they swam outdoors in the steamy, sulphurous waters of the Széchenyi Baths. Irma admired Anna's physical courage, even if it meant pushing herself further in order to keep up. After skating or swimming, Anna loved to sit with a cup of foaming hot chocolate, laughing at Irma's often absurd commentary on strangers at neighbouring tables. It was always Anna, with her mix of determination and foolhardiness, who got them into scrapes, and Irma, with her father's charm and diplomacy, who talked them out again.

Sometimes they watched the barges on the Danube or roamed the old city walls of Buda, sharing dreams of futures in which they became gangsters' molls or circus artists, wisecracking reporters or international spies, depending on the latest subtitled American film they had seen at the cinema. As they grew older, they went window-shopping along the fashionable Váci utca and discussed which fictional romantic hero each would prefer to kiss.

Despite the disturbing news from Germany, it was only after war had broken out, in the year they started secondary school, that they began to be aware of what being Jewish might mean. Both their fathers had fought in the Great War and saw themselves as patriotic Hungarians. They were not in the least devout, and no one in either of their families felt significantly different from anyone else they knew.

However, after the number of Jews who could be employed was limited by the Second Jewish Law, Anna's father struggled to keep his job at the university. Not long afterwards Irma's father voluntarily transferred ownership of his business to a non-Jewish friend in hope of hanging on to his livelihood, although many long-standing clients had already deserted him. It was around this time that Conrad left for Zürich: he was not Jewish but was unwilling to work in theatres in Budapest or Vienna that would no longer employ Jews. Some of Anna's cousins packed up and emigrated to America. At school, another pupil contemptuously informed Irma that, because her mother wasn't wholly Jewish, she was a *Mischling*, a word she'd never encountered before. She had to hold Anna back from slapping the girl.

And yet, outwardly, life went on much the same. The two friends went to school, they still had nice clothes to wear, and both even received new bicycles for their birthdays. Irma's was dark green and she was envious of Anna's shiny red machine. Sometimes they still went with their parents to dine at the little courtyard restaurants up in Buda where the gypsy violinists played. Yet, at home, Irma's parents would fall silent when she or Zsofia entered the room and she knew they'd been discussing things they didn't want Irma or her sister to hear.

One day Anna arrived at school in tears. Her adored older brother had been made to abandon his medical studies, and she had overheard her parents' fears that he might be made to undertake forced labour. A few weeks later, Irma's parents were unable to hide their anxiety after some German friends who had fled from Berlin and been living in Budapest for the past five years were suddenly taken away and put on a train to Poland. They were never heard from again. Hitler had not yet given the order to invade Hungary but everyone knew that it was only a matter of time before the tanks rolled through the streets, just as they had in so many other once proud and independent European cities. Once that happened, the possession of the right – or wrong – papers would be a matter of life or death.

One night Irma overheard an argument between her parents. Oskar was trying to persuade his wife to divorce him. The Nazis had strict classifications as to a person's degree of Jewishness, and Eva might yet save herself if she cut all ties with him. As it was, he argued, he was struggling to provide for his family in the way she deserved. Eva wept as she begged her husband never to discuss such a matter again.

A month later, over breakfast, Irma's father told her to come to his photographic studio straight after school. She usually enjoyed visiting his business, where he always found small jobs for his daughters, offering them useful roles in the adult world, but recently the place had fallen quiet and the jolly Fräulein Lantos, who greeted people, handed them their finished prints and took their payments, no longer sat at her mahogany desk by the door. However hard her father tried to pretend that all was well, Irma hated to see him so diminished.

When she arrived in her school uniform, he set the camera on its tripod, placed her in a chair against a plain-curtained backdrop and told her not to smile. After taking several exposures, he instructed her to present her profile to the lens.

'What are these for, Papa?' she asked, when he had finished.

He waved the question away. 'Everyone needs so many papers, these days. It'll be useful to have spare photos.'

He wouldn't let her join him in the darkroom, where she never tired of seeing the images on the blank sheets emerge like magic in the chemical bath, but sent her home ahead of him, saying to tell her mother he wouldn't be late for dinner but that, if anyone called at the apartment, they were to pretend to be out.

When Oskar arrived home he called Irma into his little study.

He stroked her hair as he told her he'd wanted the photographs because he was sending her to stay with Conrad in Zürich where she would be safe. He would have liked Zsofia to accompany her, but their mother had insisted that nine-year-old Zsofia was still too young to leave home. The borders had been closed since 1939 but, he explained, he had obtained a *Schutzbrief* for her, a protection document issued by the Swiss consulate that would permit her to travel by train across Austria and Germany and on into Switzerland. She was fourteen, old enough to be sensible and keep her head on what would be a difficult journey.

Irma felt a mixture of apprehension and excitement. She had no wish to be torn from her family or to leave Budapest, and had never travelled such a great distance alone before. And yet she was fond of Conrad, and couldn't deny that the idea of a journey, of independence, of being singled out for special protection, all appealed to her adolescent imagination. She knew life only from books, plays and films, and this would be an adventure.

It was only when she went into the kitchen to ask if she could help her mother and Kati, the elderly servant who lived with them, to set the table for dinner and found them both crying that she discovered her father's proposal was not something that might happen at some future unspecified date: it was to take place the following morning.

She panicked, clinging to her mother and begging her to tell her father it was impossible, she wanted to stay at home, she would die of grief if they sent her away. And if she was to go, then, please, not so soon. Let her get used to the idea and have a chance to say goodbye to friends and family. She especially couldn't go without taking leave of Anna.

But her father was implacable, most particularly so on the

point of not telling anyone about the Swiss papers, which were so very hard to obtain. Her mother helped her to pack a suitcase light enough for her to carry while Zsofia stood watching from the corner of the room, wiping away tears. When their mother's back was turned, Zsofia darted forward and tucked a miniature figure from her doll's house into a corner of the case. Knowing it was her sister's favourite, the imaginary character around whom all Zsofia's make-believe games revolved, Irma thought her heart would break.

It was impossible to sleep. Irma heard the clock that stood on the dining-room sideboard chime the hours until, around six, her mother came to get her up. Her limbs were so stiff with fear that her mother had to help her into her clothes. She watched helplessly as her mother tucked a family photograph into an inside pocket of the suitcase and added a slim tissue-wrapped box, a gift for Conrad as a small token of their gratitude.

Her father came to say it was time to go, cracking his knuckles as he stood waiting in the doorway while her mother hugged and kissed her and told her to be good and to mind Conrad, not give him any trouble. Zsofia was crying too much to kiss her goodbye, and their mother had to hold tightly to her little sister to stop Zsofia clinging to her. At the door to the apartment Kati waited with a string bag packed with provisions for the journey. Her father picked up her suitcase and silently led the way down the stairs and across the courtyard to the street door, where he'd left the car the night before.

It didn't take long to reach the station, although the streets were already busy with trams, delivery vans, horse-drawn market carts and workers hurrying to their offices. Keleti station was crowded and Irma held fast to her father's hand as he went to buy her ticket, then led her to the platform. The train was already waiting, the huge black engine hissing and blowing clouds of white steam.

'You'll come back as soon as it's safe,' he told her. 'Or we'll come to join you. Conrad will look after you. You'll see, it won't be long before we're all together again.'

She nodded, trying to believe him.

He took a deep breath and reached into the inside pocket of his greatcoat. He'd lost weight and it hung loosely from his shoulders. He seemed to hesitate for a moment and Irma's heart leaped at the thought that he had changed his mind, that he couldn't bring himself to send her away and was about to tell her to forget the whole ridiculous idea and come straight home with him.

'Here is the Swiss protection document and a new identity card,' he said, handing her a stiff white envelope. 'Keep them safe, along with your train ticket.' He paused again, licking his dry lips. 'Don't look at them until the train has left the station. You'll see that they're not in your name. It's too complicated to explain, but this is the name you must use throughout the journey. I checked your suitcase, but do you have anything else on you with the name Irma Székely? If so, you must give it to me now.'

'No, I don't think so, but—'

'There's no time for questions. You must trust me. If you do remember something with your name on it once you're on the train, you must tear it up and throw it out of the carriage window. Promise me you'll do that.'

'I promise, Papa.'

'And however upset you are, whatever you think, you must

stay on the train. It would be dangerous for you to get off and try to make your way home, do you understand?'

She nodded, feeling tears behind her eyelids.

'Give me your word.'

She nodded again, unable to speak.

'Conrad will let us know you're safe.'

He opened his arms and pulled her into a bear-hug. She gripped the lapels of his coat, inhaling its damp woollen scent.

'Please don't make me go, Papa. Please let me stay. I don't want to go.'

'It's for the best,' he said. 'You must always believe that.' He kissed the top of her head. 'Goodbye, my darling.'

Gently he prised her fingers loose and pushed her up the steep steps into the carriage, handing up her suitcase and closing the door before she could attempt to escape. A whistle blew. The engine gave out a billowing cloud of steam and the wheels began to move, slowly gaining traction against the iron rails.

37

She found a seat in a second-class compartment in the middle of two facing rows. A smiling man with a bushy moustache took her suitcase, lifted it onto the rack above her head and returned to his seat beside the window. She thanked him politely but, fearing that returning his smile would place her under some kind of unwelcome obligation, was too scared to look out at the passing landscape in case she met his eye. When she finally dared to glance around, she saw a couple of young women, who looked like students, several older men, whom she assumed were travelling on business, and a scared-looking mother with three subdued young children.

She took out the envelope her father had given her and surreptitiously examined the documents it contained. Grasping the full meaning of her new identity changed everything that Irma had previously understood about herself. When the train stopped at the first station some miles from Budapest, she had to fight the urge to get off and find her way home. She was ready to walk if she had to. She couldn't do this. She couldn't carry out her father's wishes. But she had promised. And, besides, he had warned her it might be dangerous – dangerous perhaps for her whole family – if she didn't obey.

She concentrated instead on the rhythmically passing tele-
graph poles, trying to tell herself how much she'd always
enjoyed train journeys in the past. Except those journeys had
been different: then she'd usually been going on holiday with
her family, and once with Anna's family, to stay at their summer villa on Lake Balaton. At that memory her mind froze, and
for weeks afterwards her sorrow left her stupid and tongue-tied.

At the Austrian border the train stopped. As the engine hissed
and blew more clouds of steam, sharp-eyed men in official uniforms came on board and thrust out hands for precious pieces
of paper. Outside, Nazi soldiers patrolled beside the track, making sure that everyone saw the guns they carried. The officials
seemed mainly interested in the men of military age, asking
questions and scrutinizing their papers. A German police officer also searched the suitcases belonging to the two young
students. Irma watched and copied the adults in her carriage,
keeping her gaze averted and mutely offering up her papers,
praying silently that her fraud would not be discovered and lead
to her arrest.

All was well, although the train remained stationary for
another two hours. As it finally moved on once again, heading
through flat countryside towards Vienna, she looked curiously
out of the window. All the local Austrian railway stations flew
Nazi flags or had large swastikas mounted over their entrances,
and she saw an occasional group of soldiers, their rifles beside
them, waiting on benches on platforms where her train did not
stop. She was disappointed not to see any damage from the kind
of Allied bombing reported by friends of her parents who
listened clandestinely to broadcasts from the BBC or Voice of
America.

Later, as they approached the city, she saw the famous Ferris wheel in the Prater, and was relieved that the smiling man with the moustache was among those who walked purposefully away when they were all made to get off. Those continuing their journeys were herded across to another platform and onto a streamlined new Deutsche Reichsbahn train. After another long delay and more sharp-eyed men, who inspected her papers yet again, this train carried them on towards Salzburg, passing onion-domed churches, houses with messy storks' nests on their roofs and weary-looking people on bicycles waiting at the gates of level crossings. At the first sight of the distant Alps she felt like weeping for all she was leaving behind.

It began to grow dark and the air colder. The train stopped frequently, usually, it seemed, to allow other more urgent traffic to pass – sometimes she could make out long lines of closed cattle or coal trucks and once an engine pulling open wagons with armed soldiers riding atop military equipment shrouded with tarpaulins. Hugging her coat around her, she managed to sleep for a few hours before being woken by people gathering their belongings and preparing to leave the train at Munich.

Although Kati had provided plenty of food, Irma had no appetite, not even for the slice of her favourite sour cherry cake, but she was thirsty. She had finished the tea in the small vacuum flask some time ago, and a guard had informed everyone that the dining car was solely for the use of members of the armed forces. As they drew to a halt in the huge station, she viewed with longing the brightly lit refreshment kiosk on the platform, but she had no Reichsmarks and, anyway, dared not leave either her seat or her suitcase, although she knew that she couldn't put off another visit to the lavatory at the end of the corridor for much longer.

Despite the late evening hour, the station was busy. Irma was surprised at how well dressed and confident the people looked, oblivious to the numerous men in different uniforms, some with weapons, patrolling casually among the crowd. She was stiff and exhausted, frightened and alone. She even missed the familiarity of the smiling man with the moustache. A corner seat became vacant and she took it, glad of the protection of something solid beside her, even though the glass was chilly. When the train eventually set off once more through dark fields and pine forests, she closed her eyes and managed to drift in and out of sleep.

It was barely dawn when they reached the shores of the Bodensee and the Swiss border. Everyone was made to collect their luggage, get off the train and queue nervously on the platform, where a freezing wind blew in off the lake. The men were unshaven, nearly everyone had slept in their clothes, and they were all apprehensive. As she waited her turn to enter the hastily erected immigration hall she watched others in front of her come back out in tears. She heard the whisper pass along the line: no adult refugees allowed, only the young, the old and the sick. People stood white-faced and shivering, awaiting their fate. Irma almost hoped that they would reject her, send her back, allow her to go home. But when it was her turn, the man inspected her papers, scrutinized the photograph her father had taken of her only two days ago, stamped the document from the Swiss consulate, and waved her through. As she made her way back to the train, a Red Cross worker offered her some hot soup, which she accepted gratefully.

Despite the erratic journey and long delays, when, a couple of hours later, she climbed down from the train in Zürich she somehow expected Conrad to be waiting for her on the platform. Of course he wasn't. Her father had written down his friend's address, but she had no Swiss francs with which to take a taxi or even a tram. She carried her suitcase into the middle of the vast echoing hall of the Hauptbahnhof, put it down on the marble floor and stood beside it, ignoring the streams of people forced to walk around her. Ready to drop with exhaustion, she wouldn't let herself sit on her case. She had to remain alert, constantly scanning the passing faces. Conrad had been such a frequent visitor to their apartment throughout her childhood that she was confident of picking him out, but it was a good two years since he had last seen her and she was afraid he might not recognize her now she was more grown-up. She had absolutely no idea what she would do if he did not come for her.

But he did come, waving from a distance and hurrying through the crowd.

'Irma, my dear child,' he said. 'Don't even try to speak until I get you home. A hot bath, some soup and then bed, I think. You are safe now. Whatever happens, you are safe.'

And she was. He posted the letters she wrote to her parents and to Zsofia. He pulled strings to get new Swiss papers drawn up in her own name so he could send her to school, and together they gradually established a routine. Her bedroom in his apartment was small but had everything she required, and he asked an actress friend who had daughters to take Irma shopping when she needed new clothes. He kept a manservant but no cook, so most evenings they used their ration stamps to eat a simple meal at a local restaurant. He was kind, patient and discreet, and she felt that he was growing fond of her.

And then, in March 1944, the news came that the Nazis had occupied Hungary. The mass Jewish deportations began soon afterwards. She never heard from any of her family again.

38

And yet Frank had given Delia Lily's birth certificate, proof that, while Irma had been living safely in Zürich, her friend Anna had – miraculously – either escaped deportation or survived the camps. Perhaps, Delia hoped, not only Anna but her parents and brother, too.

Delia couldn't stop staring at the piece of official paper in her hand. *Father unknown*: she understood all too well the kind of story likely hidden behind those two words. *Mother's name: Anna Körmöczy*. Lily was Anna's child.

Suddenly Delia realized why Lily had always seemed so intimately familiar: she had the same colouring and facial features as her mother, as well as Anna's spirit and determination. When Delia had believed Lily must be *her* daughter because Lily reminded her so strongly of herself at that age, it hadn't been Irma but Irma's best friend she'd been remembering.

Delia went into her dressing room and searched out her mousy brown wig from the back of a cupboard. She sat in front of the mirror and pulled it on, tucking every blonde strand out of sight. Seeking to re-absorb an identity she had for so long been too ashamed to admit, she stared at her reflection, struggling to accept that, for at least some of the years Irma Székely had secretly felt the guilt of Anna's death weigh so heavy on her shoulders, Anna had been alive.

She slipped a hand under the lining paper of the dressing-table drawer and drew out the envelope she kept hidden there. It contained two items. One was a creased black-and-white photograph taken by one of her father's assistants, which meant that, unusually, Oskar was also in it, trying vainly to pull in his stomach as he struck a studio pose beside his fashionably dressed wife and two daughters. She remembered how her mother, Eva, had chided him that, if he kept telling the assistant how to do his job, they'd never be finished. Delia could seldom bring herself to look at the image, the frail object that was all that remained of the people it depicted, but now she stared intently at her younger self: a heart-shaped face, curious eyes (despite the rather jaded expression of the photographer's child all too used to posing for a camera), curly brown hair tied back with a ribbon, and rather untidy clothes. Even then, at the start of the war, she'd felt safe and carefree, her life stretching ahead of her. Who was she? Delia Székely. Irma Maxwell. Why should she not, after all, be both?

With a fingertip she stroked the faraway faces of her parents and sister, almost able to smell the faint vanilla scent of her father's hair cream, and, for the very first time, allowed herself to feel some sympathy, even pity, for the child she'd been.

The second item was the tiny figure from Zsofia's doll's house. She knew that, the moment she touched it, she would be hit by a wave of fear, grief and guilt, by all the emotions she'd always been too afraid to face. When the death of her family had first been officially confirmed, she'd wished she'd died with them. Now she understood how lonely she'd always been, even more so since Conrad's death, how emotionally isolated she had allowed herself to become because she believed she did not deserve another family, another little sister, another best friendship.

She thought about Frank, and the temptation simply to accept the love he offered. Perhaps it might even work, now that she could explain why she would always support Lily, come what may. There was nothing Delia wouldn't do for Anna's child.

She wished she knew when Lily was due back from Rome, but the girl hadn't been in touch since the day Delia had visited the studios. She couldn't wait to see her. She felt as if a tide had turned, that Fate had given her an opportunity to make amends for what she had done, a second chance almost more precious than finding her own daughter would have been.

And then the leaden realization crept in. She picked up Frank's handwritten sheet of paper again. Anna had died when Lily was nine years old. They had lived in Birmingham, in Edgbaston. If Anna had recognized Delia Maxwell as her old friend Irma, then why had she not got in touch? And, if she'd spoken of her former school friend to Lily, why had Lily not simply sent her a note or introduced herself one night at the stage door? Or said something as soon as she discovered the name Irma Székely among Delia's papers? Delia would have been delighted to do everything she could for her, so why make up the story that Delia was her mother?

Delia shivered. She had always hoped and prayed there was no reason for Anna to have learned the truth behind Irma's abrupt and unannounced departure from Budapest. The thought was simply too unbearable, too unforgivable. But if she had ... if Lily, too, had always known yet said nothing, had instead invented the fiction of being Delia's flesh and blood ...

Delia's hands trembled as she pulled off the brown wig. She had always known it would come at last. Punishment. Retribution. It was what she deserved and she felt strangely calm and ready to welcome it.

39

The ringing telephone beside the bed roused Delia out of a fitful sleep.

'I'm so sorry to wake you. It's Peter.'

'What is it?'

'I thought you ought to know. There's been an accident.'

Half awake, Delia sat up in dread. 'What's happened?'

'It's Lily,' said Peter. 'She's not hurt, but a cyclist was. She's at a police station. I think they'd been drinking.'

'They?' she echoed. 'Who was she with?'

'Guy Brody. They'd been out late and his car hit a cyclist.'

'Is the cyclist all right?'

'He's been taken to hospital. I think he's quite badly injured.'

'That's terrible,' she said. 'Which police station are they in? I should go to her.'

'Gerald Road. It's not far from you, but you shouldn't go alone.'

'Don't be silly.'

'No, listen,' he said. 'It's common knowledge that one of the desk sergeants there has a brother-in-law who's a printer in Fleet Street and trades in tip-offs. The press will be straight on to it, unless Brody's people can silence them first. Wait there and I'll come and pick you up.'

She dressed hurriedly. Putting on her watch, she saw it was nearly two in the morning. It was mid-August, but the small hours of the night could be chilly so she took a warm sheepskin jacket from the cupboard, then, anxious there might be photographers, added a headscarf and dark glasses to her handbag before rejecting such a pointless disguise: she didn't want to appear furtive or as if she were ashamed to be associated with Lily, whatever the girl had done. She doubted she'd have enough time to make coffee, yet the wait for the doorbell seemed endless.

'I left the car at the end of the mews,' said Peter, when he arrived. 'I didn't want to wake your neighbours.'

The cobbles were slick with dew and he took her arm, even though she was wearing flat shoes. 'There's something else,' he told her. 'It was Lily driving.'

'But she doesn't know how!'

'Apparently Guy's been teaching her.'

'But she won't have a licence.'

'Precisely.'

He held the passenger door open for her and they drove the short distance in silence. The imposing stucco terraces of Belgrave Square sat silent and largely dark, facing into the majestic trees of the gardens. Delia rolled down her window and inhaled a faint earthy smell on the night air. Two minutes later they drew up outside a compact three-storey building of London brick, its windows blazing in the otherwise sleepy residential street.

'Thank goodness there don't seem to be any reporters here yet,' said Peter.

A blue police lamp hung over the door and, as she followed

him inside, Delia noticed the geraniums planted in window boxes along the ground-floor sills; the gaudy flowers seemed to possess a dream-like incongruity against the austere purpose of the place.

Peter introduced himself to the desk sergeant and asked to see Lily, introducing Delia as her mother and reminding the officer that Lily was only eighteen, not yet legally an adult. As the officer picked up the black telephone on the counter, another man rose from where he was sitting on a bench against the wall. Middle-aged, burly and florid, and wearing an expensive-looking suit, he held out his hand to Peter.

'Mr Jenks? I'm Charlie Flynn. I'm in charge of public relations for Mr Brody while he's here in England, on behalf of the producers.'

'It's good that you got here so fast,' said Peter, shaking his hand.

'I'm hoping that my client will be released as soon as he's finished making his statement,' said Flynn. 'Unfortunately matters may not be so straightforward for Miss Brooks.'

Delia noticed how the desk sergeant, once he had delivered his short phone message, only pretended to be busy, his ears obviously pricked for any gossip. She wondered how many other brothers-in-law he might have spread strategically around London.

'Is there any news of the poor cyclist?' she asked.

Flynn shook his head. 'I hope for Miss Brooks's sake that he makes a full recovery.'

Delia knew Flynn's type well. Every so often she'd come across publicists who could no longer disguise their resentment at having to shield their indulged and highly paid clients. Sometimes she couldn't blame them, having observed the kind of mess that several well-known stars had managed to walk away from unblemished. She'd heard plenty of dark rumours about Guy Brody, too. But then it wasn't Charlie Flynn's job to like him. Or to like an apparently spoiled young starlet like Lily, either.

A poker-faced female officer appeared, leading Lily by the arm, and opened a door into a bare little room with a wooden table, a dirty ashtray and some mismatched chairs. As Peter indicated to Flynn to wait outside, the officer escorted Lily in, then closed the door behind them, leaving them to speak in private. The room was clean enough, despite the scuffed walls. Lily wore a short sleeveless coral-coloured dress with only a thin scarf to keep her warm. Her cheeks were pale and her eyes seemed a little unfocused, the pupils dilated. Delia immediately took off her own jacket and put it around Lily's shoulders.

'What are you doing here?' Lily demanded, by way of thanks, although she clasped the soft sheepskin tightly.

'I'd like to help, if I can.' Delia could barely find the words, too overcome by what she now saw so clearly in Lily's face: Anna's elfin features, the same grey-green eyes, the same slightly protruding upper lip, and the same direct way of looking at people. How had she failed to recognize the likeness before?

'I don't understand why they're keeping me here,' Lily complained, her defiance barely disguising her anxiety.

Peter frowned. 'Can you tell me what happened tonight?'

'I don't know exactly,' said Lily. 'We'd been out to a club and I fell asleep in the car. I woke up because we screeched to a stop and Guy was shouting and swearing. Then I saw two men running towards us, only they didn't run to us but to someone behind us, on the ground, with a mangled bike beside him.'

Peter glanced at Delia before speaking. 'It's best you tell me the truth, Lily,' he said kindly. 'It's the only way I can help you.'

'That is the truth.'

'Who was driving?'

'Guy, of course.'

'But you have driven Guy's car before?'

'Yes,' she said impatiently, 'but only on the studio driveway. He was teaching me. So what?'

'Guy says it was you driving when you hit the cyclist.'

'*What?*' Lily's face drained of what little colour it had. 'Guy told the police *I* was driving?'

'Yes.'

'He can't have! I barely know how to work the gears, let alone drive in the dark. And why would Guy ever be stupid enough to let me?'

Delia thought of Charlie Flynn. If he had advised Guy Brody to lie, he'd only been doing his job, protecting his bankable and well-established client.

'Had you been drinking last night?' Peter asked.

Lily shrugged. 'A bit.'

'Enough not to remember clearly what happened?'

'I told you, I fell asleep. I was tired. We'd been out to a club, and we only wrapped in Rome yesterday.' She glanced at the clock on the wall. 'The day before yesterday.'

Delia wanted to ask what else Lily had been taking, but couldn't risk it in front of Peter, who seemed oddly unsympathetic to the girl's protestation of innocence.

Lily, too, seemed taken aback by his mistrust. 'It wasn't me,' she appealed to them both. 'Guy was driving.'

'Can we just get her out of here for tonight?' Delia asked Peter.

'She can come home with me and get some sleep.' She turned to Lily. 'I'll make up the daybed upstairs. Then in the morning I'll call my solicitor and we can straighten everything out.'

'I'd rather go to Smith Street,' said Lily. 'To my own bed.'

'If we're to get you released on police bail, you will have to be with a responsible adult,' Peter told her.

She looked at him levelly, a sharper glint in her eye. 'I want you to sort this out for me, Peter.'

But he didn't appear to hear, his thoughts elsewhere as if he were weighing something up. 'Wait here,' he told Lily, then turned to Delia. 'Can I have a quick word outside?'

She followed him out. He made her wait at the main door until he had checked the street for reporters or photographers, and then beckoned her out. They huddled on the pavement, away from the light cast by the blue lamp. Without her jacket, the night air made her shiver with tiredness.

'I have a feeling this is going to end badly,' he said, 'and I don't want you mixed up in it. I want you to go, disappear before the press get on to it. You can walk home from here, can't you?'

She laughed. 'You want me to disown her?'

'Yes.'

She stared at him. 'You're serious?'

'Yes,' he said.

'You think she's malicious.' She was making a statement, not asking a question. It was what Frank had said to her.

'I'm not sure it's safe to believe her,' he said carefully. 'I don't want your career to suffer any further if . . .'

He left the sentence to hang in the air. She was about to argue that Lily wouldn't lie, but pulled herself up short. If everything she suspected of Lily were true, then she was not only a liar, but an extremely clever and accomplished one.

Peter seemed to read the doubt in her eyes. 'I don't think any of us really know what she's capable of,' he said. 'I don't know Guy Brody well enough to judge which of them is telling the truth, but it's my job to protect you, Delia.'

She could vividly picture the first two railway stations where the train had stopped after leaving Budapest, of the two missed chances she'd had to get off and go back to put things right. This moment felt just as urgent, and this time she had at least to try to remedy the past.

'And it's my job to protect Lily,' she told him, hoping that, somewhere in the universe, Anna could hear her.

40

LILY

When Lily walked in and saw the men gathered around the conference table in the film company's Soho Square offices, she was almost glad that Delia had insisted on accompanying her. Not because she felt the need of the older woman beside her, but because Delia's presence would help fuel her anger.

Once she had recovered from the shock, she hadn't really been all that surprised by Guy's cynical manoeuvre or his instinct to save himself from scandal. She knew what he was. And yet a small part of her had believed he owed her some loyalty.

So she'd got it wrong. It hardly mattered. Hurt feelings were for idiots. She had nothing to cry about. And Guy would soon learn it was a mistake to underestimate her.

What truly hurt was that, until the moment she'd been jolted awake in his car by a crunch and a skid, she'd felt on the brink of an entirely new future that she had earned with her own hard work. A glimpse of a future that had shown her not only how completely consumed she'd become by the past, but also, more importantly, how she might seek to escape from it. Even the accident and subsequent police involvement had initially been a nuisance that Guy would sort out. It wasn't until they told her how Guy had lied to the police, and that, as a result, she'd have to go and stay with Delia, that she'd seen how easily she could be sucked back into her old existence.

At first Peter had tried to persuade her not to come to this meeting, telling her it was best to leave him and the other executives to deal with the problem. Contemptuous, she'd dug in her heels, forcing him to give way. But then he'd stuck to his guns when she wanted to go and pick up clean clothes from her Smith Street flat. Concerned that the police would, after all, have tipped off the press, he'd insisted on sending an assistant for whatever she needed. Luckily she'd remembered that Delia had some Benzedrine in her bathroom cabinet, and had managed to pocket the half-empty canister.

The men stood when she came in with Delia. Peter introduced the grey-haired man bowing formally to them as Max Lewis, the film company's lawyer. Lily had met the PR man, Charlie Flynn, once or twice before he'd turned up at the Gerald Road police station. James was also there, although the film director had the grace to look embarrassed, as if he knew very well that someone had cooked up a story. Guy, however, had the brass neck to come around the table, kiss her cheek and, with a solicitous hand on her elbow, guide her to a chair. It was all she could do not to jerk her arm free of him.

Taking her place beside Delia, she was aware of how vividly her youth singled her out. Never mind, these old fools would soon find out what she was capable of.

Max Lewis coughed lightly. 'I'm pleased to say that the news from the hospital is much better than we hoped. The cyclist was concussed but regained consciousness overnight and there appears to be no lasting head injury. He has, however, broken his leg and will have a valid claim for compensation. As Miss Brooks was driving, Mr Brody's motor insurance won't provide cover. And there is the additional problem that she has committed a criminal offence by driving without a licence.'

Lily stared at a spot on the wall, waiting to discover how the others would respond.

Delia looked at Guy. 'Perhaps this is the time to correct any misunderstanding about what happened,' she suggested courteously.

Everyone else turned to Guy, who cracked his slow smile. 'First of all I'd like to hear how this mess is going to be resolved,' he said. 'Charlie, what's your advice?'

'Well, the police have yet to bring charges,' the PR man replied. 'I had a useful chat with the sergeant at Gerald Road. I'm sure we can straighten things out. If we can agree payment directly with the cyclist, the whole thing can be put behind us.'

'He'll have to accept payment with no admission of liability,' said the lawyer. 'And sign a confidentiality agreement.'

'Of course,' Flynn agreed.

'And if gossip leaks out anyway?' asked James. 'What then?'

'Then I suggest we select a sympathetic journalist to whom Miss Brooks can give a candid yet heart-warming interview about the pressures of fame at such a young age,' said Flynn. 'Throw in a little childhood adversity, *Rebel Without a Cause*, that kind of thing. Shouldn't be too hard to turn the tide of opinion our way. Might even work to our advantage.'

'Except that my daughter wasn't driving.' Delia's voice was clear as a bell.

Lily closed her eyes, willing herself not to round on Delia and tear into her with the truth that she wasn't *her* daughter, she was *Anna*'s daughter. Remember Anna? But that moment would have to wait. Meanwhile she didn't know which was the more sickening: Delia's persistence in the delusional belief that Lily was hers, or her maudlin faith that she could magically put everything right.

'We're not after the bubblegum girl-next-door image for Lily,' Flynn responded. 'A little unruliness – shall we call it? – may be no bad thing.'

'That's not the point,' said Delia. 'Is it, Peter?'

Lily stared at Peter. She knew he still doubted that she hadn't been driving. She knew, too, that she deserved his mistrust, but that didn't stop her despising him for it.

'If the police do decide to prosecute Lily for driving without a licence,' Peter said carefully, 'that would have serious consequences for Lily and therefore for all of us. But if Guy were to accept responsibility, it would merely be an unfortunate accident. He wasn't incapable through drink, so at worst it'd be a slap on the wrist.'

'I think you're missing the point,' said Flynn.

'Which is?' Peter asked.

'It would still be a story. Out late with an eighteen-year-old? He's a married man, a war hero. Women love him and men admire him. I'm sure none of us want to damage that image.'

'What if I do?' said Lily.

Flynn's smile showed his teeth, and his eyes glittered. 'Then we'd have to consider closing down the movie as of now,' he said. 'Of course that would be hugely disappointing, particularly for James, and costly for the American producers who have put up the money, but there we are. Better to cut our losses sooner rather than later.'

James looked horrified. 'Come on, you two,' he appealed to Lily and Guy. 'You've seen the rushes. You've been working brilliantly together. The best is yet to come.'

Guy waved a hand nonchalantly 'I have a pile of other scripts my agent wants me to read.'

'Let me talk to Lily alone,' said Delia.

'No,' said Lily. 'I don't need to be spoken to. Guy was driving. That's the story.'

Flynn leaned forwards. 'Lily, sweetheart, if you shoot down this project, you'll never work again.' He laid his open palms on the polished surface of the table. 'So help me, that's the truth.'

'I'm afraid he's right,' said Peter.

'So what?' Lily looked at each man in turn. 'I don't care.'

'Lily, please,' begged Delia. 'You're only hurting yourself.'

Lily flinched as Delia reached out to touch her.

Guy laughed. 'Don't worry, Delia. She thinks she's still in character!' He shook his head in derision. 'Don't kid yourself that stars are born, that people other than us are going to recognize your natural talent and give you a break simply because they just can't help themselves. It won't happen. Stars are made, and by people like us. And if we unmake them, that's it. The carnival's over.'

Lily made an insolent slow handclap. 'Bravo, Guy. What script did that come from?'

'Don't be naive, Lily,' James said crossly. 'Sure, you can run to the papers with the story that Guy was driving, or even that he tried to blame you, but all that will happen is that people like Charlie here will take a few people out to lunch and guarantee far juicier stories and access to far bigger stars in return for not printing a word you tell them.'

Lily was taken aback. He was wrong about her being naive – she understood very well how power was wielded from behind the scenes – but she did lack the experience to know precisely how such things were achieved. It didn't matter, though. She refused to be a victim. She despised the Hollywood legend that limited women to a choice between doomed love or tragic death. Anna had drilled it into her that she had to be a survivor. She knew nothing else.

'I have other stories,' she said. 'About you, Guy. Perhaps your fans would like to hear how loudly you snore. And about you, Peter. And, James, that sweet young actor in Rome who played one of the musicians. The police here might like his name. I bet he's enough of a romantic fool to have kept hold of your letters and photos.'

Lily felt the rage grow inside her. She wanted to be a movie actor. She wanted to create something new, to have people tell her she was good at what she did. She didn't want to give up that little kernel of a new life. But the rage told her that what mattered more was to take revenge, not to care what people thought, not to worry about being liked, never to cry.

'Don't do this,' said Delia.

'I haven't finished yet.'

'Please, you're only hurting yourself.'

Lily appealed to the men around the table. 'I have secrets to tell about Delia, too.'

'I know,' Delia said quietly. 'It's no good, Lily, you can't do me any harm. I already know.'

41

Lily ran. The sincerity in Delia's eyes made it impossible to stay. Her kindness was hateful, almost as intolerable as the revelation that, all this time, Delia had been feigning ignorance. When had she found out? How? Was it thanks to that creep Frank Landry, always skulking around and nosing into things that didn't concern him? She hated them all.

Rounding a corner she found herself in a street market and had to slow down to make headway against the crowd of shoppers. She ducked down the nearest alley. A smell of discarded and rotting vegetables hung in the air and, too late, she realized the narrow space was lined with shops selling pornographic magazines. Two men loitering in front of some lurid posters outside a basement strip-club turned and leered at her, moving to block her path.

'Hello, darling. Where are you off to in such a hurry?'

'You want to get past? Give us a little kiss first, then.'

Something in her fierce expression caused them to move aside and find the courage to jeer only once she was walking away. She emerged onto a wider street and, regaining her bearings, headed for a coffee bar she remembered visiting once before. She was relieved to find an unoccupied table away from the window. The effects of the Benzedrine she'd taken that morning were wearing off, and she suddenly felt utterly spent, as if all her energy was draining away through the soles of her feet and into the floor. She ordered a double espresso with hot milk. She hadn't eaten properly for days, but couldn't face any of the pastries displayed in the window. Besides, she liked the feeling of hunger. It was familiar, and it fed her anger.

They had no idea who she was, those over-confident men in their expensive suits who'd simply expected her to do as she was told. They had not lived, as she had done, perched under the rafters of someone else's house. They had not tended a mother who woke screaming in the night, went white with terror at the sight of barbed wire or fell cowering to the ground, begging for her life in an incomprehensible language, when a dog barked at her in the street.

They didn't understand that Lily was afraid of nothing. She had grown up with nothing and could get by without any of them. Until she was nine years old she'd lived in a large detached suburban house belonging to the Jacobs family. They had generously responded to their synagogue's appeal for help by offering Lily's seventeen-year-old mother and her tiny baby a cramped attic flat in return for whatever light housework Anna was well enough to do.

It never seemed to occur to Anna that the situation had been offered as a temporary respite, and she'd simply dug in, satisfied with the little she had. Her education in Hungary had ended when she was barely fifteen, yet she spoke several languages. Mr Jacobs had once told Lily that he'd offered many times to help her mother find a proper job where she could make use of her languages, but Anna had refused in any circumstances to utter a word of German. And ironically, although the Jacobses owned a chain of local delicatessens, in their home Anna maintained subsistence rations and hoarded food. She darned and mended every garment, yet could be transported with joy by the scent of even the smallest sliver of soap.

Anna had guarded their isolation. The Jacobs children were a decade older than Lily and had their own friends. Once Lily started school, Anna discouraged her from accepting any invitation from her classmates, or from bringing anyone home. Lily knew she stuck out as an odd, spiky child, dressed in hand-me-downs, who never joined in any after-school activities, and with a mother who scuttled away from any attempt at conversation by teachers or other parents. Too protective of Anna ever to protest, she simply got used to being on her own.

Anna was never healthy, her body too worn down by malnutrition compounded by typhus and pneumonia. But when Lily was seven or eight, something happened that, overnight, gave her mother fresh energy and purpose. Mrs Jacobs always made a point of telling Anna when the family would be out so, if they wanted, she and Lily could come downstairs and listen to records or the radio. Lily, whose school friends were always chattering about their favourite comedy programmes, was thrilled when, one Sunday lunchtime, her mother took her downstairs and turned on the set in time for *Billy Cotton's Band Show*. Anna seemed impatient until the bandleader introduced a new guest, Delia Maxwell, who would be singing her latest hit single. Then Anna leaned forwards in her chair, clasping her thin hands between her knees. Her deep-set eyes shone and her thin mouth was curled into a kind of snarling smile that Lily, at the time, took for a sign of pleasure. Lily was overjoyed to see her mother made almost beautiful and vital again, as well as by the prospect of them sharing such a frivolous entertainment.

'Listen,' Anna commanded, as Delia Maxwell began to sing.

So often deprived of music, laughter, abundance of any kind, Lily was enraptured by the haunting, silky voice that suggested so many trembling and unknown emotions.

When the song ended, Anna turned down the radio, went to the cabinet and pulled out two LPs, handing them to her daughter. Each bore a different photograph of the same radiant and smiling young woman wearing impossibly glamorous evening gowns, identified only by the single word, *Delia*. Lily didn't understand why her mother wanted her to take note of this dazzling creature, but she felt breathless with anticipation.

'She stole my life,' said Anna. 'When you grow up, I want you to take hers and destroy it.'

Even though Lily had no comprehension of how she, a child, could inflict any kind of mark upon such an otherworldly and obviously powerful creature, she had made the solemn promise that her mother demanded. She could still remember the bitter disappointment she felt when her mother abruptly switched off the radio, put away the two records, and marched them back up to their frugal rooms under the rafters.

Except in her nightmares, Anna seldom spoke of the camp, and Lily learned never to ask questions. After Anna's death, she watched a television documentary about the Holocaust and finally understood the full significance of the number tattooed on her mother's arm. Now able to understand what lay behind Anna's constant vigilance and dread, she saw how, in her mind, her mother had been incapable of leaving the camp where she had survived for over a year and where her parents, uncles, aunts and cousins had all been murdered.

If, as a young teenager, Lily had ever been tempted to forget about Delia Maxwell, those documentary images of atrocity made it impossible to shirk her promise – which was what those men around the table in the film-company offices could never understand.

42

Distracted by the rising noise in the coffee bar, Lily realized it must be lunch hour. As she looked around, eight young office girls trooped in together. They were similarly dressed and perhaps two or three years older than her. As they squeezed past to reach the few remaining seats at the back, one stopped and, with her hand on the back of the free chair across the table from Lily, asked if the seat was taken.

'No, help yourself,' said Lily, still immersed in her thoughts of the past. As the young woman sat down, Lily reached for her purse, ready to pay the bill and leave.

'Gosh, it's you!' exclaimed the young woman. 'Lily Brooks. Oh my goodness, I can't believe it! I absolutely love "Tell Me How It Ends". Can I have your autograph?'

She began rummaging in her handbag, and Lily had little choice but to smile politely and wait for her to produce a pen and a scrap of paper.

As Lily scribbled her name and 'good luck', the young woman beckoned to her friends who'd found places at adjoining tables. 'Look! It's Lily Brooks!'

Everyone turned to stare first at the noisy young woman and then at Lily, and several of the other girls got up and moved towards Lily's table. Lily was completely hemmed in as they crowded around, each of them demanding her signature.

'No,' she protested. 'I'm sorry, there's too many. I have to go.'

'It's just an autograph,' said the nearest girl, thrusting the back of an envelope in front of her.

Lily looked around helplessly. 'I'm sorry, I can't. Not now.'

She stood up and tried to make her way through a press of bodies unwilling to let her pass. 'Please,' she begged. 'Another time. Please let me go.'

She managed to reach the entrance where a man stood aside to let her out, looking at her curiously as the young women behind her shouted insults.

'Selfish cow!'

'Too stuck up for her own good!'

She escaped into the street, relieved to let the door close on the ugly voices, and walked swiftly away,

Nothing was going right today. She didn't regret her defiance at the meeting, but she had miscalculated the threats she'd made. It was rare for her to make that kind of mistake and she was more shaken than she cared to admit. She was forever haunted by memories of her mother's extreme and silent distress at the recognition of any kind of error, however small. The wrong postage stamp, a mislaid bus ticket or running out of milk: any one of these everyday lapses could leave Anna shaking with fear, watched in incomprehension by her little daughter. Later Lily understood how, within her mother's vivid inner world, Anna remained convinced that even the smallest mistake could provoke fatal brutality. Sometimes it would take days for Lily to calm her down, to stop her trembling or waking in the night with worse nightmares than before.

Lily had never regarded herself at those times as too young to cope. She had never experienced any life other than looking after her mother and being alert to anything that might upset her. She had been bereft when Anna died, not knowing what to put in place instead of her perpetual vigilance and care.

She stopped in the narrow Soho street, causing lunch-hour pedestrians to elbow her and mutter as they pushed past. She was suddenly so tired of everything having to be a calculation. And now, in spite of the rigid control she exerted over herself, her actions had backfired anyway.

Looking up, she saw how near she was to the offices of RMJ Records. Almost instinctively, she crossed the road, relieved to head for a familiar haven. As she entered, and told the young man on reception that she wanted to see Peter Jenks, a decision formed in her head about what she intended to do next.

Peter, who had only recently returned from the ill-fated meeting, greeted her apprehensively, holding up his hands in a gesture of surrender as if he thought she might fly at him and attack him physically.

'Lily, I don't know what's going on, but—'

'Didn't Delia tell you?'

'No. None of us wanted to dignify your attempts at intimidation, especially against your own mother. They were unworthy, Lily. I know you're young, but what you were threatening us all with was blackmail, pure and simple. It's unacceptable and highly offensive.'

Lily wasn't listening. She was trying to work out whether Peter was lying, preferring not to deal with the consequences of the truth, or whether Delia had kept quiet, in which case, why?

Delia hadn't been responsible for creating the lie that Lily was her daughter. It would be all too easy for her to present herself as the tragic dupe of a cruel pretence. Why had she not seized the opportunity to do so?

Not that it mattered. Lily had made a promise all those years ago and, to carry it out, she needed to retrieve control of the present situation.

'Lily!' said Peter. 'You have to take this seriously!'

'Is Guy still saying I was driving?' she asked.

Peter had the grace to look a little shamefaced. 'No.'

She gave a snort of contempt. 'So my threats worked.'

'Not any more.' Peter drew himself up. 'I'm not going to spell it out, but whatever hold you imagine you have over me, you can forget it from now on. I will take full responsibility towards my wife and family for my actions.'

'But I'm still under contract to RMJ Records?'

He looked surprised. 'Yes.'

'And to finish making the film?'

'Well, yes, but—'

'Then that's what I want to do.'

Peter was lost for words.

'There's no problem with that, is there?' Lily demanded. 'They can't fire me just because we had a heated discussion after I refused to collude in a deliberate falsehood about a car accident, can they?'

'Put like that, no. But you have to work with these people, Lily. There are two or three weeks of shooting yet to go.'

'They're professionals. They've already sunk a lot of money into the project. And Guy and I understand one another. We'll make it work.'

She watched him wrestle silently with the conflicting arguments. At last he shook his head in confusion.

'Oh, Lily, what are we to do with you? Sit down and let's try to have a proper talk. Get to the bottom of why you behave like this.'

'You sound like one of my old teachers.'

Ignoring her remark, Peter went to one of the buttoned leather sofas beside the fireplace. 'When I was your age we had a war to fight,' he said. 'I was leading a squadron at twenty-two. So I'm not going to patronize you by saying you're young and don't understand life. You're obviously more than capable of taking your own decisions, but I don't understand what it is you really want. When you first sang "Tell Me How It Ends" you told everyone at the awards ceremony how proud you were to be Delia Maxwell's daughter. And she's done nothing but support and defend you – as a mother should,' he added quickly, as if forestalling her objection. 'But what's happened? She's not the only one to blame for your unhappy childhood. What more do you expect her to do to prove herself to you?'

Lily bit back her instant riposte: *I want nothing from her!*

'What *did* Delia say after I left?' she asked instead.

'She said Guy had to tell the truth and take the consequences. Then she left.'

Why should Delia continue to defend her? Was it possible that Lily had misinterpreted Delia's words and that Delia still remained in ignorance of her true identity? Lily pushed aside the repugnant alternative, which was that this might be Delia's way to make amends. If she'd even once set eyes on her old school friend and seen how she'd destroyed Anna's life, she'd accept why that could never be possible. But, either way, it was clear that Delia hadn't confided anything in Peter, and if she hadn't told him, it was unlikely she'd told anyone else.

Peter patted the seat beside him. 'Come and sit down.'

She took a seat on the sofa opposite and stared at him warily.

'You and I need to trust each other if we're to go on working together,' he said. 'Agreed?'

Lily nodded, not bothering to hide her aversion.

'You know,' he went on, 'I don't fully agree with what Guy said earlier, that stars aren't born. Some are. You see, I've watched some of the rushes. James wanted to show Davey and me how well the songs were working. You might not yet have your mother's incredible voice, Lily, but you can certainly act. You have a brilliant future ahead of you in the movies, if that's what you want.' He paused for effect. 'But that will only happen if other people are prepared to work with you.'

'I get the point,' she answered drily, although she could feel her rebellious heart beating faster with the exhilarating potential of his words.

'You will have to apologize,' he said. 'This is only your first film. You haven't yet earned the right to behave like a prima donna.'

'I didn't start the quarrel with Guy,' she objected. 'He had no right to expect me to carry the can for him, especially when he didn't even have the courtesy to let me know what he was up to.'

'Charlie Flynn made that decision, not Guy,' Peter said impatiently. 'That's what he's paid for. Anyway, what I'm trying to find out is what *you* want. Do you want to act? Do you want it enough to pipe down and let me try to recover your position?'

For the first time in her life, she was tempted to feel a jab of regret over her past actions. Peter had always been kind to her, and she was almost sorry for the crude naivety of her attempt to gain control over him. But, she reminded herself, it was his fault for kissing her. He should have known better than to compromise himself. Nevertheless, he was now offering her something she really wanted.

'Why would you do that?' she asked.

'Because you'll make a lot of money for RMJ Records.'

When he said no more, and didn't smile or make a joke of his words, she found she was disappointed. She looked up and saw he was studying her, his eyes full of pity. That made her angry. *Don't say you're doing it for Delia's sake*, she thought. *Anything but that.*

He must have sensed her fury, for he sighed. 'Why do you always have to make it so hard for everyone? I want to help you because I think you could become a truly great film actress and because you deserve a chance at it.'

Despising herself for how badly she wanted to cry with relief, she made her response sound as grudging as possible. 'Just get me back on set. Make them stick to the contract, or else I will make real trouble for you all.'

43

Peter was right: although the accident was successfully squared away, with no adverse publicity and a generous pay-out for the injured cyclist, it wasn't so easy for Lily to repair the damage, especially with James, who forced her to take a couple of days off by reshuffling the schedule to shoot scenes for which she was not required. Peter offered to accompany her on her first day back on set, but she refused, afraid that Guy and James would regard it as a sign of weakness. She wasn't happy, either, when Peter said that Frank Landry, as RMJ Records' head of security, might look in on her from time to time to make sure she was being treated with respect. Peter's accompanying look made it clear that Frank's occasional presence wasn't negotiable, and she guessed he'd also be there to report on whether or not she was behaving herself.

As luck would have it, on her return they were to shoot an early sequence in the story where Lily's character, the gifted ingénue, and Guy's, the fading star, admit they are in love and run away to get married. Their first location was an ornate Victorian bandstand in a large park in the depths of south London. The late summer weather was ideal, and the crew's spirits seemed lifted by being amid greenery in the open air.

Lily was nervous. James hid his animosity behind a frosty formality that his crew immediately sensed and imitated. Although Guy greeted her with professional amiability, she was not looking forward to their love scenes. Sure enough, when directed to take her in his arms, he pressed himself against her as he had that morning against the fountain in Campo de' Fiori – a demonstration not of desire but of power. What she was not expecting from their first kiss, however, was the sharp, sour taste of raw onion. She recoiled and heard James exasperatedly shout, 'Cut!' Guy gave a satisfied grin, pulled out a handkerchief and spat something into it before turning to wink at the boom operator.

She'd known he'd find a way to retaliate, but that didn't stop her hissing at him, 'You pig!'

He laughed, snaking his arm around her waist to pull her close again ready for the second take. He took a deep breath and expelled it straight into her face.

Keep your eye on the prize, Lily ordered herself. She looked up at him, smiled as enigmatically as she knew how, and melted into his arms. 'That Academy Award you said you wanted?' she whispered sweetly into his ear. 'If you're not careful, it'll be me winning it, not you, just like it is in the script.' She turned to call to James: 'Sorry about that. I'm ready now.'

When they broke for the crew to set up the next shot, rather than retreat to the trailer caravan that served as her dressing room, Lily made a point of queuing at the catering truck with everyone else. She laughed unobtrusively at their banter, doing her best to signal that she could take a joke and that she fully appreciated her role was to help their jobs run smoothly. When she was sure that no one was looking, she swallowed the extra couple of pills she'd hidden in a pocket of her costume.

The rest of the morning went well as Lily did her best to channel her steely resolve to act Guy off the screen into her character's eager romantic excitement. It must have worked, for James demanded more close-ups and reaction shots of her than of Guy, a comparison she was certain Guy would also have noted. Wrapping at lunchtime, she walked across the grass to her trailer, pleased with how she'd handled her return to the lion's den. As she climbed the steps and opened the door she waved gaily to the row of fans pressed against the park railings fifty yards away. Several of them began screaming in delight. It was only as her eyes adjusted to the dim light inside the caravan that she saw she had a visitor.

'I'm sorry to turn up like this,' said Delia, rising from the banquette seat, 'but you've been avoiding me.'

Determined to mend fences wherever she could, Lily kept her tone light and mild. 'Not intentionally, I've just been busy.'

She accepted Delia's customary embrace, then went to brush her hair at the built-in dressing-table as an excuse to sit as far away as she could. Delia's lush, pampered body seemed to take up too much room in the tight space of the trailer, and her sickly perfume lingered on the enclosed air.

'How's it gone today?' asked Delia. 'Is Guy behaving himself?'

'If you don't count his bad breath.'

Although Delia laughed, sounding relieved at Lily's lack of hostility, she soon looked serious again. 'I thought perhaps we should talk.'

'What about?' Lily put down the hairbrush and bought a little more time by peering into the mirror to touch up her frosted lipstick. It was clear that Delia had come here to say something important, perhaps even for a final showdown, but she was damned if she'd offer any assistance.

'You do believe I want to help you, don't you, Lily?'

'Of course.'

'Then why do you fight me?'

Lily shrugged at her reflection in the mirror. 'I'm a fighter. I've had to be.'

Delia frowned. 'You made me promise not to ask you about your past, and I haven't. But is there anything you'd like to know about me, about my family and where I grew up?'

When Anna had grown steadily frailer, her flesh shrinking away, the only thing Lily had had to cling to, the only thing that ever gave her a sense of power and purpose, had been her promise to bring about Delia's ruination. The urge now to tell Delia about her mother's death, the desolate funeral with only the loyal Jacobs family there to place their stones on the freshly dug grave, was overwhelming. *You*, she wanted to scream right in Delia's face, *you killed her! Why are you here when she isn't?*

Instead she acted the part of the alienated teenager whose moody behaviour could be overlooked. 'Not really,' she answered.

'I can tell you about my family, about my childhood in Budapest, and everything that happened during the war. I have a photograph of my parents with my little sister Zsofia that I can show you. If that's what you want, you only have to ask.'

Delia was almost begging, but for what? *Did* she know that Lily was Anna's daughter? Surely she must. In which case, was she simply too afraid – too *guilty* – to come straight out with it?

Either way, Delia's confusion gave Lily a pleasurable sense of being back in control. Delia's discomfort felt right. It was only a tiny piece of the price she ought to pay.

A new thought struck her: perhaps Delia was only hesitating because she wasn't yet certain what *Lily* knew.

'A photograph of my grandparents?' Lily asked, turning to face Delia so she could watch her reaction.

The hesitation was minimal. 'Yes.'

Delia smiled but Lily was certain she'd caught a glimpse of fear behind her eyes that revealed her reluctance to bring the truth out into the open unless she absolutely had to. Very well. It would be easy enough to go on convincing Delia that she had no inkling of it.

'Maybe later,' Lily said. 'I've enough emotions swirling around my head trying to stay in character. Perhaps once the movie is finished.'

'Of course,' said Delia. 'Whatever you like. I just wanted you to know that – well, that I'll always be here for you.'

Lily turned back to the mirror and smiled gratefully at Delia's reflection. It would work to her advantage to let Delia continue to be her mother, at least until she found the means to bring her promise to an effective conclusion.

44

FRANK

I'd been annoyed when Peter asked me to drop in on the film set once in a while to keep an eye on Lily and make sure she was all right. He'd explained it was because there'd been 'an unpleasantness', which had been cleared up, and he'd rather not discuss it, but it might cause difficulties for her. I couldn't see Lily being anyone's victim, or understand why he should feel the least bit protective towards her. I wondered what could have softened his attitude. I doubted it was because Delia had confided in him: if she had, he'd also know that I'd uncovered the truth and not shared it with him. I prayed Delia hadn't been foolish enough to spin yet more stories to protect the girl from whatever trouble she'd got herself into.

I had every reason to want to see the back of her. Since I'd given Delia Lily's birth certificate, Delia had made excuses not to see me, fobbing me off whenever I'd called to suggest dinner or some other outing. Yet I remained fairly confident that, if only this business with Lily could be resolved, there was every chance that Delia would return my feelings. However, I needed to be certain I wasn't deluding myself before I could make the right decision about whether to call and arrange to meet Evelyn's son. I still had her envelope in my breast pocket. Time was running out before she flew back east and I had yet to make up my mind what to do for the best. Was the boy my son? And, even if he was, had I left it too late to be his father?

Acting on Peter's request, I turned up very early one morning to where James Sinclair was shooting his film in a leafy square in Bayswater. If I had hoped to escape my emotional confusion by paying attention to how a film was made, I soon discovered that the process consisted mostly of long periods of hanging around while, at any one time, only three or four of the dozens of people present appeared to do any work. I caught a glimpse of Lily when she arrived, walking swiftly from the car to her trailer, which was parked on a blocked-off side street beside numerous other vehicles. She scowled when she spotted me, probably regarding me correctly as Peter's spy. Not that I'd been expecting much of a welcome. It was the first time I'd seen her since her birthday party and I was rather shocked by the change in her. She'd lost weight and, without make-up, had dark rings under her eyes. I supposed the pressure of maintaining her lies must be taking its toll.

I went up to one of the middle-aged women who sat smoking in a huddle of canvas-backed camping chairs behind the camera and lighting equipment, asked if I could borrow a copy of the script, and went over to an old wooden bench beneath a tree. The gardens in the square had run to seed and the once-handsome stucco terraces, with their pillared entrances, had also seen better days. The sun, already gaining height, cast shadows on the tired summer grass. The bench was covered with powdery green lichen and still bore a metal plaque in memory of a nineteen-year-old who had fallen in the Great War, placed there by his parents.

To begin with I couldn't make head or tail of the unfamiliar layout of the annotated and well-thumbed pages, but eventually I grasped how to read them. I'd regarded a film director as a glorified ringmaster but, as I began to grasp the almost military logistics involved in bringing together the many different skills required to turn these lines into a real and dramatic world, my respect increased not only for James Sinclair but also, grudgingly, for Lily and her co-star, Guy Brody.

When she finally emerged from her trailer, in full camera make-up and a simple costume of a plain short-sleeved white dress, she radiated a kind of hard, shiny defiance. Her brittle fragility was almost painful to watch and, seeing her up close, I was amazed that no one else appeared to notice the obvious effects of amphetamine use in her black, dilated pupils.

I felt no sympathy for her. I'd be only too delighted to watch her trip herself up and have her lies exposed. And if an opportunity arose for me to sabotage her career and cause her to be expelled from Delia's world for ever, I'd seize it without a second thought.

I moved to a position behind the camera but out of everyone's way so that I could watch the scene between Lily and Guy Brody being played out on the wide front steps of a house facing into the gardens. In the script, Lily's character thinks that Guy's is about to say goodbye before returning to America, but then he surprises her with a proposal of marriage. I knew better than anyone how Lily's 'smile when your heart is breaking' routine was all an act and yet, once she went in front of the camera, I finally saw why James Sinclair had wanted to use her in place of Delia – not that Delia's own style wouldn't have been superb, but Lily had directness, an emotional ruthlessness, that stemmed from more than just her youth. I wondered what Guy Brody made of his co-star, and whether future audiences would even notice that he was also on screen.

The essential manipulation that lay at the heart of her performance fuelled my anger at her trickery. Her deception had been well planned and deliberate. Whether prompted by opportunism, pure mischief, or something more darkly personal I had no idea, but I hated her for taking up so much of Delia's time and attention and leaving nothing for me. I loved Delia while Lily wanted only to hurt her. Why on earth did Delia choose to go on with this charade? I knew she made excuses not to see me only because she didn't want me probing further into Lily's background, but her continued indulgence of Lily was surely placing her in danger. I wished she'd trust me.

I was impatient for the day to end. I'd arranged to meet Celeste that evening and was already anticipating what a heart-to-heart with Delia's oldest friend might – perhaps inadvertently – reveal that would help me to make sense of Delia's flawed decisions.

My telephone rang as I was leaving the flat for my appointment with Celeste. I almost let it go unanswered, but the possibility of it being Delia made me rush back inside. It was Evelyn, who had got my number through Directory Enquiries. She was coming to London the following day and it would be wrong, she said, for her to return to her husband without having introduced me to her son.

45

Celeste had suggested that we dine together at a Hungarian restaurant in Soho. I arrived as she was being seated. It was already
busy and she had to squeeze into her place on the upholstered
wooden bench. The wall behind her was covered with framed
caricatures and cartoons, and the air was blue with cigarette
smoke. She smiled easily when she saw me. Her former air of
dejection had vanished, chased away, I hoped, by the excitement
of her new business venture.

'Conrad used to bring me here,' she said, after our greetings.
'After 1956, when so many Hungarians fled the Soviet occupa-
tion, it became a place for the émigrés to meet up. And,' she
added drily, 'the food is interesting.'

I glanced at the menu – goulash, smoked goose and cold cherry
soup – although the noisy laughter, gossip and argument rising
from the other tables suggested that the clientele was not there
primarily for the cuisine. Somehow it was easy to picture Conrad Durand sitting and smoking at one of these tables, at once
both convivial and observant.

'Did Conrad bring Delia here, too?' I asked.

'No, not often,' she said.

'I'd have thought she'd have felt at home, hearing her own language around her.'

'I think it was more to do with not resurrecting the past,' she said. 'Hungary was something she'd left behind.'

'But presumably Conrad could meet up with old friends here?' I asked. Once the waiter had taken our orders, an idea began to form: perhaps someone there might have known the families of either Irma Székely or Lily's mother, Anna Körmöczy, back in Budapest before the war. And, if I couldn't start by asking direct questions about them, perhaps I could begin by finding out more about Conrad Durand.

Celeste looked at me shrewdly. 'You shouldn't be jealous of a dead man, you know.'

I felt myself colouring. She was right: I was jealous. But I still suspected Celeste was blinding herself to the probability that Conrad had fathered Delia's child.

'That's not why I'm asking,' I told Celeste. I couldn't bring myself to share my immediate preoccupation, which was that, before leaving my flat, I'd arranged to meet Evelyn and her son the following morning. She was flying home in a couple of days and I was desperate to know where I stood with Delia before meeting Simon.

'You wanted me to find out what happened to Lily to make her so angry and manipulative,' I said instead. 'And that's what I'm trying to do. In my experience, the most unlikely leads can turn out to be rewarding. Conrad was obviously very well con-nected. One of those connections might lead back to some useful family background in Hungary.'

Celeste didn't look convinced, but she nodded reluctantly.

'Very well, I'll introduce you to some people here who might be able to help. But before you go digging, I'm going to tell you something important because I think you really need to hear it. Conrad was a very private man, very discreet, but he and I became real friends. He had a gift for friendship and he and I understood each other.' She took a deep breath. 'I've never told anyone this, not even Delia, but the love of Conrad's life was killed in the war. His name was Jozef.'

I coloured even more, this time from the shame of my determination to misjudge a man everyone had repeatedly told me was loyal and generous.

'My theory,' she went on, 'is that having to take care of Delia so soon after Jozef's death helped Conrad recover from his grief. From then on he poured all his energy and love into her.'

'I see. And thank you for telling me.'

'You're never to mention this to anyone,' she ordered me.

'Of course not.' I blurted out my next question before I could stop myself. 'So who did father Delia's child?'

'That's none of your business,' she said firmly. 'That's between Delia and Lily.'

With so many secrets, so many layers of deception and misconception, how was I ever to find my feet on firm enough ground to make the decision that faced me: was I willing to give up Delia to be with my son? Or give up my son to be with her?

If Simon was my son.

If Delia wanted to be with me.

As a waiter served our food, I tried to imagine introducing Delia to my family. We weren't close, but I wondered what my parents and sister would make of our relationship, and she of them.

On the other hand, how would my parents react if I suddenly presented them with a grandson they'd known nothing about? Evelyn had said she'd been looking at schools for Simon. Would I be able to afford the fees? If I were named as co-respondent in a divorce, would she even win custody of the boy?

I had no appetite for the stew with sour cream and dumplings placed before me. My misery prompted me to confide in Celeste after all.

'You've guessed that I'm in love with Delia?'

'Yes.' Her smile was sympathetic. 'But, before you ask, I have no idea what her feelings might be.'

'But you are still worried about Lily?'

'I don't like her. I think she's a spoiled brat with no real affection for Delia at all. But I don't want to lose Delia's friendship because of her.'

I sighed. In the end, all my dilemmas returned to the same fundamental question: why was Delia covering up for Lily? Why go on pretending when the truth was bound to be revealed eventually? Could it be because Delia herself had something to hide? And, if so, how harmful could her secret be?

I felt Celeste's hand on mine. 'Don't go running towards ruin, Frank,' she said. 'Try to break free.'

I started to protest, but her fingers tightened their grip.

'I can see it in your face,' she said. 'And I understand. It's like a sickness. I—'

She stopped herself, but I could guess what she'd been about to say: that she, too, had suffered by loving Delia.

She recovered herself. 'The only time I've ever seen Delia positively glow with love has been for Lily,' she said. 'No man is ever going to compete with her daughter.'

'I can't walk away,' I said, forcing down my fury at all the harm Lily had done. 'Lily isn't to be trusted. And Delia's going to end up badly hurt.'

'Do what you feel is right about Lily,' she said, 'but please be Delia's friend, and don't try asking for more. Not yet anyway.'

I was desperate to know how different Celeste's advice would be if she knew that Lily wasn't Delia's daughter and had faked it from the beginning. Would she still counsel me to stay away? Unable to tell her the truth, I had to pretend to agree. But her ignorance proved how dangerously isolated and alone Delia was, and how vulnerable that made her to attack. Only I knew enough to protect her.

46

The lift attendant, clad in green Harrods livery, announced the fourth floor and pointed me in the right direction. It had been decades since I had visited the pet department but, trying to come up with a suitable place to engineer a supposedly chance meeting with a six-year-old boy, I'd remembered what a treat it used to be when my mother had brought me here at about his age. It didn't look as if it had changed much, and I was amazed at how instantly the sharp smell of fresh sawdust, mixed with the cloying sweetness of animal dung, swept me back in time to those occasional special shopping trips in town.

I lingered deliberately in front of the cages, recalling my childish fascination at the little tortoises scrambling in slow motion over each other's backs, the glass boxes of white mice and fancy rats, the thrill of a snake and, of course, the sad and lonely puppies that I had begged to take home. I rounded a corner and came across another remembered scene: a small boy neatly dressed in grey shorts, shirt and sleeveless jumper being photographed with a long-tailed monkey on his shoulder. He was holding tightly to the red leather leash and beaming excitedly. With the picture taken and the animal removed, his mother turned to me with feigned surprise.

'Why, hello,' said Evelyn, holding out her gloved hand. 'How funny to run into you. What brings you here?'

'I'm tempted to buy a dog,' I said, shaking her hand politely.

'Simon, this is an old friend, Mr Landry.'

He held out a small polite hand. 'How do you do?'

He had light brown hair and blue eyes, but I couldn't see any other immediate family resemblance. My sister in Nottingham had two girls whom I hardly ever saw, so it was no good comparing him to my nieces. Perhaps I should have made a flying visit home to ask my mother for the family album so I could remind myself of what I'd looked like at his age. However hard I tried, I failed to remember Evelyn's husband's features sufficiently to judge if the boy took after him.

I held Simon's hand, touched his skin yet, contrary to so many of my dreams, I felt no instant shock of recognition, no visceral sense that here was my own flesh and blood. I was suddenly and stupidly nervous. What was he seeing? A man of nearly forty, who had been one of life's drifters. I had nothing to offer the boy.

He disengaged his hand and turned to Evelyn. 'Can I have a dog, Mummy?'

She stroked back his hair. 'No, darling, I'm sorry. We can't take a puppy with us on the aeroplane.'

He looked downcast but didn't argue or whine. He seemed a bright little chap but so very young. Were they really planning to leave him in some chilly boarding school thousands of miles from home? I'd never understood why a certain class of Englishman considered that necessary at such a tender age. A madcap idea came to me about becoming a kind of guardian-uncle figure who could visit him at school, take him out for tea and cake and get to know him without ever having to bust up other people's lives – or my own. Even as I pictured myself sitting beside him to watch the cricket at Lord's, I knew it was a ludicrous fantasy.

'Perhaps they'd allow a lion cub to fly,' I joked, hearing the slightly hysterical tone in my voice. 'They sell those here, you know. And alligators and baby elephants.'

He looked at me seriously. 'I've seen elephants. And lots of monkeys. And there are tigers in the jungle. A friend of Daddy's has a tiger skin on the floor that he shot himself.'

I looked at Evelyn, beseeching her to give me a sign: was he my son? She gave a tiny nod, holding my gaze. So it was true. I was a father. I looked at the boy again, but felt nothing. I didn't know it was possible to feel so empty.

'It seems silly to take a photo of him with a monkey when the gardens at home are so often overrun with them,' she said, forcing a lightness into her voice that she couldn't possibly feel. 'But it'll make a nice present for his grandparents. They've got used to having him around the last few weeks and will miss him.'

Simon turned and looked up at her. 'They'll have me for half-term holidays once I'm at school, though, won't they?'

She ruffled his hair and smiled. 'They will. Lucky them.'

A disloyal thought struck me: did she want me back in her life only to help her precipitate a break so she could come to live in England and not have to be parted from her child? I scotched the idea immediately. Ironically, given that she'd been a married woman conducting a clandestine affair, I'd never known Evelyn be anything but straight and true. It was one of the things I'd loved about her.

Loved. If I'd had any doubts, I knew then for certain that I no longer loved her. That realization felt like a huge milestone in my life. For so long I had regarded my love for her as something so powerful that it would endure for ever. I had kept the little flame alive for the past seven years and now I watched it go out. I felt disillusioned, diminished – and liberated.

All I could offer was to acknowledge my son, if that was what she wanted, but it was no good pretending she and I could ever be together.

'May I take you for a cup of coffee?' I asked. 'And an ice-cream soda, if that's allowed?'

Evelyn looked at her watch. 'The photographs will be ready in half an hour, so that will pass the time nicely, won't it, Simon?'

'What about the toy department?'

'After we pick up the photographs.'

He wasn't too impressed at having to sit quietly while we drank our coffee, even with his choice of a chocolate milkshake in front of him, but he was too well behaved to make a fuss.

'Why didn't you tell me?' I asked quietly. 'When we still had time to decide differently.'

'I've already explained.' She paused before looking at me directly. 'Are you over all that now, all that trauma? Because I'm not so sure you are.'

'I'm fine,' I said, bitter that her lack of belief had denied me the chance to be a father, that she had instead chosen a bully who no longer loved her. Did I really owe her anything?

She stared into her coffee cup and shook her head sadly, saying something so softly that I didn't hear.

'What did you say?' It came out more harshly than I intended.

'I thought you'd be different,' she said. 'I thought by now you'd have got over whatever happened to you out there.'

She looked miserable, and I discovered that, after all, she had retained the power to move my emotions, to make me wish wildly that I could wave a magic wand and make everything come straight again. She was right. I had been in a bad way, suffering from flashbacks and strange attacks of panic that must have frightened her. I'd thought I was in control when I wasn't. I glanced at the boy, his head bowed over his milkshake, and longed for the clarity I'd always felt when flying, for that purifying mental escape up through the grey overcast and out into a gin-clear sky. If only the rest of life could be as simple as that.

'I think this was a mistake,' she said. 'I should have just walked quietly away when I saw you by the perfume counter the other day.'

'I'm truly sorry.'

'I'm sorry, too. I really am.'

'I don't know how we start to unravel it,' I said. 'It's too complicated. But if there's anything you need from me, anything I can do to help, you know I'd never—'

She nodded without looking at me, then got to her feet, holding out a hand. 'Say thank you to Mr Landry for your drink, Simon, and let's go and see if the photographs are ready.'

As I sat and watched Evelyn walk away, I knew that she would never tell the boy the truth. I recalled how I'd spoken to Delia about the story of Orpheus and Eurydice, and held my breath to see if either of them would turn to look back. Neither did.

47

Celeste's introductions at the Hungarian restaurant bore fruit, and the following morning I returned to Greek Street for a quiet word with the owner. Victor, she had told me, wasn't Hungarian but had lived in Budapest before the war and, rumour had it, once worked for British military intelligence there. I told him a vague lie about having a client who wanted to trace his family history and asked if he knew anyone who might remember the families of either Irma Székely or Anna Körmöczy.

The name Körmöczy meant nothing to him, but his face lit up at the mention of Székely: he had known Oskar and Eva before the war. They had been good friends of Conrad Durand. Victor had met them when they all used to dine together at the restaurant where he'd trained in Budapest.

'They were fun,' he said, 'good company and generous-hearted.'

He appeared unaware that they had any connection to Delia Maxwell and, as Celeste had also warned me that he was famously indiscreet, I kept that to myself. In any case, his face immediately clouded over.

'But I heard there was some kind of fuss about them after I left,' he said, 'some odd scandal, one of those things that seem to blow up out of nothing. That must have been during the war.'

I was intrigued, but, doing my best to disguise it, waited to hear more.

'In any case,' he went on, 'what does it matter now? They died so terribly, all of them.' He shook his head. 'So many old friends gone.'

I told him I'd be interested to speak to anyone who might know what had happened, however trivial, and he offered to ask around. He proved as good as his word. The following day he rang me with the name and telephone number of the sister-in-law of one of his regular patrons, who might remember something about the old scandal. She had grown up in Hungary before the war, he said, and then was sent to Auschwitz-Birkenau. She was the only one of her family to survive.

I telephoned Miriam Cuthbertson immediately. To my surprise, she agreed to see me and offered precise directions to her house in Hertfordshire. As I drove there I tried not to think too much about Simon and Evelyn. I could picture the boy's face perfectly, and knew the image would never leave me. Although, now I'd had time to think about our chance meeting, I doubted that Evelyn had really meant to offer me a second chance. She had made her choice long ago in that hotel room in Kuala Lumpur. Nonetheless, I regretted I hadn't handled our meetings better. I should have asked more questions and established what kind of life she and her son were returning to. And I could have left it open for her to contact me again if she ever changed her mind. I accepted what she'd said about my problems – I had suffered a kind of shell shock – but if she'd told me she was having our child that might have been enough to snap me out of it and our lives could have turned out very differently.

But there was no going back in time. The war and its aftermath had cast long shadows over too many lives.

I located the Cuthbertsons' house without too much trouble. It had been built fairly recently, with one of those driveways that curved past the front entrance and exited back onto a leafy road through a second gateway. The front door faced a semi-circular lawn bordered by a beech hedge. Victor had told me that Miriam's husband was an eminent surgeon.

She answered the door herself. She was perhaps in her early forties and tall for a woman, with the straight, slim figure of an athlete. The day was warm, yet she wore a pleated tartan skirt with a heather-coloured twin-set that looked like cashmere. Her gold wristwatch and double strand of pearls were discreetly expensive. She gave me an equally thorough once-over before inviting me in and then, as we each caught the other's eye, we both smiled.

She showed me into a large sitting room with a bay window overlooking a garden dotted with fruit trees that clearly predated the house.

'This plot used to be an orchard.' She spoke clearly with only the trace of a foreign accent. 'We'll get a good crop of apples in a month or so.'

A tray with cups, milk, sugar and a plate of biscuits was laid out ready. As she went to fetch the coffee I looked around: chintz curtains, comfortable sofas, family photographs in silver frames, copies of *Country Life*. It was hard to imagine a greater contrast with the newsreels I'd seen of the Nazi concentration camps. Perhaps that was the point.

'So you've been talking to Victor,' Miriam said, when she returned with a silver coffee pot. 'He spreads gossip like wildfire, which of course his customers enjoy, but sometimes it's necessary to set the record straight.'

'Please do,' I said. 'That's why I'm here.'

'Are you able to tell me why you want to know?'

I smiled. 'I'm afraid not.'

'Very well. How do you take your coffee?'

'Without milk, thank you. So you knew Oskar and Eva Székely in Budapest?'

'No, I never met them,' she said. 'I come from Pécs, not Budapest, but I heard all about the scandal because I became friends with the poor girl at the centre of it.'

I couldn't see how this girl could be Delia, and Lily, of course, hadn't been born, but I held my breath and waited.

'She believed that it was all their fault that she was in Birkenau,' she went on. 'That was why I wanted to speak to you. The only people to blame for any single one of us being in those camps were the Nazis. Everyone else did the best they could. It cannot be right after all this time to hold people to account for doing what they could to survive or to help their loved ones survive.'

As if readying herself to tell the story, Miriam pushed up the sleeves of her soft woollen cardigan, revealing the numbers tattooed in blue ink on her inner arm. She caught me looking and, rather than pull down her sleeve to cover them, she held out her arm to show me.

'One of my husband's colleagues is a plastic surgeon,' she said, 'but having it removed wouldn't change anything, would it?'

I began to ask myself whether it was a mistake to have come, whether I was about to hear a story I would regret learning, but there was no turning away from it now.

'So what happened?' I asked. 'What was the supposed scandal?'

'Simply a man doing everything in his power to save his child,' she replied, 'but at the expense of someone else's daughter. I make no excuses. What he did was wrong, but it was human. And for you to understand that, I must tell you the whole story, not just little parts of it. Only that entire slice of history can sufficiently explain what he did, and why he should be absolved. Do you understand?'

'Yes, a little,' I said. 'I flew for the RAF. I was shot down and spent a few months in a PoW camp. I know it's not the same thing at all, but towards the end, when we were moved from one place to another, we saw some of the other people on the road, saw enough to believe everything we heard later about the death camps.'

She nodded. 'Very well. I will tell you Anna's story, as I heard it when I knew her in Birkenau.'

'Anna?' Even though I was half expecting a familiar name, I was shocked to hear the same name as Lily's mother. Was it a coincidence or another long shadow of the past reaching out?

'Anna is enough,' said Miriam. 'I don't know if she's still alive, or if she'd even have wanted to go on living. So many chose not to, you know. In any case, I don't want you to find her. I want this to be an end.'

If Miriam was speaking of Anna Körmöczy, then I could have told her it was too late to find her, that Anna had survived and somehow come to England, only to die here when her daughter was nine years old. I had no wish to speak her name, either. Much as I wanted to hear Miriam's story, I had a terrible foreboding that I was going to wish I hadn't.

48

This was the story Miriam Cuthbertson told me.

Anna was at school in Budapest when the war began. She had never particularly thought of herself or her family as Jewish, but she gradually discovered that how they regarded themselves was no longer important. Within a year, the authorities informed her father that he could no longer teach at the university and that her older brother would have to abandon his medical studies. When she was twelve she found her mother weeping because her brother was being sent for labour service where men were forced to work under such brutal conditions that many of them never returned.

Before her brother left, he told Anna that he would do his best to escape, and that meanwhile they must both try to persuade their parents to leave Hungary by any means possible. It was her brother who told them that the Swiss Consulate was not only issuing diplomatic protection documents, which offered safe passage to neutral Switzerland, but also turning a blind eye to an underground organization that was copying them as fast as they could. He was marched away before he could obtain one to save himself, but the pain of his absence made Anna's father all the more determined to save his daughter.

All Anna knew was that papers – real or fake, she was never told – were procured. She was to travel alone because a child alone would face fewer checks and difficulties than a family group. The *Schutzbrief* required her photograph and it would have to be expertly fixed. Secrecy was vital, so they appealed to Oskar Székely, the father of Anna's closest school friend who ran a photographic portrait studio. Anna was forbidden to tell even her best friend anything about their plans.

When Anna's father returned to Oskar's studio to collect the precious protection document with the photograph attached, he found the place locked and silent. He went straight round to the family's apartment, but that, too, was apparently deserted. The following day Anna's best friend was absent from school. Anna never saw her again.

It soon leaked out that Anna's school friend had been seen boarding a train at Keleti station, and Anna's father let it be widely known that Oskar Székely had stolen the papers that would have secured Anna's escape, affixing a photograph of his own daughter so he could send her to safety in Switzerland in place of Anna.

As, of necessity, the Jewish community banded closer together, Oskar Székely was shunned. And Anna's father never recovered from the betrayal. He lost the will to resist. And, after news came that Anna's brother had died of typhus, both of her parents seemed to resign themselves to their fate.

As Anna turned fifteen, she felt the walls of her domestic world close in around her. Jews were no longer allowed telephones and it wasn't long before dubious officials began to appear at their door demanding whatever they wanted – first a sewing machine, then the family's vacuum cleaner and bed linen, and finally even her mother's wedding ring. Any gold belonging to Jews, they were informed, was now the property of the Reich.

Responsibility for her parents lay heavily on Anna's shoulders. She refused to admit how much she minded the loss of her childhood friend and instead found comfort in her steadily growing hatred and anger at what Irma had done. Had Anna been the one on that train steaming out of Hungary, away from the intensifying cruelty of the Nazi regime, perhaps her parents might have held on to just enough hope for the future to help them survive. But there was no good news to be found anywhere, and by the time Hitler occupied Hungary in March 1944, bringing first the yellow stars and curfews and then the ghettoes and deportations, Anna accepted that they were all trapped.

One night in April, against a background of air-raid alarms, soldiers pounded on their door and hustled them away, permitting each of them to take only an armful of possessions. They were marched to a disused brick factory where they found thousands of other Jewish people crammed together. Oskar Székely and his wife were, no doubt, among them. Anna and her parents remained there for a month, poorly fed, in dishevelled and unwashed clothes, her father unshaven, before being crammed into an overcrowded cattle truck on a train travelling north to Poland. They were lucky and managed to stay together in the same truck.

On arriving at Auschwitz-Birkenau, men and women were separated. She never saw her father again. There was then a further separation, with any women under fourteen or over forty ordered to a different line. Anna was told that her mother was going for a shower.

Left alone, she was stripped of most of her clothes and other belongings and given a ragged blue-and-white-striped dress and headscarf to wear instead. They shaved her head, tattooed her arm with a number and herded her to a hut where she was assigned a narrow wooden bunk. Miriam, who had been in the camp for several months, had the bunk next to hers. She was ten years older and similarly alone and grieving for the family she now knew had been gassed within hours of their arrival.

The next day they were all put to work, watched over constantly by SS guards with savage dogs. After the first month, all that most of them could think about was their hunger and the itching of the lice. But Anna's hatred of her former friend burned inside her and kept her alive. She would tell anyone who would listen, over and over again, that none of this suffering should have been happening to her: it should have been inflicted on the school friend who had stolen her chance to escape.

Towards the end of that first winter, rumours began to spread that any day now the advancing Soviet troops might reach the camp. Soon the starving prisoners were rounded up and made to leave. They walked for days. It was freezing cold, and many died before they reached the trains that were intended to carry them into Germany. The SS guards shot those who couldn't keep up. Anna and Miriam were separated. A few managed to escape into the woods, but Miriam never discovered what became of Anna.

The surviving prisoners were eventually transported to other camps further west. The overcrowding and the gradual collapse of the Third Reich made conditions worse than ever. Liberation by the Allied troops finally arrived just in time for those, like Miriam, who had managed to stay alive. She met her future husband in the displaced-persons camp to which she was sent. He was a military doctor and, once he had completed his national service, he arranged for her to join him in England where they married. She had always hoped that Anna, the young girl who had kept her company through some of the darkest nights of her life, had also found some kind of security and peace, and that, once the hatred that had kept her alive had served its purpose, she would have been able to let it go.

49

I didn't interrupt Miriam's story and, when it was over, I was at a loss for words. I had no doubt that the school friends she described were Delia and Lily's mother, Anna Körmöczy. I wanted desperately to believe that the teenage Delia had had no idea of her father's treachery when she made use of those documents, that she might remain ignorant of it even to this day.

But Lily knew, of that I was now convinced. She had known when she waited in the rain that night outside the BBC concert hall with the intention of infiltrating Delia's life.

Miriam appeared remarkably composed after talking about her time in the concentration camp. I could hardly imagine how she could have accustomed herself to describing events with which most of the world was still attempting to come to terms. I felt enormous respect and admiration for her, and a kind of scorching shame at myself because, as I'd listened, I'd cared only about the details relevant to my own small and self-ish concerns. She clearly recognized the personal nature of my interest, for she repeated her earlier words.

'I want this to be an end. This is merely the story as I learned it from Anna. There are those who might tell it differently, but they are almost certainly all dead. The war is over. Enough damage has been done. If there was a scandal, it must now be forgotten – and forgiven. That's the only reason I invited you here.'

'I appreciate your honesty,' I said. 'It can't be easy, having to revive such memories.'

She smiled. 'I don't have to revive them. They never leave me, not for an instant.'

She rose to her feet. I saw no need to prolong my stay and so thanked her again and followed her to the door. As I shook her hand in farewell, I held it for an extra moment.

'I'll do my best to follow your wishes,' I told her, still trying to reassure myself that Irma Székely's betrayal of her best friend had been unwitting.

'The hardest thing I've had to learn,' Miriam said, 'is that people must always be forgiven for surviving. Even me.'

She waited at the door until I had driven out of the gate.

As I headed back into town I wrestled with her words, searching for reasons to exonerate Delia from any conscious wrongdoing.

When I'd been a PoW, we had staked out our little territory by relying on civilized rules based on a code of honour. It seemed to matter more than anything that we upheld that code, with the men who had been there longest often reinforcing it the most vigorously. Stealing anything, however small, from one another was seldom forgiven.

But the theft had been Delia's father's decision, not hers. She was only fourteen. It was wartime. Even though the Swiss protection document had borne Anna's name, I tried telling myself that Delia might not have fully understood the switch that had been made. And, even if she had, any attempt to undo the wrong by removing her own photograph and returning it to Anna might have risked destroying the document so that neither girl could have been saved. Perhaps she had no choice but to obey her father. There were many excuses I could make. But I was not Anna. And I was not Lily.

Anna's father had publicly accused Oskar Székely. Anna must have concluded that Delia knew the papers had been intended for her and, at whatever point, had understood the momentous consequences of her actions. If Anna had later witnessed Irma Székely's success as Delia Maxwell, and read about her glowing beauty and pampered life, no wonder she had instilled in her daughter such a desire for revenge.

Lily's plight reminded me of the stories that still appeared occasionally in the papers about isolated Japanese fighters who remained unaware that the war was over. They were so loyal to the Emperor that they'd stayed hidden in the jungle, prepared to fight on and refusing to surrender. And that was the trouble here – Lily was still fighting a war that had ended before she was born. And it was unlikely she would ever surrender.

As I drove through Hendon I tried to work out how much Delia already knew. I had given her Lily's birth certificate, so she must now be aware of Lily's identity – which also explained why she'd shut me out since then: I had been an unforgivably blind and blundering messenger.

But what if she had already known or suspected? Until now I'd assumed her submission to Lily's deceit had stemmed from grief and guilt over the fate of her own daughter, but what if its purpose had been to hide her own secret?

How had Delia lived all these years with the knowledge of what she had done? I ought to despise her attempts to woo Lily back not with honesty but with a lavish birthday party or the offer of a house with a swimming pool. But it was no good: I was in love with her. I had allowed Evelyn and my son to walk away because of my feelings for her. What she'd done was wrong but, as Miriam had just told me, it was human.

And, meanwhile, however much Delia might convince herself that giving Lily everything she demanded might eventually win her over, the girl's hatred remained real and dangerous.

50

LILY

It was the trees that Lily remembered, dense evergreens that added to the stillness of the place. Summer was past its best and one or two of the deciduous trees were already showing autumnal tints. She had taken a taxi from the station in Birmingham, telling the driver to wait without even considering the cost. She wondered what her mother would make of such extravagance, or of Lily's lavishly rising income.

Mr and Mrs Jacobs had arranged for Anna's modest grave here in the Jewish burial ground, a small section of a much larger municipal cemetery. By the time of the stone-setting, on the first anniversary of Anna's death, the ten-year-old Lily had begun to get used to living in the children's home, and had wanted to tell the family gathered dutifully around the new headstone – for which they had also paid – that they had no need to feel embarrassed about having placed her there. Living so closely with other children, and especially with adults who'd never known her mother, had confirmed what Lily had always accepted, that she was odd, strange, too intense, not a normal child. She hadn't been surprised that even a family as conscientiously kind and generous as the Jacobses had chosen not to keep her.

The stone-setting had been the last time she'd seen them, although she'd never forgotten the straightforward constancy of their support. Afterwards, during her two years in the children's home, they'd continued to send cards and small gifts on her birthday. She was never entirely sure why that stopped when she had gone to live with her new foster parents in Worcester – perhaps because she adopted their surname, or the Jacobses hoped it would be a fresh start for her – but in some ways it had been a relief not to have to write the obligatory thank-you letters pretending that she was happy.

It had been because the primary-school kids had made fun of her impossible surname that Mr and Mrs Brooks had suggested taking theirs. She'd minded less than she'd expected about taking that further step away from her mother. No one had ever understood Anna, and Lily had found it increasingly hard to keep explaining why she had no relatives or siblings, or why she'd arrived at the children's home with not a single toy or book and very few clothes, or why she didn't know how to skip or use a swing, or play cards or board games, and countless other things that normal kids took for granted. But, Lily had told herself, none of that had ever mattered because she possessed her own special secret: the promise she had made not only to her mother but also to all the other dead and unavenged family members who had inhabited Anna's unseen world.

In Rome Lily had picked up a smooth pebble from one of the paths in the Borghese Gardens and kept it to place on Anna's grave on the anniversary of her death. Most of the neighbouring plots had numerous piles of stones, some constructed like small cairns, tokens of remembrance left by those who visited. Anna's grave had barely a dozen. Once Lily had moved to Worcester, it simply hadn't been possible to make the journey. She didn't feel guilty about it. Her mother had never been one for empty pieties. And, besides, Lily freely recognized that she was here now as much for herself as for Anna.

She balanced the Italian pebble on top of the headstone and felt a surge of pride in all that she had achieved in pursuit of keeping her promise. In a few short months she had taken Delia's place in the recording studio, on fashion shoots, in front of the movie cameras, in a hotel suite above the Spanish Steps, in chauffeur-driven cars, and even in her world-famous co-star's bed. Lily was exhausted, almost at the end of her strength, but it had been worth it.

'Are you proud of me, Anya?' she whispered to the earth. 'Have I done what you wanted? Can you sleep quietly now?'

The thick foliage of the surrounding trees absorbed all sound, as if emphasizing the silence of the well-kept graves.

It had been worth it, hadn't it?

She mustn't think like that! Even though, recently, it was dawning on her that keeping her promise might have been a way for a lonely and confused child to comfort and sustain herself, she mustn't allow herself to weaken now. Her mother's suffering must not go unanswered.

Not even a bird sang. She had come here to reinforce her focus and purpose, but there was no answering sign from Anna. Lily was alone, as she had always been. But there was no point in crying. There was nothing to cry about. She must simply finish what she had to do. Her feelings were of no importance.

She turned to walk back to the waiting taxi. The idea of another six o'clock start the next morning, of an hour in make-up, of a long day divided between interminable waiting in her trailer and placing everything she had to give in front of the camera seemed like an impossibly uphill struggle. She should have stayed in bed on her only day off, not spent it sitting on slow and grimy trains. Perhaps, when she got back to her Smith Street flat, she would ring that new private doctor she'd been told about and ask for one of his supposedly miraculous vitamin injections.

'Lily?'

The voice was tentative, querying.

Lily turned and saw a conservatively dressed couple in their mid-thirties. Not the usual type of fan. Did they really expect her to sign an autograph in the middle of a cemetery? She smiled politely and tried to keep moving.

'You don't recognize me,' said the woman. 'I thought it was you when I first saw you on the television a few weeks ago, but I wasn't sure.'

Lily stopped and looked at the woman more closely.

'Irene Davis.' The woman touched her hands to her chest. 'Irene Jacobs as was. This is my husband, Stanley. We've been tidying up my father-in-law's grave. How are you?'

'Miss Irene, of course! How do you do?'

Irene beamed with pleasure. 'I'm well, thanks. Married with two little boys.' She took her husband's arm affectionately and smiled up at him. 'My parents retired to Israel. My brother David runs the business now. They'll be so happy to hear that I've seen you. They often talk about you and wonder how you are.'

'Very well, as you can see.' Lily felt slightly breathless with unexpected gladness. 'It's good of them to think of me. Please send them my warmest regards. They couldn't have been kinder to us when we lived in your house.'

'I will. They'll be thrilled at your success, Lily. How many weeks have you been in the top ten now? Oh, but they'd have loved to see you for themselves. You remember Harry, my younger brother? He's in London working in advertising now. Perhaps you'll run into him.'

'You never know!'

'You're visiting your mother's grave?' Stanley Davis gave her a sympathetic look.

'Yes.' Lily gazed back in that direction, comforted that Anna's presence there was recognized by people other than herself.

'Oh, but—' Irene stopped, colouring in embarrassment. 'I'm sorry, only I thought I read that you said that Delia Maxwell—'

Lily went cold. She saw from Irene's puzzled frown that she had made the connection faster than she had herself.

'Oh, that!' Lily tried to wave aside the contradiction. There was no adequate way to smooth away the lie in front of Irene. 'Not exactly a publicity stunt, but you know . . .'

Confronted with the inevitability of exposure, her actions seemed suddenly tawdry and mean.

It had been worth it, hadn't it?

Hoping Irene would find it too awkward to ask for clarification, she wondered how quickly she could disengage and escape to the safety of her taxi. Even as she told herself it didn't matter what Irene thought, an unwelcome memory rose of the young women in the Soho coffee bar, whose admiring attention had so quickly turned to yelled insults.

Fighting panic, Lily sought strength in the shock branded in her memory when she'd learned that her mother, emaciated and ill, was the same age as the radiant young woman depicted on the record sleeves that Anna had held out to her.

Lily looked at her watch. 'Goodness, is that the time already? I'm so sorry to run off, but you know what it's like with Sunday trains.' She held out a hand to each of them in turn, hoping they'd be too polite to detain her with further questions. 'So lovely to see you again, Irene. Do please remember me to your parents. Goodbye.'

She walked away without looking back. In her head a clock started to tick. Even if Irene chose not to spread word of Lily's real identity, it could only be a matter of time before the truth emerged.

51

Lily was almost too exhausted to be angry at finding herself in a television-studio green room with the last person she wanted to see. Her punishing six-days-a-week shooting schedule had provided a valid excuse to avoid Delia, but now Lily was being made to sing with her – and on live television. She liked the immediacy of a live show, but she was inexperienced and hadn't had enough time to prepare. Plus, in spite of Davey's new arrangement, the song they wanted her to sing was old-fashioned sentimental rubbish. But it had been the TV producer's idea, so Peter and Delia had ignored her objections.

James, too, had encouraged her to go along with what they wanted, saying that the early-evening pop programme was a perfect showcase. He was probably right: it had already featured several groups and singers from the new music scene coming out of places like Liverpool and Manchester. But Lily ought to be singing alone, not helping Delia to re-launch her career.

She had dressed provocatively in a scarlet dress with long sleeves and a short hemline. It hung more loosely than when she'd bought it, but she liked the way the high ruffled neck accentuated the emerging sharpness of her jawline and cheekbones. She'd accentuated her eyes with thin black eyeliner – a trick she'd learned from the professional make-up artists whose constant smoothing and stroking she'd grown to detest. Yet the expected reaction when she arrived was disappointing: Delia had looked at her with concern rather than envy and Peter kept offering her the hospitality plates of sugary biscuits or sandwiches with curling edges.

Lily had imagined it would be Delia on the back foot in this milieu – she was the past and Lily and the other young guests the future – yet she seemed to know everyone, even their names, right down to the floor manager. She was wearing one of Celeste's new designs, a slinky silver skirt with a sleeveless silver lamé top with diamanté around the neck. Lily was forced to admit that Celeste had achieved a clever, pared-down tribute to Delia's signature look that, with a subtly different haircut, made Delia look poised and sophisticated. Yet, even without the huge skirts, she still somehow seemed to take up all the space, sucking the air out of the room so that Lily found it hard to breathe.

Since her visit to Anna's grave she'd been struggling against a small inner voice of reason, warning that the situation she had created was going to end badly. She wasn't sure how much longer she could keep going, and wondered what would happen if she simply told everyone that Delia was a liar, a thief and little better than an executioner, then walked away to leave Delia to sort out the mess.

Peter came to where she stood with her back against the wall and she forced a smile.

'Nervous?' he asked.

Lily had never understood small talk, but she knew exactly how to act the part of the up-and-coming star, naturally exuberant yet also grateful and slightly overawed. It was the role she'd been playing all week in front of the movie cameras.

'I'm sure Delia's experience will carry us through,' she said brightly, and caught a glimpse of relief in his answering nod.

'I know it seems like a corny number,' he said, 'but I get why the producer suggested it. It's modern and ironic to revive something old-fashioned, and it is a rather ingenious way of facing head-on how you two singing together will always be a bit of a tear-jerker.'

'Davey's done a great job with it.' Lily smiled, teeth gritted. So far as she was concerned, 'When You Wish Upon A Star' was a childish song from a Disney cartoon, no matter how some smart-alec TV producer tried to spice it up.

'And Davey says your voices blended perfectly in rehearsal.' Peter patted her arm with a patronizing smile. 'Just wait. You may be surprised by how well it works out.'

'And you'll be happy to say, "I told you so."' She was too tired to disguise her sarcasm, but Peter's sigh made her feel chastised, like she was a little kid.

I don't want to be here any more, she wanted to say. *I've done enough. I want to stop being Delia's daughter and be left alone.*

Delia came to join them, casting a quick eye over Lily as if assessing her state of mind.

Leave me alone!

'Are you ready?' asked Delia. 'Do you want to do a few quiet breathing exercises before we're called?'

'No, I'm fine.'

'I might get a drink to ease my throat,' said Delia. 'Can I get you something?' As she spoke, she reached out and straightened one of the frills on Lily's dress.

It was all Lily could do not to knock her hand away. 'Let me get it,' she said. 'What do you want?'

Delia looked apologetic. 'Weak tea with lemon, please.'

'And if it's lukewarm, all the better,' added Peter.

Delia laughed. 'True, I'm afraid. But I can get it myself.'

'No, don't worry,' said Lily. 'I'd rather keep busy until we're on.'

An idea had come to her and she wanted to see it through before second thoughts could spoil it. As she walked over to where the food and drinks had been laid out she could feel rather than see Delia and Peter exchange looks about her behind her back. Well, let them. She still had some tricks up her sleeve.

She had brought a large bag with her containing make-up and spare clothes, and quickly retrieved it from where she'd left it under a chair. The woman behind the tea-urn followed her instructions to add extra water and three lemon slices and then Lily carried the Russian tea glass to the end of the long table where she could turn her back to the room. She reached into the bottom of her bag and quickly poured in a dose of Nembutal, stirring in the clear, odourless liquid and hoping the extra lemon would mask the bitter taste. She screwed the lid back on the bottle, pushed her bag out of sight on the floor beneath the table and, taking a glass of water for herself, returned to Delia.

'Thanks, Lily. That's sweet of you.'

She watched Delia purse her lips at the first sip.

'Is it too sour?' Lily asked, widening her eyes in contrition. 'I specially asked for extra lemon.'

'No, no, it's fine. Good for my vocal cords.'

'I can get you another.'

Delia shook her head and swallowed the rest of the tea as Peter looked at his watch.

'They'll be ready for you any second.'

Moments later an assistant floor manager came to call them. Delia put aside her glass and lightly touched Lily's shoulder. 'I know that appearing with me wouldn't have been your choice,' she said, 'but let's create something memorable, shall we?'

Lily followed Delia along a corridor and down some stairs to a door with a red light above it. The assistant floor manager tapped lightly and waited for a young man inside to open it and beckon them into the studio, a finger over his lips. As they silently awaited their cue, standing behind the cameras and out of sight of the assembled audience, Lily surreptitiously watched Delia as she swayed slightly and put a hand to her forehead. Lily leaned in close. 'Mother and daughter,' she whispered. 'What an act!'

Delia stared at her, her shock at Lily's derision already hazing over as the barbiturate took hold.

The audience burst into applause at the end of the previous number and the unwieldy camera swung around to face the DJ who was presenting the show. As he prepared to introduce them Lily took Delia firmly by the arm, willing her to keep her concentration long enough to be on camera when she began to slur her words before a live audience of millions.

'Keep going!' she whispered. 'Focus!'

Delia nodded and seemed to rally, shaking her head to chase away the fuzziness.

As they were handed microphones and the moment came for them to step forwards, the DJ's voice and the applause seemed to recede. Lily was suddenly returned to the silence beside Anna's grave. *Where are you, Anya? I'm doing what you wanted. I am doing my best. Are you here to see? Do you even care any more?*

She looked at Delia in desperate search of the anger and energy she needed. As if responding to the applause, Delia raised her head and opened her eyes wide. She shot Lily a brilliant smile and stepped forward, turning back to hold out a hand to her. As they had rehearsed, Delia sang the opening lines of 'When you wish upon a star.'

Her voice was strong and pure, vibrating with a tenderness that only a mother could feel. Lily came in on cue with the following lyrics and then, as their voices joined, she listened with satisfaction as Delia's voice began to falter. Delia blinked repeatedly, her eyes clouded over and then, before Lily could catch and support her, she staggered and fell to the studio floor.

52

FRANK

I was watching the show – Peter had told me Delia would be appearing – and jumped to my feet when she fell to the floor in an apparent faint. Just before the cameras swung away to an agitated DJ, I saw Lily throw herself down beside her. No doubt the audience saw a distressed daughter but, just before Delia collapsed, I'd caught a fleeting and unmistakable look of exultation on her face. After a few minutes of studio chaos, during which the DJ failed to offer any reassuring words about Delia's condition, I began to be seriously worried.

I had nothing else to do, so I turned off the set and drove straight to the hospital nearest to the television studios. They insisted that Delia wasn't there, so I found a phone box and rang Mary Jenks, desperate to find out if she knew what was happening. Luckily Peter had already called her and she was able to tell me that Delia had been taken by ambulance to a private clinic.

As I drove to Harley Street, I saw that the newspaper vendors had already changed their bills for the West End finals and I stopped to buy a copy of the *Evening News*. Delia's collapse live on television only a few months after her mysterious disappearance was bound to make headlines, sparking every rumour the journalists could invent, with drug addiction or a nervous breakdown now heading the list. I was pleased that Peter had had the foresight to admit Delia to the hospital under an assumed name in hope of throwing reporters off the scent.

He was with her when I got there. He kept me waiting for a few minutes, then came out of her room evidently anxious, and told me she was still drowsy, but would like to see me for a minute or two. I went in. She looked frail and delicate in the high bed, a hospital gown pulled up around her neck. She smiled bravely and held out a hand, which I took and kissed.

'I'm glad you came,' she said. 'Sorry I've been out of touch.'

'It doesn't matter. Anyway, it seems I slipped up tonight,' I said lightly. 'It's supposed to be my job to make sure you come to no harm.'

'So silly,' she murmured. 'It must have been a chill. Just one of those things.'

I didn't say that, according to my research, in fifteen years of performing all over the world she had never once succumbed to a chill.

'How do you feel now?' I asked. 'What do the doctors say?'

'That I'll be fine and can go home in the morning.'

She didn't meet my eyes, and I wondered what they'd really said. 'And they've checked you over thoroughly?' I asked.

'They've all been wonderful.'

'Do you want me to fetch you anything? I can go over to your house and get anything you need.'

She shook her head with a smile. 'Peter's already sent someone.'

I pulled up a chair and sat beside her, taking her hand again.

'Don't look at me like that, Frank.'

'I'm worried about you.'

'Don't.'

She spoke sharply, as if she suspected what I wanted to say. At some point I would have to tell her that I knew about Anna Körmöczy, that I now understood why Lily had targeted her, and that I only wanted to protect her, but a warning look in her eyes made it clear she didn't wish to hear any of it. I squeezed her hand and raised it to my lips once more.

'I'll leave you to rest,' I said. 'But anything you want, you have only to call.'

'You're very kind. I think I'll sleep well tonight.'

Peter was hovering in the corridor. 'Wait for me,' he said. 'I'll just say goodnight and then I could do with a stiff drink.'

Fifteen minutes later we were tucked into a quiet corner of a nearby pub.

'So tell me what happened,' I said.

He shook his head in bewilderment. 'I've no idea. One moment she was fine, looking marvellous, excited about singing live. She's an old hand at this, never really suffers from nerves. But the next . . .'

'What does Lily say?'

'She was sweet. Very upset, of course, and in fact quite unexpectedly caring and concerned. She wanted to come in the ambulance, but I arranged for someone to take her home. Ordered her not to answer the door or speak to any reporters.'

I nodded, turning my whisky glass around on the table in front of me.

'All hell's going to break loose tomorrow,' he said. 'Whatever we tell the press, it'll be front-page news.'

'It already is. I've got an *Evening News* in my car if you want me to fetch it.'

'It can wait,' he said grimly.

'Lily will be pleased,' I said.

'What do you mean?'

'You know what I mean,' I said. 'She's been waiting to see Delia fail.'

'She's not all bad, Frank. And I had a talk with her about that other business,' he said awkwardly. 'I made it clear she could threaten all she liked, but I wasn't going to do what she wanted unless I judged it was right.'

'And?'

'She's been behaving herself. Filming is going well. She's got her head down and turned up on time every day. Well, you've seen that for yourself. I've had no complaints about her from James Sinclair.'

'And tonight?'

'She wasn't keen on the song, but she went along with it without kicking up too much of a fuss.'

I wondered if, after all, I had overreacted and been too quick to assume that Lily must somehow have been responsible for Delia's collapse.

'How was she with Delia?' I asked.

'Fine. Even took the trouble to fetch her a cup of tea just the way she likes it.'

I recalled Lily's look of exultation: was this confirmation of my suspicions? 'How long between Delia drinking the tea and her collapse?' I asked.

'A few minutes at most. Why?'

'And how long was she unconscious?'

'It took her a while to come round,' he admitted. 'That was why I insisted she go to hospital. But she refused to have any tests, insisting she simply got too hot under the studio lights.'

Was that because it had occurred to Delia, too, that Lily might have spiked her tea? What should I do? If I told Peter straight out he'd laugh in my face. He couldn't possibly accept such a possibility unless I explained everything I knew. But could I – should I? – break my promise to Delia? As I tried to calculate how little I could get away with telling him, he looked at me sternly.

'What's going on, Frank?'

'I ought to speak to Delia first.'

'I have a duty to protect her. If you have something to say, now's the time to spit it out.'

It was his squadron leader's voice, and it reminded me of how much I owed him.

I told him everything.

He listened in silence, his serious expression growing stonier as I stumbled to the end. 'I think I need another drink,' he said, and rose abruptly to walk over to the bar.

I sat tight. I couldn't blame him for being furious. Now that I had laid it all before him, the scale of my disloyalty was uncomfortably clear. Our long friendship had been based on trust and I had betrayed it.

He returned to the table carrying a second glass for me, but his expression remained cold.

'I'm sorry, Peter.'

He nodded. 'I've been paying you to work for me. If what you've told me isn't handled correctly, it could have an impact on the whole company, on the people I employ, on the shareholders. I didn't expect to be kept in the dark, then ambushed like this in the middle of a crisis.'

Peter had always been hard but fair, and I respected him for it. I'd let him down.

'You're right, and I apologize,' I said. 'I'm not playing down my part in this, but right now we need to talk about whether Delia is still in danger.'

'This has gone far enough, Frank. You can't honestly believe Lily would ever hurt Delia physically?'

'You don't think she could have put something in Delia's tea tonight?'

'I was there,' he said, 'and never noticed anything wrong until the moment she fainted.'

'I was watching on television,' I said. 'I caught the look on Lily's face just before Delia fell to the floor.'

But he wasn't listening. 'I can't believe Delia's lied to me all this time. She's let me go on treating Lily as her daughter when, from what you say, she's known for weeks that she can't be.'

I wanted to argue that Delia hadn't really lied to us and that she had every right to choose what she shared about her past, but the defence was beginning to sound hollow even to my ears.

Peter's hurt was beginning to show. 'Why didn't she come to me?'

I could have told him that I had begged Delia to confide in him, but what was the use?

'When have I not been on her side and fought for her best interests?' he continued. 'You say Delia stole that Swiss document from her best friend at school? From Lily's real mother?'

'She was fourteen, Peter. It was her father who stole the papers.' I knew my refusal to blame Delia was because I was in love with her, but I couldn't fight it.

'But she used them,' he said. 'She was aware of the consequences.' He shook his head, bemused. 'It seems she has plenty to hide. Perhaps I've never known the real Delia at all.'

'You're missing the point.' I began to grow impatient. 'You have to admit it's possible that Lily did spike Delia's tea.'

'Delia says she had a chill.'

'She'll never speak against Lily.'

'Delia herself might taken something to calm her nerves, accidentally took too much and now doesn't want to admit it,' Peter countered.

'You've always said how professional she is. Have you ever known her risk a performance?'

'No,' he agreed, 'but I think she was more anxious than usual tonight about singing with Lily.'

I was astonished that he couldn't – or wouldn't – see what I felt was staring us in the face. 'I know for certain that Lily has access to drugs,' I said. 'She's been popping pills on set. I've seen the effects.' I held up my hands to forestall his protest. 'If my hunch is right, then at the very least Lily succeeded in humiliating Delia on live television, but what if she meant to do far worse?'

'Now you're being paranoid.'

'Lily has deliberately wormed her way close to Delia right from the start,' I said. 'And now we know why. To take revenge for her mother.'

'I freely admit the girl's a handful,' said Peter, 'but that's a very long way from accusing her of – what? Attempting to poison Delia? That's ridiculous.'

'I think we'd be fools to rule it out,' I said stubbornly. 'Why trust her? She's lied about everything else.'

'And you've explained all that,' he responded. 'Delia's enjoyed the very best in life while Lily's mother had nothing. No wonder the poor kid is so angry.'

'Which is precisely why she's dangerous.'

But he was clearly not convinced.

'Whatever game Lily's playing, it has to stop,' I urged, 'and you have to help me.'

Peter turned to study me. He knocked back the last of his whisky and put down the empty glass. 'I'm sorry, Frank, but you're on your own. I hope you understand that I can't keep you on the payroll, not after you've kept back such vital information.' He stood and held out his hand. 'No hard feelings, I hope?'

I shook it, and watched him leave the pub.

53

DELIA

Peter arrived at the hospital at dawn to smuggle Delia out of a back door and into his waiting car, but not early enough to evade the huddle of reporters and photographers already camped at the entrance to her mews.

She knew from the reluctance with which he handed over the pile of morning papers he'd brought with him that she wasn't going to enjoy looking at them. The headlines were brutal and several papers ran the same grainy photograph of Lily kneeling beside her as she lay unconscious on the studio floor. She guessed the picture was a still taken from the recording, either pirated or officially released to garner publicity for the TV show. It was disturbing to see herself like that.

Although Peter assured her that Lily had promised she wouldn't speak to the press, she'd clearly disobeyed his instruction, and three papers led with variations on 'Tragic Delia' accompanied by anxious quotes from Lily about her fear that her mother was breaking down under the pressure of years of stardom. The *Daily Mail*, quoting 'a source close to the singer', also wrote about a growing feud between the two women, describing how Lily had snubbed Delia by arriving late for the lavish party her mother had thrown for her birthday. Every paper reminded readers of Delia's earlier and still unexplained absence, with many directing the reader to an inside page where they embroidered their previous lurid speculations.

'Our press people did all they could,' Peter told her, 'but we lost control of the story the minute they got hold of that photograph.'

'What's happening to me?' she asked. 'Why has the press turned against me?'

'They haven't,' he said. 'Not really. You know what they're like. Tomorrow's fish-and-chip paper.'

'But why has Lily made it worse?'

When he didn't answer she looked up from her reading and saw him frown.

He caught her look. 'Are you ready to tell me the truth?' he asked.

She recoiled in alarm, rapidly calculating how much he might already know. 'About what?'

'You and Lily,' he said. 'I can't help either of you if you don't trust me. And it can't be long before the whole story comes out.'

Had Lily told him? What else had Lily said while she'd been unconscious?

'She's not your daughter,' Peter said.

'No,' she admitted. 'My daughter died. Who told you?'

'Frank.'

She nodded, unexpectedly feeling a rush of relief that the truth was out at last. 'It was never lack of trust in you, Peter. It was not knowing for sure who Lily is or what she wants. And it wasn't Frank's fault, either, that he didn't tell you. I made him promise not to.'

Peter waved that issue aside, although she could see that he was pained by Frank's role in the deception. 'I've tried to understand,' he said. 'But Frank has told me more than he's yet told you. He's spoken to a woman who knew Lily's mother, Anna.'

Delia winced: hearing the bare fact spoken aloud was like a physical blow. 'I didn't know he'd done that. He had no right.'

'Anna and the woman he spoke to were in a concentration camp together.'

'I only found out recently that Anna had survived,' she said. 'That was when I learned Lily was her daughter. Before that I'd no reason to hope Anna had survived. She should have come to me. I'd have done anything to help her.'

'This woman said Anna blamed you, that she hated you.'

Delia nodded. Peter was telling her only what she had always known must be true.

'Frank thinks she taught Lily to do the same,' he went on.

'And that's why I can't abandon her,' Delia said earnestly. 'You must see that. No matter what she does, I have to support her, for Anna's sake.'

'I'm afraid it may be too late for that,' he said. 'The past can't be undone so easily.'

'No, I suppose not.' Delia felt all the fear and hope she'd been holding inside suddenly slump away, leaving her blank and hollow. Only now did she see how much of her life had been built on guilt and regret.

'What really happened last night?' he asked. 'Frank reckons Lily put something in your tea.'

Delia was still unwilling to make that judgement.

'Was it just a chill? You have to be honest with me.'

'Whatever Lily's done, it's my fault,' she pleaded. 'It began with me. I stole Anna's papers, although I didn't know they were hers until the train had left Budapest. My father had made me promise to keep going. He said we could all be in danger if I tried to come back. But it was my choice to stay on that train.'

'How old were you?' he asked gently.

'What does it matter? At the Swiss border they asked if my name was Anna Körmöczy and I lied and said yes so that I could get to safety. I stole my friend's life.'

'And if her daughter is now trying to steal yours?'

'I fainted, that's all.'

'Not because Lily drugged your tea?' he asked. 'I lay awake last night going over it again and again. One minute you were fine, the next you were out for the count.'

She couldn't admit to him that, as she'd felt herself falling, she had for a split second genuinely believed she was about to die. It had been terrifying, and she'd wanted desperately to live.

'If she did slip me a Mickey Finn,' she said, trying to make light of it, 'she probably only meant to make a fool of me in front of the camera.'

Peter indicated the spread of newspapers. 'And that's not bad enough? On top of all her lies about being your daughter?'

'Whatever she's done, I have to try to understand what happened to her.' Delia was arguing with herself as much as with him. 'I gave away my own daughter. She died and I wasn't there to comfort her. I know what it's like to lose everyone you love. But I was lucky. I had Conrad. Someone has to love Lily.'

'And if she tries to sabotage you again?'

'Then perhaps that's what I deserve.'

Peter sighed in exasperation. 'I had one or two pilots in the squadron who spouted rubbish like that after they'd lost one too many of their friends. I grounded them until they saw sense. If

I hadn't, they'd have been a danger to themselves and other people. You can't change the past, Delia. Millions died and, in comparison, you barely suffered, but you can't make up for that now by offering yourself as a sacrifice.'

'I refuse to believe she intended serious harm.'

'Maybe not, but she's gone too far this time.'

'I don't care. We have to find a way to help her.'

Peter sighed heavily. 'I'll do my best to sort this mess out but, to be honest, I'm not sure we can. Lily's a crazy, mixed-up kid. How crazy we don't yet know, but she's certainly damaged by what happened to her mother.'

He held up his hands as she started to object.

'Let's just blame Hitler for that,' he said. 'But at the very least she's shown that she's capable of formidable and remorseless long-term planning. You're the one who needs protection.'

'I won't involve the police.'

'Not yet,' he agreed. 'But perhaps she'd agree to speak to a psychiatrist. I've been given the name of a good chap in Harley Street.'

Delia felt a wave of sadness at where her attempts to make amends had brought them all. 'She looks so like her mother,' she said. 'Anna was so warm and funny, although she could also be fierce, just like Lily.'

Peter tapped the pile of newspapers. 'Lily is still saying you're her mother.'

'I'm sorry I misled you, Peter.'

'So am I,' he said tersely. 'But we need to look to the future. We have to start putting the record straight.'

'Where will that leave Lily?'

He shrugged. 'That's up to her. No one forced her to tell that lie. And I think Frank's right that her intention is to kill off your career. It's time to fight back.'

Maybe it was the memory of her younger self, the girl she'd been before the war had taken away her world, but a little spark flared in her. Would it really be so wrong, after all her years of hard work, to want something for herself? It was Anna, not Lily, whom she'd wronged. Surely she had tried hard enough to atone for the past.

Peter was studying her. 'You're Delia Maxwell,' he said. 'You can be bigger than ever, if that's what you want.'

She took a deep breath. It *was* what she wanted. She loved performing and recording and was hungry for more. How could it help Anna now, or hurt Lily, if she were to go on making the most of her singing career? She could use her money and fame to help Lily. And Lily was not Anna. She shivered, reliving the moment when she began to lose consciousness. How, after last night, could she owe Lily anything?

'I'll set up for you to give an exclusive interview to Stella Parsons,' he told her. 'It can be syndicated worldwide. You'll have to say that Lily found out you'd given a baby up for adoption, and then went on to dupe you. You don't have to explain anything that happened in the war, only that she's an imposter who has taken advantage of your kindness and generosity, and how devastated you were when you learned how your own daughter had died of polio. We could even organize an emotional meeting with the couple who adopted her.'

'Oh, no – please.'

'We may have no choice but to pull out all the stops,' he said. 'You can be sure that, if the film company feel they're too invested to drop Lily, they'll fight back. And you've seen their tactics. Today's papers are already spicing up the idea of a feud between the two of you. It will be all too easy to fan those flames and for the press to have you clawing at each other's throats. You have to get your story out there first. And be ready to fight for your career.'

'Is there no other way?'

'No, Delia. It's time to choose. It's you or Lily.'

54

LILY

James had sent Lily home. The last twenty-four hours had been a blizzard of people wanting her attention, from the reporters crowding around and shouting at her as she'd rushed from her front door to the waiting car first thing this morning, to the hair and make-up and costume people, all pretending they weren't casting sideways looks at her and planning to gossip afterwards about the 'feud' between her and the woman they still believed was her mother. And there was Peter and his PR people, plus the film PR people, including that creep Charlie Flynn, and then James telling her to go home, and finally more reporters hustling her again as the car dropped her off outside her door in Chelsea. Now she couldn't even look out of her first-floor window without some photographer popping a flash.

It was August, the silly season for the press, and the reporters were desperate to fill their pages. Nevertheless, Delia's collapse had unleashed an unexpected firestorm, and although that made Lily very happy – she wanted to dance on the ashes of Delia's career, to feed the flames and make it end faster – she also wanted it to be over so she could rest.

Most of all she wanted to be able to finish shooting the movie. She craved those moments when she could focus herself down to a few lines in a script, to looking at nothing except Guy Brody's face, seeing only the character he played. In a few short weeks their characters had fallen in love, he had made her a star, they had married, his career had failed, he drank, she rescued him, he drank some more, and now they were playing out the final scenes in which he would kill himself and her character's heartbreak would be complete, yet the show would go on. Next week they were supposed to be filming the finale in which her character would appear on stage and introduce herself as his grieving widow, but today that idiot James had suggested they postpone 'until Lily feels up to it'. Didn't he understand that work was the only thing that was keeping her going?

All right, so she'd missed her mark once or twice when she'd returned on set after lunch, and Guy had kept waving his hand in front of her face as if she couldn't see him, but there'd been no need for James to wrap before they'd even finished the scene or to make a big deal about it in front of all the crew.

And then as she was changing out of her costume Guy had appeared in her dressing room and delivered a lecture about how many pills she was taking.

'I don't care what you do to yourself,' he'd said, 'except you can't be on camera with your pupils permanently dilated. You need to cut back. Think more about what you're doing.'

As usual, he had driven home his unchanging message – that he expected her, without argument, to do whatever he said – by pushing her down on the daybed and forcing himself inside her. It no longer took him very long to finish and he left immediately afterwards, giving her the usual kiss on the head as a reward for being a good girl. She often imagined him telling himself how happy and grateful she must be for his attention.

The best thing about wrapping this film would be that she'd never again have to submit to Guy Brody.

Left alone in her dressing room, she'd longed to sleep, even a ten-minute nap, but hadn't dared take anything to knock herself out. Instead she'd washed and found fresh underwear before calling for an assistant to fetch whatever morning papers she could find. On the way home she'd sat in the back of the car and looked at what had been written about the abrupt end to 'When You Wish Upon A Star'. Although she'd miscalculated how much Nembutal she'd put in Delia's tea, the coverage was more than she could have hoped for. A photograph of Delia lying unconscious on the studio floor graced several front pages along with Lily's words of daughterly concern about what Delia's sinister collapse might signify for her mother's future career.

One newspaper had got hold of the photograph of Lily holding hands with Guy Brody at Pinewood as they'd walked away from his silver Jaguar and had led with speculation about an off-screen romance. No one so far seemed to have dug up the story of Guy mowing down a cyclist: she'd keep that up her sleeve.

But now the rest of the afternoon stretched ahead and she was stuck here. When she'd landed the movie role and begged for her own place, this little Smith Street flat, with its elegant first-floor windows and high ceiling, had seemed ideal. But living alone was harder than she'd expected, especially coming back here after the intensity of filming, with the added tension of constantly anticipating when Guy would next decide to ambush her.

She'd never been much of a reader and, although she had a television, she'd grown tired of dramas about kindly policemen and handsome young doctors, let alone the smug families in adverts for gravy or soap powder. She wanted a life of her own. She wanted to be a movie star and drive a convertible in Hollywood and be on the cover of *Vogue*. She wanted Delia to be a distant memory.

She went to check the mirrored cabinet in her bathroom. Perhaps she ought to make another appointment with her private doctor to get a new prescription. She took out one of the pill canisters and unscrewed the lid. Tipping the contents into the palm of her hand to see how many she had left, she must have somehow bumped her elbow for she watched helplessly as most of them disappeared down the plughole. With a shaking hand she carefully returned all but one of the remaining few blue pills to the canister. Bending to drink from the cold tap, she swallowed it. She shouldn't really take another so soon, but right now she needed it.

What was she supposed to do to pass the time? If she went out, the reporters would hound her. It wouldn't be dark enough until late in the evening to hope to escape their attention. Peter Jenks and Charlie Flynn had both stressed how important it was not to say a single word to any of them, no matter how hard they tried to pester and cajole her into some reaction. Wear dark glasses, smile and stick to 'No comment', they'd said. Well, she could do that. She certainly couldn't sit here on her own for hours on end.

Lily put on the sunglasses she'd bought in Rome and let herself out into the street. It was only fifty yards from her front door to the King's Road where she was sure she could find protection among the well-heeled shoppers heading for Peter Jones.

She was immediately surrounded by clamouring reporters

and photographers. She held up a hand to shield her face and kept repeating, 'No comment, no comment', but they dogged her every movement, making it impossible to walk in a straight line along the pavement. She felt a firm hand on her elbow and was about to shake it off when she recognized Frank Landry beside her.

'Stick close to me,' he said, holding out his other arm to fend off the men who were elbowing each other to get closer to her.

She didn't like Frank and didn't want to go anywhere with him, but right now she didn't seem to have much choice. He led her around the corner, still pursued by the press pack. Passers-by turned to stare.

'This is hopeless,' he said, letting go of her for a second to flag down an approaching taxi that showed a yellow light. The driver failed to spot him amid the melee and drove on.

'There's a coffee bar along here somewhere, isn't there?' he asked, taking hold of her again.

'I'm not going anywhere with you!'

'Then I'll take you home. You and I need to talk.'

She tried to pull free. 'No. Leave me alone.'

He tightened his grip, hurting her arm.

'Let go of me, you creep!'

'Don't make a scene.'

She stopped dead, resisting his attempt to keep her moving, and turned to challenge him. 'Why shouldn't I?' She looked around at the avid faces of the reporters. A camera bulb popped, and passing shoppers lingered on the pavement, craning between the reporters' heads to see what the commotion was about. 'That's what they want, isn't it?' she demanded. 'Another splash.'

'Not here. Not like this.'

Her laugh sounded shriller than she'd meant it to be. 'I can do what I want!'

He leaned in closer. 'You want the front page? Fine. Shall I tell them all about Lily Körmöczy?'

55

Lily stared helplessly at Frank, unable to find the right words. Even though she'd been anticipating the moment for months, now her secret had been uncovered she was shocked by how naked she felt.

He jerked her arm, pulling her around in the direction of her flat. The photographers went on taking pictures, but the small crowd gave way and let them through. 'Come on,' he said. 'Give me your door key.'

He hustled her indoors and up the stairs. She tried to head for her bedroom where she could shut the door on him, but he grabbed her arm again, led her into the living room and pushed her down onto the sofa. She refused his offer to get her some tea or a glass of water.

'How long have you known?' she asked.

'Long enough.'

She licked her dry lips. 'Who else knows?'

'Peter.' He stared at her, his blue eyes cold and hard. 'And Delia.'

Lily shut her eyes as the world she'd worked so hard to create came tumbling down. For a while she couldn't think at all but then, as the ruins settled around her, the bizarre realization surfaced that she minded about Delia.

'How long has she known?' she asked.

Frank's face showed only contempt. 'Long enough to support you, help you, stand aside for you even after she knew you couldn't possibly be her daughter.'

The thought was present before she had time to censor it. It was true: Delia *had* been kind and generous, and had cared about her when no one else did. *Had* cared: no one would defend her now.

Frank was still speaking. 'Even last night after you tried to poison her she—'

'*Poison* her?'

'You put something in her tea.'

'I didn't *poison* her.'

'You could have killed her.'

'What? No! I never meant to hurt her.'

'You're lucky Peter hasn't called in the police.'

Lily had learned a great deal from the hours she'd spent at Gerald Road police station. She'd done nothing, yet had witnessed how easily powerful men could band together to get what they wanted. They could do what they liked. She could go to prison!

'You admit you spiked her tea?' Frank asked.

'Yes, but only to make her look stupid. It's just that I—'

She had misjudged the dose. She thought of Guy earlier today, waving his hand in front of her face after she'd taken an extra pill at lunchtime and then James sending her home. She tried to arrange the words that would explain everything but the fog in her head wouldn't let her. Seeing Frank's anger and disdain, she knew it was useless.

'What happens now?' she asked.

'I don't know,' he said. 'But it's all going to come out, how you lied to everyone and tried to destroy Delia's career. I imagine people will be queuing up to be the first to drop you.'

'But I'll have to finish the movie.' She felt a shiver of fear at all she was about to lose. 'They can't just abandon it, not after so much time and money.'

'I'm sure they can find ways to wrap it up without you. Rewrite the ending, use a body double. They have all kinds of tricks.'

'What about all the PR people? They can make this come right. That's their job, isn't it?'

'Why should they?'

'Because I'm good! James says so. Even Guy Brody. I want to work.'

Frank shrugged and she saw the hatred in his eyes. She couldn't blame him. He'd been half in love with Delia before he'd even met her.

'I'll still be under contract to RMJ Records, won't I?' she asked.

'That's up to Peter. It'll be easy for him to release you if he wants to.'

'You don't understand,' she pleaded. 'I promised my mother. I had to keep my promise.'

'You couldn't have deceived Delia more cruelly.'

'You don't know what she did to my mother.'

'Yes, I do. But it's too late, Lily. It's over. If you want my advice, you should see a shrink.'

'I'm not crazy!'

'No? How many pills did you take today?'

She remembered what had happened to one of the older girls in the children's home, a girl who wouldn't do as she was told and kept going off with a man who waited at the street corner in his car. When the staff tried to stop her she scratched and spat and swore. They told the rest of the kids where she'd been taken. Everybody feared the red-brick asylum, always visible on the crest of the hill. Some girls were only in the children's home because their mothers had been taken away to the asylum and had never come home. Let it be a lesson to you, the staff had said. She didn't want to end up there.

'If I see a doctor, will they let me come back? At least finish the movie?'

'I don't know,' Frank said. 'I don't care.'

'So what *do* you want?'

'I want you to go away and leave Delia alone.'

'Go where?'

'Back to your foster parents. You're clever. You'll work something out. You're good at pretending to be someone else. Or you could go back to being Lily Körmöczy.'

'I can't be her again!' she cried. 'I don't want to. I've had enough!'

She had nowhere to go. *What are you crying for?* She heard Anna's voice. *You've got nothing to cry about.* She must pull herself together. Crying only ever made everything worse.

And suddenly she saw it: there was nothing more she could do to fulfil her promise to Anna. She was free of it. Free, she suddenly comprehended, of a promise that had shackled her in a bond of servitude. The realization was like waking up at the end of an illness to find that the disease that had gripped her for so long had finally left her body. She experienced a strange mixture of shame, liberation and abandonment.

Lily had always told herself that the close attention her

mother had belatedly paid her in the last year or so of Anna's life had been love. But it wasn't. Delia, ironically, had shown her what love could be. Lily now understood how, from the moment Anna had shown her those images of Delia on the record sleeves, all her mother's actions had been directed towards honing Lily as an instrument of revenge. After her mother's death, the promise Lily had made had consumed the remainder of her childhood. Now she was released, but what was left to take its place? What purpose did she have?

She remembered the intoxicating sense of freedom she'd felt in Rome and knew that, if she was to survive, she had to reclaim it. She must keep working. Her close study of Delia had been an apprenticeship. She knew how to angle her face perfectly to the key-light and how to reduce her emotions to a focal point before the camera lens. She knew where to find the magic. She'd spent her life preparing for this. She couldn't give it up. She wouldn't.

Her lies would be exposed and the truth would come out. There'd be a scandal and she'd be blamed. But she would do whatever they asked – apologize, make good, prostrate herself if necessary – so long as they would let her go on working.

56

DELIA

Delia had never liked giving press interviews, finding them either repetitive or intrusive. She'd encountered Stella Parsons several times before and disliked her on every occasion. She knew she'd have to be on her guard, for Stella had a nose for a good story and no loyalty to anything but her own reputation. The smart society magazine for which she wrote profiles of the famous had been the first to showcase the latest young photographers whose stark black-and-white portraits had become status symbols, and it was a mark of her toughness that, in her late forties, she hadn't yet been forced to make way for someone younger.

Peter had arranged for the interview to take place in his office at RMJ Records. Afternoon tea would be served, and Stella and Delia could talk for as long as they liked. Delia was grateful that Celeste had not only managed to create a new outfit for her at such short notice but had rushed over to Knightsbridge that morning to make last-minute adjustments. Her friend had been a tower of strength since her collapse, and Delia had gladly accepted her offer to accompany her to Soho.

Celeste sat quietly beside her in the taxi as Delia mentally rehearsed how she'd tell her story. It was now inevitable that the truth would come out, and Peter had impressed upon her that she'd only get one chance to give her version of events. The slant Stella would take for her story would be crucial in setting the right tone and securing public opinion.

With Lily appearing to fall apart all too publicly, Delia knew she couldn't prevaricate any longer. But could she forgive herself if she told only half of the truth and destroyed Lily in the process? On the other hand, what would her future be if she didn't?

'Lily wants to destroy you,' Peter had insisted. 'You have to accept that she's not going to stop. You can't stay silent.'

And then she'd been revisited by the fear she'd felt as she fell to the studio floor – the fear of dying. She didn't believe that her extinction would offer Lily any real comfort. And she had done her best to make amends. It would have to be enough.

Celeste went with her up to Peter's office, giving her a hug before she went in. Stella, whip-thin and impeccably groomed, was already seated on one of the buttoned leather sofas, chatting with Peter. The two women greeted one another courteously and then he left them to it.

'So,' began Stella, her pen poised over her shorthand notebook, 'I want to know everything! Shall we start with your disappearance? Where did you go?'

'I took a train to the Lake District,' Delia answered quietly. She would choose her own moment to drop her bombshell.

'Why? Can you explain what was going through your mind at that moment?'

'Not really.' Delia smiled. 'I'd begun to suspect that Lily might be the daughter I gave up for adoption and I was frightened it wouldn't be true. Yet I was equally frightened that it *would* be, that I'd found her again.'

'Why frightened?' asked Stella. 'Did you fear being judged by your fans as an unwed mother?'

'Not really,' said Delia. 'I was more afraid that she'd see through me, or hate me for giving her up, that I wouldn't know how to be a mother and I'd end up driving her away again.'

'Do you think it's wrong to encourage unwed mothers to give up their babies?'

'Every case is different,' said Delia. 'I was young and had lost my own family. I'm not sure I could've looked after my baby very well.'

'It wasn't because you preferred to pursue a career?'

'I'd hardly begun singing at that point,' Delia objected.

'So how did you react when you saw the newspapers and learned that Lily had announced to the entire world that she was your daughter?'

'At the time, I was thrilled.'

'At the time?' Stella echoed. 'You sound as if that changed?'

'Yes, it did. You see, Lily Brooks is not my daughter.'

'What?'

'My daughter died in a polio epidemic.' Delia had rehearsed her answer. 'However, by the time I discovered the truth, Lily already had a number-one hit so I remained silent in order to give her career the best chance I could.'

'Even though she'd deceived you?'

'I suppose I persuaded myself that she'd also deceived herself.'

'So how did it all happen?' Stella's pen was racing across the page of her notebook. 'How did you find out?'

Delia had begged Peter to let her pretend it had all been an unhappy misunderstanding, that Lily had meant no harm, but Peter had made her promise to expose the full heartlessness of Lily's exploitation, had persuaded her that, if she didn't, Lily would use that failure against her. She had to tell the truth.

'Well, obviously, we had people check into the records,' she said. 'And friends had already become suspicious.'

'Of what?'

'They'd observed her studying me on stage so she could copy me, and making herself up to look like me.'

'You're suggesting that she *knew* she wasn't your daughter?'

'It seems that she'd been searching through my private papers and, by chance, found out that I'd had a child who would have been the same age. That's how the pretence began.'

'You think it was deliberate from the start?'

'She's a very ambitious young woman.'

'So, when you were in the Lake District and Lily made her dramatic announcement that she was your daughter, she knew she was telling a lie?'

'Yes.'

'But she's so young! It was such a daring thing to do. Is she really so calculating?'

'She staged it as a publicity stunt to launch her career.'

Stella flipped back to the previous page of shorthand. 'You said, when you read about it, you believed her to be your daughter and were thrilled?'

'Over the moon,' Delia agreed.

'And when you found out the truth?'

'I felt ill, distraught, frightened.' Delia silently acknowledged that this was true: she had felt all those things when she'd finally allowed the enormity of Lily's deception to hit her. Lily had not only led her to believe she'd found her child, but had also steadily undermined her confidence, persuading her to accept that she was too old, a has-been, a failure. But none of that was true. She felt a weight lift from her shoulders. She had every right to reclaim her life!

'When you fainted on camera the other night, Lily was right there beside you,' said Stella. 'What really happened?'

'I don't suppose we'll ever know for sure.'

'You think Lily might have had a hand in your collapse?'

'As I say, we'll never know for sure.'

'If this is all true—'

'It is.'

'Then this is your chance to set the record straight. What would you say to her fans? What about the film she's making? Her acting ability has certainly been good enough to fool you.'

Delia hesitated. She had never in her professional life belittled a fellow performer's work. The image came to her of Lily at Pinewood miming to playback on the dingy nightclub set, and she felt a rush of tenderness towards the character of the aspiring young singer. She refused to lie about Lily's work.

'She's magical,' she said. 'Given a chance, she could be a great movie actress.'

Stella's pen hovered higher than ever. 'After everything she's done, you're saying she deserves a second chance?'

Delia closed her eyes and was immediately back on the platform at Keleti station, with the damp smell of her father's wool coat and the hissing of the engine. Conrad had once said to her that, as her mother and father went to their deaths, they must have felt some comfort in the knowledge that she at least was safe and would survive. She hadn't been able to tell Conrad that she'd never been able to forgive her father for buying that crumb of comfort at the expense of Anna and her parents.

'We both have a lot to forgive,' she said.

'But why should anyone ever trust Lily again?' Stella demanded. 'A girl so cold and wicked.'

Delia knew she ought to go back to the agreed script: this interview was about *her* career, *her* future. But something in her rebelled. She had sung her heart out all over the world, asking for forgiveness for getting on that train, but the subsequent chain of events had grown too huge ever to be resolved by one person's regret.

Conrad had always told her that work was the only thing that counted. If anything could save Lily, it would be her work. What Delia had recognized weeks ago on that draughty sound stage at Pinewood was Lily's connection to an audience, albeit one that remained invisible behind the camera. It wasn't technique or talent that mattered, it was connecting with other people. She and Lily were survivors, but they hadn't survived simply to sing or to act: they had to reach out and touch people's emotions, to make up for all those others who were absent from their lives.

Delia took a deep breath. She had to have faith in her own instincts and tell her own truth. And this time it would be the whole truth, regardless of the consequences. It was time to stop hiding and reclaim the schoolgirl who had gone skating with Anna and got in and out of scrapes. She straightened her back and fixed Stella with a confident stare. 'Lily is brave, resourceful, funny and determined,' she said, 'just like her real mother.'

'How do you know? Did Lily tell you that? How can you be sure she didn't say it to manipulate you?'

'Because Lily's mother was my best friend at school.'

'Now I'm confused. When did you discover this?'

'Only very recently.'

'What was her name?'

'Anna Körmöczy.'

'You'll have to spell that!'

For the first time since Delia had sat on the train and read Anna's name on the Swiss protection document, she was able to remember her childhood friend without pain. And in that moment she knew she loved Lily in the same way that she had loved Anna. It wasn't about who Lily was, or might have been, or what she had or hadn't done: Delia loved her – as a friend or a daughter or a friend's child, it wasn't important.

'This is extraordinary!' Stella interrupted her thoughts. 'Tell me more.'

'I believe that Lily has always known that her mother and I had been friends in Budapest. It's why she came looking for me.' Delia took a deep breath. 'Because she also knew that her mother spent over a year in a Nazi concentration camp because of me.'

'What? Hold on. Go back. You and Anna were school friends, and then what?'

'In 1943 my father stole papers that would have granted Anna safe passage to Switzerland. He gave them to me and I used them. I took a train to Zürich and spent the rest of the war there with Conrad Durand. Anna and her family were sent to Auschwitz.'

'What about your own family?'

'They went there, too, and they died. But Anna survived. Maybe it was luck, maybe it was her courage and determination. I don't know the rest of her story. But now you know Lily's past you can understand why she has been so angry and defiant and unhappy. So, yes, she does deserve a second chance.'

'And if she goes on creating havoc or trying to harm you or your career?'

'That will be her choice.'

'And you honestly want me to print this?'

'Yes. It's time to put the past to rest.'

'Aren't you afraid of what your fans will make of it?'

'My fans are wonderful,' said Delia. 'I've always been so grateful to them. I'd like you to print this: my fans supported Lily when they thought she was my daughter. I ask them now to go on supporting her as Anna Körmöczy's child.'

'Well,' said Stella, 'I certainly never expected to walk away with such a scoop. It's an incredible story.'

Delia, exhausted, was relieved when Stella stood up and quickly and professionally shook hands, ready to leave. At the door she turned back, a smile on her face.

'I've got the perfect title,' she said. ' "Tell Me How It Ends".'

57

FRANK

Delia handed me a glass of whisky. 'For old times' sake,' she said, with a smile.

We were standing in her rooftop living room. She had not yet drawn the curtains and, with the nights drawing in, the cityscape was already a sea of distant twinkling lights, a view that only accentuated my melancholy mood.

'I have to thank you,' she went on.

'For what?' I was amazed. I had come here at her invitation ready to apologize for all my meddling. Since Stella Parsons's article, the papers had picked over every last bone of the story and I was responsible. I had forced Delia's hand by delving into matters that didn't concern me and, God knows, if someone had done that to me, I wouldn't have been smiling and offering them a drink.

'I don't know what you said to Lily,' Delia said, 'but it seems to have made all the difference. I haven't seen her – I'm not sure how she and I go on from here – but Peter's told me that the demons are gone. He even persuaded the American producers to let her finish the movie.'

I couldn't hide my scepticism, and she laughed.

'Don't be so cynical, Frank! She's very young and people *can* change. Even you, you know. I'm certainly learning how good it feels to let go of the past. I feel whole again, like a balloon, filling with air, ready to float into a blue sky.'

'I wish Peter would forgive *me* so easily,' I said, trying not to sound bitter. Even though it was my fault, the loss of Peter's trust still hurt.

'I told him you weren't to blame,' she said earnestly. 'That it was me who insisted on not telling him.'

'Thank you. Mary's been fighting my corner, too. But I guess, once things have been smashed up, you can't make them like they were before.'

'No, but—' She stopped and smiled again. I'd never seen her smile so readily. 'Do you remember, after the bombing in London stopped, how quickly the rubble was softened by a covering of rosebay willowherb? And the craters became playgrounds? No one tried to pretend the damage wasn't there, yet everything changed.'

I thought about the past and how hard I'd tried to remake my life. I'd gone up to Oxford and done my best to care about being picked for the college second eleven or not being caught by the university bulldogs without my gown, but it had all felt like it was happening to someone else. My war had been a picnic compared to other people's experiences, yet even a survivor like Miriam Cuthbertson had been able to make a new life for herself where I had failed. I looked at Delia. With a simple dress and her new haircut she was full of optimism and energy. I had to speak.

'If it hadn't been for Lily,' I began, 'do you think we could have—'

She silenced me with a light hand on my sleeve. 'Don't, Frank.

That's the same as saying, "If it wasn't for the war . . ." Lily has been like one of those aftershocks following an earthquake or a volcano. She's merely a consequence of a much bigger upheaval. So it's no good saying, if it wasn't for her. We wouldn't even have met if she hadn't already turned my life upside down. And she only entered my life because of what had gone before.'

'Then what about the future?' I asked.

'Well, what are your plans?'

'I've been offered a job in West Africa,' I said. 'If I take it, I'll leave within the next few weeks.'

'Then you must promise to let me know whenever you're back in London.'

I thought of how I'd sat there that night in the rain, feeling sorry for myself as the voice on the stereo of a woman I'd never met filled the room. Since then she'd told me not to pin my hopes on her. She'd never offered any real encouragement. I'd simply filled in the gaps myself with wishful thinking, just like on that night before we met. That had to stop.

I finished my whisky, put the glass back on the drinks tray and turned to her. 'I wouldn't have missed knowing you for the world.'

'You must listen to my new album when it comes out,' she said, moving with me towards the stairs. 'There's a song on it that was written just for you.'

She waited at her door long enough to wave when I turned back for a final look. I walked away up the mews feeling somehow set free. All the things I had lost – love, friendship, fatherhood – perhaps they weren't entirely lost. Perhaps I had merely been clinging to them too tightly.

58

LILY

Three years later

It was Brett who'd bought the tickets and dragged Lily along to the concert at the Hollywood Bowl. She'd been aware – who could fail to be? – of Delia's ever-widening fame. With original music inspired by soul and Motown, she was selling more records than ever before. The number with which she'd closed tonight had just won a Grammy and had also featured in the soundtrack to a film tipped to win several Academy Awards. Brett had pointed out that Lily and Delia were more than likely to encounter one another at this year's ceremony, where Lily, too, was nominated for a second Best Actress award.

Lily had been dating Brett for nearly a year. A cinematographer, he understood the demands of her career and was happy to sidestep the razzmatazz of her stardom. After the runaway success of the film she'd made with Guy and James, and with her image lent a dangerous and ambiguous edge by Stella Parsons's revelations, she'd made another four in swift succession and was signed up for two more. Although she and Brett were seldom in the same place for more than a few weeks at a stretch, they kept in touch through long late-night phone calls and she was finding it hard to imagine life without him.

Brett was the only person she'd ever really talked deeply with about her childhood, her conflicted feelings towards Anna and her shame at what she'd done to Delia. And so she'd trusted his judgement when he said it was time: Delia's concert was on a date they'd both be in Los Angeles and, however it worked out, Lily was ready for some kind of resolution.

It had been easy enough to wangle an invitation to the after-party but, even with Brett holding her hand, it took all of Lily's acting expertise to walk into the noisy, overheated room. Hollywood people had short memories, yet there'd be enough here to remember the furore of three years ago and to fall silent, watching what would happen once Delia spotted the new arrival. Lily gripped Brett's hand, anxious about her own visceral reaction and terrified that Delia would publicly repudiate her.

She located Delia in the throng before the singer noticed her, and was taken aback by the simplicity of the immediate rush of warmth and affection she felt at seeing her again. This woman had saved her, championed her, made it possible for her to go on working when work had been the only thing keeping her together. And she looked wonderful, with a compelling mixture of gaiety and authority that had previously been muted by her habitual reticence. Lily felt tears prick her eyelids.

Delia must have sensed a current run through the room. She turned and, looking towards the door, saw Lily.

Lily tensed, waiting for the blow to fall.

'Lily! Oh, Lily, it's you!'

People stood aside to make way as Delia came forwards. With

cigarettes and champagne glasses in hand, they watched the two stars avidly as Delia opened her arms and Lily stepped into them.

'You've come at last.' Delia retreated enough to reach up to touch Lily's hair. 'I've seen all your films. I'm so proud of you.'

Overcome, Lily looked around at Brett. He smiled and came to join her.

'Look at you,' he said. 'There'll be no stopping you now.'

ACKNOWLEDGEMENTS

Having always loved the heroines of film noir and the 'women's pictures' of the 1940s and 1950s, I set out to write a novel inspired by them. I hope that readers will recognize and enjoy the deliberate references to three favourite films: *All About Eve* (1950), based on a short story by Mary Orr, written and directed by Joseph L. Mankiewicz, and starring Bette Davis and Anne Baxter; *Laura* (1944) based on a novel by Vera Caspary, directed by Otto Preminger, and starring Gene Tierney and Dana Andrews; and *A Star is Born* (1954) written by Moss Hart (based on an earlier screenplay), directed by George Cukor, and starring Judy Garland and James Mason.

I'm always grateful for the patience, support and encouragement of friends and family. My thanks to Ed Bazalgette and Simon Fellowes for answering specialist background questions, to Lisa Cohen for notes on an early draft, and to Merle Nygate for being such a great writing buddy.

Each book increases my appreciation for my exceptional editor Jane Wood and the wonderful team at Quercus, and my rock of an agent, Sheila Crowley and her brilliant team at Curtis Brown. Special thanks to Hazel Orme for her fine copyediting and Andrew Smith for a stunning cover design. It's a privilege to work with you all.